Praise for *The Steel Kiss* and Jeffery Deaver

'[An] edge-of-the-seat thriller . . . breathlessly entertaining fiction.'   *Irish Independent*

'Darkly witty . . . unsettling.' *New York Times Book Review*

'Deaver at his best and when you are Jeffery Deaver this means the best of the best.'   *Huffington Post*

'Grips comprehensively, with every individual detail.'
                                                        Independent

'A master of misdirection.'   *Evening Standard*

'The art of writing blockbuster thrillers is not easily mastered but Deaver has it at his fingertips.'   *Daily Express*

'The most creative, skilled and intriguing thriller writer in the world . . . [Deaver] has produced a stunning series of bestsellers with unique characterisation, intelligent characters, beguiling plots and double-barrelled and sometimes triple-barrelled solutions.'   *Daily Telegraph*

'Jeffery Deaver is a master at crafting intricate crimes that are solved through guile, tenacity and sheer creative genius.'
                                                        Harlan Coben

Also by Jeffery Deaver

Mistress of Justice
The Lesson of Her Death
Praying for Sleep
Speaking in Tongues
A Maiden's Grave
The Devil's Teardrop
The Blue Nowhere
Garden of Beasts
The Bodies Left Behind
Edge
The October List

THE RUNE SERIES
Manhattan is My Beat
Death of a Blue Movie Star
Hard News

THE LOCATION SCOUT
SERIES
Shallow Graves
Bloody River Blues
Hell's Kitchen

THE LINCOLN RHYME
THRILLERS
The Skin Collector
The Bone Collector
The Coffin Dancer
The Empty Chair

The Stone Monkey
The Vanished Man
The Twelfth Card
The Cold Moon
The Broken Window
The Burning Wire
The Kill Room
The Burial Hour

THE KATHRYN DANCE
THRILLERS
The Sleeping Doll
Roadside Crosses
XO
Solitude Creek

A JAMES BOND NOVEL
Carte Blanche

SHORT STORIES
Twisted
More Twisted
Trouble in Mind

JEFFERY
DEAVER

The Steel
Kiss

HODDER &
STOUGHTON

First published in the United States of America in 2016 by Grand Central
Publishing

First published in Great Britain in 2016 by Hodder & Stoughton
An Hachette UK company

First published in paperback in 2017

1

A CIP catalogue record for this title is available from the British Library

B Format Paperback ISBN 978 1 473 61861 9
A Format Paperback ISBN 978 1 473 61851 0
eBook ISBN 978 1 473 61850 3

Typeset in Sabon MT by Palimpsest Book Production Limited, Falkirk,
Stirlingshire

Printed and bound by Clays Ltd, St Ives plc

Hodder & Stoughton policy is to use papers that are natural, renewable and
recyclable products and made from wood grown in sustainable forests. The
logging and manufacturing processes are expected to conform to the environmental regulations of the country of origin.

Hodder & Stoughton Ltd
Carmelite House
50 Victoria Embankment
London EC4Y 0DZ

www.hodder.co.uk

To Will and Tina Anderson and the boys . . .

The enemy is within the gates; it is with our own luxury, our own folly, our own criminality that we have to contend.

– Cicero

TUESDAY

I BLUNT FORCE

CHAPTER 1

Sometimes you catch a break.

Amelia Sachs had been driving her arterial-blood-red Ford Torino along a commercial stretch of Brooklyn's Henry Street, more or less minding pedestrians and traffic, when she spotted the suspect.

What're the odds?

She was helped by the fact that Unsub 40 was unusual in appearance. Tall and quite thin, he'd stood out in the crowd. Still, that alone would hardly get you noticed in the throng here. But on the night he'd beaten his victim to death, two weeks before, a witness reported that he'd been wearing a pale-green checked sport coat and Braves baseball cap. Sachs had done the requisite – if hopeless – posting of this info on the wire and moved on to other aspects of the investigation . . . and on to other investigations; Major Cases detectives have plenty to look after.

But an hour ago a patrolman from the 84th Precinct, walking a beat near the Brooklyn Heights Promenade, had spotted a possible and called Sachs – the lead gold shield on the case. The murder had been late at night, in a deserted construction site, and the perp apparently hadn't known he'd been witnessed in the outfit, so he must've felt safe donning the garb again. The patrol officer had lost him in the crowds but she'd sped in the direction anyway, calling in backup, even if this part of the city was an urban sprawl populated by ten thousand camouflaging souls. The odds that she'd find Mr Forty were, she told herself wryly, nonexistent at best.

But, damn, there he was, walking in a long lope. Tall, skinny, green jacket, cap and all, though from behind she couldn't tell what team was being championed on the headgear.

She skidded the '60s muscle car to a stop in a bus zone, tossed the NYPD official-business placard onto the dash and eased out of the car, minding the suicidal bicyclist who came within inches of collision. He glanced back, not in recrimination, but, she supposed, to get a better look at the tall, redheaded former fashion model, focus in her eyes and a weapon on her black-jeaned hip.

Onto the sidewalk, following a killer.

This was her first look at the prey. The gangly man moved in lengthy strides, feet long but narrow (in running shoes, she noted: good for sprinting over the damp April concrete – much better than her leather-soled boots). Part of her wished he was more wary – so he would look around and she could get a glimpse of his face. That was still an unknown. But, no, he just plodded along in that weird gait, his long arms at his sides, backpack slung via one strap over his sloping shoulder.

She wondered if the murder weapon was inside: the ball-peen hammer, with its rounded end, meant for smoothing edges of metal and tapping rivets flat. That was the side he'd used for the murder, not the claw on the opposite end. The conclusion as to what had caved in Todd Williams's skull had come from a database that

Lincoln Rhyme had created for the NYPD and the Medical Examiner's Office, the folder title: *Weapon Impact on Human Bodies. Section Three: Blunt Force Trauma.*

It was Rhyme's database but Sachs had been forced to do the analysis herself. Without Rhyme.

A thud in her gut at this thought. Forced herself to move past it.

Picturing the wounds again. Horrific, what the twenty-nine-year-old Manhattanite had suffered, beaten to death and robbed as he approached an after-hours club named, so very meta, 40 Degrees North, a reference, Sachs had learned, to the latitude of the East Village, where it was located.

Now Unsub 40 – the club was the source of the nic – was crossing the street, with the light. What an odd build. Well over six feet yet he couldn't've weighed more than 140 or 150.

Sachs saw his destination and alerted Dispatch to tell her backup that the suspect now was entering a five-story shopping center on Henry. She plunged in after him.

With his shadow behind at a discreet distance Mr Forty moved through the crowds of shoppers. People were always in a state of motion, like humming atoms, in this city, *droves* of people, all ages, sexes, colors, sizes. New York kept its own clock and, though it was after lunch hour, businesspeople who should have been in the office and students, in school, were here, spending money, eating, milling, browsing, texting and talking.

And complicating Amelia Sachs's take-down plans considerably.

Forty headed up to the second floor. He continued

walking purposefully through the brightly lit mall, which could have been in Paramus, Austin or Portland, it was that generic. The smells were of cooking oil and onions from the food court and perfume from the counters near the open entranceways of the anchor stores. She wondered for a moment what 40 was doing here, what did he want to buy?

Maybe shopping wasn't his plan at the moment, just sustenance; he walked into a Starbucks.

Sachs eased behind a pillar near the escalator, about twenty feet from the open entryway to the coffee franchise. Careful to remain out of sight. She needed to make sure he didn't suspect there were eyes on him. He wasn't presenting as if carrying – there's a way people tend to walk when they have a gun in their waistband or pocket, as any street cop knows, a wariness, a stiffer gait – but that hardly meant he was pistol free. And if he tipped to her and started shooting? Carnage.

Glancing inside the shop quickly, she saw him reach down to the food section and pick up two sandwiches, then apparently order a drink. Or, possibly, two. He paid and stepped out of sight, waiting for his cappuccino or mocha. Something fancy. A filtered coffee would have been handed over right away.

Would he eat in or leave? Two sandwiches. Waiting for someone? Or one for now and one for later?

Sachs debated. Where was the best place to take him? Would it be better outside on the street, in the shop or in the mall itself? Yes, the center and the Starbucks were crowded. But the street more so. No arrest solution was great.

A few minutes later he was still inside. His drink must have been ready by now and he'd made no effort to leave. He was having a late lunch, she supposed. But was he meeting someone?

Making a complicated take-down even more so.

She got a call.

'Amelia, Buddy Everett.'

'Hey,' she said softly to the patrolman out of the 84. They knew each other well.

'We're outside. Me and Dodd. Another car with three.'

'He's in Starbucks, second floor.'

It was then that she saw a deliveryman wheel by with some cartons emblazoned with the Starbucks logo, the mermaid. Which meant there was no back entrance to the shop. Forty was trapped in a cul-de-sac. Yes, there were people inside, potential bystanders, but fewer than in the mall or on the street.

She said to Everett, 'I want to take him here.'

'Inside, Amelia? Sure.' A pause. 'That's best?'

He's not getting away, Sachs thought. 'Yes. Get up here stat.'

'We're moving.'

A fast glance inside then back to cover. She still couldn't see him. He must be sitting in the rear of the place. She eased to the right and then moved closer to the open archway of the coffee shop. If she couldn't see him, he couldn't see her.

She and the team would flank—

Just then Sachs gasped at the abrupt, piercing scream close behind her. A horrid wail of a person in pain. So raw, so high, she couldn't tell male or female.

The sound came from the top of the up escalator, connecting the floor below with this one.

Oh, Jesus . . .

The top panel of the device, which riders stepped onto from the moving stairs, had popped open and a passenger had fallen into the moving works.

'Help me! No! Please please please!' A man's voice. Then the words coalesced into a scream once more.

Customers and employees gasped and cried out. Those on the steps of the malfunctioning unit, which were still moving up, leapt off or charged backward. The riders on the adjoining escalator, going down, jumped too, maybe thinking it was about to engulf them as well. Several landed in a heap on the floor.

Sachs glanced toward the coffee shop.

No sign of 40. Had he seen her badge, on her belt, or weapon when he, like everyone else, turned to stare?

She called Everett and told him about the accident and to call it in to Dispatch. Then to cover the exits; Unsub 40 might've seen her and now was escaping. She sprinted to the escalator, noting somebody had pressed the emergency button. The stairs slowed and then halted.

'Make it stop, make it stop!' More screams from the person trapped inside.

Sachs stepped into the upper part of the platform and looked into the gaping hole. A middle-aged man – around forty-five or fifty – was trapped in the gears of the motor, which was mounted to the floor about eight feet below the aluminum panel that had popped open. The motor continued to turn, despite someone's hitting the emergency switch; she supposed that doing so merely disengaged a clutch to the moving stairs. The poor man was caught at the waist. He was on his side, flailing at the mechanism. The gears had dug deep into his body; blood had soaked his clothing and was flowing onto the floor of the escalator pit. He wore a white shirt with a name badge on it, an employee of one of the stores probably.

Sachs looked at the crowd. There were employees here, a few security people, but no one was doing anything to help. Stricken faces. Some were calling 911, it seemed, but most were taking cell phone pics and video.

She called down to him, 'We've got rescue on the way. I'm NYPD. I'm coming down there.'

'God, it hurts!' More screaming. She felt the vibration in her chest.

That bleeding had to stop, she assessed. And you're the only one who's going to do it. So move!

She muscled the hinged panel farther open. Amelia Sachs wore little jewelry. But she slipped her one accessory – a ring with a blue stone – from her finger, afraid it would catch in the gears. Though his body was jamming one set of them, a second – operating the down escalator – churned away. Ignoring her claustrophobia, but barely, Sachs started into the narrow pit. There was a ladder for workers to use – but it consisted of narrow metal bars, which were slick with the man's blood; apparently he'd been slashed when he first tumbled inside by the sharp edge of the access panel. She gripped the hand- and footholds of the ladder hard; if she fell she'd land on top of the man and, directly beside him, the second set of grinding gears. Once, her feet went out from under her and her arm muscles cramped to keep her from falling. A booted foot brushed the working gears, which dug a trough in the heel and tugged at her jean cuff. She yanked her leg away.

Then down to the floor . . . Hold on, hold on. Saying, or thinking, this to both him and herself.

The poor man's screams weren't diminishing. His ashen face was a knot, skin shiny with sweat.

'Please, oh God, oh God . . .'

She jockeyed carefully around the second set of gears, slipping twice on the blood. Once, his leg lashed out involuntarily, caught her solidly on the hip, and she fell forward toward the revolving teeth.

She managed to stop herself just before her face brushed the metal. Slipped again. Caught herself. 'I'm a police officer,' she repeated. 'Medics'll be here any minute.'

'It's bad, it's bad. It hurts so much. Oh, so much.'

Lifting her head, she shouted, 'Somebody from maintenance, somebody from management! Shut this damn thing off! Not the stairs, the motor! Cut the power!'

Where the hell's the fire department? Sachs surveyed the injury. She had no idea what to do. She pulled her jacket off and pressed it against the shredded flesh of his belly and groin. It did little to stanch the blood.

'Ah, ah, ah,' he whimpered.

Looking for wires to cut – she carried her very illegal but very sharp switchblade knife in her back pocket – but there were no visible cables. How can you make a machine like this and not have an off switch? Jesus. Furious at the incompetence.

'My wife,' the man whispered.

'Shhh,' Sachs soothed. 'It'll be all right.' Though she knew it wouldn't be all right. His body was a bloody mess. Even if he survived, he'd never be the same.

'My wife. She's . . . Will you go see her? My son. Tell them I love them.'

'You're going to tell 'em that yourself, Greg.' Reading the name badge.

'You're a cop.' Gasping.

'That's right. And there'll be medics here—'

'Give me your gun.'

'Give you—'

More screaming. Tears down his face.

'Please, give me your gun! How do I shoot it? Tell me!'

'I can't do that, Greg,' she whispered. She put her hand on his arm. With her other palm she wiped the pouring sweat from his face.

'It hurts so much . . . I can't take it.' A scream louder than the others. 'I want it to be over with!'

She had never seen such a hopeless look in anyone's eyes.

'Please, for Chrissake, your gun!'

Amelia Sachs hesitated, then reached down and drew her Glock from her belt.

A cop.

Not good. Not good.

That tall woman. Black jeans. Pretty face. And, oh, the red hair . . .

A cop.

I've left her behind at the escalator and am moving through the crowds at the mall.

She didn't know I'd seen her, I think, but I had. Oh, yeah. Seen her nice and clear. The scream of the man disappearing into the jaws of that machine had prodded everybody to look toward the sound. Not her, though. She was turning to look for *me* in the friendly Starbucks.

I saw the gun on her hip, the badge on her hip. Not private, not rental. A real cop. A *Blue Bloods* cop. She—

Well. What was that?

A gunshot. I'm not much on firearms but I've shot a pistol some. No doubt that was a handgun.

Puzzling. Yeah, yeah, something's weird. Was the police girl – Red I'm calling her, after the hair – planning to arrest somebody *else*? Hard to say. She could be after me for lots of the mischief I've been up to. Possibly the bodies I left in that sludgy pond near Newark some time ago, weighted down with barbells like the sort pudgy people buy, use six and a half times and never again. No word in the press about that incident but, well, it *was* New Jersey. Body-land, that place is. Another corpse? Not worth reporting; the Mets won by seven! So. Or she might be hunting for me for the run-in not long after that on a dim street in Manhattan, swish goes the throat. Or maybe that construction site behind club 40°, where I left such a pretty package of, once again, snapped head bone.

Did somebody recognize me at one of those places, cutting or cracking?

Could be. I'm, well, distinctive looking, height and weight.

I just assume it's me she wants. Better safe . . . I need to get away and that means keeping my head down, that means slouching. It's easier to shrink three inches than grow.

But the shot? What was *that* about? Was she after someone even more dangerous than me? I'll check the news later.

People are everywhere now, moving fast. Most are not looking at tall me, skinny me, me of the long feet and fingers. They just want out, fleeing the screams and gunshot. Stores are emptying, food court emptying. Afraid of terrorists, afraid of crazy men dressed in camo, stabbing, slashing, shooting up the world in anger or thanks to loose-wired brains. ISIS. Al-Qaeda. Militias. Everyone's on edge.

I'm turning here, slipping through socks and underwear, men's.

Henry Street, Exit Four, is right ahead of me. Should I get out that way?

Better pause. I take in a deep breath. Let's not go *too* fast here. First, I should lose the green jacket and cap. Buy something new. I duck into a cheap store to pay cash for some China-made Italian blue blazer. Thirty-five long, which is lucky. That size is hard to find. Hipster fedora hat. A Middle Eastern kid rings the sale up while texting. Rude. My desire is to crack a bone in his head. At least he's not looking at me. That's good. Put the old jacket, the green plaid one, in my backpack. The jacket is from my brother, so I'm not throwing it out. The sports cap goes inside too.

The Chinese Italian hipster leaves the store and goes back into the mall. So, which way to escape? Henry Street?

No. Not smart. There'll be plenty of cops outside.

I'm looking around. Everywhere, everywhere. Ah, a service door. There'll be a loading dock, I'm sure.

I push through the doorway like I belong here, knuckles not palm (prints, of course), past a sign saying *Employees Only*. Except not now.

Thinking: What lucky timing, the escalator, Red next to it when the screams began. Lucky me.

Head down, I keep walking steadily. Nobody stops me in the corridor.

Ah, here's a cotton jacket on a peg. I unpin the employee name badge and repin the shiny rectangle on my chest. I'm now Courteous Team Member Mario. I don't look much like a Mario but it'll have to do.

Just now two workers, young men, one brown, one white, come through a door ahead of me. I nod at them. They nod back.

Hope one isn't Mario. Or his best friend. If so, I'll have to reach into my backpack and we know what that means: cracking bones from on high. I pass them.

Good.

Or not good: A voice shoots my way: 'Yo?'

'Yeah?' I ask, hand near the hammer.

'What's going on out there?'

'Robbery, I think. That jewelry store. Maybe.'

'Fuckers never had security there. I coulda told 'em.'

His co-worker: 'Only had cheap crap. Zircons, shit like that. Who'd get his ass shot for a zircon?'

I see a sign for *Deliveries* and dutifully follow the arrow.

I hear voices ahead, stop and look around the corner. One little black guard, skinny as me, a twig, is all.

On his radio. I could break him easily with the hammer. Make his face crack into ten pieces. And then—

Oh, no. Why is life such a chore?

Two others show up. One white, one black. Both twice my weight.

I duck back. And then things get worse yet. Behind me, other end of the corridor I've just come down. I hear more voices. Maybe it's Red and some others, making a sweep this way.

And the only exit, ahead of me, has three rental cops, who live for the day they too have a chance to break bones . . . or Tase or spray.

Me, in the middle and nowhere to go.

CHAPTER 2

'Where?'

'Still searching, Amelia,' Buddy Everett, the patrolman from the 84, told her. 'Six teams. Exits're all covered, us or private security. He's got to be here somewhere.'

Wiping away the blood on her boot with a Starbucks napkin. Or trying to, futilely. Her jacket, in a trash bag she'd gotten from the coffee shop too, might not be irreparably ruined but she wasn't inclined to wear a garment that had been saturated with blood. The young patrolman noted the stains on her hands, his eyes troubled. Cops are, of course, human too. Immunity comes eventually but later to some than others, and Buddy Everett was young still.

Through red-framed glasses, he looked at the open access panel. 'And he . . . ?'

'He didn't make it.'

A nod. Eyes now on the floor, Sachs's bloody boot prints leading away from the escalator.

'No idea which direction he went?' he asked.

'None.' She sighed. Only a few minutes had elapsed between the time that Unsub 40 *might* have seen her and fled, and the deployment of the backup officers. But that seemed to be enough to turn him invisible. 'All right. I'll be searching with you.'

'They'll need help in the basement. It's a warren down there.'

'Sure. But get bodies canvassing in the street too. If he saw me he had a window to get the hell out of Dodge ASAP.'

'Sure, Amelia.'

The youthful officer with the glasses the shade of cooling blood nodded and headed off.

'Detective?' A man's voice from behind her.

She turned to a compact Latino of about fifty, in a striped navy-blue suit and yellow shirt. His tie was spotless white. Don't see that combo often.

She nodded.

'Captain Madino.'

She shook his hand. He was surveying her with dark eyes, lids low. Seductive but not sexual; captivating in the way powerful men – some women too – were.

Madino would be from the 84th Precinct and would have nothing to do with the Unsub 40 case, which was on the Major Cases roster. He was here because of the accident, though the police would probably step out pretty soon, unless there was a finding that there had been criminal negligence in the maintenance of the escalator, which rarely happened. But it still would be Madino's boys and girls who ran the scene.

'What happened?' he asked her.

'Fire department could tell you better than I could. I was moving on a homicide suspect. All I know is the escalator malfunctioned somehow and a male, middle-aged, fell into the gears. I got to him, tried to stop the bleeding but there wasn't much to do. He hung in there for a while. But ended up DCDS.'

Deceased, confirmed dead at scene.

'Emergency switch?'

'Somebody hit it but that only shuts the stairs off, not the main motor. The gears keep going. Got him around the groin and belly.'

'Man.' The captain's lips tightened. He stepped forward to look down into the pit. Madino gave no reaction. He gripped his white tie to make sure it didn't swing forward and get soiled on the railing. Blood had made its way up there too. Unemotional, he turned back to Sachs. 'You were down *there*?'

'I was.'

'Must have been tough.' The sympathy in his eyes seemed genuine.

'Tell me about the weapons discharge.'

'The motor,' Sachs explained. 'There was no cutoff switch that I could find. No wires to cut. I couldn't leave him to find it or climb to the top to tell somebody to kill the juice; I was putting pressure on the wounds. So I parked a round in the coil of the motor itself. Stopped it from cutting him in half. But he was pretty much gone by then. Lost eighty percent of his blood, the EMT said.'

Madino was nodding. 'That was a good try, Detective.'

'Didn't work.'

'Not much else you could do.' He looked back to the open access panel. 'We'll have to convene a Shooting Team but, on this scenario, it'll be a formality. Nothing to worry about.'

'Appreciate that, Captain.'

Despite what one sees on screens large and small, a police officer's firing a weapon is a rare and consequential occurrence. A gun can be discharged only in the event the officer believes his or her life or that of a bystander is endangered or when an armed felon flees. And force can be used only to kill, not wound. A Glock may not be used like a wrench to shut off renegade machinery.

In the event of a shooting by a cop, on or off duty, a supervisor from the precinct where it happened comes to the scene to secure and inspect the officer's weapon. He then convenes the Patrol Borough Shooting Team – which has to be run by a captain. Since there was no death or injury resulting from the shot, Sachs didn't need to submit to an Intoxilizer test or go on administrative leave for the mandatory three days. And, in the absence of malfeasance, she wasn't required to surrender her weapon. Just offer it to the supervisor to inspect and note the serial number.

She did this now: deftly dropped the magazine and ejected the chambered round, then collected it from the floor. She offered the weapon to him. He wrote down the serial. Handed the pistol back.

She added, 'I'll do the Firearms Discharge/Assault Report.'

'No hurry, Detective. It takes a while to convene the team, and it looks like you've got some other tasks on your plate.' Madino was looking down into the pit once more. 'God bless you, Detective. Not a lot of people would've gone down there.'

Sachs rechambered the ejected round. Officers from the 84 had cordoned off both of these escalators, so she turned and hurried toward the elevators on her way to the basement, where she'd help search for Unsub 40. But she paused when Buddy Everett approached.

'He's gone, Amelia. Out of the building.' His dark-red frames both enhanced and jarred.

'How?'

'Loading dock.'

'We had people there, I thought. Rent-a-cops if not ours.'

'He called, the unsub, he shouted from around the corner near the dock, said the perp was in a storage area. Bring their cuffs, Mace or whatever. You know rentals? They love a chance to play real cop. Everybody went running to the storeroom. He strolled right out. Video shows him – new jacket, dark sport coat, fedora – climbing down the dock ladder and running through the truck parking zone.'

'Going where?'

'Narrow-focus camera. No idea.'

She shrugged. 'Subways? Buses?'

'Nothing on CCTV. Probably walked or took a cab out of the area.'

To one of the eighty-five million places he might go.

'Dark jacket, you said? Sport coat?'

'We canvassed the shops. But nobody saw anybody with his build buy anything. Don't have his face.'

'Think we can get prints from the ladder? At the dock?'

'Oh, the vid shows he put gloves on before he climbed down.'

Smart. This boy is smart.

'One thing. He was carrying his cup and what seemed

like some food wrappers. We looked but he didn't drop 'em that we could find.'

'I'll get an ECT on it.'

'Hey, how'd it go with Captain White Tie? Oh, did I say that?'

She smiled. 'If you said it I didn't hear it.'

'He's already planning how to redecorate his office in the governor's mansion.'

Explained the posh outfit. Brass with aspirations. Good to have on your side.

God bless you . . .

'Fine. Looks like he's backing me up on the weapons issue.'

'He's a decent guy. Just promise you'll vote for him.'

'Keep up the canvass,' Sachs told him.

'Will do.'

Sachs was approached by an inspector with the fire department and gave a statement on the escalator accident. Twenty minutes later the Evidence Collection Team assigned to the Unsub 40 case arrived from the NYPD's massive Crime Scene complex in Queens. She greeted them, two thirty-ish African American techs, man and woman, she worked with from time to time. They wheeled heavy suitcases toward the escalator.

'Uh-uh,' Sachs told them. '*That* was an accident. The Department of Investigations'll be coordinating with the Eight-Four. I need you to walk the grid at Starbucks.'

'What happened there?' the woman officer asked, looking over the coffee shop.

'A serious crime,' her partner offered. 'Price of a frap-puccino.'

'Our unsub sat down for a late lunch. Some table in the back, you'll have to ask where. Tall, thin. Green checkered jacket and Atlanta baseball cap. But there won't be much. He took his cup and wrappers with him.'

'Hate it when they don't leave their DNA lying around.'

'True, that.'

Sachs said, 'But I'm hoping he ditched the litter somewhere close.'

'You have any idea where?' the woman asked.

Looking over the staff in Starbucks, Sachs had, in fact, had an inspiration. 'Maybe. But it's not in the mall. I'll check that out myself. You handle Starbucks.'

'Always loved you, Amelia. You give us the warm and fuzzy and you take the dark 'n' cold.'

She crouched and pulled a blue Tyvek jumpsuit out of the case one of the ECTs had just opened.

'Standard operating procedure, right, Amelia? Bundle up everything and get it to Lincoln's town house?'

Sachs's face was stony as she said, 'No, ship everything back to Queens. I'm running the case from downtown.'

The two ECTs regarded each other briefly and then looked back to Sachs. The woman asked, 'He's okay? Rhyme?'

'Oh, you didn't hear?' Sachs said tersely. 'Lincoln's not working for the NYPD anymore.'

CHAPTER 3

'The answer is there.'

A pause as the words echoed off the glossy, scuffed walls, their color academia green. That is, bile.

'The answer. It may be obvious, like a bloody knife emblazoned with the perp's fingerprints and DNA, inscribed with his initials and a quotation from his favorite poet. Or obscure, nothing more than three invisible ligands – and what *is* a ligand? Anyone?'

'Olfactory molecules, sir.' A shaky male voice.

Lincoln Rhyme continued, 'Obscure, I was saying. The answer may be in three olfactory molecules. But it *is* there. The connection between the killer and killee that can lead us to his door and persuade the jury to relocate him to a new home for twenty to thirty years. Someone give me Locard's Principle.'

A woman's voice said firmly from the front row: 'With every crime there is a transfer of material between perpetrator and the scene or the victim or most likely both. Edmond Locard, the French criminalist, used the word "dust" but "material" is generally accepted. Trace evidence, in other words.' The responder tilted her head, tossing aside long chestnut hair framing a heart-shaped face. She added, 'Paul Kirk elaborated. "Physical evidence cannot perjure itself. It cannot be wholly absent.

23

Only human failure to find it, study and understand it can diminish its value."'

Lincoln Rhyme nodded. Correct answers might be acknowledged but never praised; that was reserved for an insight that transcended the baseline. He was impressed nonetheless, as he had not yet assigned any readings that discussed the great French criminalist. He gazed out at the faces, as if perplexed. 'Did you all write down what Ms Archer said? It appears some of you did not. I can't fathom why.'

Pens began to skitter, laptop keyboards to click and fingers danced silently over the two-dimensional keys of tablets.

This was only the second class session of Introduction to Crime Scene Analysis and protocols had yet to be established. The students' memories would be supple and in good form but not infallible. Besides, recording on paper or screen means *possessing*, not just comprehending.

'The answer is there,' Rhyme repeated, well, professorially. 'With criminalistics – forensic science – there is not a single crime that cannot be solved. The only question is one of resource, ingenuity and effort. How far are you willing to go to identify the perp? As, yes, Paul Kirk said in the nineteen fifties.' He glanced at Juliette Archer. Rhyme had learned the names of only a few students. Archer's had been the first.

'Captain Rhyme?' From a young man in the back of the classroom, which contained about thirty people, ranging from early twenties to forties, skewed toward the younger. Despite the stylish, spiky hipster hair, the man had police in him. While the college catalog bio – not to mention the tens of thousands of Google references – offered up Rhyme's official rank at the time he'd left the force on disability some years ago, it was unlikely that anyone not connected with the NYPD would use it.

With a genteel move of his right hand, professor turned his elaborate motorized wheelchair to face student. Rhyme was a quadriplegic, largely paralyzed from the neck down; his left ring finger and, now, after some surgery, right arm and hand were the only southern extremities working. 'Yes?'

'I was thinking. Locard was talking about "material" or "dust"?' A glance toward Archer in the front row, far left.

'Correct.'

'Couldn't there also be a psychological transference?'

'How do you mean?'

'Say the perp threatens to torture the victim before he kills him. The victim is discovered with a look of terror on his face. We can infer that the perp was a sadist. You could add that to the psychological profile. Maybe narrow down the field of suspects.'

Proper use of the word *infer*, Rhyme noted. Often confused with the transitive *imply*. He said, 'A question. Did you enjoy that series of books? Harry Potter? Movies too, right?' As a rule, cultural phenomena didn't interest him much – not unless they might help solve a crime, which happened, more or less, never. But Potter was, after all, Potter.

The young man squinted his dark eyes. 'Yes, sure.'

'You *do* know that it was fiction, right. That Hogworths doesn't exist?'

'Hogwarts. And I'm pretty aware of that, yes.'

'And you'll concede that wizards, casting spells, voodoo, ghosts, telekinesis and your theory of the transfer of psychological elements at crime scenes—'

'Are hog*wash*, you're saying?'

Drawing laughs.

Rhyme's brows V'd, though not at the interruption; he liked insolence and in fact the play on words was rather clever. His was a substantive complaint. 'Not at all. I was going to say that each of those theories has yet to be empirically proven. You present me with objective studies, repeatedly duplicating results of your purported psychological transference, which include a valid sampling size and controls, supporting the theory, and I'll consider it valid. I myself wouldn't rely on it. Focusing on more intangible aspects of an investigation distracts from the important task at hand. Which is?'

'The evidence.' Juliette Archer again.

'Crime scenes change like a dandelion under a sudden breath. Those three ligands are all that remain of a million only a moment earlier. A drop of rain can wash away a speck of the killer's DNA, which destroys any chance of finding him in the CODIS database and learning his name, address, phone number, Social . . . and shirt size.' A look over the room. 'Shirt size was a joke.' People tended to believe everything that Lincoln Rhyme said.

The hipster cop nodded but appeared to be unconvinced. Rhyme was impressed. He wondered if the student would in fact look into the subject. Hoped he did. There might actually be something to his theory.

'We'll speak more about Monsieur Locard's dust – that

is, trace evidence – in a few weeks. Today our subject will be making sure that we have dust to analyze. Preserving the crime scene is our topic. You will never have a virgin crime scene. That does not exist. Your job will be to make sure your scenes are the *least contaminated* they can be. Now, what is the number one contaminant?' Without waiting for a response he continued, 'Yes, fellow cops – often, most often, brass. How do we keep senior officials, preening for news cams, out of the scene while simultaneously retaining our jobs?'

The laughter died down and the lecture began.

Lincoln Rhyme had taught on and off for years. He didn't particularly enjoy teaching but he believed strongly in the efficacy of crime scene work in solving crimes. And he wanted to make sure the standards of forensic scientists were the highest they could be – that was, *his* standards. Many guilty people were getting off or were being sentenced to punishments far less severe than their crimes dictated. And innocent people were going to jail. He had resolved to do what he could to whip a new generation of criminalists into shape.

A month ago Rhyme had decided that this would be his new mission. He had cleared his criminal case workload and applied for a job at the John Marshall School for Criminal Justice, a mere two blocks from his Central Park West town house. In fact, he didn't even have to apply. Over drinks one night he'd mused to a district attorney he had been working with that he was thinking of hanging up his guns and teaching. The DA said something to somebody and word got back to John Marshall, where the prosecutor taught part-time, and the dean of the school called soon after. Rhyme supposed that because of his reputation, he was a solid commodity, attracting media and additional students and possibly prompting a spike in tuition income. Rhyme signed on to teach this introductory course and Advanced Chemical and Mechanical Analysis of Substances Frequently Found in Felony Crime Scenes, Including Electron Microscopy. It was indicative of his rep that the latter course filled up nearly as fast as the former.

Most of the students were in, or destined for, policing work. Local, state or federal. Some would do commercial forensic analysis – working for private eyes, corporations and lawyers. A few were journalists and one a novelist, who wanted to get it right. (Rhyme welcomed his presence; he himself was the subject of a series of novels based on cases he'd run and had written the author on several occasions about misrepresentations of real crime scene work. 'Must you sensationalize?')

After an overview, though a comprehensive one, of crime scene preservation Rhyme noted the time and dismissed the class, and the students filed out. He wheeled to the ramp that led off the low stage.

By the time he reached the main floor of the lecture hall, all those in class had left, except one.

Juliette Archer remained in the first row. The woman, in her mid-thirties, had eyes that were quite remarkable. Rhyme had been struck by them when he'd seen her for the first time, in class last week. There are no blue pigments in the human iris or aqueous humor; that shade comes from the amount of melanin in the epithelium, combined with the Rayleigh scattering effect. Archer's were rich cerulean.

He wheeled up to her. 'Locard. You did some supplemental reading. *My* book. That was the language you paraphrased.' He hadn't assigned his own textbook to the class.

'Needed some reading material to go with my wine and dinner the other day.'

'Ah.'

She said, 'Well?'

No need to expand on the question. It simply reiterated an inquiry from last week . . . as well as several phone messages in the interim.

Her radiant eyes remained steadily on his.

He said, 'I'm not sure it would be that good an idea.'

'Not a good idea?'

'Not helpful, I mean. For you.'

'I disagree.'

She certainly didn't hem or haw. Archer let the silence unspool. Then smiled a lipstick-free smile. 'You checked me out, didn't you?'

'I did.'

'You thought I was a spy? Working my way into your good graces, to steal case secrets or something?'

Had occurred to him. Then he shrugged, a gesture he was capable of, despite his condition. 'Just curious.' Rhyme had in fact learned a number of things about Juliette Archer. Master's degrees in public health and biological science. She'd been a field epidemiologist for the Transmittable Diseases Unit of the New York Institutes of Health in Westchester. She now wanted a career change, to criminal forensic science. Her home was presently downtown, the loft district, SoHo. Her son, eleven, was a star soccer player. She herself had gotten some favorable notices for her modern dance performances in Manhattan and Westchester. She'd lived in Bedford, New York, before her divorce.

No, not a spy.

She continued to gaze into his eyes.

On impulse – exceedingly rare for him – he said, 'All right.'

A formal smile. 'Thank you. I can start now.'

A pause, 'Tomorrow.'

Archer seemed amused and cocked her head playfully. As if she might easily have negotiated and won a change in the sign-on date but didn't feel like pushing the matter.

'You need the address?' Rhyme asked.

'I have it.'

In lieu of shaking hands they both nodded, sealing the agreement. Archer smiled and then her right index finger moved to the touchpad of her own wheelchair, a silver Storm Arrow, the same model Rhyme had used until a few years ago. 'I'll see you then.' She turned the unit and eased up the aisle and out the doorway.

CHAPTER 4

The detached house was dark-red brick. The color close to that of Patrolman Buddy Everett's glasses frames, the color of dried blood, viscera. You couldn't help but think that. Under the circumstances.

Amelia Sachs was lingering, her eyes taking in the warm illumination from inside, which flickered occasionally as the many visitors here floated between lamp and window. The effect could be like a strobe; the house was small and the guests many.

Death summons together those with even the most tenuous connections.

Lingering.

In her years as a police officer Sachs had delivered news of loss to dozens of family members. She was competent at it, vamping on the lines they were taught by the psychologists at the academy. ('I'm very sorry for your loss.' 'Do you have someone you can turn to for support?' With a script like that, you had to improvise.)

But tonight was different. Because Sachs didn't believe she'd ever been present at the exact moment when a victim's electrons departed cells, or, if you were of a different ilk, the spirit abandoned the corpus. She'd had her hands on Greg Frommer's arm at the moment of death. And as much as she did not want to make this trip, the pact had been sealed. She wouldn't break it.

She slid her holster east of her hip, out of sight. It seemed a decent thing to do, though she had no explanation why. The other concession to this mission had been to make a stop at her apartment, also in Brooklyn, not terribly far, to shower and change clothes. It would have taken luminol and an alternative light source wand to find a speck of blood anywhere on her person.

Up the stairs and ringing the bell.

The door was opened by a tall man in a Hawaiian shirt and orange shorts. Fifties or so. Of course, this was not the funeral; that would be later. Tonight the gathering was the quick descent of friends and relatives to support, to bring food, to both distract from the grief and to focus it.

'Hi,' he said. His eyes were as red as the lei around the neck of the parrot on his belly. Frommer's brother? The resemblance was jarring.

'I'm Amelia Sachs. With the NYPD. Is Mrs Frommer able to speak with me for a moment or two?' She said this kindly, her voice cleansed of officialdom.

'I'm sure. Please come in.'

The house contained little furniture and the pieces were mismatched and threadbare. The few pictures on the walls might have come from Walmart or Target. Frommer, she'd learned, had been a salesclerk at a shoe store in the mall, working for minimum pay. The TV was small and the cable box basic. No video game console, though she saw they had at least one child – a skateboard, battered and wrapped in duct tape, sat against a far corner. Some

Japanese manga comics were stacked on the floor beside a scabby end table.

'I'm Greg's cousin, Bob.'

'I'm so sorry about what happened.' Sometimes you fell into rote.

'We couldn't believe it. The wife and I live in Schenectady. We got here as fast as we could.' He said again, 'We couldn't believe it. To . . . well, die in an accident like that.' Despite the tropical costume, Bob grew imposing. 'Somebody's going to pay for this. That never should've happened.'

A few of the other visitors nodded at her, eyeing her clothing, picked out carefully. Calf-length skirt in dark green, black jacket and blouse. She was dressed funereally, though not by design. This was Sachs's typical uniform. Dark offers a more uncooperative target profile than light.

'I'll get Sandy.'

'Thanks.'

Across the room was a boy of about twelve, flanked by a man and two women in their fifties, Sachs estimated. The boy's round, freckled face was red from crying and his hair tousled badly. She wondered if he'd been lying in bed, paralyzed at the news of his father's death, before family arrived.

'Yes, hello?'

Sachs turned. The slim blond woman was very pale of face, a stark and unsettling contrast with the bold red of her lids and the skin below her eyes. Adding to the eeriness were her striking green irises. Her sundress, in dark blue, was wrinkled and though her shoes were close in style they were from different pairs.

'I'm Amelia Sachs, with the police department.'

No shield display. No need.

Sachs asked if they could have a word in private.

Odd how much easier it was to level your Glock at a stoned perp leveling his at you forty paces away, or downshift from fourth to second while turning at fifty, the tachometer redlined, to make sure some son of a bitch didn't get away.

Steel yourself. You can do this.

Sandy Frommer directed Sachs toward the back of the house and they walked through the living room into a tiny den that, she saw once they entered, was the boy's room – the superhero posters and comics, the jeans and sweats in piles, the disheveled bed were evidence of that.

Sachs closed the door. Sandy remained standing and regarded the visitor warily.

'I happened to be on the scene when your husband died. I was with him.'

'Oh. My.' Her look of disorientation swelled momentarily. She focused on Sachs again. 'A policeman came to the door to tell me. A nice man. He wasn't at the mall when it happened. Somebody had called him. He was from the local precinct. An Asian man? Officer, I mean.'

Sachs shook her head.

'It was bad, wasn't it?'

'It was, yes.' She couldn't deflate what had happened. The story had already made the news. The accounts were sanitized but Sandy would eventually see medical reports and would learn exactly what Greg Frommer went through in his last minutes on earth. 'But I just wanted you to know I was with him. I held his hand and he prayed.

And he asked me to come see you and tell you he loved you and your son.'

As if suddenly on a vital mission, Sandy walked to her son's desk, on which sat an old-model desktop computer. Beside it were two soda cans, one crushed. A bag of chips, flattened. Barbecue. She picked up the cans and set them in the trash. 'I was supposed to renew my driver's license. I only have two days. I didn't get around to it. I work for a maid service. We're busy all the time. My license expires in two days.'

So, her birthday soon.

'Is there someone here who could help you get to DMV?'

Sandy found another artifact – an iced tea bottle. It was empty and that too went into the trash. 'You didn't have to come. Some people wouldn't have.' Every word seemed to hurt her. 'Thank you.' The otherworldly eyes turned to Sachs briefly then dropped to the floor. She tossed the sweats into the laundry. She reached into her jean pocket and withdrew a tissue, dabbed her nose. Sachs noted that the jeans were Armani, but were quite faded and worn – and not in the factory-washed way of new garments (Sachs, former fashion model, had little regard for such useless trends). They'd either been bought second-hand or, Sachs's guess, dated to an earlier, and more comfortable, era in the family's life.

This might have been the case; she noted a framed picture on the boy's desk – the young man and his father a few years ago standing beside a private plane. Before them was fishing gear. Canadian or Alaskan mountains crested in the distance. Another, of the family in box seats at what seemed to be the Indie 500.

'Is there anything I can do for you?'

'No, Officer. Or Detective? Or—?'

'Amelia.'

'Amelia. That's a nice name.'

'Is your son coping?'

'Bryan . . . I don't know how he'll do. He's angry now, I think. Or numb. We're both numb.'

'How old? Twelve?'

'Yes, that's right. It's been a tough few years. And that's a hard age.' A tremble of lip. And then a harsh: 'Who's responsible for it? How could something like that happen?'

'I don't know. It will be investigated by the city. They do a good job.'

'We put our faith in things like that. Elevators, buildings, planes, subways! Whoever makes them has to make them safe. How can *we* know if they're dangerous? We have to rely!'

Sachs touched her shoulder, pressed. Wondering if the woman was going to dissolve into hysteria. But Sandy regained composure quickly. 'Thank you for coming to tell me that. A lot of people wouldn't.' It seemed she'd forgotten she'd said this earlier.

'Again. If you need anything.' Sachs placed one of her cards in Sandy's hand. They didn't teach *this* at the academy and, in truth, she didn't know what she could do to help the woman. Sachs was running on instinct.

The card disappeared into the pocket of jeans that had originally cost three figures.

'I'll be going now.'

'Oh, yes. Thank you again.'

Sandy picked up her son's dirty dishes and preceded Sachs out of the doorway, vanished into the kitchen.

Near the front hall Sachs once more approached Frommer's cousin, Bob. She asked, 'How do you think she's doing?'

'Well as can be expected. We'll do what we can, the wife and me. But we've got three kids of our own. I could fit out the garage, I was thinking. I'm handy. The oldest boy too.'

'How do you mean?'

'Our garage. It's freestanding, you know. Two-car. Heated 'cause I have my workbench out there.'

'They'd come live with you?'

'With *somebody* and I don't know who else it'd be.'

'Schenectady?'

Bob nodded.

'They don't own this place? Rent?'

'Right.' A whisper. 'And they're behind a couple of months.'

'He didn't have life insurance?'

A grimace. 'No. He surrendered it. Needed the money. See, Greg decided he wanted to give back. Quit his job a few years ago and started doing a lot of charity stuff. Midlife crisis or whatever. Working part-time at the mall, so he'd be free to volunteer in soup kitchens and shelters. Good for him, I guess. But it's been tough on Sandy and Bry.'

Sachs said good night and walked to the door.

Bob saw her out and said, 'Oh, but don't get the wrong idea.'

She turned, lifting an eyebrow.

'Don't think Sandy regretted it. She stuck by him through it all. Never complained. And, man, did they love each other.'

I'm walking toward my apartment in Chelsea, my womb. My space, good space.

And looking behind me, of course.

No cops are following. No Red, the police girl.

After the scare at the mall, I walked miles and miles through Brooklyn, to a different subway line. I stopped once more for yet another new jacket and new head thing – baseball cap but a tan one. My hair is blond and short, thinning, but best to keep it covered, I think, when I'm out.

Why give the Shoppers anything to work with?

I'm calming now, finally, heart not racing at every sight of a police car.

It's taking forever to get home. Chelsea's a long, long way from Brooklyn. Wonder why it's called that. Chelsea. I think I heard it was named after some place in England. *Sounds* English. They have a sports team there named that, I think. Or maybe it's just someone's name.

The street, *my* street, 22nd Street, is noisy but my windows are thick. Womb-like, I was saying. The roof has a deck and I like it up there. Nobody from the building goes, not that I've seen. I sit there sometimes and wish I smoked because sitting on an urban outcropping, smoking and watching the city, seems like the essential experience of New York old and New York new.

From the roof you can see the back of the Chelsea Hotel. Famous people stay there but 'stay' as in live there.

Musicians and actors and artists. I sit in my lawn chair, watch the pigeons and clouds and airplanes and the vista and listen for music from the musicians living in the hotel but I never hear any.

Now I'm at the building's front door. Another glance behind. No cops. No Red.

Through the doorway and down the corridors of my building. The color of the paint on the walls is dark blue and . . . *hospitalian*, I think of the shade. My word. Just occurred to me. I'll tell my brother when I see him next. Peter would appreciate that. A lot of serious in our past, so now I lean to humor. The lighting in the hallways is bad and the walls smell like they're made of old meat. Never thought I'd feel comfortable in a place like this, after growing up in green and lush suburbia. This apartment was meant to be temporary but it has grown on me. And, I've learned, the city itself is good for someone of my nature. I don't get noticed so much. It's important for me not to get noticed. Given everything.

So, comfortable Chelsea.

Womb . . .

Inside, I put my lights on and lock the door. I look for intrusion but no one's intruded. I'm paranoid, some would say, but with my life it's not really paranoia, now, is it? I sprinkle fish flakes on the fishes' sky in the tank. This always seems wrong, this diet. But I eat meat and a lot of it. I'm meat too. So what's the difference? Besides, they enjoy it and I enjoy the mini frenzy. They are gold and black and red and dart like pure impulse.

I go to the bathroom and take a shower, to wash off the worry from the mall. And the sweat too. Even on a cold spring day like this, I am damp with escape sweat.

I put the news on. Yes, after a thousand commercials, a story fades onto the screen about the incident at the shopping center in Brooklyn. The escalator malfunction, the man killed so horribly. And the gunshot! Well, that explains it. A police officer tried to stop the motor and rescue the victim by shooting it out. Didn't work. Was it Red who fired the futile bullet? If so, I give her credit for ingenuity.

I see a message on the answering machine – yes, old-fashioned.

'Vernon. Hi. Had to work late.'

Feel that tightness in my gut. She going to cancel? But then I learn it's all right:

'So I'll be closer to eight. If that's okay.'

Her tone is flat but then it always is. She's not a woman with spring in her voice. She has never laughed that I've seen.

'If I don't hear from you, I'll just come over. If that's too late, it's okay. Just call me.'

Alicia's that way. Afraid something will break if she causes any disturbance, asks too much, disagrees even if to anyone else it's not disagreement but just asking a question. Or wondering.

I can do anything to her. Anything.

Which I like, I must say. It makes me feel powerful. Makes me feel good. People have done things to me that aren't so nice. This seems only fair.

I look out the window for Red or any other cops. None.

Paranoia . . .

I check the fridge and pantry for dinner things. Soup, egg rolls, chili without beans, whole chicken, tortillas. Lots of sauces and dips. Cheese.

Skinny bean, Slim Jim. Yeah, that's me. But I eat like a stevedore.

I'm thinking of the two sandwiches I had at Starbucks earlier, particularly enjoyed the smoked ham. Recalling the scream, looking out. See Red scanning the coffee shop, not turning toward the scream, like any normal human being would.

Shopper . . . Spitting out the word, in my mind at least.

Furious at her.

So. I need some comfort. I collect my backpack from its perch by the front door and carry it across the room. I punch numbers into the lock for the Toy Room. I installed the lock myself, which is probably not allowed in a rental. They don't let you do much when you rent. But I pay on time so no one comes to look. Besides I need the Toy Room locked, so it's locked. All the time.

I undo a strong dead bolt. And then I'm inside. The Toy Room is dim except for the bright halogens over the battered table that holds my treasures. The beams of light dance blindingly off the metal edges and blades, mostly shiny steel. The Toy Room is quiet. I soundproofed it well, carefully cutting and fitting sheets of wood and acoustic material over walls and mounting shutters on the window. One could scream oneself hoarse in here and not be heard outside.

I take the bone cracker, the ball-peen hammer, from my backpack and clean and oil it and put it into its place on the workbench shelf. Then a new acquisition, a razor saw, serrated. I unbox it and test the edge with my finger. Whisk, whisk . . . It was made in Japan. My mother told me once that it used to be considered a bad thing, when she was growing up, to have a product made in Japan. How times have changed. Oh, my, this is really quite the clever device. A saw made from a long straight razor. Test the edge again, and, well, see: I've just removed a layer of epidermis.

This, which has now become my new favorite implement, I place in a location of honor on the shelf. I have the absurd thought that the others will be jealous and sad. I'm funny that way. But when your life has been thrown off kilter by Shoppers, you breathe life into inanimate things. Is that so odd, though? They're more dependable than people.

I look at the blade once more. A reflected flash from the light smacks my eye and the room tilts as the pupil shrinks. The sensation is eerie but not unpleasant.

I have a sudden impulse to bring Alicia inside here. Almost a need. I picture the light reflecting off the steel onto her skin, like it's doing on mine. I really don't know her well at all, but I think I will, bring her here, I mean. A low feeling in my gut is telling me to.

Breathing faster now.

Should I do that? Tonight?

That churning in my groin tells me yes. And I can picture her skin reflected in the metal shapes on the workbench, polished to mirror.

I reflect: It will have to be done at some point.

Just do it now. Get it over with . . .

Yes, no?

I'm frozen.

The buzzer sounds. I leave the Toy Room and go to the front door.

Then have a fast thought, a terrible thought.

What if it's not Alicia but Red?

No, no. Could that have happened? Red has such sharp eyes, which means a sharp brain. And she *did* find me at the mall.

Get my bone cracker from the shelf and walk to the door.

I push the intercom button. And pause. 'Hello?'

'Vernon. It's me?' Alicia ends many sentences with question marks. She is such a bundle of uncertainty.

Relaxing, I put the hammer down and hit the outside door release button and a few minutes later I see Alicia's face framed in the video screen, looking up at the tiny security camera above the doorjamb. She enters and we step into the living room. I smell her odd perfume, which has to me a faint scent of sweet onions. I'm sure it's not. But that's my impression.

She avoids my eyes. I tower over her; she's tiny and slim but not as bean as me. 'Hey.'

'Hi.'

We embrace, an interesting word, and I always thought it meant you brace yourself to touch somebody you don't want to touch. Like my mother near the end. My father, always. The word doesn't mean that, sure, but it's what I think.

Alicia shucks her jacket. Hangs it up herself. She's not comfortable with people doing things for her. She's around forty, some years older than me. She's in a blue dress, which has a high neck and long sleeves. She rarely wears polish on her nails. She's comfortable with that image: schoolteacherish. I don't care. It's not her fashion choices that draw me to her. She was a schoolteacher when she was married.

'Dinner?' I ask.

'No?' Again, a question when what she means is: No. Worried that one wrong word, one wrong punctuation mark will ruin the evening.

'You're not hungry?'

She glances toward the second bedroom. 'Just . . . Is it all right? Can we make love, please?'

I take her hand and we walk through the living room, toward the far wall. To the right is the Toy Room. The left, the back bedroom, the door open and the carefully made bed illuminated by a soft glow of night-light.

I pause for just a moment, eyes on the Toy Room Lock. She looks up at me, curious, but would never dream of asking, Is something wrong?

I make a decision and turn toward the left, leading her after me.

CHAPTER 5

'What happened?' Lincoln Rhyme asked. 'The scene in Brooklyn?'

This was his way of tapping the maple tree. Sachs was not normally forthcoming with details, or even clues, about what was troubling her – just like him. Nor was either of them inclined to say, 'So what's wrong?' But camouflaging the question about her state of mind under the netting of specifics concerning, say, a crime scene sometimes did the trick.

'Kind of a problem.' And fell silent.

Well, gave it a shot.

They were in the parlor of his town house on Central Park West. She dropped her purse and briefcase onto a rattan chair. 'Going to wash up.' She strode up the hall to the ground-floor bathroom. He heard pleasantries exchanged between Sachs and Rhyme's aide, Thom Reston, preparing dinner.

The smells of cooking wafted. Rhyme detected poaching fish, capers, carrots with thyme. A touch of cumin, probably in the rice. Yes, his olfactory senses – those clever ligands – were, he believed, enhanced following the crime scene accident years ago that had severed his spine and rendered him a C4 quad. However, it was an easy deduction; Thom tended to make this particular meal once a week. Not a foodie, by any means, Rhyme nonetheless enjoyed the dish. Provided it was accompanied by a crisp Chablis. Which it would be.

Sachs returned and Rhyme persisted. 'Your unsub? How are you identifying him, again? I forgot.' He was sure she'd told him. But unless a fact directly touched a project Rhyme was involved with, it tended to dissipate like vapor.

'Unsub Forty. After that club near where he killed the vic.' She seemed surprised he hadn't remembered.

'He rabbited.'

'Yep. Vanished. It was chaos, because of the escalator thing.'

He noted that Sachs didn't unholster her Glock and place it on the shelf near the front doorway into the hall. This meant she wouldn't be staying tonight. She had her own town house, in Brooklyn, and divided her time between there and here. Or she had until recently. For the past few weeks, she'd stayed here only twice.

Another observation: Her clothing was pristine, not evidencing the dirt and blood that had to have resulted from her descent into the pit to try to rescue the accident victim. Since the unsub's escape – and the escalator incident – had been in Brooklyn, she would have gone home to bathe and change.

Therefore, since she was planning on leaving again, why had she driven back here from that borough to Manhattan?

Maybe for dinner? He was hoping so.

Thom stepped into the parlor from the hallway. 'Here you go.' He handed her a glass of white wine.

'Thanks.' She sipped.

Rhyme's aide was trim and as good looking as a Nautica model, today dressed in dark slacks, white shirt and subdued burgundy-and-pink tie. He dressed better than any other caregiver Rhyme had ever had, and if the outfit seemed a bit impractical, the important part was attended to: His shoes were solid and rubber-soled – to safely transfer the solidly built Rhyme between bed and wheelchair. And an accessory: Peeking from his rear pocket was a fringe of cornflower-blue latex gloves for the piss 'n' shit detail.

He said to Sachs, 'You sure you can't stay for dinner?'

'No, thanks. I have other plans.'

Which answered that question, though the lack of elaboration only added to the mystery of her presence here now.

Rhyme cleared his throat. He glanced at his empty tumbler, sitting mouth level on the side of the wheelchair (the cup holder was its first accessory).

'You've had two,' Thom told him.

'I've had one, which you *divided* into two. Actually I've had less than one if I saw the quantity correctly.' Sometimes he fought with the aide on this, and a dozen other, subjects but today Rhyme wasn't in a truly petulant mood; he was pleased at how class had gone. On the other hand, he was troubled, as well. What was up with Sachs? But, let us not parse too finely, mostly he just wanted more goddamn scotch.

He nearly tried that it had been one hell of a day. But that wouldn't have been the truth. It had been a pleasant day, a calm day. Unlike the many times when he was half crazed from the pursuit of a killer or terrorist, before he'd quit the police consulting business.

'Please and thank you?'

Thom looked at him suspiciously. He hesitated then poured from the bottle of Glenmorangie, which, damn it, the man kept on a shelf out of reach, as if Rhyme were a toddler fascinated by a colorful tin of drain cleaner.

'Dinner in a half hour,' Thom said and vanished back to his simmering turbot.

Sachs sipped wine, looking over the forensic lab equipment and supplies packed into the Victorian parlor: computers, a gas chromatograph/mass spectrometer, ballistics examination units, density gradient measurers, friction ridge imaging hoods, alternative light sources, a scanning electron microscope. With these, and the dozens of examination tables and hundreds of tools, the parlor was a forensic lab that would be the envy of many a small- or even medium-sized police department. Much of it was now covered with plastic tarps or cotton sheets, as unemployed as their owner. Rhyme still consulted some on non-criminal matters, in addition to teaching, but most of his work involved writing for academia and professional journals.

Her eyes, he saw, went to a dim corner where sat a half-dozen whiteboards on which they used to write down evidence gathered from scenes by Sachs and Rhyme's former protégé, Patrolman Ron Pulaski. The threesome, along with another officer from CSU headquarters, would stand, and sit, before the boards and kick about ideas as to the perp's identity and whereabouts. The boards now faced away, toward the wall, as if resenting that Rhyme no longer had any use for them.

After a moment Sachs said, 'I went to see the widow.'

'Widow?'

'Sandy Frommer. The wife of the victim.'

It took him a moment to realize she wasn't speaking of the person killed by Unsub 40, but the man who'd died in the escalator accident.

'You have to deliver the news?' Forensic cops, like Rhyme, rarely if ever are charged with the difficult task of explaining that a loved one is no longer of this earth.

'No. Just . . . Greg, the vic, wanted me to tell her he loved her and his son. When he was dying. I agreed.'

'Good of you.'

A shrug. 'The son's twelve. Bryan.'

Rhyme didn't ask how they were doing. Verbal empties, questions like that.

Clutching her wine in both hands, Sachs walked to an unsterile table, leaned against it. Returned his gaze. 'I was close. Almost had him, Unsub Forty, I mean. But then the accident, the escalator. I had to choose.' Sipping wine.

'The right thing, Sachs. Of course. You had to do it.'

'It was just a coincidence I tipped to him – there was no time, zero time to put together a full take-down team.' She closed her eyes. A slow shake of the head. 'A crowded mall. Just couldn't get it together.'

Sachs was her own harshest critic and Rhyme knew the difficult circumstances of the impromptu take-down operation might dull the sting for some people but, with Sachs, they did not. He had evidence of this now: Sachs's hand disappeared into her hair and she scratched her scalp. Then she seemed to sense she was doing so and stopped. Started again a moment later. She was a woman of great dynamics, some light, some dark. They came as a package.

'Forensics?' he asked. 'On your unsub?'

'Not much at Starbucks, where he was sitting. The unsub heard Greg Frommer's scream and, like everybody else, looked toward it. I was in his line of sight. I guess he saw my piece or the shield on my belt. Knew what was going down. Or suspected. So he left fast, took everything with him. Got some trace at the table but he'd been there only for a few minutes.'

'Exit route?' Rhyme was no longer working for the NYPD, but obvious questions naturally flowed.

'Loading dock. Ron, some ECTs and some uniforms from the Eight-Four are on it, canvassing, and may have a secondary to search. We'll see. Oh, and I got a shooting team convened in my honor.'

'Why?'

'I blew away a motor.'

'You . . . ?'

'You didn't see the news?'

'No.'

'The vic wasn't stuck in the steps of the escalator. He fell through onto the gears of the drive motor. No cutoff switch there. I shot out the coils of the motor. It was too late.'

Rhyme considered this. 'No one was injured by the shot so they wouldn't put you on administrative. You'll get a no-action letter in a week or so.'

'Hope so. Captain from the Eight-Four's on my side. As long as there're no reporters trying to make their careers with stories on cops shooting guns in malls, I'll be cool.'

'I don't think that's much of a journalistic subspecialty,' Rhyme said wryly.

'Well, Madino, the captain, he managed to purgatory the situation for a while.'

'Love the word,' Rhyme told her. 'You end-ran it.' Pleased with his own verbing.

She smiled.

Rhyme liked that. She hadn't been smiling a lot lately.

She returned to the rattan chair near Rhyme and sat. The furniture made its distinctive mew, a sound Rhyme had never heard duplicated elsewhere.

'You're thinking,' she said slowly, 'if I changed clothes at my house, which I did, and if I'm not staying here tonight, which I'm not . . .' She cocked her head. 'Why'd I make the trip?'

'Exactly.'

She set down her half-finished wine. 'I came by to ask you something. I need a favor. Your initial reaction is going to be to say no but just hear me out. Deal?'

I wasn't brave enough.

Not tonight.

I didn't take Alicia to the Toy Room.

I debated, but no.

She's left – she's never stayed over – and I'm in bed, 11 p.m. or so. I don't know. Thinking of us in the bedroom earlier: unzipping Alicia's blue dress, the teacher's dress, the zipper at the back. Modest. Bra was complicated, not to undo, but the structure. Though it was hard to see for certain because, of course, we both prefer the lights dim.

Then my clothes were off too, my clothes like queen sheets on a twin bed. Her tiny hands moved fast as hungry hummingbirds. Truly deft. And we played our game. Love that. Just love it. Though I have to be careful. If I don't think of something else, it's over too soon. Trot out thoughts and memories: A steel chisel I bought last week, considering what it would do to bone. Dinner at my favorite take-out place. The screams of the victim recently in the construction site near 40° North, as the ball-peen hammer came down on his skull. (I take this as proof I'm not truly a monster. Picturing the blood, the snap, doesn't make me finish faster but dulls me a bit.)

Then Alicia and I found the pulse and all was well . . . until, damn it, really, the image of that police girl came to mind. Red. I pictured looking toward the screams from the escalator, seeing her, badge and gun and all, as she was looking toward *me*. Shadowed eyes, red hair flying. Looking *away* from the bloody escalator and the screams, looking *for* me, me, me. But, odd, though she gave me a terrible scare at the mall, though she's as bad as the worst Shopper ever, picturing her as I pulsed atop tiny Alicia didn't slow me down. Just the opposite.

Stop it! Go away!

My God, did I say that aloud? I wondered.

Glanced at Alicia. No. She was lost in whatever place she goes to at times like this.

But Red didn't go away.

And it was over. Snap. Alicia seemed surprised a little at the speed. Not that she seemed to care. Sex feeds women many different courses, like tapas, where a man wants a single entrée to wolf down and wolf fast.

After, we dozed and I awoke thinking I was still empty somehow and thought about the Toy Room, taking her there.

Yes? I'd wondered. No?

Then I told her to leave.

Goodbye, goodbye.

Nothing more than those words.

And she left.

Now I find my phone, listen to a voice mail message from my brother. '*Yo. Next Sunday. Anjelika or Film Forum? David Lynch or* The Man Who Fell to Earth? *Your call. Ha, no actually it's my call. 'Cause it's* me who *dialed* you!'

Love to hear his voice. Like mine, yet not like mine.

I then wonder what to do with my wakefulness. There are plenty of plans I have to consider for tomorrow. But instead I fumble through the bedside table drawer. Find the diary and continue writing passages. I'm transcribing, actually, from the MP3 player. It's always easier to talk, let the thoughts fly like bats at dusk, going where they will. Then write it down later.

These passages from the difficult days, the high school days. Who isn't glad to have left those times behind? I write in pretty good script. The nuns. They weren't bad, most of them. But when they insisted, you listened, you practiced, you pleased them.

Well. What a day. At school until four. Civics club project. Mrs Hooper was happy about my work. Took the secret way home. Longer but better (know why? Obvious). Past the house that drapes out cobwebs at Halloween, past the pond that seems smaller every year, past Marjorie's house, where I saw her that one time blouse open and she never knew.

Was hoping, praying I'd get home today okay and I think I will. But then there they are.

Sammy and Franklin. They're leaving Cindy Hanson's house. Cindy could be a fashion model. So pretty. Sam and Frank, so handsome, are the sort could go out with her. I don't even talk to her. I don't exist to her, I'm not on this planet. Complexion clear but too skinny too gawky too awkward. That's okay. That's the way the world works.

Sam and Frank have never slugged me, pushed me down, rubbed my face in dirt or dog shit. But never been alone with them. Know they've looked at me some, well, of course, they have. Everybody in school has. If this was Duncan or Butler, I'd get whaled on, the crap totally beaten out of me, 'cause there aren't any witnesses around. So I guess same is going to happen with them. They're shorter than me, who isn't? But stronger and I can't fight, don't know how. Flail, that's what somebody said I was doing. I looked silly. Asked Dad to help. He didn't. Put on a boxing show on TV and left me to watch it. Lotta good that did.

So now, getting beat up.

Because there aren't any witnesses around.

No way I can turn. I just keep walking. Waiting for the fists. And they're grinning. What the boys in school always do before the hitting.

But they don't hit. Sam's like hi, and asks if I live near here. A couple blocks away, I tell him. So they know now this is a really weird way for me to get home from school, but they don't say anything.

He just says nice neighborhood here. Frank says he lives closer to the tracks which is noisy and it kind of sucks.

Then from Frank: Dude. Epic in class today.

I'm like I can't say anything. What he means is Mrs Rich's class. Calc. She called on me because I was looking out the window, which she does when somebody's looking out the window to embarrass them and without looking back I said $g(1) = h(1) + 7 = -10.88222 + 7 = -3.88222$.

Yeah, one of them says. Loved her face, Mrs Bitch. You owned her, man.

Epic.

'See you 'round.' From Sam. And they just walk away.

I don't get whaled on or spit on. Or told dick bod, skinny bean, all of that.

Nothing.

A good day. Today was a good day.

I pause the recorder and sip some water. Then ease down beside the pillow holding Alicia's scent. I used to think I would date a blind woman. Tried, but couldn't find one. They don't use personals. Maybe it's too risky. Blind women wouldn't care about too tall, too skinny, long face, long fingers, long feet. Skinny worm freak. Skinny bean boy. Slim Jim. So, a blind woman was my plan. But didn't work out. I meet somebody occasionally. It works okay for what it is. Then it ends.

It always ends. It will end with Alicia too.

I think of the Toy Room.

Then I'm back to the diary, transcribing again, ten minutes, twenty.

The ups and downs of life, recorded forever. Just like my mementos on the shelves in the Toy Room: I remember the joy or sadness or anger surrounding each one.

Today was a good day.

WEDNESDAY

II THE INTERN

CHAPTER 6

'Mr Rhyme, an honor.'

Not sure how to respond to that. A nod seemed appropriate. 'Mr Whitmore.'

No nudge to first names. Rhyme had learned, however, that his was Evers.

The attorney might have been transplanted from the 1950s. He wore a dark-blue suit, gabardine, a white shirt whose collar and cuffs were starched to plastic. The tie, equally stiff, was the shade of blue that couldn't quite give up violet and was narrow as a ruler. A white rectangle peeked from the jacket's breast pocket.

Whitmore's face was long and pallid and so expressionless Rhyme thought for a moment that he had Bell's Palsy or some paralysis of the cranial nerves. Just as that conclusion was reached, though, his brow furrowed ever so slightly as he took in the parlor and its *CSI* accoutrements.

Rhyme realized that the man seemed to be waiting for an invitation to sit. Rhyme told him to do so and, smoothing his trousers and unbuttoning his jacket, Whitmore picked a chair close by and lowered himself onto it. Perfectly upright. He removed his glasses, cleaned the round lenses with a dark-blue cloth and replaced both, on nose and in pocket respectively.

Upon meeting Rhyme, visitors generally reacted in one of two ways. The majority were stricken nearly dumb, blushing, to be in the company of a man 90 percent of whose body was immobile. Others would joke and banter about his condition. This was tedious, though preferable to the former.

Some – Rhyme's partiality – upon meeting him would glance once or twice at his body, and move on, undoubtedly the same way they would assess potential in-laws: We'll withhold judgment till we get to the substance. This is what Whitmore now did.

'Do you know Amelia?' Rhyme asked.

'No. I've never met Detective Sachs. We have a mutual friend, a classmate of ours from high school. Brooklyn. Fellow attorney. She called Richard initially and asked him to consider the case but he doesn't do personal injury law. He gave her my number.'

The narrowness of his face accentuated its pensive expression, and Rhyme was surprised to hear that he and Sachs were roughly the same age. He'd have thought Whitmore a half-dozen years older.

'When she called me about taking on a possible case and told me that you were free to be an expert witness, I was surprised.'

Rhyme considered the time line implicit in his comment. Apparently Sachs had committed Rhyme to be a consultant before she'd confessed to him this was the reason she'd driven from the widow's house in Brooklyn to the parlor here last night.

I came by to ask you something. I need a favor . . .

'But of course I'm pleased that you're available.

All wrongful death litigation involves thorny evidentiary matters. And I know that will be particularly true in this case. You have quite the reputation.' He looked around. 'Is Detective Sachs here?'

'No, she's downtown. Working a homicide case. But last night she told me about your client. Sandy, that's her name?'

'The widow. Mrs Frommer. Sandy.'

'Her situation's as bad as Amelia told me?'

'I don't know what she told you.' A precise correction of Rhyme's imprecision. He doubted Whitmore would be fun to share a beer with but he would be a good man to have as your counselor, especially when cross-examining the other side. 'But I'll confirm that Mrs Frommer is facing some very difficult times. Her husband had no life insurance and he hadn't worked full-time for some years. Mrs Frommer works for a housecleaning service but only part-time. They're in debt. Significant debt. They have some distant family but nobody is in a position to help much financially. One cousin can provide temporary shelter – in a garage. I've been practicing personal injury law for years and I can tell you that for many clients a recovery is a windfall; in Mrs Frommer's case, it's a necessity.

'Now, Mr Rhyme . . . Excuse me, you were a captain on the police force, right? Should I call you that?'

'No, Lincoln is fine.'

'Now, I would like to tell you what our situation is.'

There was a robotic element to him. Not irritating. Just plain odd. Maybe juries liked it.

Whitmore opened his old-fashioned briefcase – again,

circa the 1950s – and withdrew some unlined white sheets. He uncapped a pen (not a fountain pen, Rhyme was mildly surprised to see) and in the smallest handwriting that was still possible for the unaided eye to read, he wrote what seemed to be the date and the parties present, the subject of the meeting. Unlined paper, yes, but the ascenders and descenders of the characters were as even as if they butted into a ruler.

He looked at the sparse notes, seemed satisfied and lifted his gaze.

'I intend to file suit in New York trial court – the Supreme Court, as you know.'

The forum, the lowest in the state, despite the lofty name, handled criminal cases as well as civil suits; Rhyme had testified there a thousand times as an expert witness for the prosecution.

'The complaints will be for wrongful death on the part of the widow, Mrs Frommer. And their child.'

'A teenage boy, right?'

'No. Twelve.'

'Ah, yes.'

'And for pain and suffering on behalf of Mr Frommer's estate. My understanding is that he survived for perhaps ten minutes in extreme agony. That recovery will, as I say, go into his estate and enure to the benefit of whoever is mentioned in his testamentary documents or according to determination of the probate court if he had no will. In addition, I will be filing suit on behalf of Mr Frommer's parents, whose support, to the extent he was able, he was contributing to. That will also be a wrongful death action.'

This was perhaps the least flamboyant, if not the most boring, attorney Rhyme had ever met.

'The ad damnum in my complaint – the demand for damages – is, frankly speaking, outrageously high. Thirty million for the wrongful death, twenty million for pain and suffering. We could never recover that. But I picked those sums merely to get the defendants' attention and to create a little publicity for the case. I don't intend to go to trial.'

'No?'

'No. Our situation is a little unusual. Because of the absence of insurance and any other financial support for Mrs Frommer and her son, they need a settlement quickly. A trial could take a year or more. They'd be destitute by then. They'll need money for shelter, the youngster's education, to buy health insurance, for necessaries. After we present a solid case against the defendants, and I indicate a willingness to reduce the demand considerably, I believe they'll write some checks that are minuscule to them but sizable to Mrs Frommer, and roughly in the amount that sees sufficient justice done.'

He'd be at home in a Dickens novel, Rhyme decided. 'Seems like a reasonable strategy. Now, can we talk about the evidence?'

'A moment, please.' Evers Whitmore was going to steam forward true to the course he'd set, no matter what. 'First, I would like to explain to you the intricacies of the relevant law. Are you familiar with tort law?'

It was obvious that whether he said yes, no or maybe was irrelevant. Attorney Whitmore was going to *make* him familiar.

63

'Not really, no.'

'I'll give you an overview. Tort law deals with harm caused by the defendant to the plaintiff, other than a breach of contract. The word comes from—'

'Latin for "twisted"? *Tortus*.' Rhyme had an affection for the classics.

'Indeed.' Whitmore was neither impressed at Rhyme's knowledge nor disappointed that he'd missed an opportunity to expound. 'Car accidents, libel and slander, hunting accidents, lamps catching fire, toxic spills, plane crashes, assault – *threatening* to hit a person – and battery – actually *hitting* him. Those are often conflated. Even intentional murder, which can be both criminal and civil.'

O. J. Simpson, thought Rhyme.

Whitmore said, 'So a tortious action for wrongful death and personal injury. The first step is to find our defendant – who exactly is responsible for Mr Frommer's death? Our best hope is that it's the escalator itself that caused the harm and not some outside party. Under tort law anyone injured by a *product* – anything, an appliance, car, drug, *escalator* – has a much easier time proving the case. In nineteen sixty-three a justice on the California Supreme Court created a cause of action called strict products liability – to shift the burden of loss from an injured consumer to the manufacturer even when it wasn't negligent. In strict liability all you need to show is that the product was defective and injured the plaintiff.'

'What constitutes a defect?' Rhyme asked, finding himself reluctantly intrigued by the lecture.

'A key question, Mr Rhyme. A defect can be that it was badly designed, that it had a weakness or flaw in the manufacturing or that there was a failure to adequately warn the consumer of dangers. Have you seen a baby stroller lately?'

Why would I? Rhyme's lips formed a faint smile.

Whitmore seemed immune to irony and continued, 'You'd appreciate the sticker: *Remove infant before folding stroller closed*. I'm not making that up. Of course, yes, it's called strict liability but not absolute. There *does* have to be a defect. Someone who uses a chain saw to attack a victim, for instance, is an intervening cause. The plaintiff can't sue the saw manufacturer for an assault like that.

'Now, to our case: The first question is, Whom do we sue? Was there a design or manufacturing flaw in the Midwest Conveyance escalator itself? Or was it in good working order and the mall management company, a cleaning crew or a separate maintenance company was negligent in repairing or maintaining it? Did a worker not latch it closed last time it was opened? Did someone manually open the panel while Mr Frommer was on it? Did the general contractor who built the mall render the unit dangerous? The subcontractor who installed the escalator? What about component parts manufacturers? What about the mall cleaning staff? Were they working for an independent contractor or employees of the mall? This is where you come in.'

Rhyme was already thinking of how to proceed. 'First, I'll need to have someone inspect the escalator, the controls, the crime scene photos, trace, and—'

'Ah. Now, I must tell you our situation has a *slight* wrinkle. Well, several wrinkles.'

Rhyme's brow rose.

Whitmore continued, 'Any accident involving an escalator, elevator, moving sidewalk, et cetera, is investigated by the Department of Buildings and the Department of Investigation.'

Rhyme was familiar with the DOI. One of the oldest law enforcement agencies in the country – going back to the early nineteenth century – the division was charged with overseeing government employees, agencies and anyone who contracted or worked with the city. Because he himself was rendered a quad while investigating a crime scene in a subway construction site, the DOI was involved with the investigation into how his accident happened.

Whitmore continued, 'We can use the findings in our suit, but—'

'It'll take months to get their report.'

'Exactly the problem, Mr Rhyme. Six months, a year more likely. Yes. And we can't wait that long. Mrs Frommer will be homeless by then. Or living in her relatives garage in Schenectady.'

'Wrinkle one. And two?'

'Access to the escalator. It's being removed and impounded in a city warehouse, pending investigation by the DOI and DOB.'

Hell, already major evidence contamination, Rhyme thought instinctively.

'Get a subpoena,' he said. This was obvious.

'I can't at this point. As soon as I file suit – that'll be within the next few days – I can serve a duces tecum. But a judge will quash it. We won't get access until DOI and DOB have finished their investigation.'

This was absurd. The escalator was the best evidence, possibly the only evidence, in the case and he couldn't get his hands on it?

Then he remembered: Of course, it's a civil, not a criminal, matter.

'We can also subpoena design, manufacturing, installation and maintenance records from the possible defendants: the mall, the manufacturer – Midwest Conveyance – the cleaning company, anyone else with any connection to the unit. Those we might get copies of but it'll be a fight. And the motions'll go back and forth for months before they're released. Finally, the last wrinkle. I mentioned that Mr Frommer wasn't working full-time any longer?'

'I recall. A midlife crisis or some such.'

'That's correct. He quit a high-pressure corporate position. Lately he worked jobs that he didn't have to take home at night – deliveryman, telemarketer, order taker in a fast-food restaurant, a shoe salesman at the mall. Most of his time was spent volunteering for charities. Literacy, homelessness, hunger. So for the past few years he's had minimal income. One of the hardest parts of our case will be convincing a jury that he would have gotten back into the workforce in a job like the one he had.'

'What did he used to do?'

'Before he quit he was director of marketing. Patterson Systems in New Jersey. I looked it up. Very successful company. Number one fuel injector maker in America. And he made solid six figures. *Last* year his income was thirty-three thousand. The jury awards wrongful death damages based on earnings. The defendants' attorneys will hammer home that, even if their clients are liable, the damages were minimal since he was making just enough to live on.

'I will be trying to prove that Mr Frommer was going through a phase. That he was going to get back into a high-paying job. Now, I may not succeed at that. So this is your second task. If you can make the case that the defendant, whoever it or they turn out to be, engaged in wanton or reckless behavior in building the escalator or a component part, or in failing to maintain the device, then we'll—'

'—add a punitive damage claim. And the jury, which feels bad that they can't award the widow much by way of future earnings, will compensate with a big punitive award.'

'Well observed, Mr Rhyme. You should have gone to law school. So, there we have our situation in a nutshell.'

Rhyme said, 'In other words, find out how a complex device failed and who's responsible for that failure without having access to it, the supporting documentation or even photographs or analysis of the accident?'

'And *that* is well put too.' He added, 'Detective Sachs said you were rather creative when it came to approaching a problem like this.'

How creative could one be without the damn evidence? Absurd, Rhyme thought again. The whole thing was completely . . .

Then a thought occurred. Whitmore was speaking but Rhyme ignored him. He turned toward the doorway. 'Thom! Thom! Where are you?'

Footsteps and a moment later the aide appeared. 'Is everything all right?'

'Fine, fine, fine. Why wouldn't it be? I just need something.'

'And what's that?'

'A tape measure. And the sooner the better.'

CHAPTER 7

Ironic.

One Police Plaza is considered to be among the ugliest government structures in New York City, yet it offers some of the finest views in downtown Manhattan: the harbor, the East River, the soaring 'Let the River Run' skyline of New York at its most muscular. By contrast, the original police headquarters on Centre Street is arguably the most elegant building south of Houston Street, but, in the day, officers stationed there could look out only on tenements, butchers, fishmongers, prostitutes, ne'er-do-wells and muggers lying in wait (police officers were, at the time, prime targets for thieves, who valued their wool uniforms and brass buttons).

Walking into her office now in the Major Cases Division at One PP, Amelia Sachs was gazing out the speckled windows as she reflected on this fact. Thinking too: She couldn't have cared less about either the building's architectural aesthetics or the view. What she objected to was that she plied her investigative skills here and not from Lincoln Rhyme's town house.

Hell.

Not happy about his resigning from the police consulting business, not happy at all. Personally she missed the stimulation of the give-and-take, the head-butting, the creativity that flourished from the gestalt. Her life had become like studying at an online university: The information was the same but the process of loading it into your brain was diminished.

Cases weren't progressing. Homicides, in particular, Rhyme's specialty, were not getting solved. The Rinaldo case, for instance, had been on her docket for about a month and was going nowhere. A killing on the West Side south of Midtown. Echi Rinaldo, a minor deliveryman and drug dealer, had been slashed to death, and slashed vigorously. The street and alley had been filthy, so the inventory of trace was voluminous and therefore not very helpful: cigarette butts, a roach clip with a bit of pot still clinging, food wrappers, coffee cups, a wheel from a child's toy, beer cans, a condom, scraps of paper, receipts, a hundred other items of effluvia common to New York City streets. None of the fingerprint or footprint evidence she'd found at the scene had panned out.

The only other lead was a witness – the deceased's son. Well, witness of *sorts*. The eight-year-old hadn't seen the killer clearly but had heard the assailant jump into a cab and give an address, which included the word 'Village.' A male voice. More likely white than black or Latino. Sachs had exhausted her interview skills to get the boy to recall more but he was, understandably, upset, seeing his father in the alley, cascading with blood. A canvass of cabs and gypsy drivers revealed nothing. And Greenwich Village covered dozens of square miles.

But she was convinced that Rhyme could have reviewed the mass of evidence and come to a conclusion about where, in that quaint portion of Manhattan, the perp had most likely gone.

He'd started to help then said no. And had reminded coolly that he was no longer in the criminal business.

Sachs smoothed her charcoal-gray skirt, just past the knees. She'd thought she'd selected a lighter-gray blouse, to complement, but had realized on the sidewalk in front of her town house as she left that it was the taupe one. Those were her typical mornings. Much distraction.

She now reviewed emails and phone messages, decided they were neglectable and then headed up the hall, toward the conference room she'd commandeered for the Unsub 40 case.

Thinking again about Rhyme.

Resigned.

Hell . . .

She glanced up and noted a young detective, walking the opposite way, turn toward her suddenly. She realized she must have uttered the word aloud.

She gave him a smile, to prove she wasn't deranged, and dodged into her war room, small, set up with two fiberboard tables, twin computers, one desk and a whiteboard on which details of the case were jotted in marker.

'Any minute,' said the young blond officer inside, looking up. He was in dark-blue NYPD uniform, sitting at the far table. Ron Pulaski was not a detective, as were most officers in the Major Cases Division. But he was the cop Amelia Sachs had wanted to work the Unsub 40 case with. They'd run scenes for years, always – until now – from Rhyme's parlor.

Pulaski nodded at the screen. 'They promised.'

Any minute . . .

'How much did they get?'

'Not sure. I wouldn't expect his address and phone number. But the ECT said they had some hits. It was a good call, Amelia.'

After the disaster – the word applied in several senses: the victim's death as well as losing Unsub 40 – at the mall in Brooklyn, Sachs had methodically examined the area behind the loading dock and debated where to send the Brooklyn Evidence Collection Teams; you can't search everywhere. One place that particularly intrigued her was a cheap Mexican restaurant whose back door opened onto a cul-de-sac near the loading dock. It was the only food venue nearby. There were other, faster ways for their unsub to have fled but Sachs concentrated the canvassing there, on the perhaps far-fetched theory that the restaurant would be more likely than other venues to have undocumented employees who'd be less cooperative, not wanting to give their names and addresses as witnesses.

As she'd guessed, no one, from manager to dishwasher, had seen the rather recognizable suspect.

Which didn't mean he hadn't been there, however; in the refuse bin for customers the search team had found the Starbucks cup, along with cellophane sandwich wrappers and napkins from the chain, which he'd been seen carrying as he fled.

They'd collected all the trash from that container at La Festiva, which may or may not have been a real Spanish word.

The analysis of this evidence was what they were presently awaiting.

Sachs dropped into the chair she'd wheeled here from her minuscule office. Reflecting that if they had been working out of Rhyme's parlor, the data would have been in their hands by now. Her phone sang with an email tone. It was good news from the captain at the 84, Madino. He said there was no hurry on her shooting incident report; it was taking some time to get the Borough Shooting Team together. He added that, as she and Rhyme had discussed earlier, a few reporters had called, inquiring about the wisdom of firing a weapon in a crowded mall but Madino deflected them by saying the matter was being investigated according to department procedures and didn't release her name. None of the journalists followed up.

All good news.

Now Pulaski's computer offered up a ship's-bell ding. 'Okay, here it is. Evidence analysis.'

As he read, the young man's hand went to his forehead and rubbed briefly. The scar wasn't long but it was quite obvious today, from this angle, in this light. In the first case that he'd run with Sachs and Rhyme he'd made a mistake and the perp, a particularly vicious professional killer, had clocked him in the head. The resulting injury, which had affected his brain as well as his pride and appearance, had nearly ended his career. But determination, encouragement from his twin brother (also a cop) and Lincoln Rhyme's persistence had kept him in blue. He still had moments of uncertainty – head injuries poison self-confidence – but he was one of the smartest and most dogged officers Sachs knew.

He sighed. 'Not a whole lot.'

'What is there?'

'Trace from the Starbucks shop itself, nothing. From the Mexican restaurant: DNA from the rim of the Starbucks cup but no CODIS match.'

It's rarely that easy.

'No friction ridges,' Pulaski said.

'What? He wore gloves in the Starbucks?'

'Looks like he used the napkin to hold the cup. The tech at CSU used vacuum and ninhydrin but only a partial showed up. From the tip. Too narrow for IAFIS.'

The national fingerprint database was comprehensive but only prints that came from the pads of fingers, not the very end, were usable.

But again she wondered: Had the evidence gone to Rhyme for analysis and not to the CSU lab in Queens, would *he* have been able to raise a fingerprint? The lab facility at headquarters was state-of-the-art but it wasn't, well, it wasn't Lincoln Rhyme's.

'Shoeprint from Starbucks, probably his,' Pulaski read, 'since it was superimposed over others and matched one on the loading dock and at the Mexican restaurant. Similar trace found in tread from the dock and restaurant. It's a size thirteen Reebok. Daily Cushion Two Point Oh. The trace chemical profile's here.'

She looked at the screen and read out a list of chemicals she'd never heard of. 'Which is?'

Pulaski scrolled down. 'Probably humus.'

'Dirt?'

The blond officer continued to read the fine print. 'Humus is the penultimate degree of decomposition of organic matter.'

She recalled an exchange between Rhyme and Pulaski years ago when the rookie had used 'penultimate' to mean 'final,' as opposed to the proper meaning – next to last. The memory was more poignant than she wished.

'So *soon-to-be* dirt.'

'Pretty much. And it came from somewhere else. It doesn't match any of the control samples that you or the ECT collected in and around the mall, loading dock and restaurant.' He continued to read. 'Well, not so good here.'

'What's that?'

'Dinitroaniline.'

'Never heard of it.'

'Number of uses, dyes, pesticides, for instance. But the number one: explosives.'

Sachs pointed to the chart from the murder scene itself, the construction site where Unsub 40 beat Todd Williams to death near the club a couple of weeks ago. 'Ammonium nitrate.'

Fertilizer – and the major explosive ingredient in home-made bombs, like the one that destroyed the Oklahoma City federal building in the '90s.

'So,' Pulaski said slowly, 'you think there's more to it than a robbery? The unsub was, I don't know, buying bomb ingredients near Forty Degrees North or the construction site and Williams saw it?' He tapped the computer screen. 'And look at this.' In trace collected near a footprint at the mall loading dock was a small amount of motor oil.

The second ingredient in a fertilizer bomb.

Sachs sighed. Were there terrorist dimensions to this unsub?

Though the murder had occured at a jobsite, these chemicals would not have been used for commercial demolition. 'Keep going.'

'More phenol. Like we found at the first murder scene.'

'If it's shown up twice it's significant. What's that used for?'

Pulaski called up a profile of the chemical. 'Phenol. A precursor in making plastics, like polycarbonates, resins and nylon. Also in making aspirin, embalming fluid, cosmetics, ingrown toenail cures.'

Forty had big feet. Maybe nail problems.

'Then this.' He was transcribing a long list of other chemicals onto a whiteboard evidence chart.

'Mouthful,' she said.

'Profiles as makeup. Cosmetics. No idea of the brand.'

'Need to know who makes it. Have somebody in HQ track it down.'

Pulaski sent the request.

Then they returned to the evidence. He said, 'Have a tiny shaving of metal. From the footprint in the hallway leading to the loading dock.'

'Let me see it.'

Pulaski called up the photos.

Hard to make out to the eye – whether naked or stylishly covered with drugstore-bought reading glasses, which Sachs had had to resort to lately.

She cranked up the magnification and studied the shiny bit. Then turned to the second laptop, typed her way into an NYPD database of metal trace, which, as it turned out, Lincoln Rhyme had established several years earlier.

Together they scanned the database. 'Something similar

there,' said Pulaski, standing over her shoulder, as he pointed at one of the photos.

Yes, good. The tiny fleck was from the process of sharpening a knife, scissors or razor.

'It's steel. He likes a sharp blade.' He'd beaten the victim to death outside 40° North but that didn't mean he wasn't interested in dispatching victims with other weapons as well.

On the other hand, he might recently have done nothing more than carved up the family's chicken dinner with a knife he'd just dramatically edged, tableside.

Pulaski continued 'And some sawdust. Want to see?'

She looked at the microscopic images. The grains were very fine.

'From sanding, you think?' she mused. 'Not sawing?'

'I don't know. Makes sense.'

She clicked a finger against a thumbnail. Twice. Tension rippled through her. 'The analyst in Queens didn't tell us the type of wood. We need to find that out.'

'I'll request it.' Rubbing his forehead with one hand, Pulaski scrolled through more analyses with the other. 'Looks like hammers and bombs aren't enough. This guy wants to poison people too? Significant traces of organochlorine and benzoic acid. Toxins. Typical of insecticides but they've been used in homicides. And more chemicals that . . .' He regarded a database. '. . . profile as varnish.'

'Sawdust and varnish. He's a carpenter, construction worker? Or somebody putting his bombs in wooden boxes or behind paneled walls.'

But since there'd been no reports of improvised explosive devices in the area, encased in wood or otherwise,

Sachs put this possibility low on the likelihood scale.

'I want the manufacturer,' Sachs said. 'The varnish. The type of sawdust too.'

Pulaski said nothing.

She glanced his way and noted that he was looking at his phone. A text.

'Ron?'

He started and slipped the phone away. He'd been preoccupied lately. She wondered if there was an illness in the family.

'Everything okay?'

'Sure. Fine.'

She repeated, 'I want the manufacturer.'

'Of the . . . oh, the varnish.'

'Of the varnish. And the type of wood. And brand of make-up.'

'I'll get on it.' He sent another request to the crime lab.

They turned to the secondary category of evidence – that which might or might not have come from the unsub. The ECTs had collected the entire contents of the bin where they found the Starbucks trash, on the theory that the rubbish from the coffee chain might not have been the only things the perp discarded. There were thirty or forty items: napkins, newspapers, plastic cups, used Kleenex, a porn magazine probably ditched before hubby returned home to the family. Everything had been photographed and logged, but nothing, the analysts in Queens reported, seemed relevant.

Sachs, however, spent twenty minutes looking at each item, both individual shots of the evidence in the bin and wide-angle images before the contents were collected by the ECTs.

'Check this out,' she said. Pulaski walked closer. She was indicating two napkins from a White Castle fast-food restaurant.

'Home of the slider.' Pulaski added, 'What is that, by the way?'

Sachs shrugged, she knew it was a small hamburger. No idea where the name had come from. One of the earliest fast-food franchises in America, White Castle specialized in burgers and milk shakes.

'Any friction ridges?'

Pulaski read the report. 'None.'

How hard did they try? she wondered. Recalling that Rhyme's two nemeses were incompetence and laziness, Sachs stared at the napkins. 'Odds they came from him?'

Pulaski enlarged the wide-angle shots. The rumpled White Castle napkins were directly beside the Starbucks discards.

'Could be. Our boy likes chain food, we know.'

A sigh. 'Napkins're one of the best sources for DNA. The analyst could've run them, compared it with Starbucks.'

Lazy, incompetent . . .

Then she relented.

Or was he just overworked? The story of policing.

Sachs called up the images of the opened napkins. Each contained stains.

'What do you think?' Sachs asked. 'One's brown, the other reddish?'

'Can't tell. If we had our hands on them ourselves, we

could do a color temperature to be sure. At Lincoln's, I mean.'

Tell me about it.

Sachs said, 'I'm thinking, on one napkin, chocolate and strawberry milk shakes. Reasonable deduction. And the other? *That* stain is definitely chocolate. Another stain too, less viscous, like a soft drink. From two different visits. One, he has two shakes. The other, a shake and a soda.'

'Skinny guy but he can sure pack the calories away.'

'But more important, he likes White Castle. A repeat customer.'

'If we're lucky, he lives nearby. But which one?' Pulaski was online, checking out the restaurant chain in the area. There were several.

A click in her thoughts: the motor oil.

'Maybe the oil's a bomb or maybe he goes to the White Castle in *Queens*,' she said. 'It's on Astoria Boulevard, Automotive Row. My dad and I used to buy car parts there Saturday morning, then go back home and play amateur mechanics. Maybe he picked up the oil trace getting lunch. Long shot, but I'm going to go talk to the manager there. You call the lab in Queens and have somebody go over those napkins again. Fine-tooth cliché. Friction ridges. DNA too. Maybe he ate with a friend and the *buddy's* DNA is in CODIS. And stay on the sawdust, I want the type of wood. And keep after them for the manufacturer of the varnish. And I don't want the analysts who did *this* report. Call Mel.'

Quiet, self-effacing Detective Mel Cooper was the best forensic lab man in the city, perhaps in all of the Northeast.

He was also an expert at human identification – friction ridge prints, DNA and forensic reconstruction. He had degrees in math, physics and organic chemistry and was a member of the prestigious International Association for Identification and the International Association of Bloodstain Pattern Analysts. Rhyme had hired him away from a small-town police department to work the NYPD Crime Scene Unit. Cooper was always a part of the Rhyme team.

As Sachs pulled on her jacket and checked her weapon, Pulaski made a call to the CSU to request Cooper's assistance.

She was at the door when he disconnected and said, 'Sorry, Amelia. Have to be somebody else.'

'What?'

'Mel's on vacation. All week.'

She exhaled a fast laugh. In all the years they'd worked together she'd never known the tech to take more than a day off.

'Find *somebody* good then,' she said, walking briskly into the hallway and thinking: Rhyme retires and everything goes to hell.

CHAPTER 8

'Is that . . . That's an escalator. Yes, it is. Well, a portion of one. The top part. Sitting in your hallway. But I guess you know that.'

'Mel. Come on in. We've got work to do.'

Cooper, diminutive, slim and with a perpetual, faint smile on his face, walked into the parlor of Rhyme's town house, shoving his dark-rimmed glasses higher on his nose. He moved silently; he wore his standard footgear, Hush Puppies. The men were alone. Evers Whitmore had returned to his Midtown law firm.

When no immediate explanation for the partial escalator, which was encased in a scaffolding, was forthcoming, he slipped off his brown jacket, hooked it and set down a gym bag. 'I wasn't really planning on a vacation, you know.'

Rhyme had suggested – in Lincoln Rhyme's inimitable way – that Cooper take some time off. That is, time off from his official job at Crime Scene headquarters and come in to help on the civil case of *Frommer v. Midwest Conveyance.*

'Yes, well. Appreciate it.' Rhyme's thanks were subdued, as always. He didn't have much interest in, or skill at, social niceties.

'Is it . . . I mean, I thought I should check. Are there any ethical problems with me being here?'

'No, no, I'm sure there aren't,' Rhyme said, eyes on the escalator, which reached to the ceiling. 'As long as you don't get paid.'

'Ah. So. I'm volunteering.'

'Just a friend helping in a good cause, Mel. A noble cause. The victim's widow has no money. She has a son. Good boy. Promising.' Rhyme assumed this was likely. He didn't know a thing about young Frommer, whose given name he'd forgotten. 'If we can't get her a settlement, she'll be living in a garage in Schenectady for the immediate future. Maybe the rest of her life.'

'Nothing so terrible about Schenectady.'

'The operative word is "garage," Mel. Besides, it'll be a challenge. You like challenges.'

'To a point.'

'Mel!' Thom said, stepping into the parlor. 'What're you doing here?'

'Abducted.'

'Welcome.' Then the aide scowled. 'Can you believe it. *Look* at that.' A disappointed nod toward the scaffolding and escalator. 'The floors. I hope they're not ruined.'

'They're my floors,' Rhyme said.

'You charge me with keeping them pristine. Then undermine it with two tons of mechanical device.' To the forensic tech: 'Food, drink?'

'Tea would be lovely.'

'I've got your favorite.'

Cooper liked Lipton's. He had simple tastes.

'And how's your girlfriend?'

Cooper lived with his mother but had a tall, gorgeous

Scandinavian paramour, a professor at Columbia. She and Cooper were champion ballroom dancers.

'She's—'

'We're just getting to work here,' Rhyme interrupted.

Thom lifted an eyebrow to the tech, ignoring his boss.

'Fine thanks,' Cooper replied. 'She's fine. We have the regional tango competition next week.'

'And speaking of beverages.' Rhyme looked at the bottle of single-malt scotch.

'No,' Thom said bluntly. 'Coffee.' And returned to the kitchen.

Rude.

'So. What's the caper? Love that word.'

Rhyme explained about the escalator accident and the suit that would be filed by Evers Whitmore on behalf of the widow and her son.

'Ah, right. In the news. Terrible.' Cooper shook his head. 'Never felt really comfortable getting on and off those things. I'll take the stairs, or even an elevator, though I'm not so crazy about them either.'

He walked to the computer monitor, on which were dozens of photographs of the accident site, taken by Sachs, unofficially, since she hadn't been involved in the mishap investigation. They were of the open access panel to the pit, showing the motor and gears and walls, all covered with blood.

'Died from hemorrhaging?'

'And trauma. Cut mostly in half.'

'Hm.'

'Is that the actual unit?' Cooper returned to the

scaffolding and began examining it closely. 'No blood. It's been scrubbed?'

'No.' Rhyme explained about the impossibility of getting access to the actual escalator for several months. But he hoped they could determine a likely cause of the failure from this mock-up. Rhyme's idea was to pay to borrow a portion of an identical model from a contractor in the area. Thom had found the tape measure Rhyme had requested and they'd determined there was enough clearance to get the machinery through the front door, disassembled, and put it back together in the hallway. The price for the rental was five thousand, which Whitmore would add to his legal fee and deduct from whatever they recovered from the defendant.

Workers had built a scaffolding and mounted the top plate – the access panel that had opened to swallow up Greg Frommer – along with its supporting pieces, hinges, and portions of the railing and control switches. On the floor were the motor and the gears, identical to those that had killed the victim.

Cooper was walking silently around the device, looking up, touching pieces. 'Won't be evidentiary.'

'No. We just need to find out what went wrong, why the panel at the top opened when it shouldn't have.' Rhyme wheeled closer.

The tech was nodding. 'So, I deduce that the escalator was going up at the time and just as the victim got to the top floor panel it popped up. How far open was it?'

'Amelia said about fourteen inches.'

'She ran the scene?'

'No, she just happened to be there at the time, tracking

an unsub. She lost him when the accident happened and she tried to save the vic. Couldn't.'

'And the perp got away?'

'Yes.'

'She wouldn't have been happy about that.'

'She went to see the widow and found out she's in a pretty bad way. Had the idea to hook her up with a lawyer. That's how it all ended up in our laps.'

'So, the access panel pops up – yes, I see it's on a spring. Must be heavy. The vic gets dragged underneath and then falls onto the motor and gears.'

'Right. The teeth on the front edge of the panel cut him too. That's all the blood on the walls in the pictures.'

'I see.'

'Now I want you to get inside, poke around, find out how the damn thing works. How the access panel at the top opens, switches, levers, hinges, safety mechanisms. Everything. Get pictures. And we'll try to piece together what happened.'

Cooper looked around. 'The place hasn't changed much since you resigned.'

'Then you know where the camera equipment's located,' Rhyme said, his voice taut with impatience.

The tech chuckled. 'And you haven't changed much either.' He went to the shelves on a back wall of the parlor and selected a camera and flashlight with a headband. 'Coal miner's son,' he joked, mounting it on his forehead.

'Shoot away. Go!'

Cooper climbed up inside the mockup. Silent flashes began to flare.

The doorbell sounded.

Who could this be? The stiff attorney, Evers Whitmore, was back in his office talking to friends and family of Greg Frommer. He was trying to marshal evidence to prove that, although presently underemployed, Frommer would have gone back to being a successful marketing manager in the near future, allowing the damage claim to be much higher than one based on his recent income.

Was the visitor one of his doctors? Rhyme's quadriplegic condition necessitated regular exams by neuro specialists, as well as physical therapists, but he had no sessions scheduled.

He wheeled to the closed-circuit security camera screen to see who it might be.

Oh, hell.

Rhyme typically was irritated when people arrived unannounced (or announced, for that matter).

But today the dismay was far more intense than usual.

'Yes, yes,' the man was assuring Amelia Sachs, 'I know who you're talking about. Quiet guy.'

She was speaking to the manager of the Queens White Castle hamburger joint in Astoria.

'Very tall, very skinny. White. Pale.'

The manager was, in contrast, an olive-skinned man, with a round, cheerful face. They were at the front window. He had been cleaning it himself, seemingly proud of the establishment in his care. The smell of Windex was strong, as was the aroma of onions. Appealing too, the latter. Sachs's last meal was supper yesterday.

'Do you know his name?'

'I don't, no. But . . .' He looked up. 'Char?'

A counterwoman in her twenties looked over. If she ate the restaurant's specialty, she did so in moderation. The slim woman finished an order and joined the two.

Sachs identified herself and, protocol, showed the shield. The woman's eyes shone. She was tickled to be part of a *CSI* moment.

'Charlotte works a lot of shifts. She's our anchor.'

A blush.

'Mr Rodriguez thought you might know a tall man who comes in some,' Sachs said. 'Tall, very thin. White. He might have worn a green checkered or plaid jacket. A baseball cap.'

'Sure. I remember him!'

'Do you know his name?'

'No, just, he's hard to miss.'

'What can you tell me about him?'

'Well, like you said. Thin. Skinny. And he eats a lot. Ten, fifteen sandwiches.'

Sandwiches . . . Burgers.

'But he could be buying them for other people, couldn't he?'

'No, no, no! He eats them here. Most of the time. There's this word my mother says about eating, *scarfs* them down. And two milk shakes. So skinny but he eats like that! Sometimes a milk shake *and* a soda. How long have you been a detective?'

'A few years.'

'That's so neat!'

'Was he ever with anyone?'

'Not that I saw.'

'He comes here often?'

'Maybe once a week, every two weeks.'

'Any impression that he lives around here?' Sachs asked. 'Anything he might've said?'

'No. Never said anything to me. Just ordered, always kept his head down. Wears a hat.' Her eyes narrowed. 'I'll bet he was afraid of security cameras! Do you think?'

'Possibly. Could you describe him, his face?'

'Never paid any attention, really. Long face, kind of pale, like he didn't get out much. No beard or mustache, I think.'

'Any idea where he was coming from or where he might be going?'

Charlotte tried. But nothing came to mind. 'Sorry.' She was nearly cringing that she couldn't answer the question.

'A car?'

Again, a defeat. 'Well, I don't . . . Wait. No, probably not. He turns away from the parking lot when he leaves, I think.'

'So you watched him go.'

'You'd kind of want to look at him, you know? Not that he's a freak or anything. Just, so skinny. Eating all that and so skinny. Totally unfair. We have to work at it, right?'

The two women present, Sachs supposed she meant. A smile.

'Every time? He went that way every time he left?'

'I guess. Pretty sure.'

'Did he carry anything?'

'Oh, a couple of times he had a bag, plastic bag. I think

once, yeah, he put it on the counter and it was heavy. Kind of clanked. Like metal.'

'What color bag?'

'White.'

'No idea what was inside?'

'No. Sorry. I *really* wish I could help.'

'You're doing great. Clothes?'

She shook her head. 'Other than the jacket and hat, I don't remember, no.'

Sachs asked Rodriguez, 'Security video?' Guessing the answer.

'It loops every day.'

Yep, like she'd thought. It would've already overwritten any footage of their perp.

Turning back to Charlotte. 'You've been a big help.' Sachs directed the next comment to both of them. 'I need you to tell everybody who works here that we're looking for this man. If he comes back, call nine one one. And add that he's suspect in a homicide.'

'Homicide,' Charlotte whispered, looking both horrified and delighted.

'That's right. I'm Detective Five-Eight-Eight-Five. Sachs.' She handed cards to the manager and to Charlotte. The woman gazed at it as if the tiny bit of cardboard were a huge tip. She wore a wedding band and Sachs supposed she was already relishing the dinner table conversation tonight. Sachs looked from one to the other. 'But don't call me. Call nine one one and mention my name. There'll be a squad car here faster than I could get here. You're going to have to act like nothing's going on. Just serve him like normal, then when he leaves or sits down, call us.

Okay? Don't do anything other than that. I can rely on you?'

'Oh, you bet, Detective,' Charlotte said, a private acknowledging a general's orders.

'I'll make sure of it,' Rodriguez, the manager, said. 'That everybody knows.'

'There are other White Castles in the area. He might go there too. Could you tell the managers the same thing?'

'Sure.'

Sachs looked out of the window, free of grime, and surveyed the wide street. It was lined with shops, restaurants and apartments. Any one of the stores could have sold things that clanked and stowed them in white plastic bags for customers to take home . . . or to a murder site.

Rodriguez offered, 'Hey, Detective . . . Take some sliders. On me.'

'We can't take complimentary food.'

'But doughnuts . . .'

Sachs smiled. 'That's a myth.' She glanced at the grill. 'But I'll pay for one.'

Charlotte frowned. 'You better get two. They're pretty small.'

They were. But they were also damn good. And so was the milk shake. She finished her breakfast/lunch in all of three minutes. And stepped outside.

From her pocket she extracted her cell phone then called Ron Pulaski. There was no answer on the landline at the Unsub 40 war room at One PP. She tried his mobile. Voice mail. She left a message.

Okay, we canvass solo. Sachs started onto the sidewalk, swept by punchy wind from the overcast sky.

Tall man, pale man, skinny man, white bag. He'd been shopping. Start with hardware stores. Sawdust, varnish. Ball-peen hammers.

Blunt force trauma.

CHAPTER 9

Lincoln Rhyme had forgotten completely that Juliette Archer, his forensic student, was arriving today to begin her informal internship.

She was the visitor who'd come a-calling. Under other circumstances he might have enjoyed her company. But now his immediate thought was how to get rid of her.

Archer directed her Storm Arrow chair around the escalator and into the parlor, braking smartly in front of the lattice of wires covering the floor. She apparently wasn't used to tooling over snaky cables but then, probably concluding that Rhyme would have driven over them regularly without damage, she did the same.

'Hello, Lincoln.'

'Juliette.'

Thom nodded to her.

'Juliette Archer. I'm a student in Lincoln's class.'

'I'm his caregiver. Thom Reston.'

'Pleased to meet you.'

A moment later came a second buzzer and Thom went to answer the door again. He and a burly man in his thirties entered the parlor. The second visitor was dressed in a business suit, pale-blue shirt and tie. The top button of the shirt was undone and the tie pulled loose. Rhyme never understood that look.

The man nodded a greeting to all but directed his gaze at Archer. 'Jule, you didn't wait. I asked you to wait.'

Archer said, 'This is my brother, Randy.' Rhyme recalled she was staying with him and his wife because her loft downtown was being modified to make it more accessible. The couple also happened to live conveniently near John Marshall College.

Randy said, 'It's a steep ramp out front.'

'I've done steeper,' she said.

Rhyme knew the tendency of people to mother, or baby, those with severe disabilities. The practice drove him crazy, as it apparently did Archer, as well. He wondered if she'd eventually grow immune to coddling; he never had.

Well, he thought, the brother's presence settled the matter. No way were two people – amateurs no less – hanging out here while he and Mel Cooper struggled to make a case against the manufacturer or the mall or whoever had been responsible for the death of Sandy Frommer's husband.

'Present, as promised,' Archer said, eyes taking in the parlor-*cum*-lab. 'Well. Look at this. The equipment, instruments. And a scanning electron microscope? I'm impressed. Power problems?'

Rhyme didn't answer. Any words might discourage their rapid exit.

Mel Cooper swung from scaffolding to floor, looking toward Archer. She blinked as the beam of his flashlight stabbed her eyes.

'Oh, so sorry. Mel Cooper.' A nod, rather than an offered hand, considering the wheelchair situation.

Archer introduced her brother and then, returning her attention to Cooper, said, 'Oh, Detective Cooper. Lincoln said some nice things about you. He holds you up as a shining example of a forensic lab—'

'Okay,' Rhyme said quickly, ignoring the inquiring but pleased glance from Cooper. 'We're in the midst of something here.'

She eased forward, looking over other equipment. 'When I was doing epidemiology, we used a GC/MS sometimes. Different model. But still. Voice-activated?'

'Uhm. Well. No. Mel or Amelia usually run it. But—'

'Oh, there's a voice system that works well. RTJ Instrumentation. Based in Akron.'

'Is there?'

'Just mentioning it. An article in *Forensics Today* about hands-free in the lab. I could send it to you.'

'We subscribe,' Cooper said. 'I'll look forward to—'

Rhyme muttered, 'As I was saying, this case we're working on, very time-sensitive. Came up suddenly.'

'Involving, let me guess, an escalator to nowhere.'

Rhyme was irritated at the humor. He said, 'Probably would have been best to call. Could have saved you both the trouble—'

Archer said evenly, 'Yes. Well, we *did* agree for me to be here today. You never got back to me about the exact time. I emailed.'

The corollary was that if anyone was to have called it should have been he. He tried a new tack. 'My error. Entirely. I apologize for your wasted trip.'

Drawing a dry gaze from Thom at the rampant insincerity. Rhyme pointedly ignored him.

'So, we'll have to reconvene. A different time. Later.'

Randy said, 'So, Jule, let's head back. I'll get the van. Then guide you down the ramp and—'

'Oh, but everything's scheduled. Will Senior's got Billy for the next few days. And Button's got a playdate with Whiskers. I've changed all my doctors' appointments. So.'

Button? Whiskers? Rhyme thought. Jesus H. Christ. What've I got myself into? 'See, when I agreed you could come, there was a lull. I could be more . . . instructive. Now, I wouldn't be able to be very helpful. So much going on. This is really a *very* pressing matter.'

Pressing matter? I actually said that? Rhyme wondered.

She nodded but was staring at the escalator. 'This would have to be that accident. In Brooklyn, right? The mall. A *civil* case. There didn't seem to be any thinking it was criminal. That means, I'd guess, lawsuits against a number of defendants. Manufacturer, real estate company owning the mall, maintenance crews. We know what *those* are like.' She wheeled about. 'Who doesn't love *Boston Legal*? And *The Good Wife*?'

Who know what the hell they are?

'I really think it's best—'

Archer said, 'And this is a mock-up. You couldn't have the actual escalator here? Off limits to civil lawyers?'

'Removed and impounded,' Cooper said, drawing a glare from Rhyme.

'Again, I apologize, but—'

Archer continued. 'What's so pressing? Other plaintiffs clamoring for a piece of the pie?'

Rhyme said nothing. He simply watched her wheel

closer to the scaffolding. Now his eyes took her in more closely. She was dressed quite stylishly. A long forest-green hounds tooth skirt, a starched white blouse. Black jacket. An elaborate gold bracelet of what seemed to be runic characters was on her left wrist, the one that was strapped, immobile, to the arm of her wheelchair. She maneuvered the Storm Arrow with a touchpad, using her right hand. The chestnut hair was up in a bun today. Archer had apparently already begun to learn that when your extremities are out of commission, you do all you can to minimize tickles and irritations from hair and sweat. Rhyme presently used far more mosquito repellent – organic, at Thom's insistence – than he had before his accident.

'Jule,' Randy said. 'Mr Rhyme is busy. Don't overstay your welcome.'

Already have, he thought. But his smile was smeared with regret. 'Sorry. Really would be best for everybody concerned. Next week, two weeks.'

Archer herself was staring at Rhyme, eyes unwavering. He stared right back as she said, 'Don't you think another body would be helpful? Sure, I'm a newbie at forensics but I've done epidemiologic investigation for years. Besides, without any real evidence, doesn't look like fingerprints and density gradient analysis'll be called for. You'll be doing a lot of speculative work on issues of mechanical failure. We did that all the time in sourcing infections – speculation, not mechanics, of course. I could do some of the legwork.' A smile. 'So to speak.'

'Jule,' Randy said, blushing. 'We talked about that.'

Referring, Rhyme guessed, to a prior conversation on

joking about her disability. Rhyme himself delighted in baiting the condescenders, the overly sensitive and the politically correct, even – especially – within the disabled community. 'Gimp' was a favorite noun of his; 'cringe' a verb.

When Rhyme didn't respond to Archer's persistence, her lips tightened. 'But,' she said breezily, 'if you're not interested, that's fine. We can take a rain check.' There was an edge to her voice, and this solidified his decision. He hardly needed attitude. He was doing her a favor taking her on as an intern.

'It is best, I'm afraid.'

Randy said, 'I'll get the car, bring it around. Really, Jule. And wait at the top of the ramp.' Turning to Rhyme: 'Thanks,' he said, nodding effusively. 'Appreciate all you're doing for her.'

'Don't mention it.'

'I'll see you out,' Thom said.

'Mel, get back to work,' Rhyme grumbled.

The tech climbed into the scaffolding once more. The camera flashes resumed.

Archer said, 'See you in class next week, Lincoln.'

'You can come back, of course. Intern here. Just a different time.'

'Sure,' she said flatly. And wheeled into the hallway with Thom. A moment later Rhyme heard the door close. He wheeled to the video screen and watched Archer, in defiance of her brother, tool easily down the ramp and park on the sidewalk. She looked back and up at the town house.

Rhyme wheeled to the computer monitor, on which

were displayed the pictures Amelia Sachs had taken. He studied them for a few minutes.

Then exhaled a long sigh.

'Thom! Thom! I'm calling you! Where the hell are you?'

'About eight feet away, Lincoln. And, no, I haven't gone deaf recently. What are you so politely requesting?'

'Get her back in here.'

'Who?'

'That woman who was just here. Ten seconds ago. Who *else* would I be talking about? I want her back. *Now*.'

Ron Pulaski was on a sidewalk that was cracked into trapezoids and triangles of concrete rising like bergs in an ice floe. The chain link he stood beside was topped with razor wire and was grafitti'd, defaced with letters and symbols more cryptic than usual because the tagger's canvas was mesh. Who would deface chain link? he wondered. Maybe all the good brick walls and concrete abutments were taken.

Listening to his voice mail.

Amelia Sachs wanted him. He'd snuck away from their war room in One PP, believing that she'd follow up on the White Castle lead and return to Manhattan in a few hours. But apparently she'd found something to move the case forward. He listened to the message again. Decided she didn't need him immediately. Not like there was an emergency. She wanted him to aid in a canvass of an area where Unsub 40 had been spotted a few days ago and to which he returned from time to time. Maybe he lived there, maybe shopped.

Pulaski didn't want to talk to her. He texted.

Lying was easier when your thumbs, not your voice, communicated. He'd get there as soon as he could, he said. He was out of the office briefly.

Nothing more than that.

His message, though, when he thought about it, wasn't exactly lying. He wasn't in the office and as soon as his business was completed he'd join her for the canvass. Still, when he was on the street, patrolling, his approach was: Failure to disclose is deception too.

Phone duty finished, the young officer was back to being vigilant. Extremely so. He was in the 33, after all, and so he had to be.

Pulaski had just hit the sidewalk from the transit complex of Broadway Junction and was walking along Van Sinderen Avenue. This part of Brooklyn was a mess. Not particularly filthy, no more so than other parts of the city, just chaotic. Canarsie and Jamaica trains rattling overhead. The IND underground. Autos and trucks aplenty, edging past, honking, cutting in and out. Hordes of people on the sidewalks. Bicycles.

The officer stood out — his race was represented by about 2 percent of the residents here, where Ocean Hill, Brownsville and Bed-Stuy merged. Nobody hassled him, nobody seemed even to notice him, everyone being on their own missions, which in New York City always seemed urgent. Or they were focused on their mobiles or conversations with their friends. As in most 'hoods, the majority, vast majority, of locals just wanted to get to and from work, hang with people they knew in bars or coffeehouses or restaurants, go shopping, take walks with the kids and dogs, get home.

But that didn't mean he could ignore those here who *might* take more than a casual interest and wonder why this scrubbed white boy with a suburban haircut and a baby-smooth face was sauntering down the broken pavement in a hard black and brown part of town. The 33, as in the last digits of its ZIP code, was statistically the most dangerous part of New York City.

After Amelia Sachs had left One PP, Pulaski had given it a few minutes and then lost his NYPD uniform and dressed down. Jeans, running shoes, combat-green T-shirt and black leather jacket, shabby. Head down, he'd left headquarters. He'd hit a nearby ATM, cringing mentally as he saw the bills flip out. Am I really fucking doing this? he thought, using a modifier that would only rarely, and in extreme situations, escape his rosy lips.

Over the river and through the woods . . . to bad guys we will go . . .

Leaving behind the transit hub now, he walked to Broadway, past the car repair garages, building supply outfits, real estate offices, check cashing and salary advance storefronts, bodegas, cheap diners with flyblown, handwritten menus on cards in windows. As he moved farther away from the commercial streets, he passed apartment blocks, mostly three- or four-story. Lots of red brick, lots of painted stone in beige and brown, lots of graffiti. On the horizon were the towering projects of Brownsville, not far away. On the sidewalk were cigarette butts, trash, malt liquor cans and a few condoms and needles . . . and even crack tubes, which seemed almost nostalgic; you didn't see that scourge much anymore.

The 33 . . .

Pulaski was walking fast.

One block, two blocks, three blocks, four.

Where the hell is Alpho?

Ahead, on the same sidewalk, two kids – yeah, young but together weighing four Pulaskis – eyed him hostilely. He had his Smith & Wesson Bodyguard on his ankle, his private weapon. But if they wanted to perp him, they'd perp him and he'd be on the ground and bleeding before he could snag the punchy gun from its holster. But they turned back to their joints and grave conversation, letting him pass without another look.

Two more blocks and, finally, he spotted the young man he'd been searching for. Back at One PP he'd taken a furtive look at a precinct activity report from the 73 and had a rough idea of where to go, where Alpho might be hanging. The kid was on his mobile and smoking, a cigarette not weed, in front of GW Deli and Phone Card store.

GW. George Washington? Then Pulaski thought, for some reason: Gee Whiz?

The skinny Latino was in a wife-beater T-shirt, exposing arms that didn't see a lot of pushups. Street Crimes surveillance had gotten some solid pix of him, which was why Pulaski recognized him immediately. Alpho had been brought in, questioned and released a few times. But he'd never been busted and was still, Narcotics believed, in business. Had to be true. You could tell. From the posture, from the wariness, even while concentrating on the phone call.

Pulaski looked around. No obvious threats.

So get this over with. Pulaski strode toward Alpho, glanced his way and slowed.

The young man, a grayish tint to his dark skin, lifted his head. Said something into the mobile by way of farewell and slipped the cheap flip phone away.

Pulaski eased closer. 'Hey.'

'Yo.'

Alpho's eyes scanned up and down the street, like skittish animals. Didn't spot anything worrisome. Then back to Pulaski.

'Nice day, huh?'

'S'all right. Guess. I know you?'

Pulaski said, 'Alphonse, right?'

A stare in response.

'I'm Ron.'

'So who?'

'Kett. At Richie's in Bed-Stuy.'

'He cool. How you know him?'

Pulaski said, 'Just know him. Hang with him some. He'll vouch.'

Eddie Kett would vouch for Ron Pulaski, not because they were buddies but because a few days ago, while breaking up a fight, off duty, Pulaski had found out that Eddie had been carrying a pistol when he shouldn't've been, which was never. He also had some pills on him. The meds had interested Pulaski, who'd suggested he could forget about the weapon and Oxy charges in return for a favor, provided Kett never said a word about it. Kett had wisely chosen that route and had pointed him in Alphonse's direction, happy to play character reference.

Looking up and down the street, both men now.

'Kett, he okay.' Repeating. Stalling. Alphonse was his

name but on the street it was mostly Alpho or, to cops and gangbangers, *Alpo*, after the dog food.

'Yeah, he's okay.'

'I'ma call him.'

'Why I mentioned him, why I came to you. He said you could hook me up.'

'Why not him? Help you, I mean.' Alpho wasn't calling Eddie Kett, Pulaski noticed. Probably believes me. You'd have to be an idiot to come to the 33 without somebody vouching.

'Eddie doesn't have what I need.'

'I'ma say, brother, you ain't lookin' fuckin' strung out. Whatchu want?'

'No brown. No C. Nothing like that.' Pulaski shook his head, looking around again for threats from anyone. Male or female. Girls were just as dangerous.

Pulaski also scanned for uniforms and plainclothes and unmarked Dodges. He sure didn't want to run into any compatriots.

But the streets were clear.

He said in a low voice, 'There's some new shit I heard about. It's not Oxy but it's like Oxy.'

'I ain't hear about that, brother. I hook you up with weed, with C, with speed, methballs.' Alpho was relaxing. This wasn't the way undercover busts worked.

Pulaski pointed to his forehead. 'I got this thing happened to me. Crap beat out of me, a couple years ago. I started getting these headaches again. They came back. I mean, big time. They're crap, totally. You get headaches?'

'Cîroc, Smirny.' Alpho smiled.

Pulaski didn't. He whispered, 'These are so bad. I can't do my job right. Can't concentrate.'

'What you do?'

'Construction. Crew in the city. Ironwork.'

'Man, those skyscrapers? How you fuckers do that? Climb up there? Fuck.'

'Almost fell a couple times.'

'Shit. Oxy fuck you up too.'

'No, no, this new stuff's different. Just takes the pain away, doesn't mess with your mind, doesn't make you woozy, you know?'

'Woozy?' Alpho had no clue. 'Why you ain't get a prescription?'

'This stuff they don't write paper for. It's new, underground labs. Heard you could get it here, in BK. East New York, mostly. Guy named Oden? Something. He makes it himself or runs it in from Canada or Mexico. You know him?'

'Oden? No. Ain't hear of him. What's this new shit called?'

'Heard a name. Catch.'

'It's called Catch?'

'What I'm saying.'

Alpho seemed to like the name. 'Like it grabs you, you know, catches you, it's so strong.'

'Fuck. I don't know. Anyway, I want some. Bad, man. I need it. Gotta get these headaches under control.'

'Well, I ain't got none. Never hear of it. But hook you up a dozen. Regular, I mean. One bill.'

Little lower than the general street price. Oxy went for about ten bucks per. Alpho was grooming for future sales.

'Yeah, okay.'

The exchange happened fast. As they always should. The plastic bag of OxyContin swapped for a handful of twenties. Then the dealer blinked as he looked at the wad Pulaski had slipped him. 'Brother, I telling you: *one* bill. That five right there.'

'Tip.'

'Tip?'

'Like a tip at a restaurant.'

Confused.

Pulaski smiled. 'Keep it, man. I'm just asking, can you check around? See if you can find this new shit for me. Or, at least, who this Oden guy is, where I can get some Catch from him.'

'Dunno, brother.'

A nod at Alpho's pocket. 'Bigger tip next time, you point me the right way. I mean *bigger*. M and half. Maybe more, it's righteous information.'

Then the skinny man gripped Pulaski's forearm. Leaned close, radiating the smell of tobacco, sweat, garlic, coffee. 'You ain't no fuckin' cop?'

Looking him back in the eyes, Pulaski said, 'No. I'm a guy gets headaches so bad I can't get it up sometimes, and who lies in the bathroom and pukes for hours. *That's* what I am. Talk to Eddie. He'll tell you.'

Alpho looked once more at the scar on Pulaski's forehead. 'I'ma call you, brother. Digits?'

Pulaski punched in Alpho's number, and the gangbanger reciprocated.

Burner phone to burner. The age of trust.

Then Pulaski turned and, head down, walked back in

the direction of the Broadway Junction transit complex.

Thinking it was pretty funny that he could very well have said to Alphonse Gravita that yeah, I am a cop, but it doesn't matter because this isn't an undercover operation at all. Not a soul in the NYPD – or in the world – knows about it. That wasn't buy money I just handed over but my own, which Jenny and I can't afford to give away.

But sometimes when you're desperate, you do desperate things.

CHAPTER **10**

Not good. Not good at all.

She's ruined it. Red, the cop, the Shopper.

She's taken it away from me. My wonderful White Castle. Stolen it.

And she's walking here and there in Astoria, looking for clues – to me.

A little luck here, just like in the mall – when she was right next to the deadly escalator. Here I was fortunate too, spotting her first, a half block away from White Castle.

Red, walking inside, like a hunter.

My White Castle . . .

Two minutes later and – if I hadn't seen her – I'd've pushed in, hungry, mouthwatering. Tasting burger and shake. Then eye-to-eye with Red. She could draw her gun faster than I could get my bone cracker out of my backpack, or my razor saw.

Luck saved me again.

Did her luck get her here?

No, no, no. I was careless. That's it.

I am furious.

Remembering, yes: I threw away trash when the Shoppers came after me in the mall. I dumped the Starbucks litter nowhere near Starbucks but somehow they must've found it. And that means they found the other things I'd thrown out too. In the trash bin of that Mexican place behind the mall. I thought the help would grow blind and mute, or get shipped back to Juarez. It didn't occur to me that Red would stoop to garbage. She'd have nabbed a White Castle napkin or receipt. Fingerprints? I'm pretty careful. When I'm in public I try to use far ends of fingers (the top quarter of tips are pretty useless for prints, oh, I know my stuff) or I dunk napkins in soda or coffee, turn them to mush.

But I didn't think that time.

Speaking of hands: My palms're nice and sweaty now, fingers – my long, long fingers – shaking a little. I'm mad at myself but mad at her mostly. Red . . . Taking my White Castle away, making me finish up too fast with Alicia.

Now, watching her at some distance, I see her move sveltely down the street. Into and out of stores. I know what she's done: asked a server at White Castle or all the servers and customers too, Hey, did you see the bean boy? The praying mantis? Long John, Slim Jim? Oh, sure we did. Funny, funny looking. Hard to miss.

Now, the good news is that she won't find my favorite store where I often go before or after my burgers, not on this street, not nearby. It's a subway stop away. Still, there are other connections she might make.

Have to take care of this.

Everything good in my mind's now knocked aside: the visit to my brother later today, fun fun fun with Alicia tonight, the next death on my schedule.

Plans have changed.

So has your luck, Red. Get yourself red-y. The joke sours, I'm so angry. When she steps into a bodega to ask some questions about the bean boy *I* step out onto the sidewalk. Moving wide around the White Castle, where they know about me now.

My wonderful White Castle. Where I can never go again.

I hike my backpack higher on my shoulder. And move fast.

'You were right,' Rhyme was saying. 'Your deductions.'

Though he reflected he hardly needed to tell her this. Juliette Archer, he'd decided, was somebody who wouldn't draw conclusions unless she had a good – no, *extremely* good – basis for knowing they were accurate.

She wheeled closer.

Rhyme continued, 'Though the reason we have to sue right away isn't other plaintiffs. Or only that. It's that the victim's widow and her son are in a bad way.' He explained about the lack of insurance, their debt. About the garage in upstate New York, their soon-to-be – perhaps long-term – home.

Archer offered no opinion about Schenectady but the stillness in her face suggested she appreciated the hardship that loomed. He described the additional issue of Frommer's complicated employment history. 'The attorney's building the case to prove that this was a temporary slump. But that might be hard to do.'

Archer's eyes shone. 'But if you can prove the defendant did something particularly egregious or careless, there may be punitive damages.'

Maybe, as Whitmore suggested of Rhyme himself, Archer should have gone to law school as well.

Boston Legal . . .

'To *threaten* them with punitive damages,' Rhyme reminded. 'We want to settle, and settle quickly.'

Archer asked, 'When can we have access to the real deal? And all the evidence?'

'Could be months.'

'But can we make a case for liability from just the mock-up?'

Rhyme said, 'We'll see.' He explained what Whitmore had told him about strict products liability and negligence, the possibility of an intervening cause that would shift liability away from the manufacturer.

'Our job, first, is to pinpoint the defect.'

'And find a very careless and a very rich defendant,' she said wryly.

'That's the strategy. Thom!'

The aide appeared.

Rhyme said to Archer, 'Why don't you explain your medical situation to him?'

She did. Unlike Rhyme, she had not suffered a trauma to her spine; doctors had discovered a tumor that wound around the fourth and fifth cervical vertebrae (Rhyme's injury had been at the fourth). Archer explained about the series of treatments and surgery that would ultimately render her as disabled as Rhyme, if not more so. Her life at the moment was consumed with adapting to the condition by changing careers to one more suitable to a quadriplegic and learning from an experienced patient – Lincoln Rhyme, as it turned out – what to expect and how to cope.

Thom said, 'I'm happy to play the role of your caregiver too if you like, while you're here.'

'Would you?'

'Delighted to,' he said.

She wheeled about and faced Rhyme. 'Now what can I do?'

'Research escalator accidents, particularly this model. Whitmore said that might be admissible. And get the maintenance manuals. A contractor leased us a part of the escalator but they haven't delivered the documents yet. I want to know everything about it.'

'Let's see if the company or the city is ordering inspections of similar models.'

'Yes, good.' He hadn't thought of this.

'Computer I can use?'

Rhyme pointed out a desktop nearby. He knew she could use her right hand on the controller but keyboarding was not a possibility. 'Could you set Juliette up with a headset and microphone. For computer three.'

'Sure. Over here.'

Her self-confidence suddenly dimmed and for the first time since he'd met her, Archer seemed uneasy, presumably for having to rely on someone else's help, other than her brother's. She was looking at the computer as if it were a stray dog whose tail was not wagging. Arguing with Rhyme about starting her internship had been different. They were equals. Here she was having to rely on an able-bodied person. 'Thank you. I'm sorry.'

'This is the least of my trials and tribulations.' Thom fitted her with the headset and a touchpad for her right hand. Then he booted up the computer. 'You can print out anything you find. But we don't do that much. Easier for everybody to use the monitors.' Rhyme used a page-turning frame but that was mostly for books, magazines or documents that arrived in hard-copy form.

'Those *are* some of the biggest screens I've ever seen.' Archer's good cheer had returned in part. She murmured something into the headset and Rhyme saw the screen change as a search engine popped up. 'I'll get to work. First, everything I can find about the escalator itself.'

Mel Cooper called, 'Do you want the model and serial number?'

'Model is MCE-Seventy-Seven,' Archer said absently, staring at the screen, 'I've got the serial too. Memorized them from the manufacturer's info plate when I came in just now.'

And she slowly recited the lengthy numbers into the microphone. The computer responded dutifully to her low, melodic voice.

CHAPTER 11

Still playing infrastructure paparazzo with his digital camera, Mel Cooper continued to prowl about within the scaffolding enshrouding the escalator.

'How did they get it in?' he called. 'This thing is huge.'

'Removed the roof, cut holes in all the floors, lowered it in by helicopter. Or maybe it was angels or superhcrocs. I forget.'

'Legitimate question, Lincoln.'

'Irrelevant question. Therefore *il*legitimate. What are you seeing?'

'Give me a minute.'

Rhyme sighed.

Speed. They needed to move fast. To help Sandy Frommer, of course. But also, as Archer had thought and Whitmore had confirmed, to get a settlement before spurious plaintiffs appeared, hoping for a windfall. He had explained: 'The other passengers on the escalator who leapt off. The injuries were minor – or nonexistent – but that doesn't mean they won't sue. And then,' the lawyer had added, 'there'll be those who claim emotional distress because they simply *saw* a gruesome accident and their lives will be changed forever. They'll never get on an escalator again . . . Nightmares. Eating disorders. Loss of income from taking workdays off. Yes, it's true.

Nonsense, but true. This is the world of personal injury law.'

Archer now called from the computer station she was parked in front of: 'The city's suspended the operation of all MCE-Seventy-Seven models pending inspection. Reading from the *Times*. There are fifty-six installed in New York City, nearly a thousand elsewhere. No other reports of malfunctions.'

Interesting. Rhyme wondered if an inspection might find something beneficial to their case. He wondered how fast it would be concluded.

Finally Cooper joined Rhyme and slipped the SD memory card out of the Sony camera. He loaded it into a computer slot and called up the pictures on a high-def monitor. The screen was big enough that dozens of images fit side by side.

Rhyme moved closer.

'Here're the parts that seem relevant.' The tech stepped to the screen and pointed. 'The panel that popped up. It serves as both a step – the top, immobile step – and an access panel for maintenance and repairs. Hinged on the far side, away from the escalator stairs. I'd guess the weight about forty or so pounds.'

Archer called, 'Forty-two.' She'd found specifications, she explained, in a Midwest Conveyance installation and maintenance manual.

Cooper continued, 'And it's assisted by a spring so when the catch is released the door pops up about sixteen inches.'

Consistent with Sachs's observation and photos.

'A worker can lift it all the way from there and use a

rod to keep it open – like the sort used to support car hoods.' Pointing, Cooper indicated images he'd taken. 'To close the door workers lower it by pushing it down or, I'd guess, standing on it, until a triangular bracket on the bottom of the door meets a spring-fed pin on a fixed bar. Here. The bracket pushes the pin in until the panel's all the way down and the pin snaps into a hole to lock it closed.'

'How is it released?' Rhyme asked.

'Push-button switch in a receptacle behind a locked cover on the side of the escalator. Here. Circuit runs to the servo motor here. It retracts the pin, releasing the access panel.'

'So,' Rhyme mused. 'What could have caused it to pop? Ideas? Come on, think.'

Archer: 'The latching bracket broke off.'

But an examination of Sachs's pictures seemed to show that it was still attached to the bottom of the access panel.

'Maybe the pin snapped,' Rhyme said. 'The de Havilland Comet. Nineteen fifties.'

Both Archer and Cooper looked his way.

He explained: 'First commercial jetliner. Three of them exploded in midair because of metal fatigue – a window failed at high altitude. Fatigue is one of the main mechanical failure modes. Other modes are buckling, corrosion, fouling, fracture, impact, stress, thermal shock, a few more. Fatigue occurs when a material – could be metal or anything else – is subject to cyclical loading.'

'The jetliner,' Archer offered. 'Pressurization over and over.'

'That's what happened. Right. In that case, there were square windows and doors, where the stress was concentrated in the corners. The redesigned planes had round ports and windows. Less stress and fatigue. So the question here is, did the opening and closing of the access panel on the escalator lead to fatigue on the part of the latching pin?'

Cooper highlighted the latch. 'No signs of wear on this one but it's new. I wonder how old the original was, how many times the door had been opened and closed.'

Rhyme felt once more the frustration at not having the actual evidence before him.

He heard a sound of a jostled table as Juliette Archer maneuvered closer to him, clumsily manipulating the chair's controller with her right finger; handling a two-hundred-pound wheelchair deftly took considerable practice.

New to the game . . .

'The one that failed, in the mall, was six years old,' she said.

'How did you find that out?'

'Press releases from Midwest Conveyance, announcing they'd been awarded the contract for the escalators at the mall. Seven years ago. Construction occurred the next year. According to maintenance recommendations, the unit should be inspected and lubricated five times a year. Allowing for breakdowns and unplanned repairs, I'd say the door was opened and closed fifty times.'

Rhyme looked at Cooper's picture of the pin holding the triangular bracket that kept the panel shut. It was only about an inch long but thick. It seemed unlikely that the pin would fatigue with that limited number of openings.

Archer added, 'And one of the maintenance steps is to examine the pin for excessive wear. Presumably for fatigue too.'

'What's it made of? Steel?'

Archer said, 'That's right. All the escalator parts are steel, except for a few housings that had nothing to do with the accidents. And the exterior pieces. They're aluminum and carbon fiber.'

She certainly had attacked the manual and specification sheet quickly.

Rhyme said, 'Even if it was in good shape, the latch might have come loose and the pin might not have fully reseated itself. Vibrations could have worked it loose.'

Maybe . . . Lot of speculation in this case.

'Who made the locking mechanism?'

Without looking at the documents she'd loaded onto her screen she said, 'The manufacturer. Midwest Conveyance. Wasn't a separate company.'

Rhyme said, 'Possibly metal fatigue, possibly maintenance issues. What else might've caused it to open?'

'Could somebody,' Archer asked, 'have hit the switch accidentally or as a prank?'

Cooper called up some pictures. 'Here's the switch. It's on the outside of the unit, on the bottom, near the emergency cutoff.' He pointed. 'But it's behind a small locked door.'

Rhyme said, 'Amelia checked on that. She looked over the CCTV. She said nobody was near the access switch when the panel opened.'

Archer's face screwed up with an ironic frown. 'And that video?'

'The Department of Investigations impounded it.'

She cocked her head as her eyes slipped to Cooper. 'We're civilians but you're NYPD, right?'

'I'm not here,' he said quickly.

'You're—'

'I'm unofficial. On vacation. If I were to get official investigative material now I'd be sent on permanent vacation.'

Scanning the photographs. 'What else could be the culprit?' Rhyme mused.

'Okay. No one pushed the button intentionally. Maybe a short circuit or other electrical problem activated the switch. It tripped the motor – it's called a servo – and that retracted the pin and popped the door.'

'Let's look at the wiring.'

Mel expanded the pictures he'd taken inside the escalator. Rhyme noted that a wire ran along the interior wall from the push-button switch on the outside. The switch wire ended in a plug inserted in one of the outlets on the side of the servo unit inside.

'The connections're exposed,' Cooper said.

'They are indeed,' Rhyme said. He gave a brief smile.

An instant later Archer too grinned. 'I get it. A bit of metal or foil or something conductive might've drifted onto the plug and completed the connection. The servo pulled the pin back and the door popped up.' She added, 'I couldn't find any similar incidents involving this model escalator. Escalators can be dangerous. But usually it's getting clothes or shoes caught in the mechanism.

That happens more than you'd think. A hundred and thirty-seven people died last year in escalator accidents around the world. The worst single disaster, some years ago, was an explosion in the London Underground. Dust and particles accumulated and then caught fire and blew up. Like a grain elevator explosion. Have you ever seen those?'

'They don't happen in Manhattan very often,' Rhyme said absently, mulling over what she'd told him.

'I have,' offered Mel Cooper. 'Seen one.'

Rhyme grimaced at the irrelevance. 'And the defect is—'

'That Midwest Conveyance didn't shield the plugs,' Archer said. 'Would have been easy. Recess them, put them under a covering. Something like that.'

Cooper offered, 'Or they shouldn't use plugs at all. Hardwire the switch and the servo motor. Maybe the company wanted to save money.'

The first hint there might have been punitive-level behavior on the part of the manufacturer.

'Who makes—?'

Archer answered his question before he finished it. 'Just like the locking mechanism. Both the servo motor and the switch were made by Midwest Conveyance. Their component parts unit. And a division. Not a subsidiary. They can't hide behind the corporate veil.'

Cooper said, 'I thought you were an epidemiologist.'

'*Boston Legal*. Believe me. It's really very good. I also like *Better Call Saul*.'

Cooper said, '*L.A. Law* too.'

'Oh, it's good.'

Please . . .

Rhyme was puzzling out how foreign substances could have tricked the servo motor into opening the door.

'I have an idea,' Archer said.

'What's that?'

'You're a scientist. You like empirical evidence.'

'The highest deity in my pantheon,' Rhyme said, not much caring how pretentious it sounded.

She nodded toward the escalator. 'Does it work?'

'The drive motor, gears, servo motor and switch do. And it's plugged in.'

'So let's experiment. Turn it on and try to get the panel to open.'

Rhyme had a thought. He turned toward the kitchen and shouted, 'Thom! Thom! I need a drink.'

The aide appeared in the doorway. 'A little too early, as I recently pointed out.'

'Too early for a Coke?'

'You never drink soda. There isn't any in the house.'

'But if I recall, there's a deli right around the corner.'

The hardware stores – there were two of them within hoofing distance of the White Castle – had been a bust.

No one recalled seeing a customer fitting the description of Unsub 40. And neither of them sold ball-peen hammers. So for the past hour Amelia Sachs had pounded the sidewalk, canvassing the other shops along the windblown, littered sidewalks of this workaday 'hood: the body shops, auto parts stores, phone card outlets, car services, wig stores, taquerias, dozens of other places. One clerk in a drugstore was 'pretty sure' he'd seen, on the street, a man matching the description of Unsub 40 but couldn't remember exactly where he'd been, what he'd been wearing, if he'd been carrying anything.

The sighting possibly confirmed White Castle Charlotte's belief that he'd come in this direction. But as to a destination – that was still a mystery. And of course there were bus stops and subway stations he might have walked to, or garages where he might park his car – even if he hadn't used the hamburger joint's lot. She also checked for CCTVs in the commercial outlets but none of the lenses were focused on the sidewalk, just on the doors, parking lots and interiors. Besides, there were scores of cameras and even if the unsub had stepped inside a surveilled store or taken a shortcut through a parking lot, she didn't have the manpower or time to go through hundreds of hours of video. Todd Williams's killing was a terrible crime but it wasn't the only terrible crime within the five boroughs of New York City. In this business you always had to balance.

And the balance rule applied to your personal life too.

Mobile phone out. She made a call.

'Amie.'

'Mom. How you feeling?'

'Good,' Rose Sachs said, which, from Rose Sachs, might mean good or might mean bad or might mean any stop in between. The woman didn't let a lot out.

'Be there soon,' Sachs told her.

'I can get a cab.'

Sachs chuckled. 'Mom.'

'All right, dear. I'll be ready.'

Looping back, she canvassed stores and shops on the opposite side of the boulevard.

And finally had a solid hit: at a gypsy cab company. She gave the hirsute, lanky manager a description of their unsub and the man immediately frowned and said in a thick Middle Eastern accent, 'Yes, I think so. Very skinny man. Had big bag of White Castle hamburgers. Big bag. For skinny man, funny.'

'You remember when?'

He couldn't exactly, but agreed it might have been two weeks ago – possibly the day Todd Williams was murdered. Nor could he recall who the driver was and the service kept no records of destinations but he said he'd query his employees and find out more.

She lowered her eyes to him. 'This is important. The man is a killer.'

'I will start now. Yes, I will do that.'

She believed him. Mostly because of his uneasy eyes when he had glanced at her proffered shield, which told her that not all his licenses were in seamless order; he would be certain to cooperate, in exchange for her tacit agreement not to send the Taxi and Limousine Commission to visit.

Turning south, she began walking back toward her car, parked at the White Castle lot. A few stops at locations that seemed like unlikely ones for leads: a wig shop, a nail salon, a windowless computer repair operation. Then onto the sidewalk again. Suddenly Sachs noted something from the corner of her eye. Movement. Not unusual here, though on this blustery day the sidewalks were largely deserted. But it had been a special sort of movement. Fast, deflecting. As if somebody didn't want to be seen.

She unbuttoned her jacket and, right hand lounging near her Glock, was looking around. She was at an auto repair operation with a number of vehicles, from motorcycles to box trucks, all parked helter-skelter, many of them dismantled to varying degrees. The person who'd moved in close by, if a person it was and not a shadow or swirl of trash or dust, had slipped between two of the larger trucks, a bright-yellow Penske rental and a twenty-foot white van whose only logo was two massive breasts in spray paint, bold red.

Running the odds that Unsub 40 had been coming for his multi-burger lunch once more and had recognized her from the mall and begun to follow.

Not likely but not impossible either. She tapped her Glock and moved closer to the trucks. No further sign of the shadow. Sachs continued into the lot, weaving through the vehicular graveyard. The wind snapped her jacket tail up and down and fanned her hair dramatically. Bad shooting mode. She pulled a rubber band from her pocket and bound the strands into a ponytail. A look around once more. The only living things visible were seagulls and pigeons, a curious and bold rat. No, two. Were the birds or rodents the movement she'd seen? Paper trash skidded along sidewalk and street, then soared. Maybe that was the intruder, yesterday's *New York Post*.

No sign of threat.

Her phone hummed, startling her. She looked down. The ID showed Thom's name. As always, when he, not

Rhyme, called, she felt a tap in her heart that there might be bad medical news. She answered quickly. 'Thom.'

'Hey, Amelia. Just wondering if you're going to be staying here tonight. Having dinner?'

She relaxed. 'No, I'm taking my mom to an appointment. And she's staying over at my place.'

'Can I make a care package?'

She laughed, knowing it would be a very good care package indeed. But the logistics of collecting it – driving all the way to Rhyme's – were problematic. 'No, thanks. But I really appreciate it. I . . .'

Her voice faded as, in the background through the speaker she heard words spoken by someone who sounded familiar.

No. Couldn't be.

'Thom, is Mel there? Mel Cooper?'

'Yes, he is. You want to talk to him?'

I sure as hell do. She said politely, 'Please.'

A moment later: 'Hi, Amelia.'

'Hey, Mel. Uhm, what're you doing at Lincoln's?'

'He vacationed me. Though that's a verb I can see he's not very happy I used. I'm helping him with the Frommer case.'

'Goddamn it,' she said.

A silence.

Cooper put an end to it with, 'I . . . Well.'

'Put Lincoln on.'

'Oh-oh,' the tech whispered. 'Look, Amelia, the thing is—'

'And not speaker. Headset.'

Her finger disappeared into her hair and she scratched. A sign of the tension – frustration at the case. And anger.

Rhyme. It was bad enough he'd quit the business; now she had to deal with fucking interference?

There was a rustle through her speaker as Cooper or Thom placed the headset on Rhyme. Most conversations with him, of course, occurred via speakerphone. Not much chance for privacy. She didn't want anyone else to hear what she was about to say.

'Sachs. Where—?'

'What's Mel doing there? I needed him for the Unsub Forty case. You stole him.'

A pause. 'I asked if he'd help me on the Frommer litigation,' Rhyme countered. 'There's lab work we have to do. I didn't know you wanted him.'

She snapped, 'Queens HQ wasn't doing everything it should have.'

'I didn't know that. How would I know? You never said anything.'

And why would the subject even come up with you? she thought. Then she muttered, 'How could you just move him to a civilian case? I'm not even sure you can do that.'

'He took some time off. He's not on duty.'

'Oh, bullshit, Rhyme. Vacation? I'm running a *murder*.'

'You were at the mall, Sachs. You saw what happened. *My* victim's as dead as yours.' Lincoln Rhyme didn't play defense well.

'The difference is your escalator's not going to kill anyone else.'

No response to that.

'Well, I don't think I'll need him for much longer.'

'How much is that? In terms of hours? Minutes preferably.'

He sighed. 'We have to come up with a defendant in the next day or so.'

'So, *days* then,' she muttered. 'Not hours.'

Minutes were off the table.

He tried conciliation, though it dripped insincerity. 'I'll make a call or two. Who're you working with at Crime Scene?'

'Who I'm working with is not Mel. That's the problem.'

'Look, I—' This was from Mel Cooper, who had surely deduced what was happening.

'It's okay,' Rhyme said to him.

No, it wasn't. She fumed silently. Professional and personal partners for years, they never fought about matters close to the heart. But when it came to cases, tempers could flare.

'I'm sure you can run some questions by him. He's nodding. See. He's happy to do that.'

'I can't run questions by him. He's not a clerk at Pep Boys.' She added, 'On speaker.'

There was a click.

Cooper was saying, 'Amelia—'

'Okay, Mel. Listen. Ron will give you the details. I need some napkins analyzed for friction ridges and DNA. And we need the brand name of some varnish. And the type of wood from sawdust samples.' She added firmly, for Rhyme's sake, not Cooper's, 'I need somebody really good. As good as you.'

The last *was* a bit petty, sure. She didn't care one iota.

'I'll make a call, Amelia.'

'Thanks. Ron will send you the case number.'

'Sure, of course.'

Then Sachs heard a woman's low voice: 'Is there anything I can do?'

Rhyme was saying, 'No, keep going with that analysis.'

Who was that? Sachs wondered.

Then he said, 'Sachs, look—'

'I have to go, Rhyme.'

She disconnected. Reflecting that it had been years since she'd hung up on him. She remembered when. During their first case.

At that moment Sachs realized that she'd been so focused on the phone call – and on her anger at Rhyme's 'vacationing' the technician she needed – that she'd lost awareness of her surroundings: a mortal sin for any street cop – especially since she'd just seen what might have been a hostile.

Then she heard them; gritty footsteps coming up behind her, close. Her hand went to her Glock but it was too late to draw the weapon. The assailant was by then only a yard or so away.

CHAPTER 12

'So. Didn't work.' Juliette Archer was speaking of the experiment to pour Coca-Cola into the escalator, mimicking a clumsy shopper, and short-circuit the switch, opening the access panel.

'Yes, it did,' Rhyme said, drawing a frown from her and Cooper. 'The experiment was successful. It simply proved a supposition contrary to what we were hoping for: that Midwest Conveyance built an escalator that was *not* defective in regard to liquids.'

The manufacturer had considered that riders might spill drinks on their upward or downward journey and had protected the electronics and motor with a piece of plastic that turned out to be a runoff shield. The liquids would flow into a receptacle, nowhere near the servo motor that released the pin to open the access panel.

'Onward, upward.' Rhyme ordered Cooper to continue experimenting: He was to physically strike the switch and servo motor with various objects to simulate mechanical interference: broom handle, hammer, shoe.

No response. The deadly access panel would not open.

Archer suggested the tech jump on the panel over and over again. Not a bad thought, and Rhyme told Cooper to do so, though with Thom standing by on the floor below to spot the man if he fell.

No effect. The locking pin wouldn't retract. The bracket would not shift in position. Nothing they could do would open the door, except pressing the button intended for that purpose, the button tucked safely away in a recessed receptacle, behind a locked cover.

Thinking, thinking . . .

'Bugs!' Rhyme called.

'You can't put microphones in the Department of Investigations office, Lincoln,' Cooper said uneasily.

'My mistake. "Bugs" is not correct; that's a very limited biological order. Hemiptera. Aphid or cicada, for instance. I should have been more accurate. The broader "insect," of which "bug" is a subcategory. So I want *insects*. Although a *bug* would do.'

'Oh.' Cooper was relieved, though obviously confused.

'Good, Lincoln,' Archer said. 'A roach could have gotten inside and shorted out the switch or the motor, sure. Midwest Conveyance should have taken that into account and built in screens. They failed to do that, so the escalator's defective.'

'Thom! Thom, where are you?'

The aide appeared. 'More soda?'

'Dead insects.'

'You found a bug in your soda? Impossible.'

'"Bugs" again,' Rhyme said with a scowl.

After the explanation Thom prowled the town house for critters – he was such a fastidious housekeeper that he had to extend the search to the storage area above the top-floor ceiling and the basement to come up with a few pathetic fly corpses and a desiccated spider.

'No roaches? I'd love a roach.'

'Oh, please, Lincoln.'

'There's that Chinese place on the cross street . . . Could you just find me one or two roaches. Dead is fine.'

With a grimace, Thom went off on his small-game hunt.

But even rehydrated, the various creatures he came back with couldn't make the switch engage, or short out the servo motor, when they were placed against the contacts in the receptacle containing the plug.

As Cooper and Archer discussed other possible reasons the escalator could be considered legally defective, Rhyme found himself staring at the coatrack on which was hung one of Sachs's jackets. His mind wandered back to her hard words earlier. What the hell was she so upset about? She had no particular claim on Mel Cooper. And how was *he* supposed to know she was having trouble with the lab?

Then his anger skidded around to himself for wasting time thinking about the frisson between him and Sachs.

Back to work.

Rhyme ordered Cooper to clean all the lubricant off the pin and bracket and then close it again, to see if the pin would not fully extend to the locking position because the fitting was dry and therefore would be more likely to open because of random motion. Even without the grease, though, it secured the door perfectly when closed.

Goddamn it. What had happened? Whitmore had said the product need not have been *negligently* – carelessly – built but it did have to be defective. They had to find some reason it had opened when it shouldn't have.

He muttered, 'It's insect-proof, it's waterproof, it's

shockproof . . . Was there lightning when the accident happened?'

Archer checked the weather. 'No. Clear day.'

A sigh. 'Okay, Mel. Write down our paltry finds on the chart, if you would.'

The tech walked to a whiteboard and did so.

The doorbell sounded and Rhyme looked at the monitor. 'Ah, our barrister.'

A moment later lawyer Evers Whitmore entered, walking perfectly upright, in a sharp navy-blue suit, every button occupying every hole. He carried his anachronistic briefcase in one hand and a shopping bag in the other.

'Mr Rhyme.'

He nodded. 'This is Juliette Archer.'

'I'm an intern.'

'She's helping on the case.'

Whitmore didn't even glance at her wheelchair or seem to be curious that the woman was as disabled as her mentor – or how her condition might help or hinder the investigation. He nodded a greeting then turned to Rhyme. 'I have this. Mrs Frommer asked me to deliver it to you. By means of thanks. She made it herself.' From the shopping bag he extracted a plastic-wrapped loaf, tied with a red ribbon and displayed it as if he were proffering Plaintiff's Exhibit One. 'She said it was zucchini bread.'

Rhyme wasn't sure what to make of the gift. Until recently his clients had primarily been the NYPD, FBI and other assorted law enforcers, none of whom sent him baked goods in gratitude. 'Yes. Well. Thom. Thom!'

The aide appeared a moment later. 'Oh, Mr Whitmore.'

JEFFERY DEAVER

The reluctance to use first names seemed to be contagious.

'Mr Reston. Here's a loaf of bread,' the lawyer said, handing it over. 'From Mrs Frommer.'

Rhyme said, 'Refrigerate it or something.'

'Zucchini bread. Smells good. I'll serve it.'

'That's all right. We don't need any—'

'Of course I will.'

'No, of course you won't. We'll save it for later.' Rhyme had an ulterior motive for being contrary. He was thinking that the only way Juliette Archer would be able to eat any of the pastry was to have Thom feed her, and this would make her feel self-conscious. She was using the fingers of her right hand but not her arm. The left, with its intricate bracelet, was, of course, strapped to the wheelchair.

However, Archer, who seemed to get Rhyme's strategy and not much care for it, said in a firm voice: 'Well, I'd like some.'

And Rhyme realized that he'd broken one of his own rules; he'd been coddling her. He said, 'Good. I will too. And coffee. Please.'

Thom blinked at the reversal . . . and the politeness.

'I would care for some coffee, as well. Black please.' From Whitmore. 'If not inconvenient.'

'Not at all.'

'Any chance of a cappuccino?' Archer asked.

'One of my specialties. And I'll bring some tea, Mel.' The aide disappeared.

Whitmore walked to the chart. He and the others looked it over.

Wrongful Death/Pain and Suffering Civil Lawsuit

- Location of incident: Heights View Mall, Brooklyn.

- Victim: Greg Frommer, 44, clerk with Pretty Lady Shoes in mall.
    - Store clerk, left Patterson Systems as Director of Marketing. Will attempt to show he would have returned to a similar or other higher-income job.

- COD: Loss of blood, internal organ trauma.

- Cause of action:
    - Wrongful death/personal injury tort suit.
        - Strict products liability.
        - Negligence.
        - Breach of implied warranty.

- Damages: compensatory, pain and suffering, possibly punitive. To be determined.

- Possible defendants:
    - Midwest Conveyance, Inc. (manufacturer of escalator).
    - Owner of property mall is located on (to be identified).
    - Developer of mall (to be identified).
    - Service maintaining escalator if other than manufacturer (to be identified).

- General and subcontractors installing escalator (to be identified).
- Cleaning crew.
- Additional defendants?

- Facts relevant to accident:
  - Access panel opened spontaneously, victim fell into gears. Opened about 16 inches.
  - Door weighed 42 pounds, sharp teeth on front contributed to death/injury.
  - Door secured by latch. On springs. It popped open for unknown reason.
  - Switch behind locked panel. On video no one appeared to push switch.

- Reasons for failure?
  - switch or servo motor activated spontaneously. Why?
    - Shorted out? Other electrical problem?
    - Insects, liquid, mechanical contact? Not likely factors.
    - Lightning? Not likely factor.
  - Latch failed.
    - Metal fatigue – possible, not likely.
    - Mechanical contact. Not likely.

- No access to Dept. of Investigation or FDNY reports or records at this time.

- No access to failing escalator at this time (under quarantine by DOI).

Archer explained to Whitmore that she'd found no other similar accidents – in escalators made by any company, not just those in the product line of Midwest Conveyance. Then Mel Cooper gave the lawyer the details of their attempts to get the door to pop open spontaneously due to some outside factor or a flaw in the manufacturing of the unit.

'None of the theories worked on the mock-up,' Rhyme told him.

'It doesn't look very promising, I must say,' Whitmore offered. His voice sounded no more discouraged at this bad news than it would be enthusiastic had the conclusions gone in their favor. Still, Rhyme knew he would be troubled. Whitmore wouldn't be a man who took setbacks easily.

Rhyme's eyes were scanning the scaffolding, up and down. He wheeled closer, staring, staring.

He was vaguely aware of Thom arriving with a tray: the baked goods and beverages. Vaguely aware of conversation among Cooper and Archer and Whitmore. Vaguely aware of the lawyer's monotonous voice replying to something Archer had asked.

Then silence.

'Lincoln?' Thom's voice.

'It's defective,' Rhyme whispered.

'What's that?' his aide asked.

'It *is* defective.'

Whitmore said, 'Yes, Mr Rhyme. The problem is we don't know *how* it's defective.'

'Oh, yes we do.'

*

'Scared me a bit there,' Amelia Sachs snapped, her voice sharp as the wind. 'Possibility the perp might've been around.' She removed her hand from the grip of her Glock.

The person who'd come up behind her just after her mobile call to Rhyme was Ron Pulaski, not Unsub 40 or any other assailant.

The young officer said, 'Sorry. You were on the phone. Didn't want to interrupt.'

'Well, next time circle wide. Wave. Or something . . . You see anybody looking like our unsub nearby, a few minutes ago?'

'He's here?'

'Well, he *does* like his White Castle. And I saw somebody shadowing me. You see anything?' she repeated impatiently.

'Nobody like him. Just a couple kids. Looked like a drug trans going down. I headed for 'em but they took off.'

They might've been what she'd seen. Dust. Seagull. Gangbangers swapping bills for C.

'Where were you? Tried the office and your mobile.' She noted he'd changed clothes, swapping his uniform for street.

He was looking around too. 'After you left I got a call. I had to talk to a CI, Harlem. The Gutiérrez case.'

Took her a moment. Enrico Gutiérrez. Wanted in a homicide – possibly murder, more likely low-grade manslaughter – that had been one of the first cases Pulaski had run, with another detective in Major Cases. One drug dealer had killed another, so there was little energy to close the case. She guessed the confidential informant had stumbled on some leads and called Pulaski. She said, 'That old thing? Thought the DA'd given up. Hardly worth the time.'

'Got the word to clean the docket. Didn't you see the memo?'

Sachs didn't pay attention to a lot of memos that circulated through One Police Plaza. Public relations, useless information, new procedures that would be rescinded next month. Reinvigorating cases like Gutiérrez's didn't make a lot of sense but, on the other hand, it wasn't for line detectives or patrol officers to question. And if Pulaski wanted to move up in the world of policing, word from on high had to be heeded. And memos taken seriously.

'Okay, Ron. But lean toward Unsub Forty. If our boy's got fertilizer bombs and poisons he's playing with, in addition to hammers, this's our priority. And answer your damn phone.'

'Got it. Sure. I'll fit in Gutiérrez best I can.'

She explained what Charlotte and the manager at White Castle had said. Then added, 'I've canvassed most of the stores around here and gotten to half of the streets he'd take to subways, buses or apartment complexes.' She gave him the locations she'd been to and told him to keep going another few blocks. She told him too about the gypsy cab service where the unsub had possibly been spotted. 'I want you to follow up with them. We need that driver. Keep up pressure.'

'I'll handle it.'

'I've got to get my mother to an appointment.'

'How's she doing?'

'Hanging in there. Operation's in a few days.'

'Give her my best.'

A nod, then she returned to her Torino and fired up the big engine. In twenty minutes she was cruising along the streets of her neighborhood. She felt a comfort as she headed into the pleasant residential 'hood of Carroll Gardens. The place had been much scruffier when she'd grown up here. Now it was the bastion of PWSM. People With *Some* Money. Not enough to afford this kind of square footage in Manhattan and not willing to flee the city limits for suburbia. Gentrification didn't bother Amelia Sachs. She spent plenty of time in the bad parts of town and was glad to return home to a well-tended enclave with gardenias in unmolested flowerpots on the street, families bicycling through the parks and a high saturation of aromatic coffee shops (though she wouldn't mind banishing hipsters to SoHo and TriBeCa).

Well, look at this: a legitimate parking space. And only a block from her house. She could park practically anywhere if she left her NYPD placard on the dash. But she'd found this wasn't a wise practice. One morning she'd returned to her car to find *Pig* spray-painted on the windshield. She didn't think the word was much in use anymore and pictured the perpetrator as an unfortunate, aging anti-Vietnam-War protestor. Still, the cleaning had cost her four hundred bucks.

Sachs parked and walked along the tree-lined street to her town house, which was classic Brooklyn: brown brick, window frames painted dark green, fronted by a small verdant strip of grass. She let herself in, locked the door behind her and went into the front hallway, stripping off her jacket and unweaving the Glock holster embracing the weapon from her belt. She was a gun person, in her job and as a hobby, a champion in handgun competitions on police and private ranges, but at home, around family, she was discreet about displaying weapons.

She set the Glock in the closet, on a shelf near her jacket, then stepped into the living room. 'Hi.' She nodded a smile to her mother, who said goodbye to whomever she was speaking to on the phone and put the handset down.

'Honey.'

Slim, unsmiling Rose Sachs was a contradiction.

This, the woman who would not speak to her daughter for months when she quit her fashion modeling job to go to the police academy.

This, the woman who would not speak to her husband for even longer for believing he'd encouraged that career change (he had not).

This, the woman whose moods would drive father and daughter out into the garage on Saturday mornings and afternoons to work on one of the muscle cars they both loved to soup up and drive.

This, the woman who was there every minute for her husband, Herman, as he faded to cancer and who made sure her daughter never wanted for a single thing, attended every parent-teacher conference, worked two jobs when necessary, overcame her uncertainty about Rhyme's and her daughter's relationship and quickly accepted then fully embraced him disability and all.

Rose made her decisions in life according to immutable rules of propriety and logic that were often beyond anyone else's comprehension. Yet you couldn't help but admire the steel within her.

Rose was contradictory in another way too. Her physical incarnation. On the one side, pale of skin from the weak stream of blood struggling through her damaged vessels, but fiery of eye. Weak yet with a powerful hug and vise grip of a handshake. If she approved of you.

'I was serious, Amie. You don't have to take me. I'm perfectly capable.'

Yet she wasn't. And today she seemed particularly frail, short of breath and seemingly incapable of rising from the couch – a victim of the body's betrayal, which was how Sachs thought of her condition, since she was slim, rarely drank and had never smoked.

'Not a problem. After, we'll stop at Gristedes. I didn't have a chance on the way here.'

'I think there are things in the freezer.'

'I need to go anyway.'

Then Rose was peering at her daughter with focused and – yes – piercing eyes. 'Is everything all right?'

The woman's perceptive nature was undiminished by her physical malady.

'Tough case.'

'Your Unsub Forty.'

'That's right.' And made tougher by the fact that her partner had goddamn stolen the best forensic man in the city out from underneath her – for a civil case, no less, which wasn't nearly as urgent as hers. It was true that Sandy Frommer's life and her son's would be drastically altered without some compensation from the company who'd changed their lives so tragically. But they wouldn't die, they wouldn't be living on the street, while Unsub Forty might be planning to kill again. Tonight. Five minutes from now.

And more galling: She was the one who'd convinced Rhyme to help the widow, setting him on his typically obsessive-compulsive trail of the defendant who'd been responsible for Greg Frommer's death.

Your initial reaction is going to be to say no but just hear me out. Deal? . . .

Sachs was examining the contents of the fridge and making a grocery list when the doorbell chimed, the first tone high, the second low.

She glanced at her mother, who shook her head.

Neither was Sachs expecting anyone. She walked toward the front hall, not bothering to collect her weapon, on the theory that most doers don't ring doorbells. Also: she kept a second Glock, a smaller one, the model 26, in a battered, faded shoe box beside the front door, one round chambered and nine behind it, a second mag nestling nearby. As she approached the door she removed the lid, turned the box to grabbing position.

Sachs looked out through the peephole. And froze to statue.

My God.

She believed a gasp issued from her throat. Her heart was pounding fiercely. A glance down and she replaced the lid on the camouflaged weapon case, then stood completely still for a moment, staring at her hollow eyes in a mirror set in a gilt frame on the wall.

Breathing deeply, once twice . . . Okay.

She unlatched the door.

Standing on the small stone porch was a man of about her age. Lean, his handsome face had not seen sun for a long time. He was wearing jeans and a black T-shirt under a denim jacket. Nick Carelli had been Sachs's lover before Rhyme. They'd met on the force – both cops, though in different divisions. They'd lived together, they'd even talked about getting married.

Sachs had not seen Nick in years. But she remembered vividly the last time they'd been together in person: a courthouse in Brooklyn. They'd exchanged brief glances and then the bailiffs had led him away, shackled, for transfer to state prison to begin his sentence for robbery and assault.

CHAPTER 13

'It is an exciting concept,' said Evers Whitmore in a tone that belied the descriptive participle.

Which didn't mean he wasn't truly ecstatic; it was just so very hard to read him.

He was referring to Rhyme's theory of the escalator's defect: It didn't matter whether the access panel opened because of metal fatigue, bad lubrication, a curious roach shorting out the servo motor, even someone's pushing the switch accidentally. Or an act of God. The defect was in the fundamental design of the unit – that if the door opened for any reason, the motor and gears should have stopped immediately. An automatic cutoff switch would have saved Greg Frommer's life.

'Had to be cheap to install,' Juliette Archer said.

'I would imagine so,' Whitmore said. Then he tilted his head and looked at the unit in Rhyme's hallway carefully. 'I have another theory too. What does the access panel weigh?'

From Rhyme and Archer in unison: 'Forty-two pounds.'

'Not that heavy,' the lawyer continued.

Archer: 'The spring was a convenience, not a necessity.'

Rhyme liked this one too. Double-barrel legal theories. 'They should never have added a spring. Workmen could unlatch the panel and use a hook to pull it up, or just lift it. Good.'

The attorney got a call on his mobile and listened for some time, asking questions and jotting notes in his perfectly linear handwriting.

When he disconnected he turned to Rhyme, Archer and Cooper. 'I think we may have something here. But to understand it fully, you need some background in the law.'

Not again . . .

Rhyme nonetheless lifted a please-continue eyebrow and the lawyer launched into yet another lecture.

'Law in America is a complicated creature, like a platypus,' Whitmore said, removing and cleaning his glasses once again (Rhyme could only think of them as spectacles). 'Part mammal, part reptile, part who knows what else?'

Rhyme sighed; Whitmore missed the impatience waft and kept up the narrative. Eventually he got to his point: The Frommer case would be largely determined by 'case law,' not legislative statutes, and the court would look to precedent – prior similar decisions – to decide if Sandy Frommer could win a judgment against Midwest.

With what hovered near enthusiasm in his voice, Whitmore said, 'My paralegal, Ms Schroeder, found no cases where escalators were considered defective because of the lack of interlocks. But she did unearth several cases of heavy industrial machinery – printing presses and die stampers – in which liability was found when the devices continued to work after access panels were opened. The facts are close enough to support a finding that Mr Frommer's injury occurred because of a design defect.'

Archer asked, 'Is it possible to find escalators made by other companies that *do* have an interlock switch?'

'A good question, Ms Archer. Also researched by Ms Schroeder. I'm afraid, though, that the answer is no. Because Midwest Conveyance seems to be the only escalator manufacturer on earth that makes a product with the ill-chosen feature of a pop-up access panel. However, she did find an *elevator* manufacturer whose cars have a cutoff – to apply the brakes in the event the car starts to move when a worker is in the shaft with the access panel open.'

'And that would be a good case to cite,' Archer said, 'since "escalator" sounds a lot like "elevator."'

Impressing Whitmore once again apparently. 'It does indeed. I've found there's an art to subliminally guiding the jury to favor your client. Now, again, I don't intend to go to trial but I'll include a reference to those cases when I contact Midwest Conveyance about settlement. Now we have our theory. A sound one. A good one. I'll spend the next few days preparing the complaint. After we file I'll subpoena the company's engineering records, history of complaints, safety reports. If we're lucky we might find a CBA memo that shoots them in the foot.'

Archer asked what that was; apparently her TV show legal education had failed her on this point. As for Rhyme, he had no clue either.

Whitmore added, 'Cost-benefit analysis. If a company estimates that ten customers a year will die because of its carelessness in building a product and that it will have to pay out wrongful death judgments of ten million dollars in compensation but that it will cost *twenty* million dollars to fix the problem ahead of time, the manufacturer may choose to release the product anyway. Because it's economically more sound.'

'Companies actually make that calculus?' Archer asked. 'Even though they're signing death warrants for those ten people?'

'You may have heard of U.S. Auto. Not too long ago. An engineer wrote an internal memo that there could be gasoline leaks, resulting in catastrophic fires, in a very small percentage of sedans. It would cost X amount to fix it. The management decided it was cheaper to pay the wrongful death or personal injury judgments. And they went with that decision. Of course the company's out of business now. The memo came to light and they never recovered from the public relations disaster. The moral of the story, of course, is—'

Archer said, 'To make the ethically right choice.'

Whitmore said, '—to never commit decisions like that to paper.'

Rhyme wondered if he was joking. But there was no smile accompanying the words.

Whitmore continued, 'I'm assembling information on Mr Frommer's earning potential – how he would have returned to a white-collar job like he used to have. Managerial. To increase our claim for future earning potential. I'll take depositions from the wife and his friends, former fellow workers. Expert medical witnesses on the pain and suffering he experienced. I want to hit Midwest with everything we can. A case like this, I believe, they'll do whatever they must to avoid trial.'

His phone hummed and he glanced at the screen.

'It's Ms Schroeder, in my office. Maybe some new cases we can use.' He answered. 'Yes?'

Rhyme noticed that the attorney had stopped moving. Completely. Not a twist of neck, shift of weight. He stared at the floor. 'You're sure? Who told you? . . . Yes, they're credible.' At last a splinter of emotion crossed the man's face. And it wasn't positive. He disconnected. 'We have a problem.' He looked around the room. 'Is there any way we could set up a Skype call? And I need to do so immediately.'

'You have a minute?' Nick Carelli asked Amelia Sachs.

She was thinking, manically because of her shock at his presence, how odd it was that he didn't look much different, all these years later. All these years spent in prison. Only his posture had changed. Still in good shape otherwise, he was now slouching.

'I . . . I don't . . .' Stammering and hating herself for it.

'I was going to call. Thought you'd hang up.'

Would she have? Of course. Probably.

'I came by, gave it a shot.'

'Are you . . . ?' Sachs began. And thought: Finish your goddamn sentences.

He laughed. That low, happy laugh she remembered. Took her right back, a wormhole to the past.

Nick said, 'No, I didn't escape. Good behavior. Called me a model prisoner. Parole board, unanimous.'

Summoning reason, at last. If she got rid of him fast,

maybe he'd try to come back later. Hear him out now. Be done with it.

She stepped outside and closed the door. 'I don't have much time. I've got to get my mother to the doctor's.'

Shit. Why say that? Why tell him *anything*?

His brow furrowed. 'What's wrong?'

'Some heart issues.'

'Is she—'

'I really don't have a lot of time, Nick.'

'Sure, sure.' Looking her over fast. Then back to her eyes. 'I read about you in the paper. You've got a partner now. The guy used to be head of IR.'

Investigation Resources, the old name of the division that Crime Scene was part of. 'I met him a couple times. Legend. Is he really . . . ?'

'He's disabled, yes.' Silence.

He seemed to sense niceties were clinkers. 'Look, I need to talk to you. Tonight, maybe tomorrow, could we get coffee?'

No. Gate closed, window shut, water over dam, under bridge.

'Tell me now.'

Money, a recommendation for a job? He was never getting back on the force; a felony conviction precluded that.

'Okay, I'll make it fast, Ame . . .'

Using his pet name for her grated.

He took a breath. 'I'll just lay it all out for you. The thing is, about my conviction? The 'jacking, assault? You know all the details.'

Of course she did. The crime was a bad one.

Nick had been busted for being behind a string of hijackings of merchandise and prescription drug shipments. In the last one, before he was caught, he'd beaten a driver with his pistol. The Russian immigrant, father of four, had been in the hospital for a week.

He leaned forward, eyes drilling into hers. He whispered, 'I never did it, Ame. Never did a single thing I was arrested for.'

Her face flushed, hearing this, and her heart began throbbing. She glanced back through the curtained window that bordered the door. No sign of her mother. She'd also looked away to buy a moment to wrestle with what she'd just heard. Finally she turned back. 'Nick, I don't know what to say. Why is this coming up now? Why are you here?'

And her heart continued to beat frantically, like the wings of a bird cupped in your hands. She thought: Could it be true?

'I need your help. Not a soul in the world is going help me but you, Ame.'

'Don't call me that. That's the old life. That's not now.'

'Sorry. I'll tell you fast, I'll explain.' He inhaled long and then said slowly, '*Donnie* was the one working the hijackings. Not me.'

Nick's younger brother.

She could hardly comprehend this. The quiet one of the two siblings, the younger, was a dangerous criminal? She recalled that the hijacker had worn a ski mask and was never identified by the truck driver.

Nick continued, 'He had his problems. You know.'

'The drugs. Drinking, sure. I remember.' The two

brothers were so very different, not even resembling each other. Donnie was almost rat-like in manner and nature, Sachs remembered thinking back then, feeling uneasy with the spontaneous image. In addition to the looks, Nick got the confidence, Donnie the uncertainty and anxiety – and the need to numb both of those. She'd tried to engage him in conversation when they went out to dinner, tell jokes, ask about his continuing-education classes but he'd grow shy and evasive. And occasionally hostile. Suspicious. She believed he was envious of his elder brother for having a former fashion model girlfriend. She remembered too how he would disappear into the men's room and return buoyant and talkative.

Nick continued, 'The evening it all went down, the bust . . . Remember, you were on night watch?'

She nodded. As if she could ever forget.

'I got a call from Mom. She thought Donnie'd started using again. I asked around and heard he might be meeting somebody near the Third Street Bridge. Had some deal going down.'

The ancient bridge, over a hundred years old, spanned the Gowanus, a sludgy canal in Brooklyn.

'I knew something bad was going to happen, if it hadn't already. That 'hood? Had to be. I headed over there right away. I didn't see Donnie but around the corner was the truck, the semi, parked, the doors open. The driver was on the ground, bleeding from his ears, the truck was empty. I called nine one one from a pay phone, anonymous, reported it. Then I went straight to Donnie's apartment. There he was, stoned. And he wasn't alone.' He was now staring into her eyes; his were fierce. She had to look down. 'Delgado, remember him? Vinnie Delgado.'

Vaguely. A gangbanger in BK. Bay Ridge, maybe. Not really connected, not high up anyway. A piece of scum, acting like the Godfather, even though his base of operation was a dive of a magazine/tobacco store. Dead, she also believed – executed for encroaching on a serious crew's turf.

'He got Donnie to work for him. Helping Delgado's crew 'jack and move some stuff off trucks, get it to the fences, middlemen. Promised Donnie all the 'ludes and coke he wanted.'

Sachs was furiously assessing. Then told herself: Stop. Truth or lies, none of this was her business.

'Delgado and his minder told me there was a problem. Apparently one of the Five Families wasn't happy about the 'jackings Delgado had been running, the Gowanus in particular. They'd had their eye on that truck. Huge score of prescription drugs, remember? Delgado said somebody needed to take the fall. He gave me two options. Point the finger at Donnie, in which case Delgado would have to take him out, since he'd spill everything in prison. Or . . . me. Somebody could do the time and keep his mouth shut.' A shrug. 'How's that for a choice?'

'You didn't contact OCT?'

He laughed. The NYPD Organized Crime Task Force was good – but it was good at marshaling big cases against high-profile mobsters. They could have done little to keep Donnie Carelli alive.

'What did Donnie say?'

'When he sobered up I talked to him. I told him what Delgado had said. He was crying, gone all to pieces.

What you'd think. He was desperate, begging me to save him. I said I'd do it for him and Mom. But it was his last chance. He had to get clean.'

'What happened then?'

'I took some of the merch Donnie had and some money, threw it in my car. Wiped the piece Donnie had, the one he'd beaten the driver with, and got my own prints on it. Then made another anonymous call, reported my tag number being at the scene.

'Detectives got me the next day at the station house. I just confessed. That was it.'

'You gave up everything, your whole life? Your years on the force? Just like that?'

He whispered harshly, 'He was my brother! I didn't have any choice.' Then his face softened. 'You remember what we talked about then? About me being on the force, not sure about it?'

She did. Nick didn't have blue in his soul. He wasn't a cop the way she was, or her father was . . . or Lincoln Rhyme had been. He was biding his time until he could find something else – a business, a restaurant. He'd always wanted a restaurant.

'I wasn't meant to be a cop. I was going to get out sooner or later. I could do the time and live with that.'

She thought back. 'And Donnie did get clean, right?'

After he'd gone to jail Sachs had stayed in touch with the family, though not Nick. She'd attended Harriet Carelli's funeral and Donnie had indeed been sober there and every other time she'd seen him. She and the younger brother fell out of touch, however, after she met Lincoln Rhyme.

'He did. For a while. But it didn't stay that way. He didn't do any more work for Delgado that I heard but he went back on C and then H. He died a year ago.'

'Oh, no. I'm sorry. I didn't hear.'

'Overdose. He hid using pretty good. They found him in a hotel in East Harlem. Been there for three days.' Nick's voice caught.

'I did a lot of thinking inside, Amelia. I thought I did the right thing, and I guess I did. I kept Donnie alive for a few years. But I decided I want to prove I'm innocent. I don't care about a pardon or anything like that. I just want to be able to tell people I didn't do it. Donnie's gone, Mom's gone. I don't have any more family might be disappointed to hear the truth. Delgado got capped years ago. His crew's gone. And I want you to know I'm innocent too.'

She saw what was coming.

He continued, 'There's evidence in the case file that'll exculpate me. Contacts, detectives' notes, addresses, things like that. There'll be people out there still who know I didn't do it.'

'You want the file.'

'I do.'

'Nick . . .'

He touched her arm, lightly and fast. His hand receded. 'You've got every right to walk right back inside and close the door. Never see me again. After what I did.'

And the sin wasn't just the crime. What he also did was cut everything off from her, from the instant of his arrest. Yes, he'd done it to protect her. He was, by his admission, a crooked cop. And waves spread from people like that, lapping against anyone nearby. She, an ambitious, rising star on the force, might have been tainted if they'd remained in contact.

So? she asked herself. Walk right back inside and close the door?

She said, 'I have to think about it.'

'That's all I'm asking.'

She steadied herself for an embrace, or a kiss, prepared to resist, but all Nick did was stick his hand out and shake hers, as if they were business associates who'd just concluded a successful real estate deal. 'Wish Rose the best . . . if you want to tell her it was me here.'

He turned and strode away.

She watched him go. After half a block, he looked back at her fast, and on his face was that boyish smile she remembered so clearly from so many years ago. A nod, then he was gone.

CHAPTER 14

Attorney Evers Whitmore logged onto one of Rhyme's computers and loaded Skype.

He typed in an account and Skype's electronic *da-da-da* tone of dialing filled the room. Rhyme moved closer so that both he and Whitmore were visible to the callee, as they could see in the bottom right-hand corner of the monitor.

'Juliette?' Rhyme asked. 'Do you want to move closer?' She was out of view of the webcam.

'No,' she said. And remained where she was.

A moment later an image fluttered onto the screen. A balding man in a white shirt with rolled-up sleeves was glancing at some papers in front of him. The desk he sat behind was paved with stacks of documents.

He looked up at the webcam. 'You're Evers Whitmore?'

'That's right. Attorney Holbrook?'

'Yes.'

'Now, I will tell you that also present are Lincoln Rhyme and to my right, though not visible, Juliette Archer, who are consultants working with me.'

Cooper and Thom were absent. Whitmore had thought it best – an NYPD detective and a civilian with no connection to the case might hamper the conversation that was about to happen.

'Accordingly, I am invoking the work-product doctrine. Are you willing to accept that they are cloaked by the attorney-client privilege as well?'

Holbrook looked up, handed a document to someone who had fire-engine-red nails and then returned to the lens of the camera. 'Sorry. What?'

Whitmore repeated his request.

'Yeah, sure,' Holbrook said. There was a tone of 'Whatever' in his voice. Even though he was chief general counsel of Midwest Conveyance, maker of the deadly escalator, the man seemed far from either defensive or aggressive. Distracted mostly. And Rhyme now knew why.

The attorney concentrated on his webcam once more. 'Been expecting to hear from somebody who represented Greg Frommer and his family. You're the attorney of record?'

'I am.'

'I've heard about you,' Holbrook said. 'Your reputation, of course. Trans Europe Airlines, B and H Pharmaceuticals. You brought them to their knees.'

Whitmore gave no response. 'Now, Attorney Holbrook . . .'

'Damien's fine.'

Good luck with that, Rhyme thought.

Whitmore: 'Yes. You understand why I'm calling?'

'The press conference was a half hour ago. I assumed the attorney representing Frommer's family would hear. And therefore I'd get a call.' Holbrook turned to the side and said, 'I'll be right there. A few minutes. Get them some coffee.' Back to the camera. 'Do you have any theories of defect?'

'We do.'

Holbrook offered, 'Design flaw, no interlock to shut off the motor if the access panel opened accidentally?'

Whitmore glanced toward Rhyme then returned to the webcam. 'I'm not prepared to discuss our theories.'

'Well, that's a good one. And I'll go one further. The spring-loaded access panel.' The lawyer actually chuckled. 'Our design department added that because of workers' comp claims from maintenance people who claimed lifting the door pulled out their backs. Probably spurious . . . But we went with a spring anyway. And you'll probably find out, after the accident, our safety team went to every location that had escalators with spring-loaded access panels installed and detached the springs – before the city inspection. I know, sir, this's a case made in heaven for your client. You could have introduced post-accident modification to show admission of defect on our part. Under other circumstances we would've written a check, and a big one. Mrs Frommer's going through a rough time, I'm sure. And my heart goes out to her. But, well, you *did* hear the news. I'm sorry.'

'My paralegal hasn't gotten to bankruptcy court yet. We haven't read the filings.'

'It's Chapter Seven. Full liquidation. We've been in trouble for a while. Chinese competitors. Germans too. Way of the world. The accident, your client's husband, well, that accelerated our decision, sure. But our bankruptcy was going to happen in the next month or the month after anyway.'

Whitmore said to Archer and Rhyme, 'In filing for bankruptcy Midwest is protected by an automatic stay.

That means we can't sue unless we go to court and have the stay lifted.' Back to the screen and Holbrook. 'I'm hoping for some courtesy information here.'

Holbrook shrugged. 'I'm not going to throw up walls if I don't have to. What do you need to know?'

'Who's your insurer?'

'Sorry. Don't have one. We're self-insured.'

Whitmore's face might have registered dismay at this. Rhyme couldn't tell.

The in-house counsel continued, 'And I have to tell you, there's nothing left, asset-wise. We've got probably a million in receivables and forty million in hard assets. Zero cash. Zero stock. Versus nine hundred million debt, most of it secured. Even if you get the bankruptcy stay lifted and the judge agrees you can file the suit *and* you win – which, I'm sure you know, the receiver'll fight tooth and nail – you'll walk away with a judgment that won't even cover your photocopy costs, sir. And that'd be two or three years from now.'

Whitmore asked, 'Who would have maintained the escalator?'

'I'm afraid to say – for your sake – we did. Our parts and service division. No outside maintenance company for you to bring an action against.'

'Was the mall involved at all with the unit?'

'No. Other than superficial cleaning. And as to the contractors who installed the units, I can tell you our safety team inspected every unit carefully and signed off on them. It all falls on our shoulders . . . Look, sir, I truly am sorry for your client. But there's nothing here for you. We're gone. I've worked for Midwest Conveyance my whole life. I was one of the founders. I rode the company down to the end. I'm broke.'

But you and your loved ones are alive, Rhyme thought. He asked, 'Why do you think the access panel opened?'

The lawyer shrugged. 'Take ten thousand car axles. Why do they work fine, except one, which cracks at eighty miles an hour? Why are twenty tons of lettuce perfectly harmless but a few heads from the same field are contaminated with *E. coli*? In our escalator? Who knows? Something mechanical about the latch, most likely. Maybe the bracket on the access panel was mounted with a screw made in China of substandard steel. Maybe the retracting pin missed tolerance but wasn't rejected by the quality-control robot because of a software hiccup. Could be a thousand things. Fact is, the world's not perfect. You know, sometimes I'm amazed that things we buy and put in our homes and stake our lives on work as well as they do.' A pallid smile. 'Now our outside counsel's arrived. I have to meet with them. It's no consolation, sir, but there are a lot of people here who will have many a sleepless night about Greg Frommer.'

The screen went dark.

Archer snapped, 'Was that bullshit?'

'No. It's an accurate statement of the law.'

'There's nothing we can do?'

The lawyer, completely unemotional, was jotting notes in his microscopic writing, all block letters, Rhyme noted. 'I'll check the filings and court documents but he's not going to lie to us about confirmable information at hand. Under bankruptcy law a judge will sometimes lift a stay if there's an outside insurance company – one that could pay a liability claim like ours. Being self-insured, though, no stay. The company's immune. Judgment-proof.'

'He said we could try other defendants,' Archer said.

Rhyme pointed out, 'Though he wasn't very damn encouraging about that.'

Whitmore said, 'I'll keep looking but' – a nod at the blank screen – 'Mr Holbrook had every incentive to try to blame someone else, for his company's reputation, if nothing else. He didn't see a likely cause of action, and I don't either. This is a classic product liability situation, and we're helpless to pursue it. I'll go see Mrs Frommer and give her the news in person.' The lawyer rose. Fixed both buttons on his suit jacket. 'Mr Rhyme, please submit a bill for your hours. I'll pay that myself. I thank you all for your time and effort. It would have been a productive experience.'

Sachs, here's the thing. I'm out of the business. Well, the criminal *business.*

After dropping her mother back at the town house, following her doctor's appointment, Sachs had driven to Manhattan and was alone in their war room at One PP, her task to make sense of the evidence in the Unsub 40 case and to prod the new officer at the Crime Scene Unit (an older woman technician who was *not* as good as Mel Cooper) to complete the analysis she needed: the examination of the White Castle napkins that might contain their perp's friction ridges and additional DNA, and to identify the sawdust and varnish from the earlier scenes.

Well, that was her ostensible mission.

In fact, she was staring out the window, recalling Rhyme's words to her of a month ago.

I'm out of the business . . .

She'd argued with him, tried to pry open the clamshell of his determination. But he'd been adamant, irritatingly deaf to the bullet points of her side of the debate.

'Everything comes to an end,' her father had told her one crisp, glary Saturday afternoon as he took a breather from their joint project of installing a rebuilt carburetor in their Camaro. 'It's the way of the world and it's better to accept that. Dignify, don't demean.' Herman Sachs was, at the time, on a leave of absence from the NYPD, undergoing a series of cancer treatments. Sachs accepted almost everything the calm, shrewd and humorous man had taught and told her, but she furiously declined to buy either of those points – the ending and the acceptance – despite the fact that he proved himself right, at least as to the first, by dying six weeks later.

Forget it. Forget Lincoln.

You've got work to do. Staring at the evidence charts.

Crime Scene: 151 Clinton Place, Manhattan, construction site, adjacent to 40° North (Nightclub)

- Offenses: Homicide, Assault.
- Victim: Todd Williams, 29, writer, blogger, social topics.
- COD: Blunt force trauma, probably ball-peen hammer (no brand determined).
- Motive: Robbery.
  - Credit/debit cards not yet used.

- Evidence:
  - No friction ridges.
  - Blade of grass.
  - Trace:
    - Phenol.
    - Motor oil.

- Profile of suspect (Unknown Subject 40).
  - Wore checkered jacket (green), Braves baseball cap.
  - White male.
  - Tall (6 feet, 2 inches to 6 feet, 4).
  - Slim (140–150 lbs.).
  - Long feet and fingers.
  - No visual of face.

Crime Scene: Heights View Mall, Brooklyn

- Relevance to case: Attempted apprehension of subject (not successful).
- Additional elements of profile of suspect.
  - Possibly carpenter or works in trades?
  - Eats large amounts of food.
  - Likes White Castle restaurant.
  - Lives in Queens or other connection with borough?
  - High metabolism?

- Evidence:
  - DNA, no CODIS match.

- No friction ridges sufficient for ID.
- Shoeprint, likely unsub's, size 13 Reebok Daily Cushion 2.0.
- Soil sample, likely from unsub, containing crystalline aluminosilicate clays: montmorillonite, illite, vermiculite, chlorite, kaolinite. Additionally, organic colloids. Substance is probably humus. Not native to this portion of Brooklyn.
- Dinitroaniline (used in dyes, pesticides, explosives).
- Ammonium nitrate (fertilizer, explosives).
  - With oil from Clinton Place scene: Possibly constructing bomb?
- Additional phenol (precursor in making plastics, like polycarbonates, resins and nylon, aspirin, embalming fluid, cosmetics, ingrown toenail cures; unsub has large feet, so – nail problems?)
- Talc, mineral oil/paraffinum liquidum/huile minérale, zinc stearate, stearic acid, lanolin/ lanoline, cetyl alcohol, triethanolamine, PEG-12 laurate, mineral spirits, methylparaben, propylparaben, titanium dioxide.
  - Makeup? No brand determination. Analysis to return.
- Shaving of metal, microscopic, steel, probably from sharpening knife.
- Sawdust. Type of wood to be determined. From sanding, not sawing.
- Organochlorine and benzoic acid. Toxic (insecticides, weaponized poisons?)

- Acetone, ether, cyclohexane, natural gum, cellu-
lose (probably varnish).
  - Manufacturer to be determined.
- Napkins from White Castle, probably unsub's.
Will resubmit for additional evidence.
  - Stains suggest unsub drank several bever-
  ages.

Crime Scene: White Castle Restaurant, Astoria Boulevard, Astoria, Queens

- Relevance to case: Unsub eats here regularly.
- Additional elements of profile of suspect.
  - Eats 10–15 sandwiches at a time.
  - Had been shopping at least once when ate
  here. Carried white plastic bag, something
  heavy inside. Metallic?
  - Turned north and crossed the street (toward
  bus/train?). No sign he owned/drove automo-
  bile.
  - Witnesses didn't get good view of face, probably
  no facial hair.
  - White, pale, maybe balding or crew cut.

- Used a car service on Astoria Blvd. around day of
Williams's murder.
  - Awaiting word from owner of gypsy cab
  company.

From what was found at the scenes, Sachs and Pulaski
had concluded Unsub 40 might be a tradesman. But even

if so, did workers carry around tools late at night, especially a rare one like the ball-peen hammer he'd used to kill Todd Williams? And if a tool like that had nothing to do with his job, his carrying it suggested design – a perp on the hunt for a victim. But why? What the hell are you up to, Mr Forty? How much money could Todd Williams've had on him to justify killing? You didn't use any of his credit or debit cards, or sell them – they would have shown up by now. Stolen plastic has a very short shelf life. You didn't try to suck his bank account dry. Williams had been straight, for the most part, but she'd learned from friends of a few gay encounters. There was a rough-trade club about three blocks from the construction site where he was killed, yet extensive canvassing of the place uncovered no evidence that Williams had ever been there.

Any other reasons for the unsub to kill you?

Williams had been a former programmer by profession and now he wrote about social issues on his blog but there was nothing controversial that she'd seen. The environment and privacy were his main topics. Nothing anyone could take offense at. And as for the bomb making and poisoning theories – related to terrorism possibly – the evidence was sketchy and her instinct said those were dead ends.

Maybe the motive was that which was the least helpful to investigators: Williams had witnessed some other crime and the lean perp – maybe a hit man, maybe a professional burglar – had seen him and clipped him. And yet . . . and yet . . .

Come on, Rhyme . . .

She needed somebody to brainstorm with. But it can't be you now, can it?

Out of the business . . .

And what was up with Ron Pulaski? He'd been acting particularly odd. He'd questioned the wisdom of Rhyme's retirement, firmly calling his boss on the decision. ('It's crazy!' To which he received back: 'I've decided, Rookie. Why bring it up for the thousandth time. Quit. Asking.')

Was this his distraction? Though maybe Ron's mood had nothing to do with Rhyme. She again considered illness in the family. Or the officer himself. His head injury. Then too: He was a husband and father, trying to make ends meet on a patrolman's salary. God bless . . .

Her phone buzzed. She looked down and felt a prickle along her scalp.

Nick.

Sachs didn't hit answer. She closed her eyes.

After the humming stopped, she glanced at the phone. He'd left no message.

What to do, what to do?

In days past, Sachs might have wandered down to the file room at One PP or, depending on where the *People of the State of New York v. Nicholas J. Carelli* files were stored, driven to the archives in New Jersey. In either case she might have dawdled outside the room downstairs – or spent the drive – pondering Nick's request. Yes or no?

Now, with every case file for the past twenty-five years scanned and sitting in a big fat database somewhere, this debate occurred here, at her desk, as she looked over a sliver of vessel-filled New York Harbor. Leaning back in lazy posture, now she was staring at the screen.

The propriety of downloading the file? No objections she could see. Sachs was an active-duty officer, so she had legitimate access to all files and there were no regulations about sharing them with civilians in closed cases. And if Nick found something that proved his innocence, he could come to her and she could tell the brass she'd decided to look into the matter on her own initiative. And then – this was non-negotiable in her heart – hand the matter over to an Internal Affairs investigator and step away entirely.

No, legality wasn't really the issue. Some endeavors, of course, could be completely legal yet stunningly bad ideas.

Nick's other options would be to find a lawyer to reopen the case and petition the court for review. Though, Sachs had to admit, her handing him the file would make his quest a thousand times easier.

Yet why had it fallen to *her* to help him?

Their years together – not so many in number but intense, consuming – flashed past. She couldn't deny that the memories were tugging her in the direction of doing what he'd asked of her. But there was a broader issue. Even if she hadn't known him, his story was compelling. Earlier this evening she'd looked up Vincent Delgado. Unlike high-level organized crime figures, who were essentially businessmen, Delgado was a megalomaniac, probably borderline psychotic. Vicious, prone to torture. He would have killed Donnie Carelli without blinking an eye, might even have threatened to kill their mother, Harriet, if Nick didn't roll over to the Gowanus 'jacking. Yes, if everything he said was true, he was guilty of obstructing justice, though the statute of limitations would have run out a long time ago. So he was in all ways innocent.

Yes, no?

What bad could come of it?

Sachs turned from the computer back to the evidence boards on the Unsub 40 case.

And what would you say, Rhyme, if you were here? What insights?

But you're *not* here. You're hanging with the ambulance chasers.

Then her eyes slipped to the unblinking cursor.

Archived File Request
Case File Name: People v. Carelli
Case File Number: 24-543676F
Requesting Officer Shield: D5885
Passcode: ********

Yes, no?

What bad could come of it? she asked herself again.

Sachs removed her hands from the keyboard, closed her eyes and leaned back in the chair once more.

CHAPTER 15

Juliette Archer and Lincoln Rhyme were alone in the parlor.

The notes from the now-defunct *Frommer v. Midwest Conveyance* – the hard copies of the pictures Sachs and Cooper had snapped, the printouts from Archer's research – sat in ordered rows. Even in defeat Mel Cooper was as organized as an operating room nurse.

Earlier today, upon hearing that the case was over, Rhyme indulged himself with an encouraging thought: that he was relieved of the burden of mentoring his student. Yet now he wasn't as buoyed by that idea as he initially had been. He found himself saying to her, 'There *are* a few things you could help with, if you're interested, a couple of other projects I'm working on. Not as intriguing as a case. Research. Esoteric elements of forensics. Academia. But still.'

She maneuvered her chair to face him and her countenance suggested she was surprised. 'You didn't think I was going to leave, did you?'

'No. I was just saying.' An expression he detested when coming from someone else's lips and he liked it no more now that *he'd* uttered it.

'Or you were hoping?' Her smile was coy.

'Your presence was helpful.'

His highest compliment, though she wouldn't know that.

'It's unfair what happened. No money, no recourse for Sandy Frommer.'

Rhyme said, 'But that's your situation.' A nod at the wheelchair. Because her disability stemmed from the tumor, not an accident, she had no one to recover settlement money from. 'I was lucky. I got a large settlement from the construction company that built the scaffolding the pipe fell from.'

'Pipe? Is that what happened?'

He laughed. 'I was playing rookie. At the time I was head of the Crime Scene Unit but I couldn't keep from searching a scene myself. A killer was murdering police officers. I had to get down in the site and dig for evidence. I was sure *I* could find the clue that would lead to him, and no one else could. A good example of the adage: One's character is one's fate.'

'Heraclitus,' she said, her eyes amused. 'They'd be so proud, the good sisters of Immaculata, my remembering *something* they taught me. Of course, fate sometimes has nothing to do with who you are and what you do. Two assassination attempts on Hitler. They both were perfectly planned and they both failed. *There*'s fate for you. No design, no justice. Sometimes you get the golden apple. Sometimes you're screwed. Either way . . .'

' . . . you cope.'

Archer nodded.

'Something I've been wondering.'

'Yes, it's true,' Rhyme announced in a bold voice. 'A ninhydrin solution *can* indeed be prepared in a mixture of non-polar solvents. "The exhibit is immersed in the working solution and allowed to develop in dark, humid conditions for two to three days, avoiding high temperatures." That's a quotation from the Department of Justice's fingerprint manual. I tested it. They're accurate.'

She fell silent as she looked around the lab, congested with equipment and tools and instruments. Finally: 'You're avoiding the question that's coming, aren't you?'

'Why I quit working for the police.'

Archer smiled. 'Answer or not. Just curious.'

He gestured with his working hand toward one of the whiteboards in the far corner of the room, snubbing them with their backs. He said, 'That was a case about a month ago. There's a notation at the bottom of the board. *Suspect deceased. Prosecution terminated.*'

'That's why you quit?'

'Yes.'

'So you made a mistake and somebody died.'

Inflection is everything. Archer's comment ended in a lazy question mark; she might have been asking legitimately if this was the case. Or she might have been dismissing what happened and chiding him for backing away from a profession in which death was a natural part of the process: A human's ceasing to exist is, of course, the prime mover of a homicide case. A corollary is the possible death of the suspect during apprehension . . . or, occasionally, a lethal injection gurney.

But Rhyme gave a shallow laugh. 'No. In fact, the opposite happened.'

'Opposite?'

He adjusted the chair slightly. They were now facing

each other. 'I didn't make a mistake at all. I was one hundred percent accurate.' He sipped from the tumbler of Glenmorangie that Thom had poured ten minutes before. He nodded toward the liquor and then turned to Archer but again she declined a beverage. He continued, 'The suspect – a businessman from Garden City named Charles Baxter . . . You ever hear of him?'

'No.'

'The case was in the news. Baxter defrauded some rich folks out of about ten million that, frankly, they would hardly've noticed. It's all about the decimal point, of course. Who really cared? But that's not the prosecutor's – or my – call. Baxter broke the law and the assistant district attorney brought the case, got me on board to help find the cash and analyze the physical evidence – handwriting, ink, GPS logs that let us follow him to banks, trace evidence from where the meetings took place, false identity documents, soil from where money was buried. It was easy to run. I found plenty of admissible evidence to support grand theft, wire fraud, a few other counts. The ADA was happy. The perp was looking at three to five years.

'But there were some questions about the evidence that I didn't find the answers to. Eating at me. I kept analyzing, getting more and more evidence. The prosecutor said don't bother; she had all she needed for the conviction she was after. But I couldn't stop.

'I found a very small amount of oil in his personal effects, oil that's used almost exclusively in firearms. And some gunshot residue and drug trace. And several different kinds of trace that led to a particular location in Long Island City. There was a big self-storage facility in the neighborhood. The detective I was working with found that Baxter had a unit there. Baxter didn't tell us about it, he said, because there was nothing there that had to do with the financial fraud, just personal things. But we got a warrant and found an unregistered handgun. That moved the charge up to a different class of felony and, even though the ADA didn't want to pursue it – Baxter had no history of violence – she didn't have any choice. Firearms possession carries a mandatory sentence in New York. DAs have to prosecute it.'

Archer said, 'He killed himself. Facing that.'

'No. He went to the violent felons' wing on Rikers Island, got into a fight and was killed by another prisoner.'

The facts sat between them, in silence, for a moment.

'You did everything right,' Archer said, her voice analytical, not softened to convey reassurance.

'Too right,' Rhyme said.

'But the gun? He shouldn't have had it.'

'Well, yes and no. True, it was unregistered so it technically fell within the law. But it was his father's from Vietnam. He'd never shot it, he claimed. Didn't even know he still had it. It was just stored away with a bunch of memorabilia from the sixties. The gun oil I'd found he said he probably picked up at a sporting goods store buying a present for his son a week before. The gunshot residue could have been transferred from cash. The same with the drugs. Half the twenties in the New York metro area have traces of cocaine, meth and heroin on them. Gunshot residue. He never tested positive for any controlled substances and he'd never been arrested on any drug charges. Never been arrested before at all.' Rhyme offered what he knew was a rare smile. 'Gets worse. One of the reasons for the fraud – his daughter needed a bone marrow transplant.'

'Ah. I'm sorry. But . . . You were a cop. Isn't that the cost of doing business?'

Exactly Amelia Sachs's argument. She might have used those very words. Rhyme couldn't remember.

'It is. And am I traumatized and lying – well, sitting – in a therapist's office? No. But there comes a time when you get off the carousel. Everything comes to an end.'

'You *needed* to find the solution.'

'Had to have it.'

'I understand that, Lincoln. Epidemiology's the same. There's always a question – what's the virus, where's it going to hit next, how do you inoculate, who's suscep-tible? – and I always *had* to find the answer.' She'd loved the field of epidemiology, she'd told him when first asking about being his intern. But she could hardly continue to be a field agent. And the office work in that endeavor was far too routine and boring to hold her attention. Crime scene, even in the lab, she reasoned, would keep her engaged. As with Rhyme, boredom was a demon to Juliette Archer.

She continued, 'I got dengue fever once. Pretty serious. I *had* to find out how the mosquitoes were infecting people in Maine, of all places. You know dengue's a tropical disease.'

'Don't know much about it.'

'How the hell could people in New England get dengue?

I searched for months. Finally found the answer: a rain forest exhibit in a zoo. I traced the victims back to visits to the place. And, wouldn't you know, I got bit while I was there.'

Character is fate . . .

Archer continued, 'It's a compulsion. You had to search the crime scene where you were injured and find out the answer to the gun oil and drugs. I had to find those goddamn mosquitoes. An unanswered riddle is the worst thing in the world for me.' Her striking blue eyes lit up again. 'I love riddles. You?'

'Games? Or life?'

'Games.'

'No. I don't do that.'

'I've found they help you expand your thinking. I collect them. Want to try?'

'That's all right.' Meaning absolutely not. His eyes were on the evidence boards whose backs were to them. Another sip of whisky.

Archer nonetheless said, 'Okay. Two sons and two fathers go fishing. Each one catches a fish. They return from the trip with only three fish. How can that be?'

'I don't know. Really, I—'

'Come on. Try.' She repeated it.

Rhyme grimaced but he found himself thinking: One got away? They ate one for lunch? One fish ate another?

Archer was smiling. 'The thing about riddles is that you never need more information than you're given. No fish sandwiches, no escapes.'

He shrugged. 'Give up.'

'You're not trying very hard. All right, the answer?'

'Sure.'

'The fishing party included a grandfather, his son and grandson. Two fathers, two sons, but only three people.'

Rhyme barked an involuntary laugh. Clever. He liked it.

'As soon as you got the idea of four people in your head, it's almost impossible to dislodge it, right? Remember: The answers to riddles are always simple – given the right mind-set.'

The doorbell hummed. Rhyme looked at the video monitor. Archer's brother, Randy. Rhyme was mildly disappointed she'd be leaving. Thom went to answer the door.

She said, 'One more.'

'All right.'

'What one thing do you find at the beginning of eternity and at the end of time and space?'

'Matter.'

'No.'

'Black hole.'

'No.'

'Wormhole.'

'You're guessing. Do you even know what a wormhole is?' she asked.

He did. But he hadn't really thought that was the answer.

Simple . . .

'Give up?'

'No. I'm going to keep working at it.'

Thom appeared a moment later with Archer's brother. They spoke for a few minutes, polite but pointless conversation. Then brief goodbyes and brother and sister headed out of the arched doorway of the parlor. Halfway through Archer stopped. She wheeled around. 'Just curious about one thing, Lincoln.'

'What's that?'

'Baxter. Did he have a big house or apartment?'

What was this about? He thought back to the case. 'I recall that he did. In his asset statement it was listed at three million Why do you ask?'

'Just wondering why he needed a storage unit in Long Island City – where the gun was found. You'd think he could store things in his house. Or at least in a storage place closer to home. Well, just a thought. Good night now.'

'Night,' he said.

'And don't forget our riddle: eternity and time and space.'

She wheeled from sight.

Computers saved my life.

In several ways. In high school, I could excel at something not sports (tall is good for basketball but skinny bean isn't). Computer club. Math club. Gaming. Role-playing online – I could be whoever I wanted to. Appear however I wanted to appear, thank you, avatars and Photoshop.

And now: Computers make my career possible. True, I don't really look a *lot* different from many people on the street. But just *some* different can be enough. People say they like different but they don't really – unless it's to look at and laugh at and boost themselves up. So, running a business online, in the safety of my Chelsea womb, is perfect for me. I don't have to see people, talk to them in person, endure the gawking, even if it's with a smile on their faces.

And I make a tidy living to boot.

I'm now sitting at – yes – my computer, smarting from the loss of my White Castle. At the kitchen table. I type some more. Read the results of my search. Type another request. Zip, zip, I get more answers. I like the sound the keys make. Satisfying. I've tried to describe it. Not a typewriter, not a light switch. Closest I can come is the sound of fat raindrops on a taut camping tent. Peter and I went camping a half-dozen times when we were kids, twice with our parents (not as much fun then; father listened to a game, mother smoked and turned magazine pages). Peter and I had fun, though, especially in the rain. I didn't have to be embarrassed going swimming. The girls, you know. And the boys in good shape.

Tap, tap, tap.

Funny how time seems to work to your advantage. I heard some people say, oh, wish I'd been born in this time or that time. Romans, Queen Victoria, the '30s, the '60s. But I'm lucky for the here and now. Microsoft, Apple, HTML, Wi-Fi, all the rest of it. I can sit in my room and put bread on my table and a woman in bed occasionally and a bone-cracking hammer in my hand. I can outfit the Toy Room with everything I need for my satisfaction.

Thank you, computers. Love your raindrop keyboards. More typing.

So. Computers saved my life by giving me a business of my own, safe from the Shoppers out there.

And they'll save my life now.

Because I'm learning all I can about Red, Amelia Sachs, detective third-grade with the New York City Police Department.

I almost solved the problem of her earlier. Almost cracked her skull to splinters. I was following her near the White Castle, hand in my backpack, on the lovely hammer handle, smooth as a girl's ankle. Moving close. When some other man showed up, who knew her. A cop, I had a feeling, one who worked for her, it seemed. Little white boy, skinny as me, okay, not quite, and shorter but he looked like trouble. He would have a gun and radio, of course.

I settled for getting Red's license plate from that sexy car of hers.

All the helpful information I'm learning about her is pretty neat. Daughter of a cop, partner of a cop – well, former cop. Lincoln Rhyme, a famous guy. Disabled, which is what they call it, I've learned. In a wheelchair. So we have something in common. I'm not disabled exactly. But people look at me the way they look at him, I imagine.

Typing and typing hard. My fingers are long and big, my hands are strong. I break keyboards once every six months or more. And that's not even when I'm angry.

Type, read, jot notes.

More and more about Red. Cases she's closed. Shooting competitions she's won (I'm keeping *that* in mind, believe me).

Now I *am* growing angry . . . Yes, you can buy White

Castle burgers at grocery stores. I will do that. But it's not the same as going into the place, the tile, the smell of grease and onions. I remember going to one near where we grew up. A cousin, Lindy, was visiting from Seattle. Middle schooler, like me. I'd never been out with a girl before and I pretended she wasn't a relative and I imagined kissing her and her kissing me. Went to lunch at White Castle. Gave her a present, for her shiny blond hair, to keep it dry: a clear plastic rain scarf, all folded up tight like a road map in a little pouch, deep blue and embroidered in a Chinese design. Lindy laughed. Kissed my cheek.

A good day.

That was White Castle to me. And Red has taken it away.

Mad, mad . . .

I come to a decision. But then: It's not a decision if you don't decide. I have no choice in the matter. As if on cue, the door buzzer blares. I jump at the sound. Save the file on the computer, slip the hard copies away. I click the intercom.

'Vernon, it's me?' Alicia says/asks.

'Come on up.'

'You're sure it's okay?'

My heart is slamming, at the prospect of what's coming. For some reason I glance back at the Toy Room door. I say into the intercom box, 'Yes.'

Two minutes, here she is, outside the door. I check the camera. She's alone (not brought here at gunpoint by Red, which I actually imagine happening). I let her in and close and lock the door. I think involuntarily of a stone closing onto a crypt.

No turning back.

'Are you hungry?' I ask.

'Not really.'

I was, not any longer. Considering what's about to happen.

I start to reach for her jacket, then remember, and let her hang it up. Tonight she's in her thick schoolteacher blouse, high neck. She looks at the darting fish.

Red and black and silver.

The question is a lump, throbbing prominently in my brain, right where I would crack the bone of someone I wanted to kill.

Do I really want to do this?

My anger at Red oozes out to my skin and burns.

Yes, I do.

'What?' Alicia asks, looking at me with that wariness in her eyes. Must have said the word aloud.

'Come with me.'

'Uhm. Are you all right, Vernon?'

'Fine,' I whisper. 'This way.'

We walk to the door of the Toy Room. She looks at the complicated lock. I know she's seen it. And is curious. What would he want to hide? she'd be wondering. What's in the den, the lair, the crypt? Of course she doesn't say a word.

'Close your eyes.'

A hesitation now.

I ask, 'Do you trust me?'

She doesn't. But what can she do? She closes her eyes. I grip her hand. Mine is trembling. She hesitates and then grips back. Sweat mixes.

Then I'm guiding her through the door, the halogens shooting off the steel blades and blinding me. Not her. True to her word, Alicia keeps her eyes closed.

Lincoln Rhyme, lying in bed, near midnight, hoping for sleep.

He'd spent the last hour reflecting on *Frommer v. Midwest Conveyance*. Whitmore had called and in his somber, well, *dull*, cadence reported that he'd discovered no other potential defendants. Attorney Holbrook was right. The cleaning crews could not possibly have done anything to cause the access panel to open, and the attorney's private eye had tracked down the crew that had dismantled the escalator for the Department of Investigations. The worker had confirmed that the door covering the access panel switch had indeed been closed and locked, confirming what Sachs had said: that no one could, accidentally or on purpose, have opened the panel and caused the accident.

So the case was officially dead.

Now Rhyme's thoughts eased to Amelia Sachs.

He was particularly aware of her absence tonight. He could not, of course, feel much of her body beside him when she was here, but he found comfort in her regular breathing, the layered smells of shampoo and soap (she was not a perfumista). Now he sensed an edge to the silence in the room, somehow accentuated by the aroma of inanimate cleansers and furniture polish and paper from the rows of books against the wall nearby.

Thinking back to their harsh words earlier, his and Sachs's.

They had always argued. But this had been different. He could tell from her tone. Yet he didn't understand why. Cooper was truly gifted. But the New York Police Department Crime Scene Unit was filled with brilliant evidence collection technicians and analysts, with expertise in hundreds of fields, from handwriting to ballistics to chemistry to remains reconstruction . . . She could have had any one of them. And, hell, Sachs herself was an expert at forensic analysis. She might prefer somebody to man the gas chromatograph/mass spectrometer or scanning electron microscope, but Rhyme himself didn't run those. He left that to the technical people.

Maybe there was something else on her mind. Her mother, he supposed. Rose's operation would be weighing on her. A triple heart bypass in an elderly woman? The medical world was nothing short of miraculous, of course. But considering the massively complex and vulnerable machine within our skin, well, you couldn't help but think every one of our hours was borrowed.

Since *Frommer v. Midwest Conveyance* no longer existed, tomorrow Mel Cooper would be back in the CSU fold. And she could use him to her heart's content.

Sleep crowded in, and Rhyme now found himself thinking of Juliette Archer, wondering about her life in the future. She seemed to have what it took to be a solid forensic scientist but at the moment his musings were about something else: her coping with disability. She still had not fully accepted her condition. She would have a long and dark way to go before she did it. If, in fact, she chose to do so. Rhyme recalled his own early battle, which culminated in a fierce debate about assisted suicide.

He'd faced that choice and chosen to remain among the living. Archer was nowhere near that confrontation yet.

How would she choose?

And what, Rhyme wondered, would he think about her decision? Would he support it or argue against finality?

But any debate within her was years off; most likely he wouldn't even know her then. These ruminations, grim though they were, had the effect of lulling him to sleep.

It was perhaps ten minutes later that he started awake, his head rising as he heard, in his thoughts, Archer's low, alto voice. What one thing do we find at the beginning of eternity and the end of time and space?

Rhyme laughed out loud.

The letter 'e.'

THURSDAY

III EXPLOIT

CHAPTER **16**

Morning, a Chelsea morning. Chelsea light streams through the open shutters.

I'm in the Toy Room, transcribing the diary once again. Sister Mary Frances's diligence is revealed in the perfectly scripted words I form on the thick paper.

We played Alien Quest today. Long time, the three of us. Sam and Frank and me. The popular boys and me! Sam's dad has money. He sells things, medical stuff, I don't know what it is but the company pays well and even gives him a car! So Sam has all the games and all the platforms.

Funny, even before I ran into them that day outside of Cindy's house, coming home a different route, the safe route, they never gave me any shit. But that didn't mean they'd be interested in hanging out. But they ARE. They're A Team, ha, don't mean on teams even though they are. Mean the top crowd, the clique crowd, the A Team crowd. Handsome, cool, they could have any girl, any time. But they want to hang with me.

It's Tye Butler, Dano, their friends, sort of goth sort of redneck, yeah even in Manhasset, Long Island. It's THEM who push and gawk and say, Bean Pole and Dick Freak. Stuff like that. Sam heard about Butler saying something and he went to find him and said, Leave Griffith alone. And Butler did.

Don't see them real often. Sam and Frank. The teams, the girls. But that's what makes it real. They're like, Hey, Griffith, what's going on? And it's epic cause they use my last name, what the in people do. Hey, Griffith, you want a Coke? Then we go separate ways for a few days or a week.

Can't talk to them serious. Of course. I'd like to, talk about being/feeling different. Can't talk to anybody, really. Dad, yeah right. In between games. Which is never. Mom, sometimes. But she doesn't get it. She has baking and her friends and her crafts and her food and after six thirty, forget it. My brother's okay but off doing other things.

But talking to Sam and Frank?

I decided no. Might break something is how I feel.

I put the diary and the recorder away. I stretch and stand up and walk to the futon, look down, scanning Alicia's body. Pale, really pale. Mouth kind of open, eyes kind of shut.

Pretty, even in the messy clothes, the twisted sheets.

Beside the bed is a band saw, which is really quite a wicked piece of machinery. If they had one during the Middle Ages, imagine how many people would have renounced the devil. Slice, slice, off with a finger.

Off with whatever.

A voice makes me jump. 'Vernon.'

I turn. Alicia is stirring. Blinking against the halogen lights.

She sits up, blinking and stretching too. 'Morning,' she says, shy and cautious.

This is a word she's never said to me before. A first, staying over.

A first, her seeing the Toy Room. Which no one else has ever done – and which I thought would never, ever happen.

Letting someone into my sanctuary, letting someone see the *real* me was hard to do, so very hard. I could never explain it right but it was like risking everything to let her in. One-night stands, fucking to exhaustion, that's easy. But, like, taking a woman to a gallery exhibition showing paintings you're hopelessly passionate about – that's a chance that's so risky. What if she laughs, what if she looks bored, what if she decides you miss her mark completely?

And wants to go away.

But last night, walking into the Toy Room and, on my command, opening her eyes, Alicia was as delighted as I've ever seen her. She gazed over the workbench, the saws, the tools, the hammers, the chisels. My new implement, the razor with the tiny teeth, my *favorite*. My child. I loved seeing her pale brow and cheeks, lit by the blue-white reflections shooting from all the steel surfaces.

But what really entranced her was what I constructed with those tools.

'You *made* these?' she asked last night.

'Did,' I told her uncertainly.

'Oh, Vernon. They're works of art.'

And, hearing that, my life was about as perfect as it could be.

A good day . . .

But just after that, last night, we grew very, very busy and, after, fell fast asleep. Now, this morning, she wants to see more of my handiwork.

Before I can turn away or hand her a robe she's out of bed, and Alicia does in her way what I have done by sharing the room with her. Because now, in the light, she remains naked and I can see her scars clearly. This is the first time she's allowed me to view them full. The high-necked dress or blouse covers them when she's clothed. The thick sheltering bra and high panties when she's half naked. And when we're in bed, the lights are always low to nonexistent. Now, though, here's every inch of her body to see in sun-splayed clarity: the slashed breast and thigh, the burned groin, the patch where her arm bone poked through her pale skin after being so fiercely bent.

I hurt for this woman – because of these scars and the scars within, all going back to her husband, years ago, that terrible time. I want to make her whole, make her perfect again, untwist the arm that her husband twisted, unburn her low belly, mend her breast. But all I have are my steel tools and the best they could do is the opposite of my good intent: cutting and crushing and snapping flesh.

What I *can* do, though, is to ignore the troubled skin, which is not at all difficult, and show her – it's quite obvious now – how much I desire her. And, I think, here is yet another way I can help heal the other scars, the ones inside.

Alicia looks up at my eyes and comes close to smiling. Then she enwraps her bothered flesh with a sheet stained from us both because it's what any normal couple would do upon waking. She walks to the shelves, and once more looks over the miniatures I've built with my panoply of tools.

I construct almost exclusively furniture. Not toys, not Kids-R-Us plastic or mismatched wood glued together by children in China. But fine-worked, quality pieces, only tiny, tiny, tiny. I spend days on each piece, sometimes weeks. Turning legs on a model maker's lathe, using a fine razor saw to make even seams, lacquering chests of drawers and desks and headboards with ten coats of varnish, so they are smooth and rich and dark as a still autumn pond.

Alicia says: 'This's as good as anything you'd find in an artisan's workshop in High Point. North Carolina, you know. Where they make real furniture. Vernon, amazing.' And I can tell from her face she means it.

'You told me you sold things for a living. eBay and online. I just assumed you bought things and marked them up and sold them.'

'No, I wouldn't like that. I like making things.'

'You shouldn't call them "things." They're more than things. They're works of art,' she repeats.

I might be blushing. I don't know. And for a moment I want to hug her, kiss her, but not in the way I usually grip her and taste her finger or mouth or nipple or groin. Just hold my lips against her temple. This might be what love is but I don't know about that and I don't want to think beyond this moment.

'It's quite a workshop.' She's looking around.

'My Toy Room. That's what I call it.'

'Why didn't you tell me this is what you do? You were all mysterious.'

'Just . . .' I shrug. The answer of course is Shoppers. The bullies, the rude, the people who humiliate for sport.

193

Vernon Griffith sits in his dark room and makes toys . . . Why bother to get to know a freak like him? I need somebody chic or cool or handsome.

I don't answer.

'Who buys them?'

I can't help but laugh. 'The people who pay the most are the American Girl folks. Mostly they're lawyers and doctors and CEOs, who'd do anything, spend any amount for their little girls.' I know they don't appreciate the pieces – even the ones I charge a thousand for – any more than they would a hunk of molded polyurethane. And I doubt they enjoy their children's faces when they open the package (though I suspect the kids' reaction is a milli-meter above indifference). No, what the businessmen enjoy is showing off to neighbors. "Oh, look what I had commis-sioned for Ashleigh. It's teak, you know."'

(And I always reflect on the irony of parents' buying for their adorable little ones a chest of drawers made by the same hands that have cracked skulls or sliced tender throats with a lovely *implement*.)

'Most buyers, however, love what I sell, the reviews are stellar. Oh, and look. You do historical too.' She's looking at a catapult, a siege tower, a medieval banquet table, a torture rack (one of my more popular items, which I find amusing).

'We can thank *Game of Thrones* for that. And I made a lot of Elvish and Orc things when the *Hobbit* movies came out. Anything medieval is okay as long as it's generic. I was going to do *Hunger Games* but I was worried about trademark and copyright problem. You have to be careful with Disney too. And Pixar. Oh, you have to see this.'

I find a book on my shelf, hold it up. *The Nutshell Studies of Unexplained Death*.

'What *is* this, Vernon?' She sidles close and I feel her body against mine as I flip the pages.

'Woman in Chicago, a millionaire heiress. Long time ago. She died in 'sixty-two. Frances Glessner Lee. Ever heard of her?'

'No.'

'Quite a person. She didn't do heiress, society stuff. She was fascinated with crime, murder mostly. And had dinner parties, fancy ones, for police investigators. She learned all about solving murders. But she wanted to do more. So she got details on famous murders and made dioramas – you know, like dollhouse rooms – of crime scenes. Every detail was perfect.'

The book is photographs of her miniature sets. Names like Three Room Dwelling and The Pink Bathroom. Every one features a doll of a corpse where a corpse actually lay, bloodstains where the bloodstains really were.

I think suddenly of Red. What I found out about her, Ms Shopper Amelia Sachs, is that she specializes in crime scene work. Two thoughts: She would probably appreciate the book.

The other: A miniature diorama in which a doll representing her shapely body lies on the floor of her bedroom. Skull cracked, red hair redder from the blood.

We laugh at some of the perfect detail Lee included in her work. I put the book away.

'Would you like one?' I ask.

She turns. 'One what?'

I nod toward the shelves. 'A miniature.'

'I . . . I don't know. Aren't those part of your inventory?'

'Yes. But the buyers will wait. What do you want? Any one in particular?'

She leans forward and her eyes settle on a baby carriage.

'It's so perfect.' She offers her second smile.

There are two perambulators. One made on commission and one I've done just because I enjoy making baby carriages. Couldn't say why. Babies and children do not, never have, never will figure in my life.

She points to the one that's under commission. The better one. I pick it up and hand it to her. She touches it carefully and repeats, 'It's perfect. Every part. Look at how the wheels turn! It even has springs!'

'Have to keep the baby comfy,' I say.

'Thank you, Vernon.' She kisses my cheek. And turns away, letting the sheet slither to the floor while she lies down on the bed, gazing up at me.

I debate. An hour won't delay me significantly.

Besides, it seems humane to give the person I'm going to kill today a little more time on God's earth.

*

'I want that damn thing out of here,' Rhyme was grumbling to Thom, nodding toward the escalator.

'Your Exhibit A? What am I supposed to do? It's five tons of industrial machinery.'

Rhyme was truly irritated by the device's presence. A reminder that what, yes, might very well have been Exhibit A was going to be no such thing.

Thom was looking for the paperwork that came with

the unit. 'Call Whitmore. *Mister* Whitmore. He arranged it.'

'I did call. He didn't get back to me.'

'Well, Lincoln, don't you think it might be best to let him handle it? Or do you really want me to look up "partial escalator removal services" on Craigslist?'

'What's Craigslist?'

'We'll wait for the lawyer to contact the company. At least his people knew what they were doing. The floors aren't actually scratched at all. Surprise to me.'

The doorbell rang and Rhyme was pleased to see that Juliette Archer had arrived. He noted that she was alone, no brother in tow. He suspected she'd insisted he drop her off on the sidewalk to negotiate the 'intimidating' ramp on her own. No babying allowed.

He wondered what assignment to give her. There wasn't anything that got his heart racing. Academic research for a school of criminalistics in Munich, a position paper on mass spectrometry for publication here in a scientific journal he contributed to, a proposal about extracting trace evidence from smoke.

'Morning,' she said, wheeling into the parlor. Smiling to Thom.

'Welcome back,' the aide said.

Rhyme offered, 'Do you speak German, by any chance?'

'No, afraid not.'

'Ah, well. I'll find something else to occupy your time. I think there are a few projects that aren't too boring.'

'Well, boring or not, I'm happy to work on anything you have. And forgive the dangling modifier there.'

He gave a chuckle. True, she'd just said that whether

or not *she* was boring, she'd be happy to work on any project. Grammar, punctuation and syntax could be formidable opponents.

'Breakfast, Juliette?' Thom asked.

'I've eaten already. Thanks.'

'Lincoln? What's it going to be?'

Rhyme was wheeling closer to the escalator unit. 'I don't think any one piece would weigh more than a hundred pounds. *Anybody* could take it apart. But I suppose we should wait for—' His voice braked to a stop.

Thom was asking something once again.

Rhyme didn't hear a word.

'Lincoln? . . . What . . . Well, that's a fierce gaze. I was only asking what you wanted for breakfast.'

He ignored the aide and wheeled closer yet to the scaffolding and examined the deadly access panel and, below it, the switch and servo motor operating the latch.

'What is the number one rule in engineering?' he whispered.

'I have no idea. What do you want for breakfast?'

He continued, rhetorically, 'The answer is efficiency. Designs should have no more components—'

Archer finished his sentence, more or less: '—than are necessary to perform the intended function.'

'Exactly!'

Thom said, 'Fine, fine. Now. Pancakes, bagel, yogurt? All of the above?'

'Goddamn it.' Though directed at himself, not his aide.

'What is it, Lincoln?' Archer asked.

He'd made a mistake. And nothing infuriated Lincoln Rhyme more than that. He pivoted and sped his chair forward to the nearest computer, on which he summoned the close-up pictures that Mel Cooper had taken of the interior of the escalator. Yes, he was right.

How the hell had he missed it?

In fact, he *hadn't* missed the critical fact at all. He'd noted, but unforgivably had not focused on, the very words he'd thought to himself:

The switch wire ended in a plug inserted into one of the outlets on the side of the servo unit inside . . .

One of the outlets.

He explained now to Archer: 'Look at the servo motor operating the latch. Right side.'

'Ah,' she said, a hint of disgust in her voice, as well. 'It has *two* outlets.'

'Right.'

'We saw that. We looked right at it.' Archer was shaking her head.

Rhyme scowled. 'We sure did.'

There was no reason to have a second outlet in the motor unless something – another switch, presumably – was plugged into it.

Of course, this was true of the mock-up in front of them. What of the escalator actually involved in the accident? He posed this question to Archer.

She pointed out that Amelia Sachs had taken some pictures of that one, unofficially.

'Good.' He called them up.

Thom tried again, 'Lincoln? Breakfast.'

'Later.'

'Now.'

'Anything. I don't care.' He and Archer stared at the

pictures. But they didn't answer the question; the angles were wrong and there was too much blood inside the pit where the tragedy had occurred to see clearly.

'I wonder – a second switch,' Rhyme said in a soft voice.

Archer said, 'Which malfunctioned. And, if we're lucky, it's made by a company other than Midwest Conveyance. A company with a lot of assets.'

He continued, 'Where would it be? The other switch? Anything in the documentation?'

Nothing, she reported, after scrolling through what she'd downloaded. 'How can we find out?'

'Here's a thought. The mall in Brooklyn, where the accident happened? All the escalators would be the same, right?'

'I'd assume so.'

'How's this? Whitmore hires a private eye – he must have a dozen he uses. The PI jams something into one of the escalator steps. Shuts it down.' Rhyme nodded. He liked this idea. 'They'll get a repair crew in right away. Whitmore's man could stay close and take pictures inside when they get it open.'

Thom, who'd overheard, was frowning. 'Seriously, Lincoln? You don't think that crosses some line?'

Rhyme scowled. 'What I'm thinking about is Sandy Frommer and her son.'

Juliette Archer said, 'Before you do that, can I try something?'

He quite liked the idea of sabotage. But he said, 'What do you suggest?'

'Hello?'

'Is this Attorney Holbrook?'

'Yes, who's this?' the voice resonated from the speaker of Rhyme's landline.

'My name is Juliette Archer. I work with the men you were Skyping with yesterday. Evers Whitmore. And Lincoln Rhyme.'

A moment of silence as the man recalled. 'Oh, the case. The lawyer and the consultant. About the personal injury suit. Greg Frommer.'

'That's right.'

'Yes, I think somebody mentioned your name. You're a consultant too?'

Rhyme watched her face, narrow, her blue eyes focused on the floor. She was concentrating, and hard.

'I am.'

The man muttered cynically, 'Well, we're still bankrupt. Nothing's changed. Like I said, you want to file a motion to lift the stay, go ahead. The trustee'll fight it, I doubt you'll win, but feel free.'

'No, I'm calling about something else.' Archer had the same edgy tone in her voice that Rhyme recalled from when he'd sent her away from his town house, often arriving for the first day of internship.

He wondered where she was going.

'And what's that?' Holbrook asked.

'You were courteous enough to suggest we might pursue other defendants, though none of those worked out.'

The in-house counsel sounded wary as he said, 'No, I didn't think that seemed likely. After all, Midwest Conveyance was the company that was responsible. I admitted that. And I'm sorry we aren't able to help your client, the widow.'

'Didn't seem likely,' she echoed. 'Still, you never suggested the one company that *might* be a viable defendant.'

Silence.

'You know whom I'm talking about, don't you?'

'What's your point, Ms Archer?'

'That you didn't tell us about the second switch that opens the access panel.'

'Second switch?' His tone suggested he was stalling.

'That's my question, Mr Holbrook. Who makes it? How does it work? We need to know.'

'I really can't help you, Ms Archer. I should go.'

'Did you know that Lincoln Rhyme, the other consultant on this case, has worked most frequently with the NYPD and—'

'We're not in that jurisdiction.'

'And, I was going to say, with the FBI too.'

'There are no state or federal crimes involved here. There are confidentiality agreements that preclude me from talking about companies we're in a contractual relationship with.'

'You've just confirmed that there is a second switch that could open the access panel.'

'I . . . Well. I'm terminating this conversation. I'm going to hang up now and—'

'—and after you do, I'm calling Sandy Frommer and suggesting she and her lawyer hold a press conference about Midwest's lack of cooperation in finding who really was responsible for her husband's death. I'll suggest they use the phrase "cover-up." I'm guessing that wouldn't play well in bankruptcy court, especially among creditors who'd love to get their hands on the personal assets of the executives of the company.'

A sigh.

'Help us out here. She's a widow with a son. I believed you when you said you were sorry. Go the next step and tell us. Please. Who makes the second switch?'

'Do you have time for leisure reading, Ms Archer?'

She was frowning. A glance at Rhyme. She said, 'Occasionally.'

Pages rustled, Rhyme could hear.

The lawyer said, 'I myself am a big fan of *Entertainment Weekly*. And *Fly Fishing Today*. But I still find time for *Industrial Systems Monthly*. I enjoyed the March issue particularly. Pages forty and forty-one.'

'What—'

'Goodbye, Ms Archer. I will not pick up if you call back.'

He disconnected.

'Good,' Rhyme said. 'From *Boston Law*?'

'*Legal*,' she corrected. 'But, no. I was vamping.'

Rhyme was already online. He found a digital version of the magazine Holbrook had mentioned and scrolled to the pages cited. It was an advertisement for a product made by a company called CIR Microsystems. Much of the copy was technical, none of which he understood at first glance. Featured was a gray box with wires protruding. According to a caption, it was a DataWise5000.

'The hell is it?' Rhyme asked.

Archer shook her head and went online. A few seconds of Google and she had an answer. 'Well. Listen to this. It's a smart controller.'

'I believe I've heard the term. Tell me more.'

She read for a few minutes then explained: 'A lot of products have them built in. Conveyance systems — escalators, elevators — and cars, trains, industrial machinery, medical equipment, construction equipment. Hundreds of consumer appliances: stoves, heating systems, lighting in your house, security, door locks. You can send and receive data to and from machinery with your phone or tablet or computer, wherever you are. And control the products remotely.'

'So maybe a maintenance worker sent a signal by mistake and the access panel opened? Or stray radio waves triggered it.'

'It's possible. I'm on Wikipedia. And . . . oh. My.'

'What?'

'I'm just reading about CIR Micro, the maker of the controller.'

'And?'

'The head of the place, Vinay Parth Chaudhary, is being called the new Bill Gates.' She looked over at Rhyme. 'And the company's worth eight hundred billion. Let's call Evers Whitmore. I think we're back in the game.'

CHAPTER **17**

No help from CSU headquarters on the brand of varnish or cosmetics found at the earlier Unsub 40 scenes, or the type of sawdust. Nor had there been any more insights into trace or DNA on the White Castle napkins.

But at least the car service lead blossomed.

'Got it.' Ron Pulaski held up a pad to Sachs, sitting across from him in their war room at One PP. The young officer read from his notes. 'Driver, Eduardo. He remembers the unsub, picked him up across the street from the White Castle, had a bag full of burgers. Ate them while they drove. A dozen. Maybe more. He talked to himself some. And spoke in a weird monotone. Skinny, looked down all the time. Scary. And it was the day of the murder.'

'The driver got a good look at him?'

'Not really. Just: lanky, skinny, tall. The green jacket and Atlanta baseball cap.'

Sachs asked, 'How could he not get a look at him?'

'Dirty glass. The partition, you know. Plexiglas.'

He added that the driver had dropped their unsub in downtown Manhattan, about four blocks from the murder site.

'What time?'

'About six p.m.'

Hours before the murder. What had he done during the intervening time? she wondered.

Pulaski added, 'The driver stayed at the corner where he dropped him off – had some calls to make – and watched him for a minute. The unsub didn't go to any of the buildings at the intersection near where they stopped; he walked a block away to another one. The driver could have dropped him there, but maybe our boy didn't want to be seen going into a particular place.' The young officer went online, she could see, and called up a map of the city.

He tapped a satellite image, overhead, of a building. 'Here it is. This has to be it, from what he described.'

The picture view revealed a small building, terra-cotta in color. 'Small factory, offices, warehouse?'

'Doesn't seem residential.'

Sachs said, 'Let's go take a look.'

They left One PP and headed downstairs to her car. In ten minutes they were cruising through congested downtown traffic, Sachs pumping the accelerator in low gears when she could, cutting in and out of the lanes as aggressively as ever.

Wondering, as she often did, what would they learn?

Sometimes leads provided a minor fact to help in the investigation.

Sometimes they were a waste of time.

And sometimes they took you straight to the perp's front door.

Mel Cooper was back in Rhyme's Central Park West parlor.

Sorry, Amelia, Rhyme thought. After the discovery of the potential new defendant, I need him more than you do. We'll argue later.

Evers Whitmore was present too.

The three men were staring into a dark portion of the room, where Juliette Archer sat in front of a computer, verbally commanding her computer to do her bidding.

'Up three lines. Right two words. Select. Cut . . .'

So very difficult to live life without shortcuts, Rhyme thought. Being disabled put you in a very nineteenth-century world. Everything took longer. He himself had tried eye recognition, voice recognition, a laser-emitting device attached to his ear that activated portions of the screen. He had returned to the old-fashioned way, using his hand on a joystick or touchpad. This was clumsy and slow but the technique approached normal, and Rhyme had finally mastered it. He saw that Archer needed to settle into an artificiality that was right for her.

In a few minutes she wheeled about and joined them. On the screen nearby were the fruits of her work but she began to report verbally on what she'd found, without glancing toward the notes glowing on the monitors.

'Okay. CIR Microsystems. Vinay Chaudhary's company. It's the number one manufacturer of smart controllers in the country. Revenues of two billion annually.'

'My, that's helpful,' the understated Whitmore said.

'The controller's basically a small computer with a Wi-Fi or Bluetooth connection or cellular one mounted in the machine or appliance it controls. It's really pretty simple. Say it's mounted in a stove. The controller is online with the stove manufacturer's cloud server. The homeowner has an app on his smartphone to communicate with the stove from anywhere in the world. He logs into the server and can send or receive signals to and from the controller – to shut the stove off or on. The manufacturer also is online with the stove separately, to collect data *from* the controller: usage information, diagnostics, maintenance scheduling, breakdowns – it can even be alerted to burned-out lights in the oven.'

Cooper asked, 'Any problem with the DataWise Five Thousand controller in the past? Activating when it shouldn't?'

'None that I could find but I was playing Google Roulette. Give me some time and I might find something more.'

'So how did it open the panel?' Rhyme mused. 'A stray signal ordered the controller to open the door, something in the mall itself. Or from the cloud? Or did the DataWise just short out and send the open command itself?'

Archer looked up from the computer and said, 'Have something here. Take a look at this. It's from a blog about two months ago. *Social Engineering Second-ly*. That's "second" as in the unit of time, I think. Updated every second. As opposed to Monthly or Weekly. Doesn't quite work.'

Rhyme said, 'Sometimes you can be too clever for your own good.'

He and the others read:

> *Indulgence = Death? The Dangers of*
> *The Internet of Things (IoT)*
> *Will consumer indulgence be the death of us?*

From self-foaming soap to portion-controlled, calorie-specific meals delivered to consumers' homes in time for dinner, manufacturers are increasingly marketing products geared to take over people's lives. The justification is that they are helping busy professionals and families save time – and in some instances money – and make their lives easier. In reality, many of these items are simply desperate attempts to fill the pockets of companies facing markets saturated with competing products or in which brand differentiation has all but vanished.

But there's a dark side to the convenience factor.

I'm speaking of what is called the Internet of Things, or IoT.

Thousands of appliances, tools, heating and air-conditioning systems, vehicles and industrial products sport internal computer controls that allow consumers to access them remotely. These have been around for some years in the form of home security systems, in which video cameras are, in effect, mini computers connected to your Wi-Fi or cellular service. When you're away, you log onto an Internet site – supposedly secure – and make sure no burglars are prowling through your living room or keep an eye on the babysitter.

Now the proliferation of these 'embedded devices' (that is, containing computer circuitry) is increasing exponentially.

They help us save money and make our lives so much more convenient.

Now you can turn your oven on from a remote location, turn your furnace up when you're on your way home, tell your door to unlock for an hour when the plumber's expected (and watch him at work on your security camera!), start

*your car remotely on below-zero days . . . How convenient!
What could be wrong with that?*

Who can argue with this?

Well, I can.

Let me tell you two dangers:

One: Is your data safe?

*The way most smart controller systems work is that the
appliances in your house are online with cloud servers run
by the manufacturers of those appliances. While they 'assure'
you your privacy is important, all of them collect data about
their products' performance and your usage history, often
without your knowledge. That information is routinely sold
to data miners. Some effort is made to keep your identity
anonymous but just consider: Last week a thirteen-year-old
in Fresno got the names, addresses and credit card numbers
of everyone who owned a General Heating furnace equipped
with a smart controller. It took him six minutes to download
that data.*

Two: Is your life safe?

*More troubling is the potential for injury and death when
a smart system malfunctions. Because all functions of smart
appliances are managed by the controller, not just data collection, it's possible in theory for a water heater, for instance, to
receive a signal to turn the heat up to 200 degrees, WHILE
YOU'RE IN THE SHOWER! Or, in the event of fire in your
house, the controller could lock your doors and trap you inside
your dwelling and refuse to send a signal to the fire department
reporting the blaze. Or it might even contact the authorities
and report a false alarm, leaving you and your family to die
a hideous death.*

Representatives for the manufacturers say no. There are

safeguards built in. Network keys, encryption, passcodes.

But Your Blogger recently purchased one of these controllers. The DataWise5000 by CIR Microsystems, one of the most common, found in everything from water heaters to elevators to microwaves. It was possible, by bombarding the device with ambient radio waves, to cause it to malfunction. Had the unit been installed in a car, a medical instrument, a piece of dangerous industrial machinery, a stove, the results of that malfunction could have been disastrous.

Ask yourself, is convenience worth the price of your and your children's lives?

'Bingo,' Archer said, smiling.

More sedately Whitmore mused, 'We could argue that the controller is defective because it wasn't shielded from ambient signals.'

Rhyme said, 'Who posted that? We should talk to him.'

The blog gave little personal information and no address.

Rhyme said, 'Rodney.'

'Who?' Archer asked.

'You'll see,' Rhyme said. A glance at Cooper, who smiled knowingly and said, 'I'll get the volume.' And turned down the control on the speakerphone.

Despite the reduced decibels, when the phone was answered a moment later, relentless rock music pounded into the parlor.

'A bit more,' Rhyme called to Cooper, who complied.

A voice from the other end of the line, ''Lo?'

Archer frowned in curiosity.

'Rodney! Can we lose the music?'

'Sure. Hi, Lincoln.' The chugga-chugga bass diminished to a whisper. It was not, however, *lost*.

Rodney Szarnek was a senior detective with the NYPD's elite Computer Crimes Unit. He was impressively brilliant at collaring perps and helping other investigators with the computer side of a case, though irritatingly in love with the worst music on earth.

Rhyme explained that the detective was on speaker, then told him about the case. The smart controller in an escalator might have malfunctioned, resulting in a gruesome death. 'But it's not a case, Rodney.'

'How's that?'

'It's civil. Mel Cooper's here but only on vacation.'

'And I'm confused.'

'I'm not working with the department, Rodney,' Rhyme said patiently.

'No.'

'Yes.'

'If you've quit, why have you not quit? I ask only because we're having this conversation.'

'I resigned from *criminal* practice. I'm consulting on a civil case.'

A pause. 'Oh. Well. In that case I can't really help you. You understand. Wish I could.'

'No, I know that. All I need is for you to tell us how to find the physical address of somebody who's written a blog about these controllers. We want to talk to him, maybe hire him as an expert witness. Pretend we're at a cocktail party, you and me.'

'Well, finding somebody online? That's easy enough. A WhoIs search. W-H-O-I-S. Run the .com or .net name through that. Of course, he might be using a privacy service as the domain registrant. That's so pissed-off ex-wives or pissed-off ex-husbands can't find out where the registrant lives.'

Rhyme looked to Cooper, who typed at the keyboard in front of his monitor. He nodded at the results. Rhyme read them. 'It says Privacy Plus, New Zealand.'

'Yep, that's a service to mask the physical address. And New Zealand? No court order. You're screwed.'

Rhyme said calmly, 'But we can't afford to be screwed, Rodney. Let's think harder.'

Szarnek cleared his throat. 'Well, speaking theoretically, you catch that word? The-o-ret-i-cally? To get past a privacy service, one might go online and download and install – on a flash drive, of course, to be burned later – a program like, let's just say, HiddenSurf. Then one would run that and then do a search of Russian websites for a program called, let's just say, *Ogrableniye*. Means "robbery" in Russian. Don't we love our Slavic friends' subtlety? *Ogrableniye* is a hacker code. Completely illegal. Terrible. I don't approve one bit. Because it allows people to hack into a, say, a privacy service even in, oh, say, New Zealand, and look up the physical address of someone whose IP – Internet – address you know.'

'We'd better hang up now, Rodney.'

'I'm in favor of that. Although how can we hang up if you and I haven't even been talking?'

Music rose to lofty decibels and they disconnected.

Rhyme said, 'Did somebody write all that down, know what to do? We've got to—'

Archer looked up from her computer screen and said, 'Bad news, good news.'

'What?'

'I followed his instructions. The bad news is you've already started to get Russian porn spam. But the good news: I've got the blogger's address.'

CHAPTER 18

'Too many people in this city,' Ron Pulaski said. Then seemed to regret the comment since the perp they were now seeking was in his own demented way addressing the population situation.

The young officer's complaint really was that there were too many people crossing streets against lights and that those lights were not in his and Amelia Sachs's favor.

She, however, wasn't that concerned about either limitation. True, transit was slow but they were making steady progress from One PP to the intersection where the gypsy cab had dropped Unsub 40 the night he'd murdered Todd Williams with his inelegant but effective tool. Sachs was engaging in what she called the touchless nudge – easing the car close to those blocking the way with an air of sufficient distraction to make the pedestrian feel deliciously imperiled and, accordingly, scoot out of the way.

Finally they escaped from the downtown area known in the 1800s as Five Points, the most dangerous few square miles in the United States (now far more pristine, though, some said cynically, populated by as many criminals as back in the day; the neighborhood embraced City Hall).

In ten minutes, they spotted the gypsy cab on the Lower East Side, parts of which were growing into hipster and artist enclaves. Not here. Dilapidated commercial buildings ruled, and a number of vacant lots.

In the phone conversation, arranging this meeting, the driver had said, 'You'll see me, white Ford. Dripping wet. Just clean her.' The accent had been a mystery.

Sachs nosed the Torino into a space, avoiding mounds of trash banked at the curb, and they climbed out. The short, swarthy driver, in jeans and a blue Real Madrid soccer shirt, exited his cab and joined them.

'I'm Detective Sachs. This is Officer Pulaski.'

'Hi, hi.' He shook their hands enthusiastically. Some people are nervous meeting the police, some are critical of authority, and some – a few – act like they're in the presence of rock stars.

Eduardo was going to give White Castle's Charlotte a run for the money.

'So, I happy to help. Happy.'

'Good. Appreciate it. Tell me about this man.'

'He very tall and very skinny. Weird, don't you know?'

'Any—'

'Distinguishing characteristics?' he blurted.

'Yes.'

'No, no, couldn't see much. Hat on. Braves. The team, don't you know?'

'Yes, we know.' Pulaski was looking around, taking in the empty street. Warehouses, small offices. Nothing residential or retail. He turned back to his notebook, in which he was transcribing whatever the man had to say.

'Sunglasses, he wore too.'

'Hair color?'

'Lighter, I think. But, the hat. You know.'

'And his clothes?'

'Green jacket, yellow-green. Dark pants. And a back-pack. Oh, and a bag.'

'Bag?'

'Plastic. Like he bought something and they put it in bag. He look in bag a couple times, I driving him.'

Charlotte had said the same.

'Any logo on the bag?'

'Logo?'

'Store name, picture? Smiley face.'

'Emoji! No.'

'How big was the bag?' Sachs asked.

'Not big. Strawberries.'

'He had strawberries?' Pulaski wondered.

'No, no. I mean about size of package of strawberries. Just thinking that. Or blueberries, or salad dressing or large can of tomatoes. That big,' Eduardo said, beaming. 'Exactly.'

'Any idea what was in it?'

'No. Hear something metal. Click, a click. Oh and those burgers. Ate many, many. A dozen White Castle?'

'Did he make any phone calls?'

'No. But he kind of talk to himself. I told you that on phone. I could not hear good. First, I say, "What that, sir?" Thinking he talking to me. But he said, "Nothing." I meaning, he said something. "Nothing" was what he said. Don't you know? And then he quiet after that. Just look out window. Wouldn't look at me. So couldn't really see scars. You always like scars. Police. Distinguishing things. But didn't see any.'

Pulaski asked, 'Did he have an accent?'

'Yes.'

'What was it?'

'American,' Eduardo answered. He wasn't being ironic.

'So, you stopped here. This intersection?'

'Yes, yes. I thought you want to see where exactly.'

'We do. He paid with cash?'

'Yes, yes, that's all we take, don't you know?'

'I don't suppose there's any chance you still have the money he paid you with?'

'For fingerprints!'

'That's right.'

'No.' The driver shook his head broadly.

'You waited here and saw him go into one of those buildings.' Pulaski was looking up from the notebook.

'I did, yes. I will tell you.' He pointed up the street. 'You can just see it, that one. Beige.' He wrung two syllables out of the color.

It was the one they'd found on the satellite map. From here they could make out only a sliver of the five-story building; the front was on an adjoining street. It was surrounded by a vacant lot on one side and a half-demolished building on the other.

Eduardo continued, 'I remember because I am thinking maybe whoever he was going to see was not home, or not there, and this neighborhood? No cruising medallions so he want to go back to Queens and I could make a second fare. But I saw him go through back door. That's when I left, don't you know?'

'We appreciate your help.'

'He a killer?' Eduardo grinned happily.

'He's wanted in connection with a homicide, yes.

If you see him again, if he comes by your office in Queens, call nine one one and give them my name.' She dealt out another of her cards. 'Don't do anything yourself, try to stop him.'

'No, I call you, Officer Detective.'

After he left, she and Pulaski started toward the building he'd pointed out. They got no more than a half block when she stopped fast.

'What is it, Amelia?' Pulaski whispered.

She was squinting. 'What street is that? That the building faces?'

'I don't know.' He pulled out his Samsung and loaded a map. 'Ridge.' The young officer frowned. 'Why's that familiar? . . . Hell.'

Sachs nodded. 'Yep. It's where Todd Williams worked.' She'd learned where the victim's office was and retraced his steps from the murder site back to here, canvassing for clues. She'd also tried to interview others in the ramshackle building but of the few people who had offices in the structure – only three or four, the rest of the space being empty – no one had seen anything helpful to the investigation.

'They *knew* each other. The unsub and Williams. Well, this changes everything.'

It wasn't a robbery or random killing at all.

Sachs mused, 'The unsub got here four hours before the murder. Did they stay in the building? If so, doing what? Or did they go somewhere else?'

And other questions: Did Unsub 40 come to this area often? Did he live near here?

She looked around the street. The occupied buildings

included a few tenements and what seemed to be ware-houses and wholesalers. The canvass probably wouldn't take too long. She'd assemble a team from the local precinct.

Sachs spotted a homeless man, lean and pale, foraging through a trash bin.

Approaching, Sachs said, 'Hi. Can I ask you a question?'

'Just did.' His dark face wrinkled.

'I'm sorry?'

He returned to digging through the bin. 'Just did ask me a question.'

She laughed. 'You live near here?'

'Simon Says.' He found a half sandwich and put it into his shopping bag. 'Okay. I'm being fun. Shelter up the street. Or under the bridge. Depending.' The hands and neck and calves, which were uncovered by the greasy clothing, were quite muscular.

'Did you seen anybody tall and real thin go into that building a few weeks ago? Or any other time?'

'No.' He moved on to another bin.

Sachs and Pulaski trailed. 'You sure?' Pulaski asked. 'Want another look?'

'No. Simon Says.'

Sachs waited.

The man said, 'You asked if I saw him going into the building. Nup. Didn't. You didn't ask if I'd seen him period. Which I have. Simon Says.'

'Okay, where have you seen him?'

'Now you're cooking with gas. Standing right Jiminy there.' He pointed: the far intersection, the direction they were going. 'Skinny guy, but eating like a . . . do sailors eat? No, they swear. Chimneys smoke. He was eating something, munchin' it down. Was gonna hit him up for something. But felt off. Kind of talking to himself. Not that I don't. Ha! Also, eating that way, thought he seemed greedy. Chomp, chomp, chomp. I wouldn't get anything.'

'When was this?'

'A while ago.'

'How long? A week, a few days?'

'Simon Says.'

Sachs tried, 'What do you mean by a while ago?'

'Ten, fifteen.'

'Days?'

'Minutes. He was just there.'

Jesus.

Sachs unbuttoned her jacket and glanced up the street. Pulaski too grew vigilant, looking in the directions she was not.

'He go in any particular way?' she asked.

And don't fucking Simon Says me.

'No, just standing there. I went on looking for stuff, and that was it. Didn't see him again. Could be here, could be there, could be anywhere.'

Pulaski was pressing the transmit button on the Motorola mike pinned to his shoulder. He called in a request for backup and, before she could remind him to do so, he said, 'Silent roll-up. Suspect may be unaware of our presence. K.'

'K,' came the staticky response.

Sachs got the homeless man's name, which wasn't Simon, and the shelter he sometimes stayed in. She thanked him and told him it was best to leave. She was tempted to hand him a twenty but if it came down to testifying in court about the presence of the unsub, a defense lawyer would ask if he'd been paid anything by the police.

'You better get back to the shelter. Safer.'

'Yes, ma'am. Yes, sir, Officer, sir.'

He started away.

Ron Pulaski said, 'Oh, hey, look.'

The man slowly pivoted. Pulaski was pointing at something in the street a few feet away from them. It was a twenty-dollar bill.

'You drop that?' Pulaski asked.

'Me. Ha.'

'If we take it, we have to report it. Pain in the ass.'

'Bullshit.'

Sachs, playing along. 'True. Rules.'

Pulaski said, 'You go ahead and take it. Finders keepers. Simon says.'

'Think I will. There's a reason you get half sandwiches in the trash. Nobody throws out a good sandwich.' He scooped up the money with his long, sinewy fingers and pocketed it.

Sachs nodded to Pulaski, acknowledging the good deed. It had never occurred to her to handle a donation that way.

The man wandered off, muttering to himself.

'How long, you think?' she asked.

'Before backup? Eight, nine minutes.'

'He can't've gotten very far. Let's check the ground for footprints. See if we can find which way he went, size thirteens.'

And they began to walk a lazy grid in search of tread marks. The search was, of course, slowed by the fact that each officer looked up from time to time, searching for a threat.

Just because Unsub 40 had not shot anyone yet didn't mean he wasn't willing and able to try.

CHAPTER 19

Thom had dropped Evers Whitmore and Lincoln Rhyme off in front of the building that housed the blogger's office, whose address Juliette Archer had tracked down, and driven off to park the accessible van in a lot a few blocks away.

The lawyer once again pressed the button on the intercom. *Social Engineering Second-ly*. It was on the top floor.

Still no answer.

'We can keep looking,' Whitmore said. 'There have to be other people who've researched the DataWise.'

But Rhyme wanted the man who'd written the piece that Archer had found. He wanted to know exactly what kind of ambient radio waves had caused it to activate.

Expert witness . . .

A perfect one.

Whitmore gazed around the deserted streets. 'We can leave a note, I suppose.'

'No,' Rhyme said. 'He'll never contact us. We know where he works now. Let's come back later. We can—'

'What was that?' Whitmore said quickly.

Rhyme too had heard the scrape of sole on the cobblestones. Around the corner, it seemed.

Whitmore, of course, was not given to displays of

emotion but Rhyme could tell from the lawyer's uncharacteristically darting eyes that he was concerned.

Rhyme was too.

The footsteps seemed furtive.

The lawyer said, 'I've never done criminal work, but I've been shot at twice pursuant to civil suits. The perpetrators missed both times and might have been trying only to scare me. But it was still an unpleasant experience.'

Rhyme had been shot at, as well, and could concur.

Another scrape.

From where? Rhyme had no idea.

Whitmore added, 'I also received in the mail a rat without its head. The head arrived a week later with a note suggesting I withdraw a lawsuit.' It was nerves talking at this point.

'But you didn't.' Rhyme was scanning the street, and the buildings. This was not a particularly dangerous neighborhood, statistically, but if a mugger wanted to nail someone easy, this pair would be a good choice. A slim nerdy lawyer and a gimp.

Whitmore said, 'No, the case stood. In fact, I ran some forensics on the rat, found human DNA, and my private eye got samples of personal effects of everyone connected to the case. The rodent was a gift from the brother of the defendant.' Whitmore was looking around again, up. One black window seemed particularly to bother him, though Rhyme could have told him that snipers weren't the main risk.

'You would have thought that the brother would be a rather obvious suspect. But he seemed to believe he could get away with it. I sued him for intentional infliction of emotional distress. I wasn't actually that distressed but I made a credible witness. The jury was rather sympathetic. I testified I had nightmares about rats. This was true but the opposing counsel failed to ask when. The last time was when I was eight. Mr Rhyme, did you hear that noise again?'

He nodded.

'Do you have a gun?' the lawyer asked.

Rhyme's expression, as he turned toward Whitmore: Do I look like I'm a fast-draw kind of person?

Then more footsteps, growing closer.

Cocking his head to the right, Rhyme whispered, 'He's coming from that direction.'

They remained still for a moment. There was a sound from where he'd just indicated: A click of metal.

Chambering a bullet before the mugging?

Or just planning to shoot and pilfer after they were dead?

Time to leave. Now. Rhyme gestured with his head and Whitmore nodded. Rhyme could move fast, if roughly, over the cobblestones toward one of the busy north–south avenues.

He whispered Thom's number to Whitmore. 'Text him. Have him meet us a block north, Broadway.'

The lawyer did this and slipped his phone back into his pocket. With effort he dragged Rhyme's heavy chair over the curb.

Another whisper to Whitmore: 'He's close. Move, fast.'

They started up the street, along the front of the office building.

When they arrived at the corner and hurried past it, both men froze.

Staring directly into the muzzle of a pistol.

'Oh, my,' Whitmore gasped.

Lincoln Rhyme's response was more subdued. 'Sachs. What the hell arc you doing here?'

CHAPTER 20

Rhyme watched his partner examining him and Whitmore with a perplexed frown for mere seconds before she slipped the blocky Austrian pistol back into the plastic holster with a definitive click.

The frown vanished and she turned to her right and called, 'Ron! Clear!'

Footsteps from around the corner. Rhyme watched Pulaski approach, also holstering his weapon. 'Lincoln!' A curious glance at the lawyer.

Rhyme introduced them.

Pulaski blurted to Rhyme, 'What're you doing here?'

'Just asking the same question, Rookie.'

And the answer was soon clear, once he and Sachs explained what had brought them to the building on Ridge Street in lower Manhattan, on their respective missions. The victim of the unsub whom Sachs had been on the trail of for the past several weeks, Todd Williams, was in fact the man who'd posted the blog about the dangers of DataWise5000 controllers. Since Rhyme was no longer doing criminal work she'd never had reason to mention Williams's name.

Sachs explained that she and Pulaski had run down a lead: The unsub had taken a car service from Queens to this area and the driver had seen him go through the back door of this building about four hours before Williams's death.

Rhyme said, 'Williams published a blog piece about the risks of a particular kind of Wi-Fi smart controller – the same type that we think malfunctioned in the escalator and probably caused the access panel to open. Since the widow can't sue the escalator manufacturer – they're in bankruptcy – we're considering a suit against the controller company. We were hoping Williams could be an expert witness, or at least tell us more about how the controllers could fail. But now . . . '

Sachs asked, 'You thinking what I am?'

'Yep. Your unsub reads Todd's blog about the controller, thinks it might be a nifty murder weapon – for whatever reason. Contacts Todd, arranges to meet him here. Learns what he needs to so he can hack into the controller.'

Sachs continued the likely narrative: 'Then suggests they go to the club, Forty Degrees North. But before they get there, he pulls Todd into the construction site and beats him to death with his hammer. Makes it look like a robbery. He killed him there, rather than here, to keep the investigation focused away from Williams's office.'

Whitmore said, 'I don't quite follow this, Mr Rhyme.'

Rhyme said, 'Amelia was after the perp at the mall in Brooklyn. She assumed it was a coincidence that the escalator collapsed while she was there.'

Sachs added, 'But it wasn't. Looks like Unsub Forty knew how to hack the controller and opened the door intentionally.'

'To cause a distraction and escape?' Pulaski asked. 'When he saw you were after him?'

Rhyme's face tightened at the young man's flawed thinking. 'How would he know there was a DataWise controller in the escalator?'

Blushing, the young man said, 'Sure, sure. Wasn't thinking. He'd have had it planned out ahead of time. He was at the mall – to kill either somebody at random or Frommer in particular – by popping open the access panel.'

Pulaski's Motorola crackled. He stepped aside to take the transmission.

Sachs explained to Rhyme and Whitmore, 'The unsub was spotted here about twenty minutes ago. We called in backup. That's why the weapons; we thought you might be him when we heard you on the other side of the building.'

The young officer rejoined them. 'One car patrolling the neighborhood east and north, other's pulling up here. No sign of him yet.'

Rhyme said, 'Any chance he's in the building?'

'Homeless guy said he was standing at that intersection,' Sachs said, nodding. 'He probably would have seen him if the unsub'd come this way.'

Whitmore asked, 'But I'm curious. Why would he come back here?'

Rhyme said, 'He might live nearby.' The area was mostly commercial but there were pockets of tenements and newer – that is, seventy-five- or eighty-year-old – apartments.

'Or he's worried he didn't cover his tracks well enough and came back to look for evidence. He saw us and took off.' She looked over the building. 'See if it's been broken into, Ron.'

He circled the structure and returned. 'Windows're

intact. But the back door might've been jimmied. Scratch marks.'

Rhyme couldn't feel the thud in his insensate chest but he knew this occurred . . . from the rapid pulse in his forehead. 'You said to *look* for evidence, Sachs. He could also—'

'Have come here to destroy it!' She spun toward the building.

It was at just that moment that there came a muffled *whump* from within the building. Whatever kind of incendiary device Unsub 40 had planted, it must have been quite large. Within seconds, smoke and flames began spiraling out of the ground-floor windows, which had shattered from the heat.

Rhyme caught a mouthful of smoke and ash and, coughing hard, he struggled to maneuver backward in his chair. Evers Whitmore helped him do so, kicking away a trash basket that was blocking the criminalist's escape. Ron Pulaski called Dispatch to send the FDNY.

And Amelia Sachs ran to the front door of the building, picked up a loose cobblestone and used it to smash through the glass of the door. She turned to Rhyme and shouted, 'What floor is the blogger's office on?'

'Sachs, no!'

'What *floor*?'

'The top,' he replied, still coughing hard.

She turned and leapt inside, barely avoiding the points of glass that ringed the open doorway like shark's teeth.

She's going in?

Well. Good fortune for me.

My police girl, Red, the thief of White Castle, has no idea that it's five full gallons of low-octane gas pooling in flame in the basement. An ocean of flame. The building, dry as a California pine, won't last long.

Will *she*? Will she last very long?

I was going right back home, to Chelsea, and an Internet café, to send out a few emails. But I decided to stay. I'm looking out a hall window, fifth floor, of an abandoned tenement across the street and a few doors down. Bad for living in, good for spying. I crouch, shrinking, to watch what's unfolding below me.

Can't see me here, none of them can.

Pretty sure.

No, no one's looking up. Police cars are cruising but looking on the streets and sidewalks only. They're thinking I've gone. Because who would wait around?

Well, *I* would. To see who exactly it is after me. And to see who will crisp to death, or suffocate, thanks to the gift I left. Smoke from the building is thick already. And thickening more. How can Red breathe? How can she see?

Sirens, I can hear them. Fire engine intersection horns, blaring. I love the sound, trumpeting pain and sorrow.

If it goes as planned, all the tidbits of evidence I left behind in Todd's office, careless me, will be melted to nothing. I know from Frances Lee's crime scene dollhouses how telling evidence can be – why, look how Red put an end to my precious sliders.

Burning it is best.

Burn to ash, to dust, to greasy plastic smoke.

And Red?

Myself, I never much cared for burning bones. It's not satisfying. Cracking them is better. But however she goes is good. Hair burned off, skin, fat, then the bones, fine. As long as she goes. A little pain wouldn't be a bad thing either.

Smoke is curling up like a huge black pig's tail. Help will be here soon. But the fire is progressing nicely.

I'm not close to the raging inferno but not too far either. Maybe I'll hear her screams.

Unlikely — but one can always hope.

CHAPTER 21

Smoke is wet, smoke is scaly, smoke is a creature that slides into your body and strangles from within.

Amelia Sachs was squinting through the white then brown then black clouds as she charged up the stairs to the top floor of the building dying of fire in its low heart.

She had to get inside the blogger's office. If the unsub had gone to such lengths to destroy the place, that meant there was evidence inside. Something that would lead to him or to future victims.

Go, she told herself, retched, spat, then said the command out loud.

The door was locked, of course – which was why he'd started the fire in the basement, more accessible than the room he needed to destroy. She tested the door with her shoulder. No, breaking in wasn't going to happen. You can breach a door with crowbars, battering rams and special shotgun slugs (aiming for the hinges only; you can't shoot out a lock). But you can't kick in most wooden doors.

So she'd float like an angel. As smoke ganged around her, heat too, she stumbled to the window in the hallway and kicked this one out too. Unlike the door downstairs, which left jagged shards, the window here vanished into cascading splinters, opening a wide entrance into the void. Cool air rushed past her. She inhaled deeply, relieved at the oxygen, but – from the suddenly increasing roar behind her – she realized she'd just fed the inferno, as well.

She looked out and down. Not a wide sidewalk of a ledge, but sufficient. And the window into the blogger's office was a mere five or six feet away from the open rectangle Sachs now climbed into. She was luxuriating in the clean air, sucking it voluptuously into her stinging lungs. She glanced down to the ground. Nobody beneath her. This was the back of the building, opposite from where Rhyme and the others were waiting and, she hoped, the fire department was arriving to squelch the flames.

Yes, she heard sirens. But silently commanded them: Get closer, if you don't mind.

Looking behind her. The billows of smoke were growing denser.

Coughing and retching. God, her chest hurt.

So, onto the ledge.

Sachs's animal fear was claustrophobia, not heights, yet she was in no hurry to tumble fifty feet to slick cobblestones. The ledge was a good eight inches wide, and she had to traverse only two yards to get to the Williams's office. Better without shoes but she'd have to break that window too to get inside and litter the floor with razors. Keep the footware.

Go. No time.

Her phone was ringing.

Not hardly answering at the moment . . .

Onto the ledge, gripping the window frame, and turning to face the building's exterior wall. She then eased to her right, weight on her toes, fingers digging into the seams between the soot-stained stones. Cramps radiated through her wrists.

From within the building a groan. Something structural was failing.

How bad an idea was this?

Not a question to be asking at the moment.

One yard, then the second, and she arrived at Williams's window. Inside there was a faint patina of smoke but visibility seemed good. Placing her hands on the side of the frame, gripping hard, she eased back her knee and kicked. The pane shattered into a thousand pieces, littering the floor in the tiny, dim office.

Getting inside, however, was trickier than she'd thought. A center-of-gravity issue. Lowering her head and shoulders to duck in sent her rear into the void and that started to tilt her backward.

Nope . . .

At least her hands had good purchase on the frame – the parts where no glass remained. Try sideways. Angling to her right, easing her left leg in and then shifting her weight to that limb. Sachs reached inside, seeking something to grip. A metal square, a file cabinet, she guessed. Smooth, no handle. She could feel only the side of the furniture. But recalling a Discovery Channel or some such show about rock climbing, she pictured free climbers working their fingers into the tiniest of crevices and supporting their full weight. She moved her hand to the back of the cabinet, wedged fingers between metal and the wall and started to shift her weight inside.

Tipping point.

A few inches, balanced.

Push. Now.

Sachs tumbled inside, falling on the glass-encrusted floor.

No cuts. Well, none serious. She felt a bit of sting in her knee – the joint that had tormented with arthritic pain, until the surgery. Now the ache was back, thanks to the fall. But she rose and tested. The mechanism functioned. She glanced at the smoke rolling inside from under the door. The whole office now felt hot. Could the flames have risen this fast and be roasting the oak under her feet?

She coughed hard. Found an unopened bottle of Deer Park, unscrewed the cap and chugged. Spat again.

Scanning fast, Sachs noted three file cabinets, shelves filled with paper in all forms: magazines, newspapers, printouts, pamphlets. All extremely combustible, she noted. Riffling, she saw they were mostly generic articles about the dangers of data mining, government intrusion into privacy, identity theft. She didn't immediately see anything related to the controllers Rhyme and Whitmore had been talking about or anything else that might have motivated their unsub to murder Williams, nor evidence he might have left.

In the corner, flames teased their way out from under a baseboard. And ignited a bookshelf. Across the room, another tongue of fire lapped at a cardboard box and, with no delay at all, set it on fire.

The building groaned again and the door began to sweat varnish.

Gasped at another sound: The window opposite the

one she'd climbed through, the front of the building, crashed inward. In a lick of a second her Glock was out, though the draw was mere instinct; she knew the intruder wasn't a threat but was in fact what she'd counted on for salvation all along. Sachs nodded to the New York City firefighter, perched nonchalantly on a ladder, connected to a truck forty-odd feet below.

The woman guided the top of the ladder to a hover about two feet from the windowsill. She called, 'Building's gonna drop, Detective. You leave now.'

If she'd had an hour she might have parsed the documents and found something relevant that might lead to the unsub's motive, victims past and victims future, his identity. She did the only thing available, though. Grabbed the laptop computer, ripped out the power cord and with no time to unscrew the wires connecting it to the monitor sliced the unit free with her switchblade.

'Leave that,' the FDNY firefighter said through her mask.

'Can't,' Sachs said and hurried to the window.

'Need both your hands!' Shouting was required now. The building moaned as its bones snapped.

But Sachs kept her arm around the computer and clambered out onto the ladder, gripping with her right hand only. Her legs scissored around one side and another rung. Every muscle in her body, it seemed, was cramping. But still she held on.

The operator below maneuvered them away from the building. The office room Sachs had been in just seconds before was suddenly awash with flame.

'Thanks!' Sachs called. The woman was either deaf to

her words because of the roar or was pissed that Sachs had ignored her warning. There was no response.

The ladder retracted. They were twenty feet above the ground when it jerked and Sachs finally had to release the computer to keep herself from plunging to the street.

The laptop spun to the sidewalk and cracked open, raining bits of plastic and keys in a dozen different directions.

*

An hour later Lincoln Rhyme and Juliette Archer were at one of the evidence tables. Mel Cooper was nearby. Evers Whitmore stood in the corner, juggling two calls on two mobiles.

They were awaiting the evidence from the burned-out building; the structure was completely gone. It had collapsed into a pile of smoldering stone and melted plastic, glass and metal. Sachs had ordered a backhoe to excavate and Rhyme hoped something of the incendiary device might remain.

As for the computer, Ron Pulaski had taken it downtown to the NYPD Computer Crimes Unit at One PP in hopes that Sachs's mad vertical dash hadn't been in vain; Rodney Szarnek would determine if any data on the laptop was salvageable.

The front door now opened and another figure walked into the parlor. Amelia Sachs's face was smudged, her hair askew, and she wore two bandages, presumably covering cuts from broken glass – it seemed she'd taken out at least three panes in her dramatic break-in of Williams's office.

Rhyme was actually surprised she wasn't more badly hurt. He wasn't happy she'd ignored him and taken the risk. But they'd fallen into an unspoken agreement years ago. She pushed herself to extremes and that was just who she was.

When you move they can't getcha . . .

An expression of her father's and it was her motto in life.

Sachs carried a small milk crate, containing evidence from the building – very little, however, as was often the case when a scene is destroyed by flames.

A bout of coughing. Tears ran.

'Sachs, you okay?' Rhyme asked. She'd refused a trip to the emergency room and had remained at the scorched site to excavate and to walk the grid, as soon as the fire department gave the all-clear, while Rhyme, Whitmore and Thom had returned to his town house here.

'Little smoke. Nothing.' More coughing. Sachs glanced wryly at Mel Cooper. 'You look just like somebody who works for the NYPD.

The Tech blushed.

She handed the crate to Cooper, who examined the bags.

'That's it?'

'That's it.'

He stepped to the chromatograph to begin running the analysis. Sachs, wiping her eyes, was looking over at Juliette Archer. Rhyme realized they'd never met. He introduced them.

Archer said, 'I've heard a lot about you.'

Sachs nodded a greeting, rather than offering a hand,

of course. 'You're the intern Lincoln mentioned was going to be helping out.'

Rhyme supposed he'd never mentioned that Archer was in a wheelchair. In fact, he believed he'd never told Sachs anything about his student, even the name or sex.

Sachs looked briefly at Rhyme, a cryptic glance, perhaps chiding, perhaps not. And then to Archer: 'Nice to meet you.'

Whitmore disconnected from one, then another, call, 'Detective Sachs. You sure you're all right?'

'Nothing, really.'

The lawyer said, 'Never thought when I got a call about taking on a personal injury lawsuit, it would turn out like this.'

Rhyme said to Sachs, 'So your case and our case, they're one and the same – often misstated as one *in* the same, by the way.'

From his perch near the gas chromatograph/mass spectrometer, Mel Cooper said, 'I don't quite follow what's going on.'

Rhyme explained about Unsub 40's reading Todd Williams's blog and deciding to tap him for help in hacking a DataWise controller to turn it into a weapon. 'He says, we can guess, he wants to help Williams expose the dangers of these things, down with digital society, capitalism, bullshit like that.' Rhyme nodded to the blog post, still on one of the monitors. 'Williams teaches the unsub how to hack the system and the unsub kills him. He's expendable.'

Archer added, 'He's also a liability. A news story about the escalator accident might mention the controller in the press. Williams would know who was behind it.'

Rhyme nodded and continued, 'Amelia is after him in Brooklyn and follows him into the mall, where he's going to kill his first victim.'

Archer asked, 'How do we know it's his first victim?'

A reasonable question. But Rhyme said, 'Williams was killed just a few weeks ago and I don't recall any suspicious product-related deaths in the news. We may find more, but for now let's assume the escalator was the first. The question is, was it a one-off? Or does he have more planned?'

'And why?' the lawyer asked. 'What's his motive? Using a controller to kill – it has to be a lot of trouble.'

Rhyme added, 'And it's a lot riskier,' at the same time as Archer said, 'And he's more at risk.' The criminalist grunted a laugh. 'Well, we don't know why and we don't particularly care. When we catch him, we can ask. When the hell is the computer going to be ready?'

'Ron said it should be within the hour.'

'And where the hell *is* the rookie?' Rhyme muttered. 'That other case? Gutiérrez, I think he mentioned.'

'I think so.'

'Was Gutiérrez the killer or killee?'

Sachs said, 'Perp. I don't know why it's heated up.'

'Well, we'll make do . . . '

Which brought Sachs's attention to bear on Rhyme.

'Do you mean that?'

'What?' Not understanding what she was getting at.

'"We'll make do." Are you going to help us? It's criminal now.'

'Of course I will.'

A faint smile on her face.

Rhyme said, 'I don't have any choice. We get the unsub, then Sandy Frommer can sue *him* for wrongful death.'

Rhyme recalled what Whitmore had said about intervening causes. The controller itself wasn't the cause of Greg Frommer's death; it was Unsub 40's *hacking* that had killed him. It was like someone's cutting the brake lines of a car, killing the driver. The car manufacturer wasn't liable.

A look at the lawyer. 'Sandy *will* be able to sue the unsub, right?'

'Of course. The O. J. Simpson scenario. If we're lucky this individual – your unsub – has assets.'

'I'm not un-retiring, Sachs. But our paths coincide for a while.'

The smile faded. 'Sure.'

Mel Cooper tested the evidence Sachs had found. He asked, 'Site of origin?'

'Right.'

Arson produces very distinct patterns as flames start and spread. It's at the origin site that investigators can expect to find the best evidence about the perp.

He read from the GC/MS monitor. 'Traces of wax, low-octane gasoline – not enough to link it to a particular maker – and cotton, plastic, matches.'

'Candle bomb.'

'Right.'

A simple improvised explosive device can be made from a jug of gasoline, using a candle as a fuse.

Cooper confirmed that the trace was so minimal he couldn't source any of the other ingredients in the unsub's IED. As Rhyme had suspected.

Sachs got another call, coughed a bit before taking it. 'Hello?' Nodding, listening. 'Thanks.'

It wasn't good news, Rhyme could tell.

She finished up the call and turned to the others in the room. 'Full canvass of the neighborhood. No one saw him. He must've left just after setting the bomb.'

A shrug. Nothing other than Rhyme had expected.

A moment later another call. Rodney Szarnek's name flashed onto caller ID.

Ah, let's hope for the best.

'Answer,' Rhyme commanded.

The rock music was back. But only momentarily. Before Rhyme could say, 'Shut the damn music off, please,' the officer downed the volume.

'Lincoln.'

'Rodney, you're on speaker here with . . . a bunch of people. No time for roll call. Was Todd Williams's computer salvageable?'

A pause, which Rhyme took to be one of surprise. 'Well, sure. A fall like that is nothing. You can drop a computer out of an airplane and the data'll survive. Black boxes, you know.'

'What do you have?'

'Looks like the relationship between this Williams and your unsub is recent. I found some emails between them. I'll send them to you.'

A moment later a secure email popped up on the screen. They read the first of the attachments accompanying it.

Hello, Todd. I read you're blog and I feel the same way, what society is coming to is not good and electronics and the digital world are making it a much more dangerous place then it needs to be. Their has to be some way to change the system. Money is the root of it of course as you suggest, I would like to try to help in you're cause. Can we meet?

P. G.

Archer said, 'Ah. We have initials.'

'Maybe,' Rhyme said. 'Go on, Rodney.'

Szarnek continued, 'Your unsub used an anonymous email account. Logged in from an untraceable IP. They set up a meeting for the day of the murder.'

Cooper looked over the email. 'Not particularly smart. Look at the mistakes, commas, and the homonyms. Y-O-U apostrophe R-E instead of "your." And "Their" too.'

Rhyme corrected, '*Homophones*. Same pronunciation, different spelling and meaning. Homonyms have the same pronunciation and same spelling but different meaning.'

Staring at the screen, Archer provided the classic example: 'Bark – what a dog does and a covering on a tree. Homonym.' She then added, 'But I don't think he's stupid. I think he's pretending to be. Run-on sentences, the homophones – they're obvious. But he uses the clause "as you suggest" correctly. Not "like you suggest."'

Rhyme agreed. 'And the infinitive after "to try." It's non-standard to say "try and"; you should say "try to." And using "then" for "than" would have been flagged by most usage checkers, even on a basic phone. No, you're right; he's faking.'

Szarnek broke in with, 'Now for the big find. The most *troubling* find.'

Whitmore asked, 'Which is what, Mr Szarnek?'

'For hours before the murder – while Todd and your unsub were meeting, I assume – Todd was online. He did two things. First, he bought a database. He bought it from a commercial data miner. He spoofed he was an ad agency – used a real one with an account he'd hacked – and he claimed he needed the information for market research. It was a laundry list of the products that DataWise Five Thousand controllers are found in.'

'How many?'

'A lot. About eight hundred different products, nearly three million units shipped to the Northeast of the US, including the New York metro area. Some couldn't do any real harm if a third party took control: computers, printers, lights. Others could be deadly: cars, trains, elevators, defibs, heart monitors, pacemakers, microwaves, ovens, power tools, furnaces, cranes – the big ones used in construction work and on docks. I'd guess sixty percent of them could be dangerous. Then, the second thing he bought, a database of purchasers of those products. Some are equipment manufacturers. Like Midwest Conveyance. Others are individual consumers, who bought smart appliances. Names and addresses. Again, New York and Northeast mostly.'

Archer asked, 'That's available? That information?'

Another pause. Perhaps this was one of astonishment. 'Data mining, Ms . . .'

'Archer.'

'You have no idea what aggregators know about you. The data collection is why when you buy, in this case, a smart stove you start getting direct-mail ads for other products that might be cloud-oriented. By buying the stove you've declared yourself to be in a certain demographic.'

'So he simply browses through the list and finds a dangerous product with a DataWise inside, like the escalator. He hacks in and waits so that – if he's a decent monster – it's not a child or pregnant woman riding to the second floor, and pushes the button.'

Sachs asked, 'How did he hack it? It can't have been that easy.'

No pause this time. Just a laugh. 'Well. Okay. About the Internet of Things – a phrase I completely detest, but there it is. Can I give you a brief lesson?'

'I like the brief part, Rodney.'

'Smart products from household lights all the way up to the ones I just mentioned are quote "embedded" with wireless connectivity circuits.'

Rhyme recalled this from Williams's blog.

'Now, embedded devices use special protocols – rules, let's call them – which govern how computer devices talk to the cloud and to each other in the networks. ZigBee and Z-Wave are the most popular protocols. The DataWise controller and some other companies use Wi-Swift. The protocols provide for encryption keys to make sure only legitimate users and devices are recognized but there's a moment of vulnerability when the stove or webcam and the network try to shake hands, and hackers can sniff that out and get the network key.

'To make matters worse the manufacturers are, well, don't be shocked – greedy! New software takes time to write, and that flies in the face of the time-to-market issue high-tech companies face. The longer it takes to start selling a product the greater the risk that somebody'll beat you to it. So what's happened is these smart controller companies use existing software for their embedded products – and I mean old, ancient software. Dinosaur-ware. Early Windows and Apple operating systems and some open source code, stripped of gingerbread like the Solitaire game and PaintShop. The software is more vulnerable to security exploits than if the company wrote new code that was specific to the products the smart controller's installed in.'

'Exploit?' From Whitmore. 'What's that?'

'Hacking. Finding a weakness and, well, *exploiting* it. You know the refrigerator hack a few years ago? This was epic. A product line of smart fridges was running some old software written for PCs. Hackers got inside and turned the controller into a spambot. Refrigerators around the world were writing and sending penis-enhancement emails and vitamin offers to millions of addresses. The homeowners never knew.'

'The companies that make these smart controllers? Can't they protect against hackers?' Archer asked.

'Well, they try to. They're always sending out updates with security patches. Ever logged onto your PC and you have to wait because Windows is installing updates? That's probably a security patch. Sometimes you have to install them yourself. Sometimes – like with Google – they're downloaded and installed automatically. The patch'll usually do the trick . . . until some hacker comes up with a new exploit, of course.'

Rhyme asked, 'Can he be traced when he's online and controlling the product?'

'Possibly. You'll have to talk to the controller maker about that.'

'We'll do that, Rodney. Thanks.'

They disconnected.

Sachs said, 'I'll have somebody at One PP get us the number of a contact at the controller company.' She stepped away to make a call. She completed it and said, 'They'll get back to us ASAP.'

Then simultaneously three phones in the parlor sounded. Sachs's, Whitmore's and Cooper's.

'Well,' Sachs said, reading. 'Looks like we have our motive.' Her face glowed from the phone screen as she read.

'What?' Rhyme asked.

Whitmore said, 'My paralegal has sent me a text. Probably the same as yours, Detective Sachs. A posting on several newspapers' online editions in the op-ed sections, claiming credit for the escalator death.'

'It's up here,' Cooper said. They all turned toward the display.

You're lust for things, for objects, for trinkets will be the death of you all! You've abandoned true values and in doing that lost your precious "control", that happens when you don't use your data wisely. You have rejected the love of families and friends for the addiction of belongings. You must own more and more and more until, soon, your possessions will possess YOU and, with a cold, steel kiss, send you to hell.

– The People's Guardian

Rhyme mentioned that the unsub's email to Todd Williams was signed *P. G.*

'Legit?' Cooper asked.

Curiously many people took credit for crimes that they had nothing to do with.

'No, I'm sure it's from him,' Rhyme said.

'How do you—?' Archer started. Then: 'Sure, the word "control." It's in quotation marks. And the reference to "wise" and "data."'

'Exactly. Hacking the DataWise isn't public information; only our unsub would know about it. And some of the same intentional grammatical mistakes, the Y-O-U-R-E. And the incorrect use of "that" for "which."'

Sachs said, 'Let's find out if he's done this before . . .' She went online and began a search. A few minutes later, 'Nothing in NCIC.' The National Crime Information Center compiles warrants and profile information on tens of thousands of suspects throughout the United States and some foreign nations. Sachs added that the popular press had reported no activist groups mounting attacks that were in anyway similar to what Unsub 40 had done. Nor were there any references to 'the People's Guardian.'

Juliette Archer, Rhyme realized, had wheeled away from the others and was looking over a computer screen. She called, 'I've got it.'

'What?' Rhyme asked bluntly, irritated that there were no new leads in a case in which the unsub was possibly targeting more victims right at the moment.

'The controller company. CIR Micro?' She returned to the others and nodded at the screen she'd just called up. 'That's the CEO's direct line, Vinay Chaudhary.'

'How'd you get that?' Sachs asked, seemingly irritated that the NYPD assistance she'd requested hadn't been as fast as an amateur.

'Just a little detective work,' Archer answered.

'Let's talk to him,' Rhyme said.

Sachs typed the number into her phone and apparently got Chaudhary's assistant, from what Rhyme could deduce. After an explanation, Sachs's body language, registering surprise, suggested she was on with the CEO himself. It appeared he wasn't resistant to talking with them, though – she explained after disconnecting – he wasn't free just now. He could speak to them in about forty-five minutes.

Presumably, after he had his lawyers assembled around him, like settlers circling the wagons when hostiles appeared on the bluffs over their heads.

CHAPTER 22

'Whatta we got, Sarge?' The question slipped smoothly through the officer's headset.

The DSS tactical surveillance van, plumbing today, was parked directly across from the bar and NYPD Sergeant Joe Reilly had been good eyes on the inside of the dive. He replied, 'Both of 'em, sitting, hanging. Drinkin' beers. No cares in the world.' A paunchy, gray-haired officer in Narcotics, Reilly had been a supervisor with the Drug Street Sweep program since it had started years ago; back then radios crackled like wadded-up waxed paper. Amazing they could coordinate the busts at all. Now it was all high-def digital, as if the tactical team officer he was speaking with was only feet away, not up the street in this scruffy Brooklyn 'hood.

Reilly wasn't alone in the van. Beside him, operating the camera controls, was a prim and proper stocky young African American officer, a whiz with the electronic eyes and ears, though she wore too much perfume for the sergeant's taste.

'Any weapons?' the voice in his ear asked. The undercover tac team was a half block away from Richie's bar in Bedford-Stuyvesant and they damn well better've ordered the calzone Reilly had told them to get for him. And no spinach. Ham and Swiss. Period. Soda. Diet.

Reilly peered at the screen image of the two beer drinkers under surveillance. The woman officer shook her head. Reilly said, 'Negative presenting.'

Which didn't mean the two men they were watching weren't armed to the teeth.

'Just the two of them?'

Woulda said three, it'd been three. Four, four.

'Yeah.' Reilly stretched. Hoped this wasn't a damn waste of time. There'd been good intel that a senior asshole from one of the Dominican Republic crews was meeting a local punk in Richie's. Maybe transferring something big. But the DR guy was late and the punk – skinny, twitchy – was just hanging with some unknown, a white male, youngish, acting kind of twitchy himself.

The tac officer on the radio took a sip of something, slurping, and said, 'How late is Big Boy?'

The Dominican was not only high up in the crews but tipped the scales at three hundred plus.

'Half an hour.' Reilly looked at his watch. 'Forty minutes.'

'He ain't gonna show,' the tac cop muttered. He was now chewing.

The gangbanger's absence probably wasn't cold feet, Reilly guessed. Drug suppliers at the Dominican's level are just very, very busy.

'You sure the unknown with him isn't with the DR crew?'

Reilly laughed. 'Not unless times're so hard they're hiring choirboys. White ones. And times ain't that hard.'

'Any idea who?'

'Nup. Descrip is blond, six feet, fucking piss-me-off skinny.' Reilly scanned the guy's face close up. 'You know, he's looking funny.'

'What'sat mean?' the take-down guy said, between bites.

Fuck that. I want my calzone.

'Nervous.'

'He made you, Sarge?'

'I'm sitting in a fucking plumbing van on a street in Brooklyn that's filled with plumbing supply stores. The camera lens is about the size of your cat's dick.'

'I don't have a cat.'

'No, he didn't make me. Just, he doesn't want to be with our boy.'

'Who would?'

Good point. Alphonse Gravita – aka Alpho, but more popularly Alpo, woof woof – was a shining piece of non-work. The germ of a dealer had been lucky enough to miss getting busted but he had his eye on moving up, expanding his street business from the mini mart he hung out in in Ocean Hill to Bed-Stuy and Brownsville.

'Hold on.' Reilly sat up straighter.

'The DR guy there?'

'Negative. But Alpo and his buddy . . . wait, something's happening.'

'What?' The chewing had stopped.

'Looks like a transaction . . . Pull out.' The latter spoken to the perfumed cop sitting beside him.

Bad choice of words, he decided. Or good. But she missed the innuendo.

The officer zoomed out to get a broader shot, to catch everything that Alpo and the blond man were doing. Alpo was looking around and fishing in his pocket. The blond kid was too. Then palm met palm.

'Okay, got an exchange.'

'What was it?'

'Shit. Fair number of bills. But couldn't see the product. Could you see?'

'No, sir,' the surveillance woman answered. Gardenia came to mind, the perfume, though Reilly had no clue what gardenias smelled – or looked – like.

The tactical cop radioed, 'Your call, Sarge.'

Reilly debated. They'd just seen an illegal drug transaction. They could come home with two heads. But it might make sense to collar White Boy alone, outside, and keep Alpo in play. They'd have at least one collar to their credit if they couldn't go back to the 73 with the DR scumbag in metal. The kid might also have intel about the Dominican. They could squeeze the nervous guy until he gave up plenty.

Or just let this one pass – obviously the deal wasn't that big. The blond kid could walk away and they'd hope Big Boy showed up.

Tactical: 'They're still there, just sitting there?'

'Right.'

'We move in?'

'No, don't want to lose the Alpo connection to our DR friends. Maybe take the other guy if he leaves. Until then wait.'

'The DR guy's fifty minutes late.'

Reilly made a decision.

'Okay, I'll tell you what we're gonna do. But answer the question: You order me that calzone?'

Lincoln Rhyme was saying, 'We know he's going to hit somebody again. I want a memo out to every precinct and FDNY station. Any accident involving a product, *seeming* accident, I want to hear about it. Stat. Immediately. ASAP. Whatever cliché you want to use.'

Mel Cooper said he'd take care of that and drew his phone the way he would the small revolver he wore almost quaintly on his hip.

Sachs received a text and glanced at her phone. 'The smart controller company. They want to talk.'

'Or,' Archer said, 'tell us in person how uncooperative they intend to be.'

When it came to investigative work, she was quite the fast learner, Rhyme reflected and shouted for Thom to set up a Skype call.

Soon the distinctive heartbeat of the app's ringtone pulsed through the room and a moment later the screen came to life.

It wasn't much of a wagon circling. Only two people from CIR Micro were on the screen and one of them, Rhyme easily deduced, was Vinay Parth Chaudhary himself, looking both South Asian and authoritarian. He wore a collarless shirt and stylish metal-framed glasses.

The other was a sallow-faced, solid man in his fifties. The lawyer, presumably. He was in a suit, no tie.

They sat in an antiseptic office: a bare table, on which were two monitors, bookending the pair. On the wall behind them was a slash of maroon and blue paint.

Rhyme at first thought it was a painting but saw that, no, it was directly on the wall. A stylized rendering of the company's logo.

'I'm Amelia Sachs, detective with the NYPD. We spoke earlier. This is Lincoln Rhyme, a forensic consultant who's assisting on our case.' It was just the two of them. As earlier, Rhyme had decided that the company might be less cooperative with more people present, even if the outfit wasn't any longer a target of litigation.

'I'm Vinay Chaudhary, president and CEO. This is Stanley Frost, our chief general counsel.' His voice was pleasant, calm. Hardly any inflection. He didn't appear threatened. But Rhyme supposed that men who are worth forty billion dollars rarely are.

'This is about a crime involving our products?' Frost asked.

'That's right. Your DataWise Five Thousand smart controller. An individual here in New York City intentionally sent a signal to one of those devices that was installed in a Midwest Conveyance escalator. It activated the access panel at the top. It opened. A man fell in and was killed.'

Chaudhary: 'I heard about the accident, of course. But I didn't know it was intentional. How terrible. I *do* have to say, we told Midwest to use the DataWise solely for uploading diagnostic and maintenance data and for emergency shutoff. Not to allow access.'

'We have correspondence to show that,' Frost the lawyer said.

The CEO continued, 'And the Midwest Conveyance controllers were installed several years ago. We've sent the company forty, forty-five security patches since then. They would've kept the hacker out. If they didn't install them promptly then there's nothing we can do.'

Rhyme said, 'This isn't about your liability. It's the hacker we're after, not you.'

'Your name again, please?' Chaudhary asked.

'Lincoln Rhyme.'

'I believe I've heard of you. The newspapers, or a TV show.'

'Possibly. Now, this suspect learned how to get inside the controller from somebody who'd blogged about it.'

Chaudhary was nodding. 'You're probably thinking of the *Social Engineering Second-ly* blog.'

'Yes, we are.'

'Well, the blogger used an early model and he intentionally didn't download and install the security patches. If he had, he never would have gotten the DataWise to malfunction. But he didn't say that in his blog, of course. It's much more sensational to suggest that any thirteen-year-old can run an exploit. Gets you a lot more hits on your blog when you raise the battle flag of privacy breaches and malfunctions. The DataWise has far fewer vulnerabilities than ninety percent of the systems out there.'

Frost added, 'We have a white-hat firm we work with – ethical hackers. You know the term?'

'We can figure it out,' Sachs said.

'Which spends all day looking for ways to hack into the DataWise servers our clients use. Any hint of an exploit, we send out a patch. If that blogger had done that he never would have gotten inside. What does he have to say about it?'

Sachs said, 'I'm afraid our suspect killed him after he learned how to hack into the system.'

'No!' Chaudhary actually gasped.

'It's true.'

'Well, I'm certainly very sorry about it. Terrible.'

Rhyme continued, 'The subject we're after has a list of products that use your controller and people and companies who bought those things. A very long list.'

'It's been a good few years.'

The lawyer turned to the CEO, saying nothing, but perhaps sending a signal to avoid hinting at the company's net worth, even though this wasn't about its potential liability.

Chaudhary said, an aside, 'It's okay. I want to help.'

Rhyme pressed on. 'And we have reason to believe that he's going to do this again. Kill someone else.'

The man frowned. 'On purpose? Why on earth?'

Sachs said, 'Domestic terrorist, you could say. He has a grudge against consumerism. Maybe capitalism in general. He's sent some email rants to various news organizations. You can find stories about them, I'm sure. He calls himself the People's Guardian.'

Chaudhary said, 'But . . . is he psychotic?'

'We don't know what he is,' Rhyme said impatiently. 'Now, why we're calling. I'd like to know a few things. First, is it possible to trace where he's physically located when he takes over control of a product? And it seems he'll be nearby, so he can see the incident and decide exactly when to activate the controller. And, another question, is it possible to trace his identity?'

Chaudhary answered: 'Technically, tracing, yes.

But again that's the province of each manufacturer – the webcam maker, the stove maker, the car companies. We couldn't do it from our facilities. We simply make the controller hardware and write the script – the software in the controllers. He'd be hacking into the system through our customers' cloud servers.

'But, if you knew in advance which appliance or device – I mean, the actual unit itself – he was targeting, the manufacturing company could trace his location. And even if you could he'd be using proxies to log into the cloud. You'd have to identify those. Finally, you'd have only seconds to find out before he logged out and powered down after the hack. As for identity, I'm sure he's too smart not to use burner phones, unregistered pads or computers and anonymous proxies or virtual private networks. That's Hacking One Oh One.'

This was more discouraging than he'd hoped. Rhyme then said, 'All right. One other thing: Is there some security measure you can take to stop him getting access?'

'Surely. What I was telling you a moment ago. The manufacturers of the embedded products – the stoves, HVAC systems, medical equipment, escalators – just need to install the security patches we send them. I know from his blog how that fellow – what was his name?'

'Todd Williams.'

'How he ran the exploit. Yes, there was a vulnerability. We patched it within a day of learning it and sent out the updates. That was a month ago. Maybe more.'

'Why wouldn't Midwest Conveyance have installed them?'

'Sometimes companies don't update out of laziness, sometimes business factors. Updating requires a reboot and often some tinkering with the code. That takes the whole cloud offline for a while. Their customers aren't happy with any disruption of service. Once people get used to a convenience it's impossible to take it away from them. Turning lights off remotely if you forgot, when you left the house on vacation? Keeping an eye on the babysitter in real time? Ten years ago, when that wasn't an option, you never thought twice about not being able to. But now? Everyone who has a smart product expects it to keep performing. If it doesn't they'll go elsewhere.'

'You said it wouldn't take long.'

Chaudhary smiled. 'The study of the psychology of consumers is a fascinating topic. Disappointments are remembered. Loyalties shift in milliseconds. Now, Mr Rhyme and Detective . . .'

'Sachs.'

'I have a meeting I need to attend. But before that we'll send all our customers another link to the security patches with a memo reminding them they *have* to install those patches. People's lives could be at stake.'

'Thanks,' Sachs said.

'Good luck to you. If we can help, please let us know.'

The webcam closed. And Rhyme and Sachs reconvened the team, reporting on what Chaudhary had said.

Which, while it might stymie some of Unsub 40's future attacks, was essentially of no help whatsoever in tracking him down.

Rhyme glanced at the whiteboard he, Archer and Whitmore had created for the Midwest Conveyance case. 'I want to consolidate our charts, Sachs. See what evidence we've got.'

Rather than actually transport the Unsub 40 whiteboards from Sachs's war room at One PP to the parlor here, she asked an assistant at Major Cases to take phone pictures and email them. They arrived in seconds.

Sachs now transcribed the details of the crime scenes onto the whiteboard. And added what they'd learned from Williams's computer. The team reviewed them.

Rhyme watched Sachs staring at the chart, her right index finger and thumb spinning her blue-stone ring compulsively. Shaking her head, she muttered, 'We're still waiting for the sawdust, the varnish and the DNA and friction ridges from the napkins. CS in Queens never got back to us.' A glance toward him, a cool glance, as if this speedbump was his fault. Which, he guessed, it partly was, thanks to the Cooper kidnapping.

'Let me see the micro pictures of the sawdust,' Rhyme said.

Sachs went online, into the secure CSU database, typed in the case file and conjured up the images.

Rhyme looked them over. 'I'd say mahogany. Mel?'

After a fast examination the tech said, 'Ninety-nine percent sure. Yes.'

'Ah, Sachs, you were right. Mea culpa for stealing him out from under your nose.' He'd meant this as a joke but she didn't respond. Rhyme continued, 'And you're right about sanding. The particles aren't from sawing. Suggests fine woodworking.' She wrote this down. And Rhyme added, 'No idea about the varnish. There's no database. We'll just have to see what the analysts can come up with. What's the story with the napkins?'

Sachs explained about the White Castle lead. 'I don't know why the hell it's taking so long to run DNA and enhanced friction ridge.' She snagged her phone and called the crime scene operation in Queens, had a brief conversation. Disconnected.

A scowl. 'It's taking so long because they lost them.'

'What?' Cooper asked.

'Somebody in the evidence room lost the napkins. They got tagged wrong, seems. A clerk's looking.'

It could be, Rhyme knew, an imposing quest. The evidence room was not one room at all but a number of them, which contained hundreds of thousands of items of evidence. Looking for a needle in a stack of needles, Rhyme had once heard.

'Well, fire whoever dropped the ball on that one,' he snapped.

He scanned the chart again, noting the new entries. Unsub 40 was either very lucky or very careful. The evidence gave no clear direction either as to where he lived or worked or to where he might be going to strike next, assuming he'd picked up some of the trace while assessing a future victim.

Crime Scene: 151 Clinton Place, Manhattan, construction site, adjacent to 40° North (Nightclub)

- Offenses: Homicide, Assault.
- Victim: Todd Williams, 29, writer, blogger, social topics.
- COD: Blunt force trauma, probably ball-peen hammer

(no brand determined).
- Motive: Robbery.
    - Credit/debit cards not yet used.

- Evidence:
    - No friction ridges.
    - Blade of grass.
    - Trace:
        - Phenol.
        - Motor oil.

- Profile of suspect (Unknown Subject 40).
    - Wore checkered jacket (green), Braves baseball cap.
    - White male.
    - Tall (6 feet, 2 inches to 6 feet, 4).
    - Slim (140–150 lbs.).
    - Long feet and fingers.
    - No visual of face.

Crime Scene: Heights View Mall, Brooklyn

- Offense: Homicide, escape from apprehension.
- Victim: Greg Frommer, 44, clerk with Pretty Lady Shoes in mall.
    - Store clerk, left Patterson Systems as Director of Marketing. Will attempt to show he would have returned to a similar or other higher-income job.
- COD: Loss of blood, internal organ trauma.

- Means of death:
  - Unsub 40 hacked into CIR DataWise5000 controller and opened door remotely.
  - Discussion with CIR executives.
    - Tracing the signal: only each manufacturer could do that. Difficult.
    - Probably impossible to identify him.
    - Danger of hacking could be minimized by companies' installing security patches. CIR is sending out warning to do so.
- Evidence:
  - DNA, no CODIS match.
  - No friction ridges sufficient for ID.
  - Shoeprint, likely unsub's, size 13 Reebok Daily Cushion 2.0.
  - Soil sample, likely from unsub, containing crystalline aluminosilicate clays: montmorillonite, illite, vermiculite, chlorite, kaolinite. Additionally, organic colloids. Substance is probably humus. Not native to this portion of Brooklyn.
  - Dinitroaniline (used in dyes, pesticides, explosives).
  - Ammonium nitrate (fertilizer, explosives)
    - With oil from Clinton Place scene: Possibly constructing bomb?
  - Additional phenol (precursor in making plastics, like polycarbonates, resins and nylon, aspirin, embalming fluid, cosmetics, ingrown toenail cures; unsub has large feet, so – nail problems?)

- Talc, mineral oil/paraffinum liquidum/huile minérale, zinc stearate, stearic acid, lanolin/ lanoline, cetyl alcohol, triethanolamine, PEG-12 laurate, mineral spirits, methylparaben, propyl- paraben, titanium dioxide.
  - Makeup? No brand determination. Analysis to return.
- Shaving of metal, microscopic, steel, probably from sharpening knife.
- Sawdust. Mahogany. From sanding, not sawing.
- Organochlorine and benzoic acid. Toxic. (insec- ticides, weaponized poisons?)
- Acetone, ether, cyclohexane, natural gum, cellu- lose (probably varnish).
  - Manufacturer to be determined.
- White Castle napkins missing at Crime Scene HQ.
• Cause of action in civil suit for Greg Frommer's death.
  - Wrongful death/personal injury tort suit.
    - Strict products liability.
    - Negligence.
    - Breach of implied warranty.
• Damages: compensatory, pain and suffering, puni- tive.
• Defendant: Unsub 40.
• Facts relevant to accident:
  - Access panel opened, victim fell into gears. Opened about 16 inches.

- Door weighed 42 pounds, sharp teeth on front contributed to death/injury.
- Door secured by latch. On springs. It popped open for unknown reason.
- Reasons for failure?
  - Intervening cause – Unsub 40's hacking DataWise controller.

• No access to Dept. of Investigation or FDNY reports or records at this time.

• No access to failing escalator at this time (under quarantine by DOI).

Crime Scene: White Castle Restaurant, Astoria Boulevard, Astoria, Queens

• Relevance to case: Unsub eats here regularly.
• Additional elements of profile of suspect.
  - Eats 10–15 sandwiches at a time.
  - Had been shopping at least once when ate here. Carried white plastic bag, something heavy inside. Metallic?
  - Turned north and crossed the street (toward bus/train?). No sign he owned/drove automobile.
  - Witnesses didn't get good view of face, probably no facial hair.
  - White, pale, maybe balding or crew cut.

• Used a car service on Astoria Blvd. around day of Williams's murder.

– Awaiting word from owner of gypsy cab company.

– Service has reported on the destination.

Crime Scene: 348 Ridge Street, Manhattan

- Offense: Arson.
- Victim: None.
- Relevance to case: Unsub 40 is the same person who caused Greg Frommer's death, intentionally opening the access panel of Midwest Conveyance escalator, at Brooklyn Heights Mall. Met Todd Williams and learned how to hack DataWise5000 smart controllers, which caused escalator accident.
- On night of Williams's death unsub got two lists from him:
  - Database of all products the controllers are found in.
  - Consumers who bought some of those products.
- Additional elements of profile of suspect:
  - Under name of the People's Guardian, posted manifesto. Domestic terrorism, attacking excess consumerism.
  - Can't trace the post.
  - Intentional grammatical mistakes. Probably he's intelligent.
- Evidence:
  - Improvised explosive device.
    - Wax, low-octane gasoline, cotton, plastic, matches. Candle bomb. Elements not sourceable.

*

So. This is her home.

Red's.

Amelia Sachs, the Shopper.

The Shopper who was not courteous enough to burn to death in Todd Williams's office building.

I happen to be across the street from her Brooklyn town house, dolled up in some worker's clothing, coveralls, which, well, cover all. So as not to draw attention. Tired, now toward the end of a long, long workday (though I'm largely pretending at the moment, the fatigue is true). Coffee in one hand, mobile phone in another, pretending to read texts, though in reality I've been reading how well my screed against consumerism went over in the press. Why, I've even had some likes!

Studying Red's town house carefully. A Shopper. Yes, she is and she'll suffer for it but I've softened a bit (White Castles from the frozen foods section are not bad) and I've decided, Red isn't the sadistic sort. A Shopper with a heart she is. The sort of girl who if I had asked her out wouldn't laugh in my face and let loose about string beans and sacks of bones. She'd blush and keep a pretty smile on her pretty face. 'Sorry, I have plans.'

A Shopper with a heart . . .

So when I destroy Red's life I will probably feel some regret. But I think this in passing and get back to the task at hand.

Nice place she has here. Old-time Brooklyn. Classic. Amelia *Sachs*. German name, I guess. She doesn't look German, but I really don't know what a German looks

JEFFERY DEAVER

like, now I think about it. She doesn't have braided blond hair and blue Aryan eyes.

I've been debating what to do about her. Red owns no products that have DataWise5000 controllers in them. At least not that I can find. She's not on my magic lists that Todd so helpfully got for me before his bones started to crack. Of course once a product gets out into the hands of the public, it can bob like a cork in the ocean until it washes up in someone clse's kitchen or garage or living room. But I scanned Red's house for signals, like Todd showed me, and while I found some lonely little devices sending out their wireless beacons, begging to join a network, none of them will help me turn her into a mass of broken bone or blistered flesh.

Sipping coffee, which I'm not really sipping, looking at the cell phone, which I'm not really looking at . . . pretending. I'm blending in – an impatient workman waiting for a ride home at the end of the day.

Though I'm not impatient at all.

I'm patient as stone.

Which pays off. Because only a half hour later I see something interesting.

And I realize I now have the final piece of the puzzle that will let me solve my Red problem.

All right, I think, finishing my beverage and putting the crumpled cup into my pocket (learned my lesson there!), it's time to go. We've got work to do.

CHAPTER 23

Ron Pulaski walked out the front door of Richie's bar. He felt good, almost light-headed.

He turned south and kept walking quickly, head down.

What sat in his front left pocket was minuscule but seemed like ten pounds of gold. He casually slipped his hand into his pocket and touched it for the comfort. Thank you, Lord.

And thank you, he thought too to the guy he'd been sharing a beer with a minute ago: Alpho (Pulaski didn't like to use the dog food nic, even skels deserved respect). He'd hooked Pulaski up with just what he needed. Oh, yeah.

He could . . .

'Excuse me, sir. If you could stop right there, please. Take your hand out of your pocket.'

Face burning, heart thudding, Pulaski stopped in his tracks. Knew he wasn't being mugged. But he also knew what was going down. The tone of voice, the words. He turned to see two large men, dressed in jeans and jackets, street clothes, but he knew right away who they were – not their names, but their jobs: tactical cops, undercover. He glanced at their shields, gold shields dangling from silver chains.

Shit . . .

He slowly removed his hand and kept both palms open. Non-threatening. He knew the drill; he'd been on the other side hundreds of times.

Pulaski said, 'I'm NYPD, assigned to Major Cases. I have a weapon in an ankle holster and my shield's inside my jacket.' Trying to sound confident. But his voice was unsteady. His heart slammed.

They frowned. 'Okay,' the bigger one, bald, stepped forward. His partner kept his hand near his weapon. Baldie: 'We just want to make sure everybody stays safe, you understand. I'm going to ask you to turn around and put your hands against the wall.'

'Sure.' It does no good to argue. Pulaski wondered if he'd throw up. Deep breath. Okay, control it. He did. More or less.

The officers – they smelled of a task force – got the gun and the shield. They didn't give them back. His wallet too. Pulaski was inclined to argue that one but didn't.

'Okay. Turn around.' From the other officer – blond hair in a spiky cut. He was flipping through the wallet. He clustered it, the gun and the shield in his left hand.

Both officers looked around and directed Pulaski into a doorway, out of sight of the pavement. Ah. They'd been conducting surveillance at Richie's, probably on Alphonse, waiting for a contact to show up. And they didn't want to blow the main operation by getting spotted now.

Baldie spoke into his microphone. 'Sarge, we got him. The thing is he's on the force. Major Cases . . . I know . . . I'll find out.' He cocked his head. 'Pulaski?

You running an op here? Major Cases always coordinates with us, DSS. So we're confused.'

'Not an op.'

'What'd you buy?' Baldie seemed to like doing the talking. They were close. His breath smelled of pizza. Garlic and oregano. He glanced at Pulaski's pocket.

'Nothing.'

'Look, man, we got it on video. Everything.'

Shit. The plumbing van across the street. He had to give 'em credit. There were a dozen plumbing supply stores on the block. A lumberyard truck, a taco truck, an HVAC truck . . . that might be weird. But not plumbing.

'It's not what you think.'

'Yeah, it *is* what we think, Pulaski. There's nothing we can do. It's on tape that's gotta be logged in,' the blond partner said. He seemed personally upset at the prospect of busting a fellow cop for scoring drugs. But being upset wasn't going to stop him. Either of them. It just seemed that Blondie would enjoy a collar a bit less than his partner.

'We're in this far, Pulaski. You gotta give us what you scored. If it's a misdemeanor amount it won't go so bad. You can work out something with the DA and Benevolent Association.'

They'd probably be thinking too Pulaski might be part of a sting himself – scoring drugs knowing surveillance was there and seeing if Baldie and Blondie let him go, professional courtesy. Then Internal Affairs would sweep in and take *them* down. So they'd have to treat him like any other buyer.

'I didn't score any drugs.'

There was silence.

'Search me.'

A glance between them. Blondie did. A good search. They knew what they were about.

Then Baldie was talking into his microphone. 'Sarge, nothing on him . . . K.' He disconnected and barked: 'So, the fuck's going on here, Pulaski?'

'That.' He nodded at a wad of papers Blondie had lifted from his pocket. Blondie handed it to him. He opened one small sheet of paper and handed it back.

'What'sis?'

'I had some money trouble last month. Need a couple large. Somebody put me in touch with Alpho. He hooked me up with a money man. I paid him back the last of the vig today. He gave me the marker back.'

The cops looked at the IOU.

Borrowing money at exorbitant rates of interest isn't illegal unless it's done to launder cash – though a cop's doing so probably tripped over some departmental regs.

Baldie spoke into the microphone. 'Wasn't drugs, Sarge. Juice. Paid his vig and got the note back . . . Yeah . . . I will.'

'You know, that was just fucking stupid, Officer.'

'Yeah? How fucking stupid is it to borrow some green for a friend who's losing a leg 'cause he's got cancer and no insurance?' The fear had translated into anger and he decided if you're going to make something up, pick the most outrageous story you can.

That set them back a bit. But Baldie wasn't deterred for long. 'You could've screwed up a major operation here. Your boy back there, *Alpo*, was supposed to be meeting somebody senior with a DR crew. He comes in, tips to you being blue and who knows what might've happened? He could've had a shooter with him.'

Pulaski shrugged.

'He say anything about a Dominican?'

'No. We talked sports and how fucked people can get when they borrow at twenty percent interest. My piece and shield. The wallet too.'

Pulaski took them and eased to his knees, re-holstering his weapon. He snapped the strap around the small pistol and rose. 'Anything else?' No response. Pulaski gazed at him for a moment then, without a word, he turned and walked away.

If he'd thought his heart was beating fast a few moments ago, it was like a machine gun now.

Man, man, man . . . You lucky son of a bitch, he told himself. But not really all luck. He'd planned ahead. Alpho had called him earlier and said he had a lead to Oden, the man who could supply Pulaski with the new breed of Oxy. 'Catch or whatever the fuck you call it.' They'd meet at Richie's and Pulaski would pay him two thousand for the information.

But leaving One PP, where he'd dropped off the computer from the arson scene downtown, Pulaski began to feel paranoid. What if he was seen talking to Alpho by a friend, or fellow cop? He needed an excuse for hanging with the guy. He'd bought drugs once from him but wouldn't do that again.

For some reason the IOU idea had jumped into his head. Not bad. He'd scrawled out a fake marker.

When Alpho gave him the Oden info he'd slipped it into the same pocket as the IOU. It wouldn't pass forensics – no friction ridges other than his own . . . and forget about handwriting analysis. But he guessed that the DSS cops back there weren't much concerned about him. They just wanted to get back to their pizza and the Dominican banger stakeout.

He now extracted and looked over the note Alpho had given him, memorizing the address and the other information on it. He closed his eyes and recited it a dozen times. Then ditched it down a sewer.

The hour was getting late. Lincoln and Amelia had to be wondering where he was. And he himself was curious if there'd been anything on Williams's computer that might lead to Unsub 40. But, checking his phone, neither had called. He texted Amelia that he was heading home – the Gutiérrez case had taken up more time than he'd believed it would – but if she needed anything, give him a call.

Was she mad? Probably. But nothing he could do about it.

He was going to flag down a cab but was painfully aware of how much of his own money he'd just handed over to Alpho so it was subway time. He walked back to Broadway Junction to begin the complicated journey to his wife and children. Feeling dirty, tainted. And sure that even seeing their soft, smiling faces would do little to bring him comfort.

Amelia Sachs pulled her Torino up to the curb and shut the engine off. Sat for a moment, reading texts. She slipped the phone away but still didn't get out of the car.

After leaving Rhyme's she'd gone on two missions. The first was to meet with a reporter for one of the big local papers and give him a follow-up to the People's Guardian story. As part of the article he would print the list of products that contained smart controllers – though in the online edition only, since the number of such items was so lengthy. She'd also explained what Chaudhary had said, that manufacturers were reluctant or too lazy to install the patches to improve security. The CEO was going to contact them again but she'd decided that a news story about that reticence would create some public relations pressure for them to install the security updates.

The reporter had thanked her for the tip and agreed to keep her anonymous since she hadn't cleared her contacting him with the brass at One PP. He left to further research and write up the story.

Sachs had then stopped by One PP briefly and was now here on her second mission – in Little Italy, little indeed, having been taken over by hipsters from the north and Chinese restaurants and gift stores from the south. She climbed out of the car, snagged her briefcase and walked south. Slowing her pace to a stop, she noted the man's silhouette in a window of the coffeehouse before her.

This place had been here for years, a classic espresso-and-pastry shop right out of a 1940s film. The name was Antonios (there had been only one owner by that name; the family, or the sign-painter, had never bothered with an apostrophe). Sachs preferred it to the three or four other surviving bistros here in south-central Greenwich Village, all of them resiliently resisting the chain-store approach to caffeine.

Sachs pushed inside, a bell mounted to the door jingling cheerfully, and she was assaulted by the smells of rich coffee, cinnamon, nutmeg, yeast.

Eyes still on Nick Carelli, who was scrolling through an iPad.

After a brief pause she walked up to him and said, 'Hi.'

'Hey.' He stood up, looked into her eyes and kept his gaze there. No embrace.

She sat and set the briefcase on her lap. Defensive, the way suspects being grilled sometimes crossed their arms.

'What would you like?' Nick asked.

He was drinking black coffee, and she had a memory of a cold Sunday morning, both Nick and she off duty, she in a pajama top, he in the matching bottoms, as she made two cups of coffee, pouring boiling water through a cone filter, the sound like crinkling cellophane. She would sip hers immediately while he would set his cup in the fridge for a few minutes; he liked tepid drinks, never hot.

'Nothing. I can't stay.'

Did he seem disappointed? She believed so.

'Newfangled.' He pointed to the iPad with a smile.

'A lot's changed.'

'I think I'm at a disadvantage. Don't you need to be about thirteen to master something like this?'

'That's the upper limit,' Sachs said. She couldn't help but note once more that Nick looked good. Even better than when she'd seen him last. Less gaunt than then. More upright, the slouch gone. He'd had a haircut too. His appearance seemed better now than in his younger days when he'd been, she thought, too skinny. The sprinkles of gray among the black strands helped. And the years – and prison – didn't seem to have dimmed his sparkly-eyed boyishness. A bit of frat was forever inside. Sachs had believed back then that he hadn't so much ruthlessly planned and executed the hijackings, as fallen in with the wrong crowd and, for the hell of it, thought he'd try something daring, without considering the consequences.

'So. Here you are.' She opened her briefcase and handed over three thick folders containing about eight hundred sheets of paper. The documentation on his case and related investigations. She'd skimmed the file years ago – not wanting to, but unable to resist. She'd learned that back then there'd been several hijacking rings operating in the city. Nick's arrest was one of seven in a three-month period. Some other perps had been cops as well. If he had been a sole hijacker – especially one going for a plea – the file would have been much skimpier. He flipped through one of the folders fast, smiled and touched her arm.

Not her hand. That would have seemed inappropriate. Just her forearm. Still, even through layers of wool and cotton, she felt the electricity that she remembered from years ago. Wished she hadn't. Really wished that.

He must have felt her stiffen. Certainly he saw her look away. Nick lifted his hand off her sleeve.

She said, 'You've got to be careful, Nick. You can't associate with anybody's got a record. Your PO's told you that.'

'If there's anybody who can help me and there's any

risk, or it even looks like they're connected, I'll use, you know, an intermediary to contact them, a friend. Promise.'

'Make sure.'

She stood.

'You're positive you don't have time for a fast dinner?'

'I've got to get home to my mother.'

'How is she?'

'Well enough for the surgery.'

'I don't know how to thank you, Amelia.'

'Prove you're innocent,' she said. 'That's how.'

CHAPTER 24

Policing, Nick Carelli knew, was mostly paperwork.

You wanted collars but you hated collars because of all the forms, the notes, the triplicate, quadruplicate and whatever the hell five copies of something was.

But the good news now was that the Internal Affairs cops on his case, and the regular gold shields, had really done their homework, and he had paperwork galore to prowl through. Probably there was so much because they'd thought they had a crooked cop and a crooked cop is the best kind of perp. You nail a boy in blue who's screwed up and the world's your oyster. Press, promotion, adulation from the public.

In his apartment now. Sitting at a table he'd been meaning to level with a folded piece of paper since he'd moved back in, Nick was looking through what Amelia had brought him, ream upon ream of paperwork. Looking for a key to his salvation.

He sipped coffee, black and lukewarm. Not hot, not iced. Tepid. He didn't know why, but this was the way he always drank coffee. He remembered being with Amelia and she'd make it the old-fashioned drip way – pre-Keurig days – pouring it through a cone filter. One of his favorite memories, a freezing-cold morning, sharing the ugliest pair of striped beige pajamas on earth. Her toenails blue from polish. His blue from the cold.

He'd gulped several mugs of Folgers since he'd started going through the files Ame – no, Amelia – had brought him. How many hours had it been? He didn't want to guess.

He suddenly was aware of a scent that took him back years. He cocked his head, inhaled. Yes, definitely. The source? He lifted one of the file folders. Where Amelia had undoubtedly held it. She wasn't into perfume. But she tended to use the same lotions and shampoos, which had their own distinctive fragrance. This was what he now smelled. Hand cream, Guerlain, he believed. Amazed the name came back to him.

He discarded a few other memories, with difficulty, and returned to the paperwork. Page after page.

An hour crawled past. Another. Numbing. He decided to go for a late-night run. Just five more minutes.

But finding what he so desperately wanted took only two.

Jesus. Oh, my sweet Jesus!

He was reading from a report that had been put together as part of the larger investigation into police involvement in hijackings. It was dated nearly a year after he had gone to jail. There was a photocopy of a detective's hand-written notes, very hard to read – it looked like the officer had used pencil.

2/23. Interv albert constanto olice investigation 44-3452 – operation take back subject not involved in jackings but sheet on drug missed court rants, dropped one, kicked down

*to lesser included, subject reported overheard . . . in flanni-
gan's bar key man for stolen merch, always behind scenes,
layers of protection knows 'everything' in BK, white male,
fifties, first name starts with j married nanci, 'j' is key
constanto says.*

I'll say he's key, Nick Carelli thought. For my mission
at least. Flannigan's was one of *the* underground meeting
places for organized crime operations. This mysterious
'J' figure, who'd operated in BK – Brooklyn – with connections and a wife, Nanci, would know who was who in
the hijacking scene back then. And if he couldn't directly
help Nick, he'd probably know somebody who could.
He flipped through the remaining pages, hoping to find
a transcript of the notes, which would be easier to read,
but no. There wasn't much else. And no follow-up finding
the 'J' figure and his wife Nanci.

Then he saw why.

An NYPD memo announced the end of Operation
Take Back. The commissioner praised the officers for
greatly reducing the incidence of hijackings and the
involvement of corrupt police officers in them. Many
'jackers and their police allies were behind bars; others,
against whom cases could not be made, had been driven
out of the business. The real answer was made clear in
several other memos, announcing the formation of several
anti-terrorist and -drug task forces. Resources within the
NYPD were limited, always true, and stolen TVs fall
pretty low on the gotta-stop-it scale, compared with
al-Qaeda wannabes in Westchester targeting synagogues
and Times Square.

Well, good news for him. This meant it was all the more likely J and Nanci were still free and would be able to help him.

His first reaction was to pick up the phone and call Amelia, tell her that what she'd done – betting on him – had paid off. But then he decided not to. He'd called her earlier but she hadn't picked up. He sensed she wouldn't pick up now either. Anyway, he wanted something more substantive to tell her and he still had to track down this J, convince him to help. And Nick didn't have a lot of street cred. Former cop *and* former con. That meant a lot of folks, from both sides of the swamp, wouldn't be real inclined to help him out.

Also, talking to Amelia would give free rein to those feelings again, and that was not, he guessed, a good idea.

Or was it?

He pictured her again, that long red hair, her face, the full lips. She seemed hardly to have aged while he was inside. He remembered waking up beside her, listening to the clock radio, the announcer: 'Ten-ten WINS . . . you give us twenty-two minutes, we'll give you the world.'

Reflect later, he told himself bluntly. Get your ass in gear. You've got work to do.

CHAPTER 25

Their first argument of substance.

About something small. But an essential aspect of forensic work is that something small can mean the difference between a killer killing once more or never again.

'It's *your* database,' Juliette Archer was saying to Rhyme. 'You put it together.' A concession of sorts. But then she added, 'That was, of course, a while ago, no?'

They were in the parlor. Mel Cooper was the only one present. Pulaski was home, as was Sachs, with her mother.

Cooper was holding a dry marker, glancing with his infinitely patient face from Rhyme to Archer, waiting for a conclusion to settle like a bee on a stamen. So far, only flutter.

Rhyme replied, 'Geologic shifts happen rather slowly in my experience. Over millions of years, in fact.' A subtle but acerbic assault on her position.

The issue was a simple one, having to do with the humus – decomposed earth – Sachs had found at the earlier crime scene. The composition of the humus, Rhyme believed, dictated that its source was Queens, and, because of the large amounts of fertilizer and weed killer (he too largely discounted bombs and human poisons), it was a place where an impressive lawn was important, like a country club, resort, mansion, golf course.

Archer thought Queens was too restrictive, even though Rhyme's soil database, which, yes, he'd compiled years ago at the NYPD, suggested that the trace Sachs had found came from the eastern portion of the borough, where it bordered Nassau County.

She explained her reasoning: 'I'll give you that the soil material might've *originated* in Queens. But how many gardening and landscaping businesses are there? Tons.'

'Tons?' Rhyme's tone sneered at the imprecise word.

'Many,' Archer corrected. 'It could have been shipped to a resort in Westchester, where it picked up the herbicides and fertilizer. Or a golf course on Staten Island, for a dirt trap or something there—'

Rhyme said, 'I don't think they have those at golf courses. Dirt traps.'

'Whatever they might have, the courses order landscaping supplies and soil from Queens and have them shipped to New Jersey, Connecticut, the Bronx,' she replied. 'Our unsub might've picked the trace in Bergen County, where he lives or works, and left a sample at the scene. He does woodworking at a posh country club there.'

'Possibly. But we play the odds,' Rhyme explained. 'It's more likely than not that our perp was in Queens when he picked up the humus.'

Archer would not back down. 'Lincoln, when we do medical investigations in epidemiology, tracing infectious diseases, the worst thing you can do is draw a conclusion prematurely. Do you know the myopia study?'

Nearsightedness was relevant why? Rhyme wondered. 'Missed it.' His own eyes were on the single-malt whisky bottle perfectly in focus but hovering just out of reach.

Archer continued, 'A few years ago some doctors noticed that children who slept with the lights on were more likely to develop myopia. The MDs began to create programs to modify children's sleeping habits, change the lighting in the room, arrange for counseling if children were anxious in the dark. Lots of money was spent on campaigns to reduce myopia.'

'And?'

'The researchers got the causation fixed in their head at the beginning. Lights on leads to myopia.'

Despite his impatience he was intrigued. 'But that wasn't the case.'

'Nope. Myopia is genetic. Because of *their* vision problems, *parents* with severe myopia tended to leave the lights on in their children's rooms more frequently than parents with normal eyesight. Leaving lights on didn't cause myopia; it followed *from* myopia. And that causation error set research back years. My point, in our case, is that if we're convinced he has a connection with Queens, we'll stop looking at the other possibilities. Once you get something into your head do you know how hard it is to dislodge?'

'Like the Pachelbel Canon? I truly dislike that piece of music.'

'I find it lovely.'

Rhyme said stridently, 'We know for a fact he has a Queens connection. White Castle burgers and the car service he used there. Probably some shops he goes to. The plastic bag, recall?'

'That's *western* Queens. By the East River. The soil and fertilizer are from miles away, east. Look, I'm not saying *ignore* Queens but give it gradiently less importance.'

He didn't believe he'd ever heard that adverb.

Archer persisted. 'Look for other locales in the New York City area where landscaping supplies from Queens were delivered. That's all. He might've picked up the trace in the Bronx or Newark, New Jersey.'

'Or Montana,' Rhyme mused with the cool, sardonic tone he quite loved. 'Let's get a dozen officers together and have them canvass Helena for somebody who visited an eastern Queens landscaping company for a lawn gnome.'

Patience finally depleting, Mel Cooper brandished the marker again and asked, 'What do you want me to write up on the board?'

Rhyme said, 'Put the humus originated in Queens but that our perp might have picked it up in Montana. No, let's start alphabetically. Alabama, Alaska, Arizona, Arkansas . . .'

'Lincoln. It's getting late,' Cooper said.

He asked Archer, 'Can you live with Queens with a question mark?'

'Two question marks,' she countered.

Ridiculous. Did the woman ever back down? 'All right. Two goddamn question marks.'

Cooper wrote.

Rhyme said, 'And don't forget the "well-tended lawn."' He glanced at Archer, who seemed to have no objections.

The fact was that he enjoyed this. Debate was the

heart-and-soul of crime scene work, the back-and-forth. He and Sachs used to do this all the time.

Thom appeared in the doorway. 'Lincoln.'

'Oh, I know that tone. You better get used to it, Juliette: the caregiver of the iron fist. Make sure you brush the little teeth and tinkle and hit the hay.'

'You've been up for too many hours today,' Thom said. 'And your blood pressure's been high lately.'

'It's high because you *hound* me to check my blood pressure.'

'Whatever the reason,' the aide said with infuriating cheer, 'we can't afford it to be so high. Can we?'

In fact, no, he couldn't. A quad's physical condition leads to several maladies that could be life threatening. Sepsis from bedsores, respiratory problems, blood clots and the ace of spades: autonomic dysreflexia. When an even minor irritation – like a full bladder – goes unrelieved, because the brain's unaware of it, various changes occur as the body tries to regulate itself. Often the heart rate slows and, in compensation, the blood pressure rises. It can lead to strokes and death.

'All right,' he said, surrendering. He would have fought longer but it occurred to him that he had to be a reasonable model for Archer. She too would be at risk from dysreflexia and she'd have to take the threat seriously.

'My brother'll be here any minute, anyway,' she said. 'I'll see you tomorrow.' She wheeled into the front hallway.

'Yes, yes, yes,' Rhyme muttered, staring at the evidence charts. Thinking: What do the clues tell us – where is your next move going to be, Unsub 40? And where do you hang your hat?

Is it Montana, Alabama, Westchester . . . the Bronx? Or is it *Queens*??

'Man walks into a bar. Says, "Hell, that hurt."'

Nick was speaking to the back of a man he'd snuck up behind, sitting at a bar – the other kind.

Freddy Caruthers didn't turn. He kept his eyes on the TV above the premium booze. This was happening in a somewhat classy pub in Brooklyn, Park Slope. 'Hell. I know that voice. No. No way. Nick?'

'Hey.'

Now Freddy turned, looked Nick up and down and waited all of a half second to hug him.

The man pretty much resembled a toad.

Though a friendly, cheerful one, a grin burned onto his toady face.

'Man, man, man. Heard you were out.' He backed off and gave an arm's-length gaze. 'Damn.'

Freddy and Nick went way back. They'd been classmates, public school classmates (no private schools in Sandy Hook, at least not for them). Nick was the good-looking one, the athlete. Freddy – five two then and now – couldn't swing a bat or catch a pass, let alone dunk. But he had other skills. You needed a term paper, he'd write one for you. Free of charge. You needed to know if Myra Handleman had a date for the prom, he'd tell you who and give good advice how to convince her to break it and say yes to you instead. You needed help on a test, Freddy had a knack for knowing what questions would be asked (students speculated that he broke into teachers' offices late at night – some said in a ninja outfit – but Nick suspected that Freddy simply thought the way the teachers thought).

Nick had built his cred on an impressive batting average and the class officer thing – looks too, sure.

Freddy had nurtured his differently, by working the system the way Amelia would needle-valve a carburetor. The rumor was Freddy got laid more than anybody else in high school. Nick doubted it but he still remembered that the plum Linda Rawlins, a foot taller and *Cosmo* beautiful, was Freddy's date to the junior prom. Nick stayed home with TV and the Mets.

'So. What're you up to, man?' Nick asked, sitting down. He gestured to the bartender and ordered a ginger ale.

Freddy was nursing a beer. A lite.

'Consulting.' And Freddy laughed. 'How's that for a job title? Ha! Really. Sounds like I'm a hit man or some shit. But it's like *Shark Tank*.'

Nick shook his head. No clue.

'A TV show about business start-ups. I hook entrepreneurs up with investors. Small business. I learned Armenian and—'

'You what?'

'Armenian. It's a language.'

'I know it is. But what?'

'Lot of Armenians here.'

'Where?'

'New York. I put together Armenian businessmen with money people. Not just Armenians but anybody. Lot of Chinese.'

'You speak—'

'*Nee-how!*'

'Rich.' They high-fived.

Freddy grimaced. 'Mandarin's a bitch. So, you did your time. You're out. That's good. Say, I heard your brother passed. I'm sorry about that.'

Nick looked around. He took a breath. Then, in a soft voice, told Freddy about his brother, his own innocence.

Toady eyes narrowed. 'No shit, man . . . That's heavy.'

'Donnie didn't know what he was getting into. You remember him, a child.'

'We always thought he had some problems, sure. Nobody cared. Just, he wasn't quite right. All respect.'

'No worries,' Nick said, sipping the soda he'd ordered.

'Delgado. Doesn't surprise me. Piece of crap. Total floating crap. Deserved what he got.'

Nick said, 'You treated him good – Donnie.'

'And there's no way he could've done time.' Freddy toyed with his beer bottle, peeling the wet label down. 'You did the right thing. Jesus, I don't know I could've done that.' He grinned. 'Course, my brother's an asshole. I woulda let him spin in the wind.'

Nick laughed hard. 'But now I've got to get my life back. I've lost some years. I'm going to get a business going.'

'Find a lady, Nick. Man needs a woman in his life.'

'Oh, I'm working on that.'

'Good for you. And you can still have kids.'

'You've got the twins, right?'

'And two more. Twins're boys. The four- and five-year-old're girls. The wife said enough is enough. But, hell, that's what God put us here for, right? So you need some money? I can stand you to some. Not a lot. Ten, twelve K.'

'No, no, I'm fine there, got some inheritance.'

'Shit, really?'

'But, Freddy, I do need a favor.'

'What?'

'I found out that there's somebody who might know about the 'jacking Donnie was behind. Maybe he was a fence, maybe he just took delivery of some merch. Maybe he financed the job. I'm hoping he knows I wasn't behind it. I gotta find him.'

'Who is it?'

'That's the problem. I don't have much to go on. I could ask around the 'hood, but you know—'

'Sure, nobody'd trust you. Think you were a CI or something.'

'Well, that, yeah. But mostly, if this guy was actually connected, I can't really be seen talking to him.'

'Oh, shit, sure. The parole thing.'

'That's it.'

'You need *me* to ask around?'

Nick raised his hands. 'You can say no.'

'Nick, I gotta say there was a lot of people in the 'hood who didn't believe it. They thought some other cop fucked you over 'cause you wouldn't play along. Everybody liked you. You were a golden boy. Sure, I'll help you.'

Nick slapped Freddy's arm and felt his eyes welling up. 'Means everything to me, man.'

'What kind of business you looking at?'

'Restaurant, I've decided.'

'Yeah. Ballbreaker work. But there's money to be made.

I do some Armenian restaurant deals. You ever have Armenian food?'

'No. I never have. Don't think so.'

'You'd like it. Middle Eastern, you know. I do more shoe stores and clothes and prepaid phone card operations but some restaurants.'

'My lawyer's looking for one.'

'So this guy?' Energetic, Freddy drained his beer and ordered another.

'This guy I was mentioning? Yeah. He hangs in Flannigan's. Or did.'

'Oh, then likely connected.'

'Right. His first name starts with a J. And he's got a wife named Nanci.'

'And that's it? That's all you know?'

''Fraid so.'

'Well, it's a start. I'll do what I can, man.'

'One way or another I'll make it up to you.'

'Don't worry about it.' Freddy laughed. 'Those were the days, high school. Going to Shea or up to the Bronx. Remember that feeling, early in the season? You—'

'Oh, Jesus. I know what you're going to say. You walk up the stairs before the game, into the stadium, and through the tunnel into the stands and there's the whole park in front of you like Saint Peter opened the gates.'

'The smell of everything. Wet concrete, popcorn, beer, the grass.'

'Fertilizer too, I think.'

'Never thought about that. Yeah, probably fertilizer. You know, Nicky Boy, maybe it won't be that hard to find this guy, J, and his lady . . . What's her name again?'

'Nanci. With an i.'

'Nanci. Since you went in, there's this thing called data mining.'

'What's that?'

'Let's just say you can do all the searching you need by sitting on your ass.'

'I've used Google.'

'That's a place to start. But there's more to it than that. There're services. You drop a few bills, they can find anything. I kid you not. A little bit of luck, you'll get his name, address, where he went to school, what kind of dog he has, how big Nanci's tits are and how long his dick is.'

'Seriously?'

Freddy frowned. 'Okay. Probably not the boobs and dick, but that's not *im*possible. The world has changed, my friend. The world has changed.'

FRIDAY

IV THE PEOPLE'S GUARDIAN

CHAPTER 26

At 12:30 a.m., Abe Benkoff took a last sip of his brandy and clicked off the streaming *Mad Men* episode with ten minutes left to go. He liked the show – he worked in advertising, one of the biggies in Midtown, though on Park, not Madison – but without Ruth here, it wasn't as much fun to watch. He'd save the episode for when she returned from her mother's in Connecticut the day after tomorrow.

Benkoff, fifty-eight, was sitting in his leather lounger in the couple's town house in Murray Hill. Many old buildings here but he and Ruth had found a three-bedroom co-op in a building that was only six years old. A motivated seller. That coincided with Abe's promotion to partner of WJ&K Worldwide, which meant a bonus. Which became the down payment. Still more than they could afford, technically. But with the kids gone, Ruth had said, 'Go for it.'

And they had.

Great for entertaining. And it was just a walk to his job and hers, at a publisher in Times Square.

Abe and his wife had sunk tens of thousands into the decor and appliances, stainless steel, glass, ebony. State-of-the-art kitchen – a phrase that Abe would not let a copywriter slip into an ad, though it certainly did describe the room. Brushed-steel stove and oven and other accessories.

Tonight, though, he'd cranked up nothing more than the microwave, zapping General Tso's Chicken from Hunan Host, up the street. Not so great in the calorie department but it had been a busy day, he'd gotten home late and didn't have the energy – or inclination – to whip up something healthy.

Was General Tso from Hunan province? Benkoff wondered, rising stiffly from the chair and gathering the dishes. And if not, would he be offended that he was being honored by a restaurant with roots in a different locale from his own?

Or was Hunan Host run by Taiwanese or Koreans or an enterprising couple from Laos?

It's all in the marketing, as Abe Benkoff knew quite well, and Cambodian Star might raise a few questions and discourage diners. Or Pol Pot Express, he thought, both smiling and acknowledging his bad taste.

The plates and glass and utensils he took to the kitchen, rinsed and stacked them in the dishwasher rack. Abe started to leave then paused and returned. Then rearranged the dishes and utensils the way Ruth would have wanted. They loaded the appliance differently. He believed he was right – sharp ends down – but that was a battle not worth fighting. It was like trying to convince a Dem to vote Republican or vice versa.

After a shower, he donned pajamas and, snagging a book from above the toilet, he flopped into bed. There he set the alarm for six thirty, thinking about the health club. He laughed to himself and reset it for seven thirty.

Benkoff opened to page thirty of the thriller, read five paragraphs, closed the book, doused the light and, rolling onto his side, fell asleep.

Exactly forty minutes later Abe Benkoff gasped and sat up in bed.

He was fully awake, sweating, gagging, from what was wafting through his bedroom.

Gas!

The room was filled with cooking gas! That rotten-egg stink. There was something wrong with the stove. Get the hell out! Call 911. But get out first.

Holding his breath, he instinctively reached for the bedside lamp and clicked it on.

He froze, his fingers gripping the switch. Are you out of your mind? But the light didn't, as he'd thought in a moment of icy panic, set the gas off and blow the apartment to pieces. He didn't know what might do that but apparently a lightbulb wasn't sufficient. Hand shaking, he shut the bulb out before it got hotter.

Okay, he thought, stumbling to his feet, the danger's not explosions – not yet. But you're going to suffocate if you don't get out. Now. He pulled his robe on, feeling dizzy. He dropped to his knees and breathed slowly. Still the stink, sure, but it wasn't as bad lower, near the floor. Whatever was in natural gas, it seemed to be lighter than air and at the ground level he could breathe all right. He inhaled several times and then rose.

Clutching his phone, he made his way through the darkened apartment, picking his route thanks to the ample illumination from outside, washing through the ten-foot-high windows, unobstructed by curtains. His wife insisted on this and, though he didn't care much for the glare and the lack of privacy, he silently thanked her for it now. He was sure that if there'd been curtains he might've stumbled in the dark, knocking over a lamp or some furniture, metal against stone . . . producing a spark that would ignite the gas.

Benkoff made it down the hall to the living room.

The smell was growing stronger. What the hell had happened? A broken pipe? Just his place or the entire floor? Or the whole building? He remembered the story of an apartment in Brooklyn where a gas main explosion had leveled the five-story structure, killing six people.

His head was growing lighter and lighter. Would he faint before he got to the front door? He had to pass the kitchen, where the gas probably was coming from. The fumes would be greatest there. Maybe he could open one of the windows in the den – he was just outside the doorway – and suck in more air.

No, just keep going. Most important, get out!

And resist making a phone call to the fire department now. The phone might ignite the gas. Just keep going. Fast, fast.

Dizzier, dizzier.

Whatever happened, he was so very glad that Ruth wasn't home. Pure luck that she'd decided to stay in Connecticut after her business meetings.

Thank you for that, he thought to a generic god. Abe Benkoff hadn't been to temple in twenty years. A lapse that would end next Friday, he decided – if he got out of here.

Then into the hallway and staggering toward the

front door. He stumbled once, dropped the phone, snagged it and began to crawl again. He'd get outside, slam the door behind him. Hit the fire alarm, warning the other tenants, and dial 911.

Twenty feet, ten.

The fumes weren't so bad here in the front hallway of the apartment, some distance from the stove. Five feet to safety.

A man of words and numbers, a man at home in the rarified world of offices, Benkoff now became a soldier, thinking only of survival. I'm going to make it. Goddamn it, I am.

CHAPTER 27

Lincoln Rhyme was awakened by his humming phone.

The clock: *6:17 a.m.*

'Answer' was the groggy command to the unit. 'Yes?' Directed to the caller.

'Rhyme, another one.'

He asked Amelia Sachs, 'Unsub Forty?'

'Right.'

'What happened?'

'Murray Hill. Gas explosion. Looks like he sabotaged a stove – one of the products on the list Rodney found.'

'And the vic was on the second list, the purchasers?'

'Right. Put a new kitchen in a couple of years ago. Purchase information was in the data.'

Rhyme pressed his attendant button, to summon Thom.

Sachs continued, 'Victim is Abe Benkoff, fifty-eight, advertising executive.' She paused a moment. 'Rhyme, he burned to death. Ron's pulling the vic's vitals. I'm going to get down there now, run the scene.'

They disconnected. Rhyme called Mel Cooper, summoning him back to the town house in anticipation of analyzing what Sachs would find at Benkoff's.

Thom arrived for the morning routine and in ten minutes Rhyme was downstairs, in the parlor. He turned his chair at an oblique angle and eased toward the evidence charts, looking over the findings from the past crime scenes, concerned that there might have been something they'd missed – *he'd* missed – that could have let them anticipate this attack.

Murray Hill . . .

A fancy stove . . .

Gas explosion . . .

It was always a long shot, making an educated guess from the evidence in past crimes as to where the perp might strike in the future. In essence, doing so was dependent on the unsub's visiting scenes to plan a crime, accidentally picking up evidence there and then depositing it at another scene, where it was discovered. Most serial killers or multiple doers weren't so helpful.

But Unsub 40 had such a curious agenda and wielded such an odd weapon that it seemed he would have to do some homework a day or two or even more ahead of time to make sure he'd succeed with the murder.

Benkoff's death, he thought grimly, might be the opposite of the Baxter case, the scam artist whose death led to Rhyme's retirement. There Rhyme had had too much evidence and had parsed it too carefully. Perhaps in the Unsub 40 situation he'd *missed* some clue in prior scenes that might have pointed to Abe Benkoff's apartment as the site of a future attack. And he experienced that unnerving hollowness he'd felt when he learned of the businessman's death. The uneasiness and, okay, guilt that had prompted his decision to end his career as a criminal forensic investigator.

This validated that decision. He couldn't wait for this case to be done with. And he could get back to his life in the *civil* world – he smiled at the double-duty word – once more.

His phone hummed again.

Glancing at caller ID.

'Hello?'

'I saw the news,' Juliette Archer said. 'The fire in Murray Hill. Stove malfunctioned. Was that our boy?'

'Looks like it. I was just about to call you. You free?'

'Actually, I'm on my way.'

Thinking about pain.

Breakfast in bed, just after waking, in Chelsea. I ate one sandwich – bologna, very underrated nowadays – and now am having another.

Six fifty a.m.

I'm tired after all the work last night. I tried to sleep in but couldn't. Way too excited.

Pain . . .

Because of my recent endeavors, I've studied the subject. I've learned there are various types. Neuropathic, for instance, is when a nerve is struck or impinged upon (hitting your funny bone – oh, yeah, nothing funny 'bout *that*, is there?). Not necessarily excruciating. More twitchy and irritating.

Then there's psychogenic, or somatoform, pain. This comes from environmental factors and stress and some physiologic stimuli. Migraines, for instance.

But the most common in our daily life is called nociceptive. Fancy word, I think, for when you miss the nail with your hammer and squoosh your thumb instead. A couple of fine categories of nociceptive give connoisseurs like myself much to work with. I think of Todd Williams: blunt trauma impact. Or rending with a razor saw (I used that not long before). Another: Alicia's radius bone sprouting through her flesh as her husband, dull from whisky, twisted and pulled.

And then there's thermal nociceptive pain. Cold, yes. But the worst is heat, of course. Freezing numbs. Fire makes you scream and scream and scream.

I had a pretty good view of my victim's last few minutes. I was watching him the whole time, from across the street, the roof terrace of a not-very-secure five-story walk-up. It was easy to see him through the large windows. Waking up, idiotically turning on the light on the bedside table – worried me there. Wasn't sure at that point if there was enough gas in the place to do what I hoped.

But a moment later he was walking toward the door, then crawling.

At that point I was sure there was enough gas and – feeling a bit perverse – I flicked the switch when he was only a half dozen feet from the door, safety well within his grasp.

Except it hadn't been, of course.

A simple command through the cloud and the CookSmart Deluxe stove came to life. Eleven thousand dollars buys you a very responsive appliance.

And my victim turned into a shadow in the flames, twitching and staggering, and staggering still when the smoke enshrouded him, though I caught a glimpse of him rolling onto his back, quivering, and turning pugilistic with hands and legs up. I lost sight and the smoke flowed and flowed and flowed.

At least he got a few good meals out of the fancy oven.

The job done, I left and came back here, filled with robust satisfaction, for a bit of sleep.

The People's Guardian will write another missive to the press later, reminding them that excessive consumerism is a bad thing. Blah, blah, blah. You don't have to be too articulate and clever with your manifestos after you burn someone to death. Object lessons teach best.

I roll from bed and, in my pajamas, sit groggy on the bedside, think of the busy day ahead.

I have plans for another poor Shopper.

Nociceptive pain . . .

There are plans for Red too. I know now all I need to about her habits, I think. It should be good. It certainly will be enjoyable to me, what I have planned.

I have some time, so I go into the Toy Room.

The way I work when I build a miniature is to draw a blueprint first, though it's not blue. Then I focus on each part of the item I'm making. Legs, drawers, tops, frames – whatever it might be. And I go in order of the most difficult task to easiest. Carving eighteenth-century legs, for instance, is so very hard. Spindly yet complex, with swells and knobs and sweeps, angular. I coax them out of blocks of wood. I smooth with the blade and sand carefully. Then comes assembly. The one I'm holding now is an Edwardian bed for an American Girl client, the father a lawyer in Minneapolis. I know because his check to my company includes the triplet 'esq.' after his name. I almost didn't do the job because Alicia told me of the trouble she had with lawyers after the situation with her husband. She was innocent of any wrongdoing; you'd think all would have gone well for her. But no. And it was the lawyers to thank. But I need to make a living and she wouldn't care, I don't think. Anyway, I didn't tell her.

Peering through the magnifier, I ease the dowel joints together, knowing they'll fit since I've measured twice. A joke. The old expression. Actually I measure a dozen times before cutting.

Furniture, as lessons for life.

In an hour the bed is nearly done and I look at it for some time under the ring of light on the business side of the magnifier glass. I tend to want to do some more finishing work but restrain myself now. Many pieces are ruined because the artisan didn't know when to stop (a life lesson, I was saying). But I know when to stop. In a few days, after the varnish is long dried and rubbed smooth I will pack it up in bubble wrap and foam peanuts and ship it off.

As I study the piece and make a few final touches I click on the tape recorder. I just listen now. I'll transcribe this entry of the diary later.

Quite the interesting spring. Helped them with calc, though they were pretty smart, I was surprised, for athletes. Frank and Sam. Prejudice to say, like people say I'm really smart because I'm a beanpole and geekish which I'm not. I'm okay smart and math comes easy. Science. Computers. Not other things, though.

And we are having pizza and soda at Sam's house and his father comes in and says hi to me and he's pretty nice. He asks if I like baseball, which I don't, of course, because my father sits and smokes and watches games hour after hour and doesn't talk to us. But because our father sits and smokes and watches games hour after hour, especially if it's St. Louis or Atlanta, I know enough about the game to sound like I'm not an idiot (and I know how to throw a knuckleball, ha!!! Even if not very well). And I can talk about some players. Some stats.

Frank comes over and we start talking and Sam says let's have a graduation party, and at first I think this is a mistake that he's said this not thinking because I'm here, since I've never been invited to any party at the school, but the math club party and the computer club party, but they're not really parties. Also, I'm a junior. But Frank says that's cool, a party, and then turns to me and says I'll be in charge of the music, and that's it. Which means not only am I invited but I have an important thing to do.

Music could be the most important part. I don't know – because, yeah, I've never been to a party before. But I'm going to do a good job.

I click off the recorder, inspired to get cracking. I sit down at my computer, log into several virtual private networks serially, then head to Bulgaria and one of the Shitloadistans for a proxy.

I sit back and close my eyes. Then, channeled by the People's Guardian, I begin to type.

Nick Carelli's mobile hummed.

His lawyer.

When he'd gone into the system, caller ID was in its infancy. Now it was everywhere and, he'd decided, the most important thing invented in the past hundred years.

'Hey, Sam.'

'Nick. How's it going? You adjusting well?'

'As can be expected.'

'Sure. Well. I've got a place for you to check out. I've emailed the address and the deal sheet. It's preliminary so we'll still have a lot of due diligence to do. The place is out a way so the asking isn't going to give you a coronary. You get closer to the Heights and hipsters, there's better revenue but you couldn't afford it.'

'Great, man. Thanks. Hold on. I'll check it out now.'

Nick went online and noted the address – solid, working-class and striving neighborhood in BK – and the name of the owner. 'Is he there now?' Nick was feeling the electric prods again. Impatience. He recalled Amelia's slogan: When you move they can't getcha . . .

'Yeah. He's there. I just talked to his lawyer.' Then Sam fell silent. 'Listen, Nick, are you sure you want to do this?'

'You gave me the lecture before.'

'I did, yes. It would've been nice if you'd listened to me.'

'Funny.'

'Restaurants're one of the biggest money sucks in history. This one, okay, it's got decent cash flow and a loyal clientele. I know it. I've been to it. Been around for twenty years, so it's got serious goodwill. But still, you've never run a company before.'

'I can learn. Maybe I could hire the owner to stick around, be a consultant. He's got an interest in making sure the place stays open and's successful.' The proposal was the owner would get the purchase price plus a cut of the action. 'He's gotta have a sentimental attachment to the place. Wouldn't you think?'

'I'd guess, sure.'

'It's late in the game for me, Sam. I need to get going with my life. Oh, but the other thing I asked you.'

'I checked and triple-checked. Not a hint of criminal activity. The owner, his family, any of the employees. No records. Clean with the IRS and state too. Passed a couple of audits with flying colors. And I'm working on the liquor waiver.'

'Good. Thanks, Sam. I'm so psyched.'

'Nick. Slow down. You sound like you're ready to sign the paperwork today. Don't you at least want to try the lasagna?'

CHAPTER 28

Amelia Sachs returned to the town house with what seemed to Rhyme measly evidence. Two milk crates containing a half-dozen paper and plastic evidence collection bags.

The damn unsub kept burning things up and turning evidence to ash. Water was the worst elemental contaminant of crime scenes; fire was a close number two.

These boxes she handed off to Mel Cooper, who was wearing a lab coat over his corduroy beige slacks and short-sleeve white shirt, as well as surgical cap and gloves. 'That's all?' he asked, looking toward the door, thinking perhaps that other ECTs were bringing in more evidence.

Her grimace said it all. Nothing else would be forthcoming.

'Who was he?' Juliette Archer asked. 'The victim?'

Ron Pulaski glanced through his notes: 'A fifty-eight-year-old advertising account executive. Pretty senior. Abe Benkoff. He was responsible for some famous TV commercials.' The young officer ran through some of them. Rhyme, never a TV watcher, had not heard of the ad, though, of course, he knew the clients: food companies, personal products, cars, airlines. 'Fire marshal said they're a week away from anything specific as to how it happened but off the record: There was a gas leak from a CookSmart range and oven. Six-burner gas stovetop, an electric oven. With the DataWise you can turn the stove on remotely – both the burners and the oven. It's mostly designed to shut them off if you leave and think you might have left them on. But it works the other way too. The unsub, it seemed, disengaged the pilot light sparkers – those *click, click* things – and then turned the gas on.

'The marshal said the flow had to be going for close to forty minutes, given the size of the explosion. Then the unsub turned the sparkers back on. The whole place blew. Benkoff was about five, six feet from the front door. Looked like he was trying to get out. The gas woke him up, they think.'

Archer: 'Anyone else in the place?'

'No. He was married but his wife was out of town, business trip. They had two grown children. Nobody else in the building was hurt.'

Sachs began a whiteboard for this crime scene.

Her phone hummed and she took a call. After a brief conversation she hung up. Shrugged to Rhyme. 'Another reporter about my statement to the press – about the security patches that CIR uploaded to its clients. The story's got legs.' She was pleased. Her anonymity had vanished and she was now the go-to cop for journalists writing about the use of smart controllers as weapons. Word apparently was spreading about the dangers of products embedded with DataWise5000 controllers. And, according to the reports, people were paying attention.

She added, 'Even if companies aren't intimidated into

Chaudhary's security updates, at least we can hope their customers read the stories and stay offline or unplug their appliances.'

Rhyme's computer sounded with an incoming news story on an RSS feed. 'He's sent out another chapter of the manifesto.'

Greetings:

Another lesson delivered.

My feeling is that people begin as innocents. Some philosopher, I don't know whom, said that way back. One of the famous ones. We are born sweet and pure: we do not have an inbred lust to possess Unnecessary things, to have a better car, a bigger hot tub, a better-definition television set. A MORE EXPENSIVE STOVE!!! We have to be taught that. But, I feel taught is not the right word. The right word is INDOCTRINATED. It's the product manufacturers, the marketers the advertisers that browbeat and intimadate us into purchasing bigger and better, suggesting we can't live without this or that.

Yes, think about it. Think about your Possessions. What do you have that you can't live without? Precious little. Close your eyes. Walk through your house in your mind. Pick up an object, look it over. Think about where you got it? A gift? From a friend? It's the FRIENDSHIP that's important not the token of it. Throw it out. Do this with one thing a day.

And, more important stop buying things: Buying is an act of desparation and, apart from staples like clothes and simple food, an addiction.

You do not NEED a kitchen appliance, that costs so much it could feed a family of four for a year. Well you've PAID the price . . . literally.

— The People's Guardian

'Nut job,' muttered Mel Cooper.

As good a diagnosis as any.

'If he's guarding the people why is he killing them?'

'He's only killing the ones with expensive products,' Rhyme pointed out.

'A distinction that's lost on me,' Archer said. She scanned the diatribe carefully and said, 'If he knows the premise of the philosophy, tabula rasa, he must've heard of John Locke. He's playing down his intelligence again. What look like intentional misspellings. A few *unnecessary* uppercasings — so to speak.'

Rhyme laughed at her comment; one of those words was 'Unnecessary.'

'Colon where a semi would be more appropriate. But using one means he knows how to use the other. Wrong use of "whom."'

'Okay,' Rhyme said, not much interested in the profiling. 'We've established he's corrupting Ms Peabody's English lessons on purpose. Let's get to the evidence. Where did you find that, Sachs?' It seemed there were two separate locations she'd searched; he could tell this from the separate containers.

'I did a fast grid in Benkoff's apartment. Since the unsub's using a remote, he doesn't need to be inside a victim's location. From the lists, he knows who has a product with a smart controller. But I took some samples anyway. Just in case he got in to Benkoff's kitchen and added an accelerant.'

'Ah yes,' Rhyme said. 'He might not have trusted that the natural gas would cause enough damage. Mel, check that first.'

The evidence collection bags Sachs pointed out each featured a glassine strip on which was written the room it had been collected in. The contents were several spoonfuls of ash.

Cooper began the chromatographic and spectromic analysis. As the machine ran and he noted results, Sachs continued, 'But I was thinking of the MO – that he needed to see inside the place. To make sure there was a victim present.'

Archer added, 'And remember Rodney's comment about his being "a decent monster"; he might've wanted to make sure there were no children, say, who were visiting. Or he doesn't want to hurt poorer people. The ones who don't buy the expensive products.'

'Maybe,' Sachs said, though Rhyme could tell she was doubtful. He tended to side with Sachs on this one. Unsub 40 didn't seem troubled by finely parsed ethical concerns. 'I think it was more an issue to make sure he had a victim in his sights. I found the one spot where he could see clearly into the Benkoffs' apartment. The roof across the street. A resident there saw a tall, slim man come out of the lobby just after the explosion. White male, had a backpack, dressed in overalls like a worker. And a baseball cap. I got some trace from where he probably stood.'

'Access?' Rhyme asked.

'He could've taken the fire escape, would have been less visible. But he went for the front door.'

'Lock on that apartment's door?' Archer asked.

Again, stealing the question from Rhyme.

'Old building. Old lock. Easily jimmied. No broken windows. No tool marks to speak of. Took trace from the lobby but . . .' She shrugged.

Archer said, 'Lincoln's book. Smart perps travel routes where there's heavy foot traffic, and where, therefore, the likelihood of isolating usable trace diminishes logarithmically. That's why he entered there.'

Stating the obvious, Rhyme thought, of his own observation. He'd always regretted putting that in the text. 'So what do we have,' he asked impatiently, 'from the roof?'

'For one thing, a piece of glass.' This was Archer's observation. She'd wheeled close to the examination table and was staring at a clear plastic evidence bag, which appeared to contain dust only.

'Spread it out, Mel.'

The tech did.

'I still can't see it,' Rhyme muttered.

'*Them*,' Archer corrected. 'Two, no, three shards.'

'You have microscopic vision?'

Archer laughed. 'God gave me good nails and twenty–twenty vision. That's about it.'

No reference to what He was taking away.

With the help of magnifying goggles, Cooper found and extracted the shards of glass and put them under a microscope. The image was broadcast on the screen. Archer said, 'Window glass, wouldn't you think?'

'That's right,' Rhyme said. He'd analyzed a thousand

samples of glass in his years on crime scene detail – from splinters produced by bullets, falling bodies, rocks and auto crashes to shards intentionally and lovingly turned into knives. The fracture lines and the polished sides of the tiny pieces Sachs had collected left no doubt they were from windows. Not automotive – safety glass was very different – but residential. He mentioned this.

Cooper pointed out. 'There, upper right-hand quadrant? Imperfection.'

It seemed to be a small bubble. Rhyme said, 'Old. And cheap, I'd say.'

'That's what I'd guess. Seventy-five years? Older maybe.'

Modern window glass was much closer to flawless.

'Compare them with the control samples. Where are they, Sachs?'

She pointed out several envelopes; they would contain trace samples from parts of the roof that were nowhere near the place the unsub had stood. Cooper went to work comparing the various items microscopically.

'Okay . . . No other bits of glass.'

And there'd been none in Todd Williams's office building – the unsub had broken in through the back door. And none downstairs here either. Where had he picked it up?

'Anything else, the trace?'

Cooper had to wait to run the samples through the GC/MS. He was still awaiting the results from the ash Sachs had collected. In a few minutes they were finished. He read the compiled data. 'No accelerant.'

'So that tells us he most likely didn't break in and pour gas or kerosene around the place.'

'It wasn't likely anyway,' Archer said.

'Why do you say that?' Sachs asked

'Gut feel. Almost like he's proud he's using the controller as a murder weapon. It would be . . . I don't know, inelegant to have to add gasoline.'

'Maybe,' Sachs said.

Rhyme agreed with Archer but said nothing.

'Burn the other trace. From his vantage point on the roof.'

For a half hour or so, Cooper ran various samples through the machine, the chromatograph separating the components, the MS identifying them. Rhyme watched impatiently. Finally Cooper listed them:

Diesel fuel, no brand identified. Two soil samples, indigenous to shoreline Connecticut, Hudson River, New Jersey and Westchester County.

'Not Queens with two question marks?' Rhyme said wryly. Archer smiled his way. Sachs noted this, turned back to the whiteboard on which she was writing down their findings.

The tech continued. A number of samples of soft drinks: Sprite, and regular and Diet Coca-Cola, all in various dilutions, which meant they came from cups that contained ice; the beverage was not drunk directly from can or bottle. White wine, high sugar content. Typical of inexpensive sparkling or still white.

Silence flowed into the parlor, broken only by the tap of the gas chromatograph cooling. The device worked by subjecting its samples to temperatures that were about fifty degrees Celsius higher than the boiling point of the least volatile element of the sample. An inferno, in other words.

Sachs fielded a call. She stepped aside to take it. In a corner of the parlor, she stood with head down. Eventually she nodded and relief was obvious in her face. She disconnected. 'The Borough Shooting Team was convened.' Rhyme recalled – the incident review after she parked a slug in the escalator motor to try to save Greg Frommer's life. 'Madino – the captain – says it's a good panel. Uniforms and shields from the street. I'll write up the FD/AR and that'll be it, he said.'

Rhyme was pleased for her. The NYPD had so many regulations and formalities that they could overwhelm an officer just trying to do the job.

Cooper said, 'Something else here. Traces of rubber, ammonia and the fiber, probably from paper – a paper towel.' He then ran through a lengthy laundry list of trace chemicals.

'Glazing compound,' Rhyme said absently.

'You knew that?' the intern asked, staring at the mouthful of substances, three lines long.

He explained. There'd been a case years ago in which a wife had slashed her husband's jugular with the sharp edge of a pane of glass she'd worked out of the rec room window. As he slept she drew the glass over his jugular and he bled out quickly. She'd cleaned the glass and replaced it in the window, glazing the pane back in place. (Her bizarre strategy was that no murder weapon, that is, knife or other blade, could be traced back to her. Not true, of course, since she neglected to clean from her blouse the traces of glazing compound she'd used on the window after the murder. It took officers all of five minutes to find the pane; a luminol test confirmed the presence of blood.)

Sachs took another call. A cryptic reaction. Eyes flitting from window to floor to rococo ceiling. What was this about? he wondered.

She disconnected and grimaced. She walked to Rhyme. 'I'm sorry. My mother.'

'She's all right?'

'Fine. But they moved up a test.' Her face remained troubled. He knew she was torn between the case and her only close family member.

'Sachs, go,' he said.

'I—'

'Go. You have to.'

Without a word, Sachs headed out of the parlor.

Rhyme stared after her then turned slowly, the motor of his chair uttering a soft whine, and gazed at the challenging whiteboards.

Crime Scene: 390 E. 35th Street, Manhattan (site of arson)

- Offense: Arson/homicide.
- Victim: Abraham Benkoff, 58, account director advertising agency, well known.
- COD: Burns/hemorrhaging.
- Means of death:
    - Gas leak from CookSmart Deluxe range, equipped with DataWise5000 controller.
    - No accelerant.
- Additional elements of profile of suspect:
    - Dark clothes, baseball cap.

– Observing scene to make sure only adult victim killed?

– Another message from the People's Guardian.

▪ Again playing down intelligence.

Crime Scene: 387 E. 35th Street, Manhattan (site of unsub's surveillance)

• Evidence:

– Shards of glass. Window glass, old.

– Xylene, toluene, iron oxide, amorphous silica, dioctyl phthalate and talc (glazing compound).

▪ His profession? Probably not.

– Paper towel fibers.

– Ammonia.

– Rubber fragments.

– Diesel fuel.

– Two soil samples, indigenous to shoreline.

▪ Connecticut, Westchester County, New Jersey.

– Soda, differing dilutions, several sources.

– White wine, high sugar content. Typical of inexpensive sparkling white wine.

Archer too was studying the writing carefully. 'More questions than answers,' she muttered.

Welcome to the world of forensics, Lincoln Rhyme thought.

CHAPTER 29

Sweeney Todd, now, *that* was a challenge.

Joe Heady, a carpenter at the Whitmore Theater in Times Square, was thinking of the successful revival of the Sondheim play a year ago. He and the other set builders and gaffers had had to create a working barber's chair – well, working to the extent that it would drop open on command, allowing the customer to slide into the pit below after the Demon Barber of Fleet Street had sliced open his throat.

They'd worked for months to get the chair to function seamlessly – and to create a wonderfully gothic Dickensian set.

But the set for this job? Damn child's play. Downright boring.

Heady lugged some two-by-four pieces of common-grade pine into the set construction workshop behind the theater on 46th Street and dumped them on the concrete floor. For *this* play his job was to build a large maze, the sort that a rat – make that a two-foot *holographic projection* rat – would poke through at various points in the story, which was about some family gathering and arguing and a bunch of other crap. Not a single cut throat for the entire two hours and change. Having read the script, Heady decided a little literal blood would have helped.

But a maze was what the set designer wanted and a maze she was going to get.

A big man, with bushy black-and-gray hair, Heady arranged the pieces of wood in the order in which he'd cut them and then stiffly rose. Actually grunting. Sixty-one years old, he'd given retirement a shot; he and the wife had moved here after his thirty-six years on the assembly line in Detroit. Living closer to the kids and grandkids in Jersey was great. Up to a point. But Heady wasn't ready to hang up his tools yet, and his son-in-law hooked him up with this job. Heady was basically a machinist – the Detroit thing – but handy is handy, and the theater hired him on the spot for set-building carpentry. He loved the work. Only problem: The wood weighed a lot more than it did twenty years ago. Funny how that happens.

He spread the plans for the maze on a table nearby, then plucked a steel tape measure off his belt and a pencil – an old-time pencil, which he sharpened with a locking-blade knife – from his pocket and set them beside the plans. Pulling on his reading glasses, he reviewed the schematics.

This was one of the nicer theaters on Broadway and definitely one of the best set-building workshops in Manhattan. It was large, sixty by sixty feet, with the south wall stocked with more wood than most lumberyards had in inventory. Against the west wall were the bins of hardware (nails, nuts, bolts, springs, screws, washers, you name it), hand and power tools, workbenches, paint and a small kitchen area. In the middle, mounted to the floor, were the big power tools.

The day was pleasant and the massive double doors

– large enough for the delivery of the biggest props – were open onto 46th Street. A breeze wafted in, carrying smells that Heady liked: car exhaust, perfume from who knew where, charcoal smoke from the nut and pretzel vendors. The traffic was chaotic and people in every style of clothing you could imagine streamed past constantly, surging in every direction. He'd never developed affection for Motown. But now, a convert, he was a devout Manhattanite, even though he lived in Paramus.

And he loved his job too. On nice days like this, with the doors open, passersby sometimes stopped and glanced in, curious to watch the set builders at work. One of Heady's proudest days was when someone called him to the door. The carpenter, anticipating a question about a tool or what set he was working on, was astonished when the man asked for an autograph. He'd loved the sets from the revival of *The King and I* and wanted Heady to sign the *Playbill*.

Heady heated up some water in the microwave, poured in some instant Starbucks coffee and sipped the black brew while he made notes about the cuts he was about to make. He glanced at the bench to make sure a necessary accessory was handy: sound-dampening earmuffs. He absolutely had to wear these because of a device that sat in the middle of the workshop.

The huge Ayoni table saw was the latest addition here. The bulk of the work done in set building on Broadway is carpentry – cutting, framing, joining. The Ayoni was rapidly becoming a workhorse for that task. Weighing in at over three hundred pounds, the device featured circular blades with edges sharp as shark's teeth. The steel blades were interchangeable, in varying thicknesses and tooth depth and shape – the thicker, with larger teeth, were meant for rough frames, the thinner and finer for finishing work. These wicked disks spun at nearly two thousand RPM and screamed as loudly as a jet plane's engines.

The saw would slice through the thickest wood like tearing newsprint and featured a computer chip that remembered settings and dimensions for the past fifty jobs.

To cut the two-by-four pieces for the base of the maze, Heady got a heavy, rough-cut blade from a rack on the wall. Before removing the blade presently mounted to the Ayoni, however, and replacing it with this one, he'd have to shut the power off. The unit was hardwired into the theater's electrical system, since its motor – running at a gutsy eight horsepower – drew 220 volts and many amps.

The manufacturer recommended that you shut off the power to the entire facility at the main circuit breaker before replacing blades, but here at the theater no workers ever did, since the breaker was in the basement. But perhaps because the Ayoni Corporation knew that purchasers might not always cut the main juice, the saw itself had two power cutoffs. One was the device's own circuit breaker. The second was the on/off switch that started the blade spinning. It was a bit inconvenient to reach down, to the base of the machine, find the circuit breaker and click it off, but no way was Heady going to swap blades without doing so. The tool was as dangerous as a guillotine. (He'd heard about an accident in which an assistant had fallen next to an Ayoni as it ran and instinctively reached out to steady himself. His forearm hit the blade and was severed halfway between wrist and elbow in an instant. The poor man had felt not a bit of pain for a good ten seconds, so fast and clean was the cut.)

So he now reached down and popped the breaker.

Then, just to double-check, he flipped on the power switch; nothing. He returned it to the off position. Heady now gripped the blade with his left hand and held it steady while, with a socket wrench in his right, he began to loosen the nuts fixing the disk to the shaft. He was glad that he'd taken the redundant precautions; it occurred to him that should the unit happen to start, not only would he lose the fingers of his left hand but the wrench would crush his right to a pulp.

Two thousand RPM.

But in five minutes the blade was changed safely. The power was back on. And he readied the first piece to cut.

There was no doubting the saw's efficiency; it made all the carpenters' lives so much easier. On the other hand, Healy had to admit he wasn't looking forward to spending the next few hours changing blades and slicing up the wood for the maze.

Fact was, the thing scared the hell out of him.

The waitress offered a flirt.

Mid-thirties, Nick guessed. With a pretty, heart-shaped face, black hair, black as oil, tied up tight, the curls just waiting to escape. Tight uniform too. Low cut. That was one thing he'd change if he became owner of the restaurant. He'd like a little more family-friendly staff. Though maybe the old farts in the neighborhood liked the view Hannah offered.

He smiled back, but with a different smile from hers,

polite and formal, and asked for Vittorio. She stepped away, returned and said he'd be out in a few minutes. 'Have a seat, have some coffee.'

She tried another flirt.

'Black please. One ice cube.'

'Iced coffee?'

'No. A cup. Hot coffee but an ice cube in it.'

Sitting down in the window booth she took him to, Nick looked around at the place. Nice, he assessed. He liked it right away. The linoleum would have to go – too many heel marks – and he'd lose the wallpaper and paint the walls. Maybe dark red. The place had plenty of windows and good lighting. The room could handle walls that color. And he'd put up some paintings. Find some of old Brooklyn, this very neighborhood if he could.

Nick loved the borough. Many people didn't know that BK had been a city unto itself until 1898, when it got absorbed and became a part of New York. In fact, Brooklyn had been one of the biggest cities in the country (was still the biggest borough). He'd find some prints of the waterfront and Prospect Park. Maybe portraits of some famous Brooklynites. Walt Whitman. Sure, had to have him. 'Crossing Brooklyn Ferry,' the poem – good, he'd get a ferry print. And Amelia's father – also from BK – had told him that George Washington and the colonial troops had fought the British here (and lost, but retreated safely to Manhattan, thanks to a frozen river). George Gershwin. Mark Twain supposedly named his character Tom Sawyer after a heroic firefighter from Brooklyn. He'd get pictures of them all. Maybe those pen-and-ink drawings. They were cool. They were classy.

Definitely not one of native son Al Capone, though.

A shadow over him and Nick rose.

'Vittorio Gera.' A thick man, both olive-skinned and ill-colored at the same time. His suit was one size too big and Nick wondered if the reason the restaurant was on the block was his poor health. Probably. The perfect hair, gray, was a piece.

'Nick Carelli.'

'Italian. Where's the family from?'

'Flatbush.'

'Ha!'

Nick added, 'Long time ago, Bologna.'

'We've got Italian on the menu.'

'The lasagna's good, I hear.'

'It is.' Gera sat. 'But have you ever had bad lasagna?'

Nick smiled.

The waitress brought the coffee. 'Anything for you?' she asked Gera.

'No, I'm fine, Hannah. Thank you.' She turned and left.

The man brought his weathered hands together and lowered his head. 'So, I'm Vito.'

'Well, Vito, I'm interested in your place.'

'You ever done restaurants?

'Eaten in them. All my life.'

Well, *most* of my life . . .

The large man laughed. 'They're not for everybody.'

'It's the sort of thing I'd like to do. Always have. A neighborhood place, you know. People can hang out here. Friendly. Socialize. And whatever happens to the economy, people still have to eat.'

'That's all true. But hard work. Hard work.' Looking him over. 'Though you don't seem to be the sort of man who's afraid of work.'

'No, I'm not. Now, I've gotten the deal sheet from my lawyer and I've looked it over. Seems good. And the asking price? I've got some money I inherited from my mother when she passed—'

'I'm sorry.'

'Thank you. And I'm talking to a couple of banks. Now, we're in the ballpark. About the price. A little horse trading and I'm sure we can come to an agreement.'

'Sure – you pay what I'm asking and it's an agreement.' The man was sort-of joking, sort-of not. This was business.

Nick leaned back and said confidently, 'Before we go any farther I have to tell you something.'

'Sure.'

'I'm an ex-con.'

Vito leaned forward and regarded Nick closely, as if he'd just said that he had plastic skin, take a look.

Nick kept his eyes on Vito's and a sincere smile on his face. 'The charges were armed robbery and assault. I didn't do it. I've never done any crime. And I'm working to prove my innocence and I think I'll be exonerated. Maybe I can show you that proof in a few days, maybe it'll take a little longer. But I'm really hoping we can go forward with this anyway.'

'You didn't do it.' Not a question. But an invitation to continue.

'No. I was trying to help somebody and I got caught up in the system.'

'You can't get a liquor license. That's a third of our income.'

'My lawyer's working on a waiver with the city. He thinks it'll go through. With an exoneration, there's no problem.'

'I don't know, Nick. This is a whole 'nother thing. I been here, I've been the owner for twenty years. Reputation, you know.'

'Sure. I understand.' Nick was sounding confident because he was confident. 'But my lawyer says I can get a court to issue a pardon, complete vindication.'

'I've gotta sell soon, Nick.' Vito's hands rose, palms up. 'Have some issues. Health.' He looked across the room, populated by about thirty patrons. One man wanted his check. Gera called to a waiter and pointed it out.

'Help is the problem,' he said. 'People come and go and don't show up or're rude to customers. They steal. You have to let them go. You're like a father and school-master, you know, *headmaster*, all the time. And they'll try to rob you.'

'I'm sure. A business like any other. You got to be on top of it. I was thinking maybe I could hire you to be a consultant for a while.'

'I don't know about that. The health thing. My wife and our daughter're taking care of me. She's moving back into the house. My older daughter. I'll have to take it easy. There're pros out there, you know. Consultants. Food industry consultants. They're pricey but it'd be a good idea in your case.'

'I know. But think about it, Vito. I'd be happy to pay

you. You wouldn't even have to come in. I could come see you twice a week or something.'

'You seem like a nice guy, Nick. And you didn't have to tell me about your past. Not like you're applying to be a fry cook and I check out your references. We agree and you show up at the closing, all I care about is you have a check. But you were straight with me. I gotta tell you, though, I need to think about it.'

'I don't expect anything else. And, Vito – the asking price?'

'Yeah?'

'I could go there.'

'You're not much of a horse trader.'

'I know something good when I see it. Okay, think about it. But a favor?'

'What's that?'

Nick said, 'Don't sell to anybody else without giving me a chance to pitch my case again. Just give me that chance.'

A close examination. 'All right. I'll let you know. Oh, and Nick?'

'Yeah, Vito?'

'I liked it you didn't hit on Hannah. My younger daughter.' He nodded to the black-haired waitress in the tight uniform. 'You scored points there. I'll think about it, Nick, talk it over with my family. Let you know.'

The men shook hands. 'Now, I got one other question, Vito.'

'Sure, son. What's that?'

Nick leaned back and smiled.

CHAPTER 30

'I don't know, Amie.'

Sachs poured some Twinings black tea and gave an inquiring glance to her mother.

They had returned from Rose's X-ray and EKG appointment – everything was on track for the surgery in a few days – and were sitting in the sunny kitchen of Sachs's Carroll Garden town house. Rose was living both here and in her own home, six blocks away. When the woman had appointments it was easier for her to stay here, since her doctor and the hospital where the bypass surgery would occur were nearby. And she'd recover here, after the operation.

'I don't know about *Nick*.' Rose took the NYPD souvenir mug, containing the tea, and added a shot of half-and-half. Sachs was working on a half-empty Starbucks. Tepid, like Nick's. She nuked it back to steaming and sat down across from Rose.

'Was a shock to me. Him showing up.' Sachs examined her mother, wearing a skirt and blouse, hose, a thin gold chain, as befit a thin neck. As always, she'd dressed up for her doctor's appointment as if going to church. 'I'm still not sure what to think.'

'How was it for him, inside the joint?' Rose could have a sense of humor. This had developed later in life.

'We haven't talked about it. No reason to. We don't have anything in common anymore. He's like a stranger. I don't talk to store clerks or somebody I meet on the street about personal things. Why would I talk to him?'

Sachs sensed she was explaining too much, and too quickly. Rose seemed to make this observation too.

'I just hope it works out for him,' Sachs said, ending the conversation. 'I should get back to Lincoln's. Never had a perp like this one.'

'He's a domestic terrorist? That's what the press is saying. And did you hear that story on MSNBC? People aren't taking escalators or elevators. A man had a heart attack in an office building in Midtown, walking up ten flights. He didn't trust the elevator.'

'No. I missed that. Did he die?'

'No.'

Another victim to rack up for Unsub 40.

She asked, 'What do you want me to pick up for dinner? Wait, is Sally coming over?'

'Not tonight. She has bridge.'

'You want to go? I can run you over to her place.'

'No, not feeling like it.'

Sachs thought back to the time when her mother and father had been queen and king of the neighborhood bridge club. What a time that was . . . Cocktails flowed, half of the crowd smoked like a tire fire, and the play for the last few hands was laughably inept, thanks to outrageous strategies concocted in gin and rye hazes. (Sachs had relished those party nights; she could sneak out and hang with the other kids in the neighborhood and even go for a joyride or set up a drag race. Amelia Sachs had been, her own admission, a bad girl.)

The doorbell rang. Sachs walked to the door and looked out.

Well.

Eased the door open.

'Hi,' she said to Nick Carelli. Her voice must've sounded cautious. He smiled uncertainly.

'Took a chance and drove by. Saw your car.'

She eased back and he stepped into the hallway. He was in black jeans, a light-blue dress shirt and navy sport coat. This was dressing up for Nick Carelli. He was carrying a large shopping bag and she smelled garlic and onions.

'I can't stay,' he said, handing the bag over. 'I brought you and Rose lunch.'

'You didn't call.'

'No. I wasn't far away. At a restaurant.'

'Well.' Sachs looked down. 'Thanks, but—'

'Best lasagna in the city.'

The 'but' hadn't referred to the food. She wasn't sure what it was meant to aim at. She glanced down at the bag.

Nick lowered his voice. 'I had a breakthrough last night. In the files you gave me. I found a lead. A guy I think can confirm I didn't have anything to do with the 'jacking.'

'Really? It was in the files?' Treading water verbally here. His unexpected arrival had shaken her.

'Still need to do some digging. Like being a cop all over again.'

Then she frowned. 'Nick, is he connected?'

'I don't know. Maybe. But what I told you before. I'm using a buddy from school to get the particulars. He's fine, he's clean. Never any trouble with the law.'

'I'm glad, Nick.' Her face softened.

'Uhm, Ame . . . Amelia, look, is your mother here?'

A pause. 'She is.'

'Can I say hi?'

'I'm not sure that's a good idea. I told you she hasn't been feeling well.'

A voice from the hallway called, 'I'm well enough to say hello, Amie.'

They turned to see the wiry figure in the hallway, backlit by the large bay windows against the far wall.

'Hello, Rose.'

'Nick.'

'Mom—'

'You brought lunch?'

'Just for you two. I can't stay.'

'We're not ladies who lunch,' Rose said slowly. And Sachs wondered if Rose was about to go on the assault. But her mother added, 'We're ladies who *dine*. We'll save it for tonight.' Rose was looking at the logo on the bag. 'Vittorio's. I know it. Good place.'

'Lasagna, veal piccata, salad, garlic bread.'

Another glance at the heavy bag. 'And, Nick, where are the five people coming to join us?'

He laughed. Sachs tried to.

'Come into the living room. I have the strength to converse but not to stand for very long.'

She turned.

Oh, brother. This is just plain strange. Sachs sighed and followed the other two. She diverted to the kitchen, refrigerated the food and debated getting Nick some coffee. But decided it would take too long to brew and then cool to his taste. She wanted this to be a brief visit. She returned and found Rose in her lounger, Nick on an ottoman in front of the couch, as if sitting on a backless piece of furniture testified to the temporary nature of his stay. Sachs stood for a moment and then pulled a chair from the dining table, set it near her mother and sat down. Upright, leaning forward slightly. She wondered what her California friend Kathryn Dance, an investigator with skills in body language analysis, would have concluded about her posture and the messages it was telegraphing.

'Amie told me about your brother, you taking responsibility for the crime. Your trying to prove your innocence.'

Rose was never one to withhold any stories she'd been told. Sachs had often thought it was a good thing that her mother was largely ignorant of social media. She would have been the hub of a million rumors zipping through the Internet.

'That's right. I found some leads. I hope they'll pan out. Maybe not, but then I'll still keep trying. Rose, Amelia told me you'd been staying with her off and on. That's why I took the chance of coming by today, not just to play delivery boy. I wanted to apologize to you. Both of you together.'

The woman's eyes drilled into his. To Nick's credit, he didn't look away. Sachs believed he was the picture of calm, somebody at last getting something heavy and painful off his chest.

'It was the hardest thing I ever did, cutting things off with Amelia . . . and you. Not telling you the truth about Donnie. But I couldn't risk word getting out that he'd been involved and I hadn't. Amelia can give you the details, if you want them, but I know in my heart this guy Donnie got involved with, this guy who ran a crew – a gang—'

'I know what a crew is. My husband was a police officer all his life.'

'Sure. Sorry. Well, this guy? He would've killed Donnie if I hadn't taken the fall. There was virtually no evidence against me. I was afraid if I told anybody what really happened, Internal Affairs or a prosecutor'd put two and two together and get the idea I was faking it. They wouldn't have to look very far to find Donnie. He was . . .' Nick's voice caught. He cleared his throat. 'He was just a kid, who couldn't take care of himself. Oblivious, you know. He stumbled into the whole mess and got caught up with some bad people.' Nick's eyes seemed damp.

'He was a good boy,' Rose said slowly. 'I didn't realize he had problems.'

'He wanted to get straight, but . . . addiction's tough. I should've done more. I got him into a few programs but I didn't follow up the way I should have.'

Rose Sachs was never one to pat hands. There, there, you did the best you could. She simply nodded, her lips tight. Saying, in effect: Yes, Nick, you should have. Then you wouldn't've gone to prison. And Donnie might still be alive. And you wouldn't have broken my daughter's heart.

'Rose, you might not want to have anything to do with me.' A wan smile, a glance at Amelia. 'I imagine neither of you do. And I completely understand. I just wanted to tell you I had to make a decision and I chose my brother over Amelia and you and dozens of other people. I almost didn't. I almost threw him to the wolves but I went the other way. I'm sorry.' He rose and extended his hand.

Slowly Rose took it and said, 'Thank you, Nick. Apologies are very difficult for some people. Now, I'm feeling a little tired.'

'Sure. I'll be going.'

Sachs walked him to the door.

'I know you didn't expect this. Just something I had to do. Like Donnie? In the Twelve Steps? He had to make the rounds and say he was sorry.' A shrug. 'Or he would have if he'd gotten that far.'

He gave her a spontaneous embrace. Brief. But she felt his hand trembling as it pressed against her neck – her upper spine, she reflected, exactly where Lincoln Rhyme's vertebrae had been snapped. She stepped back. And for a moment debated asking him to tell her what he'd found – this mysterious lead. But she didn't.

Not your issue, she reminded herself.

She closed the door behind him. Then returned to the living room.

'That was odd,' Rose said. 'Speaking of the devil.'

The daughter wondered about the mother's choice of word. Sachs re-nuked her coffee, sipped and threw out the cardboard cup.

'I don't know.' The older woman shook her head.

'I believe him, Mom. He's not going to lie to me.'

'Oh, I think I believe him too. I think he's innocent. That's not what I mean.'

'Then what is it?'

'Nick's decided he made a mistake back then. You should have come first.'

'He's making amends, sure. Why is that a problem?'

'Why did he contact *you* for help?'

A leading question. Sachs hadn't told her that he'd done that. Nor had she shared with her mother that she'd engaged in the legal, but morally murky, effort to download and give him his case files. She'd told her only that he claimed he was innocent, that Sachs believed him and that he was working to prove it.

'Isn't there a procedure – lawyers, review boards – for vindicating yourself?'

Sachs addressed what her mother was really asking: 'Mom. Nick'll get on with his life. I'll get on with mine. That's the end of it. I probably won't ever see him again.'

Rose Sachs smiled. 'I see. Could I please have some more tea?'

Sachs stepped into the kitchen and returned a moment later with a fresh mug. Just as she handed it to her mother, her phone hummed. She pulled it from her pocket, regarded caller ID and answered, 'Rhyme.'

'We have a positive hit, Sachs. Real time. Unsub Forty's in Times Square. Maybe going after a target right now. Get moving. I'll tell you more on the way.'

CHAPTER **31**

Sachs was speeding toward Times Square. In Manhattan on the FDR expressway, racing north.

The traffic wasn't terrible . . . but the drivers were.

They wove; her Torino wove. The consequences of an error in this mutual ballet would have been steel on steel at a speed differential of about forty miles per hour. Potentially bloody and fracturing, if not fatal.

A phone call. She hit the speaker button. 'Go ahead.'

'Here's what we've got, Sachs. Are you there? What was that? That noise?'

'Downshift.'

The sound had been like a jet engine reversing on landing.

Lincoln Rhyme continued, 'Here's what we've got. Was looking over the trace. You found makeup at one of the scenes. We isolated the brand. StarBlend theatrical makeup. And geologic soil from Connecticut, Westchester and New Jersey, all from two of the unsub's footprints. Diesel fuel. Soda in cups and cheap wine or champagne.'

'Tourists in the Theater District: buses from out of town and intermission drinks!'

'Exactly. Either he lives or works in Times Square, likes plays . . . or was planning another attack there when he picked up the trace.'

'What's the hit?'

'As soon as Archer and I figured that out—'

'Archer?'

'Juliette. The intern.'

'Oh.' The wheelchair woman with the beautiful eyes – and God-given nails. Referring to her by last name had confused Sachs.

Traffic cleared and she was cruising again.

'As soon as we figured out it was the Theater District I called COC.'

In the Community Observation Center of the NYPD, based in a cavernous, windowless room at One PP, dozens of officers scanned monitors fed by two hundred thousand CCTVs around the city. There were too many screens to monitor the entire city for a suspect, and algorithms weren't helpful when you had no facial recognition points on your unsub – just 'tall and skinny and probably wearing a baseball cap and carrying a backpack.'

But, Rhyme explained, with the evidence pointing to a fairly small area, highly concentrated with security cameras, an officer had focused on the Times Square district and spotted someone who profiled as Unsub 40 ten minutes ago.

'Where exactly?'

'Broadway and Forty-Two, going north. They lost him in a store at Four-Five Street, west. May have gone out the back entrance. Cameras're sporadic west of Broadway. Haven't picked him up again.'

Sachs skidded around a gas tanker changing lanes unexpectedly and righted the Torino. O-kayyy. The adrenaline bled out.

Rhyme was continuing, 'Mel called Midtown North. Half-dozen bodies are on their way to the intersection. ESU too.' Rhyme was unable to deploy troops, but Mel Cooper, a detective, had the authority to do so, even if his specialty was forensic science. 'And Pulaski's on his way to Twelve and Forty-Four with a team.'

The MTN team would sweep west with Sachs; Ron Pulaski's would head east, a pincer movement.

'From the evidence – any other idea where he might be headed? Specifically?'

No response.

He was talking to somebody else. Probably Cooper.

No, Sachs heard a woman's voice. Juliette Archer.

Then there was a pause.

Sachs asked, 'Rhyme?'

'What?'

'I was asking, anything from the evidence to narrow down where he is or where he's headed?'

'Some things we haven't been able to place. The broken glass, the glazing compound. Paper towels. That could be from anywhere. The humus is from Queens, or *originated* in Queens.' She wondered about the emphasis on the word. He continued, 'We've got fertilizer and herbicides, too, but you don't see rolling pastures on Broadway in Midtown. I don't mind speculating but I'm not guessing. No, we'll have to leave it up to a manhunt at this point.'

'Keep looking,' she said. 'I'll call you when I'm on scene.'

Sachs disconnected before he could respond and then veered off the highway and sped west onto surface streets.

Intersections . . . damn intersections.

Slamming down clutch and brake, squinting against the blue flashing light on the dash.

Sachs would hit the horn with one hand, downshift with the other, then grab the wheel rim again with both.

Clear right, clear left. Go! Go!

This process repeated a half-dozen times and only twice did the frantic Manhattan traffic drive her onto the curb, though three times or possibly four she came within inches of de-fendering a car gridlocked in her path.

Interesting, she reflected as she hit a clear stretch. Unsub 40 was hanging out in her father's beat. Herman Sachs had walked the streets of Times Square for years, concentrating mostly on the Deuce, 42nd Street, long before it morphed into the Disney theme park it was today. Fact was, Sachs missed the 'hood's porn, skin-game, honky-tonk days, as she suspected her father would have too.

Her mobile buzzed.

Manual transmission, phone? She chose the Samsung over fourth gear and let the transmission complain. 'Sachs.'

'Amelia. It's Bobby Killow. Patrol. MTN. Captain Rhyme gave me your number. About your unsub.'

'I remember you, Bobby.'

Killow had been a cherubic, energetic young patrol officer in Midtown North whom she'd worked with occasionally back in her pre-detective days. He was probably much the same now, though the 'young' wouldn't apply as seamlessly. 'What've you got?'

'I'm on Four-Six, been canvassing. A few people think they've seen him here. Last five minutes.'

Piercing the heart of the Theater District, 46th Street ran from river to river.

'Where exactly?'

'Few doors west of Broadway. Ducked into a souvenir store. Was looking suspicious, the wit said. Staring out the windows, like he was thinking he was being tailed. The clerk's words. When it seemed safe or clear or something – the clerk again – he stepped outside and vanished west.'

'I . . . well.'

'What was that?'

That had been a scooter driver, as oblivious as those in Rome, zipping out into her lane to see who would win the contest between a Ford Torino and a tinny Vespa knockoff.

Sachs had controlled the skid rather well, though she nearly ended up under a garbage truck. Then, tires spinning, on the way again.

'Bobby, descrip of the perp?'

'Dark-blue or black windbreaker, no logo, jeans, baseball cap in red or green – that's witnesses for you. Dark backpack.'

'K. I'm there in five.'

In fact, it took her three. She skidded to a stop at Broadway and 46th beside three Midtown North cruisers. Nodded to Bobby Killow. Yep, angelic as ever. She knew several of the octet of officers standing nearby too and greeted them.

Already the vultures were gathering: the tourists with mobile phones shooting away.

Hum of hers. Ron Pulaski was calling.

''Lo, Ron. Where are you? In position?'

'Right, Amelia.' The young officer explained he was

with a team of four patrol and six Emergency Service officers. They were on 46th Street, near the Hudson River.

'We're at Broadway. Sweep east, toward us. We'll move west.' She gave the description of the suspect and added that it was possible he lived or worked here. If so, his unique appearance meant neighbors or shopkeepers or waiters would most likely recognize him.

'If he's here because he was stalking a victim and has no other connection, well, that's something else. We'll just hope we can stumble over him before it's too late.'

They disconnected and Sachs briefed the officers in front of her. She explained that they couldn't be sure who the unsub's target was, other than someone using or near an 'embedded' product, which he would sabotage from his smartphone or tablet.

Sachs continued, 'We don't know if he's got a firearm. But he's used a hammer in the past.'

'He's the escalator killer, right?'

'That's right.'

'What other kinds of products would he be targeting?'

She told them about Abe Benkoff's stove. And recalled the lengthy list of products Todd Williams had downloaded for him, those with DataWise5000s in their hearts. 'Could be appliances, water heaters, kitchen things, heavy equipment, tools, maybe vehicles. Medical equipment too. But he's going for showy, to get attention. If you see something that could scald or crush you to death, assume it's got a controller in it and our unsub's about to push the button.'

'Jesus,' one of the officers whispered. 'Your wife and kids're in the kitchen baking cookies? And the stove could blow up?'

'That's it. Let's get started.'

As they began to sweep west, one officer muttered, 'Wonder why he picked this area.'

The answer was obvious to Sachs. Here were hundreds of stores, restaurants and entertainment venues, all presided over by towering high-definition video billboards, bullying or enticing passersby and tourists to spend, spend, spend . . .

For anyone whose agenda was assaulting consumerism, Times Square was the best hunting ground in the world.

CHAPTER 32

Canvassing.

The officers with Sachs divided into two teams, each taking a different side of the street, and were moving west.

Nothing fancy about the technique, simply asking if anyone had seen a tall thin man in a baseball cap, dark jacket and jeans, carrying a backpack. Their progress was slow. The sidewalk dense with pedestrians and vendors.

And, of course, they were watching their backs.

On the lookout for anything that might turn on them. Could he rig this car's engine to explode or catch fire? Could he command that garbage truck to lurch forward? What about the city infrastructure – a million volts and tons of superheated steam coursed inches below their feet.

Products were everywhere.

Distracting.

Sachs herself had no hits but one of the officers radioed and said he'd had a maybe – about ten minutes earlier a man fitting the unsub's description had been standing at the edge of the sidewalk, looking down at his tablet. Between Seventh and Eighth Avenues. He'd done nothing other than that; the witness – the owner of a Theater

District souvenir shop – had noted him simply because of his unusual appearance.

'Any idea where he went?'

'No, ma'am,' the officer said.

Looking around in frustration.

'Maybe that's a target zone. Assemble there.'

In a few minutes, they'd gathered where the unsub had been spotted and continued searching. No one else had seen him. So they continued west. Slowly. Looking in restaurants, shops, cars and trucks, theaters – front and stage doors. Nothing.

Ron Pulaski called from the west end of 46th Street and reported no sightings. He and his officers were continuing east. The two search teams were about a half mile from each other now.

Moving closer to Eighth Avenue, Sachs could see a theater and across from that a large construction site. An irritating noise shot toward them on the wind – a power tool's whine. As she approached, it grew very loud, a shriek that stung her ears. She'd thought the sound was coming from the jobsite – a high-rise. There were dozens of workers welding and hammering the steel skeleton into place. But curiously, no, the sound was coming through two large open doors across the street. It was the backstage area of a theater, a workshop where a carpenter was cutting wood, presumably to assemble a set for an upcoming play. Thank goodness the workman was wearing bulky plastic earmuffs – the sort that she wore when she went shooting. The huge scream of the circular saw could ruin unprotected eardrums. When the worker stopped cutting, she or one of the search team would ask if he'd spotted the suspect.

For the moment, though, Sachs and the officers with her walked through the gap in the six-foot plywood fence surrounding the construction site. The building going up was a thirty- or forty-story-high structure. Much of the steelwork and rough flooring had been done but few walls were in. The ground was congested with heavy equipment and stations for tools and supplies. Making her way farther inside, Sachs asked a scrawny worker, an unlit cigarette in his mouth, for the manager or foreman. He ambled off.

A moment later a big man in a hard hat waddled up. He was obviously displeased.

'Hello,' she said, nodding to the worker, who exuded an air of seniority. She showed her badge.

Rather than responding to her, he frowned and turned to another, younger worker, not the one who'd fetched him. 'You call 'em? I didn't say call 'em yet.'

'I didn't call nobody, Boss.'

'Who called?' the man – Boss – shouted, looking over workers nearby and scratching his large belly, encased within a seriously stressed plaid shirt. Hairs protruded from the gaps between buttons.

Sachs could make a reasonable deduction. 'Someone was *going* to call the police?'

'Yeah but,' he said, looking around for a culprit.

His assistant said to Sachs, as he nodded toward Boss, 'Iggy, he's Iggy, wanted to make sure there was a reason, you know. Not a false alarm. The company don't like cops, sorry, like *officers* on a jobsite. Looks bad, you know.'

'What did you think the problem was? Why would anybody have called?'

Iggy was mentally back with them now. 'Trespass. Looks like some guy snuck in. We aren't sure. Just wanted to check. Before we called. We woulda. Just, we wanted to check. Didn't want to waste nobody's time.'

'Was he very tall, very thin? In a dark windbreaker and jeans? Baseball cap?'

'Dunno. You looking for him? Why?'

With edgy impatience, Sachs said, 'Could you find out if that's who it was?'

'Yeah, I guess.'

'Yeah, you guess it was him. Or yeah you guess you can find out.'

'Uh-huh.'

Sachs stared. 'This man is wanted in connection with a homicide, Iggy. Could you . . . ?' A gesture with her open palm, impatient.

Iggy shouted, 'Yo, Cly!'

Another worker walked up, hiding a cigarette behind his back. This one was lit.

'Yeah?'

'That asshole you saw walking around?'

Sachs repeated the description.

'That's him.' The smoker's eyes swiveled momentarily to his boss. He was sheepish. 'I didn't call, Iggy. You didn't want nobody to call. I didn't call.'

Shit. Sachs pulled her radio off her belt and summoned her team and Pulaski's to the site ASAP.

'Any idea where he went?' she asked Cly.

'Coulda been up. He was near the west elevator.'

Gesturing at the soaring steelwork of the building.

'Are there people there to spot him?' Sachs asked. She couldn't see any workers from the ground.

'We're doing the ironwork,' the foreman said, meaning, she supposed, *obviously* there'd be people there.

'Call them and find out if he's been spotted.'

Iggy ordered his second- or third-in-command to do so. The man hopped to the task, making calls on his walkie-talkie.

Sachs asked the foreman, 'How could he have gotten out of the site?' The walls were eight-foot plywood, topped with razor wire.

Iggy rubbed his hard hat as if scratching his head. 'Entrances on Forty-Seventh. Or here, but this one, the main one, probably he would've been spotted. And nobody did or they woulda told me.'

She sent two officers in the direction of the 47th Street entrance. And said to Boss Iggy, 'Oh, and tell your men not to use the elevators.'

'They can't walk down—'

'He could have sabotaged them.'

His eyes went wide. 'Jesus. For real?'

Iggy's adjutant ended a transmission and said, 'He mighta been up there, one of the lower floors. Tall guy. Nobody was sure he was working for a sub or whatever.'

This seemed like the most likely target. Elevator cars mounted on the outside of a scaffolding track. It wouldn't take much, she guessed, for a DataWise controller to shut down the automatic brakes. Workers would slam to the ground at a hundred miles an hour.

Iggy called out, 'Freeze the elevators. All of them.

And tell the guys up there not to use them until they've been checked.'

Good. That would . . . But then Sachs reflected: Wait. No. Hell, what *am* I thinking of? No, no, got it wrong. Of course! Remember his MO. He's not going to be sabotaging the jobsite; he's here so he can *watch* where he's going to attack. He needs the high-rise as a vantage point. Just like he wasn't in Benkoff's apartment; he was across the street. Just like he was in the Starbucks so he could watch the escalator when the access panel opened to swallow up Greg Frommer.

So. What could he see from the iron skeleton here?

Then Sachs was aware of silence.

The screaming table saw in the workshop of the theater across the street had stopped. Sachs turned and hurried to the opening in the fence surrounding the construction site. From there she could see that the carpenter in the set-building workshop was gripping the mean-looking blade with one hand and wielding a socket wrench with another. The saw looked new, state-of-the-art.

And it was surely embedded with a DataWise5000.

He was his target! Unsub 40 was waiting till the man had shut the saw off and was changing the blade and then – though the carpenter thought it was safe – the unit would come to life and sever his hand or send the unsecured blade spinning through his belly or groin, or maybe into the street to hit passersby.

Sachs sprinted across the street, halting traffic with her palm, yelling toward the open theater doors, 'Get back from the saw! Get back! It's going to start up!'

But he couldn't hear through the protective earmuffs.

Sachs arrived at the doorway of the workshop. 'Stop!' No response.

The saw and the unsub's victim were still forty feet away. She then noted that the power cord to the saw extended from a fixture in the wall right next to her, a few feet away. There was, however, no plug. The cable disappeared into the wall.

No time. The unsub, somewhere high on the construction site, would have seen her and would be hacking into the saw's controller right now, to turn on the blade and slice away the hand of the oblivious carpenter. To her right was a workbench filled with hand tools, including a large pair of bolt cutters. The handle was wood – a good insulator, right? She wasn't sure when it came to 220 volts, which was what the saw undoubtedly used.

But no choice.

She yanked the tool off the rack, fitted the sharp teeth on either side of the power cable and pressed the handles together, closing her eyes as the sparks fired into the air around her.

CHAPTER 33

Moving as fast as I can, through the crowded sidewalks, putting distance between me and the theater and those who wanted to stop me, put me in jail, take me away from Alicia. Away from my brother. From my miniatures.

Shoppers! Goddamn Shoppers.

And Red, of course.

The worst Shopper of all. I so regret giving her the benefit of the doubt. I hate her, hate her, hate her now.

I was, though, I must confess, not surprised, not totally surprised, to see her in the construction site as I stood on the third floor and scanned the kill zone – the workshop behind the theater.

Still: How? How did she guess about the attack at the theater?

Not a guess, of course.

Police are smart nowadays. All that scientific equipment. DNA and fingerprints and everything. Maybe they'd found some evidence I left somewhere, evidence from when I'd been here before, preparing for the attack today. Or maybe I got spotted. Distinctive appearance, one could say. Slim Jim. Sack of bones . . .

Hell.

Moving west now, head down, slouching away some of my height.

Keep on the disguise? I wonder. I stole a hard hat and Carhartt jacket in the jobsite before I climbed to the third floor to get to business. Don't know if anybody saw Vernon the ironworker. But I decide: better to dump the outfit soon. Maybe a restroom in the subway. No – there'd be security cameras in the stations. The police would be watching them diligently. Go to Macy's, a restroom there, and shove them into a wastebasket.

A new jacket. Hat of course. A fedora again maybe, hipster. My tight crew cut, blond, is pretty distinctive.

I'll get back to the Toy Room as soon as I can. The womb. The zipping, colorful fish. I need comfort. Have Alicia come over. If I tell her to come over, she'll come over.

It's me, Vernon?

Looking behind. Nobody following. I—

Uh.

A pain in my side. I've collided with someone. Panic, at first, thinking it's a cop, cuffs out, about to arrest me. But no. A well-built, handsome man – dressed Powerful Businessman – was stepping out of a Starbucks and talking into his Bluetooth earpiece.

He rages at me: 'Jesus, you skinny fuck. Watch where you're going.'

I can only stare at his face. Red with anger. 'Apoplectic' is the word that blossoms in my head.

Handsome, he's handsome. Small nose, nice brows, solid physique. He holds his precious Starbucks toward me, not like a toast but like a gun about to fire. 'You'd spilled this on me, it would've cost you big time, you *Walking Dead* asshole. This shirt cost more'n you make in a month. I'm a lawyer.' Then talking into his phone as he walked away. 'Sorry, honey. Some skinny freak, AIDS patient, thinking he owns the sidewalk. I'm on my way home now. There in twenty.'

My heart is racing as it always does after an encounter with a Shopper. He's ruined my day, ruined my week.

I want to scream, want to cry.

I don't bother with the Macy's restroom plan. Strip off the Carhartt, the hard hat. Toss into a bin. The flesh-colored cotton gloves too. Put the St Louis cap back on. No, pick another, I tell myself. And fish in my backpack for a basic Nike black. On it goes.

Want to scream, want to cry . . .

But, eventually, those feelings go away, as they usually do, leaving in their place another desire.

To hurt. To hurt oh so badly.

*

The sparks had not been that impressive.

A quarter-inch flash of orange, accompanied by a modest puff of smoke. Had it been a scene in a movie the director surely would have called cut or redo or whatever they say and summoned the special effects pyrotechnician to multiply the cascade times ten.

What did happen, though, was the circuit breaker popped and the workshop, if not the entire theater, went dark. She herself didn't get shocked or receive a single burn from a spark.

Sachs had then held up her shield and motioned the carpenter, who'd turned and was staring at her in dismay, out of the open doorway. The unsub was still unaccounted for. He pulled off the muffs and started asking questions. She held up a wait-a-minute finger and looked around the workshop carefully. Sachs reminded herself that she'd deduced the theater was probably, but not necessarily, the attack site so she directed the other officers in the search teams to continue the sweep along the street here, particularly in the construction site, where at least they knew he'd been.

A few minutes later her phone hummed. It was Killow, her rotund, good-natured patrolman friend. 'Amelia. I'm in the jobsite. The foreman's assistant found some workers who spotted our boy. He was here – third floor. South side. Somebody saw him leaving. K.'

Third floor, south side. A perfect view of the carpenter and the saw.

'Got it. Going where?'

'Hold on.' A moment later he came back on. 'Four-Seven Street. Wearing brown Carhartt jacket and hard hat. Still canvassing. K.'

'Roger that. Keep me—'

Ron Pulaski's voice sliced through the airwaves. 'Sighting. Somebody spotted him on the corner, Four-Eight and Nine, headed north. We're in pursuit. Nothing further. K.'

'Keep on him, Ron. He'll've dumped the Carhartt and hard hat, I'm sure. Look for tall, look for skinny. He'll have the backpack – it's got his hammer or other weapons and whatever he controls the DataWise with. A phone or tablet.'

'Got it, Amelia. Sure. K.'

Hell. They'd been *so* goddamn close. So close. She

felt her teeth grinding like millstones and found her left index finger probing her left thumb's cuticle. She felt pain, told herself to stop. She didn't stop. Damn nervous habits.

The carpenter disappeared downstairs. The lights in the theater came back on. And the man returned. She learned his name was Joe Heady. She asked if he'd seen anybody resembling the unsub in or near the theater.

He thought for a moment. Then: 'No, never, ma'am. What's this all about?'

'There's a killer, somebody who's using products to kill people. He's sabotaged an escalator—'

'That story on TV?' asked the carpenter.

'That's right. A stove too. Caused a gas leak and then ignited it.'

'Right. I heard about that. Oh, man.'

'He's found a way to hack into smart controllers and take over the product. He was in the construction site, looking down at you, we think. He was going to turn the saw back on while you were holding it, I think.'

Heady closed his eyes briefly. 'That thing had started and my hand was on the blade? Jesus. Two thousand RPM. It cuts through wood like butter. I'd've lost the limb. Probably bled to death. This's all very fucked up, pardon my French.'

'Sure is,' said Sachs.

As she was jotting notes, her phone rang once more. It was Pulaski. She said to Heady, 'Excuse me, have to take this.' He nodded and walked to the kitchen area of the workshop. She watched him set a packet of instant

Starbucks coffee on the counter and heat a mug of water in the microwave. His hands quivered as he performed these simple tasks.

Pulaski said, 'Lost him, Amelia. We've expanded the search up to Five-Two and down to Three-Four. Not a bite so far.'

She sighed. 'Keep me posted.'

'Sure, Amelia. K.'

She disconnected and Heady turned to her. 'But why me? I mean, is it a labor thing? I was in the Auto Workers, Detroit, for years and I'm union here. But nobody busts unions anymore.'

'It's not you personally. He's a kind of domestic terrorist. He's injuring people who own or're using fancy products to make a statement. He says we're too reliant on them, spending too much money. That's his message. Here, the theatre? Who knows? Maybe all the self-indulgence of entertainment in Times Square.' She gave a faint smile. 'Maybe price of Broadway tickets.'

'Did I say fucked up?' Heady looked at the timer of the microwave counting down. He turned back to Sachs.

'One thing?'

'Yes?'

He glanced at the saw. 'You said he hacked into this controller or something?'

'That's right.'

'Well, the thing is, with the saw, there's just an on/off switch. You can't operate it remotely.'

'But you can upload data for diagnostics, right?'

'No. There's a chip in it to remember cutting specs. That's all.'

The microwave dinged and Heady walked toward it, reaching for the door lever.

Sachs frowned.

No!

As he opened the microwave's door, she dove forward and tackled him hard. They tumbled to the workshop's concrete floor as the ceramic cup inside the microwave exploded, sending a hundred pieces of shrapnel flying outward amid a searing cloud of steam.

CHAPTER 34

'You all right, man?' Freddy Caruthers was asking.

Nick returned to the couch after letting the little guy inside. Looking particularly toady at the moment.

Judge Judy was on the screen. Nick said, 'Wouldn't think I'd watch this, right? But I'm loving all the shows. Discovery Channel, A and E. I went in, there were fifty channels. Now, seven hundred.'

'Only ten're any good. ESPN and HBO. All I watch. *Big Bang Theory* too. It's funny.'

Nick shook his head. 'Don't know it.'

'You didn't answer me.'

'Answer you?'

'You all right?'

'Good days, shitty days. Everything in between. This's a less-shitty-than-others one.'

'That'd be a good self-help book. *The Less-Shitty-Day-Than-Others Guide to Life.*'

Nick laughed hard. And let the subject go. He didn't explain that the shittiest days were the ones when he couldn't let go of the fact that life screwed him over; none of the shit that happened was his fault. Unfair. That was something he'd talked to the prison therapist about a lot. Dr Sharana. 'Life's unfair.'

'Yeah, it can be. Let's talk about how you can deal with it, though.'

He now explained to Freddy, 'You never did time. It, what it does, is it resets you. Like you've got a clock in your gut or brain or somewhere and it turns a dial and life stops moving. Then you get out and, man, it's chaos. The traffic, the people moving.' He nodded. 'Just the TV programs. All those channels, I was saying. Everything. It can be too much. Like a mixture that's too rich in the carb.'

But this gave him a moment's pause, since it put in mind Amelia Sachs, who was an expert at setting carburetors and getting even the most troublesome choke to do what she wanted.

'A book I read when I was a kid,' Freddy was saying.

'A book?'

'When I was a kid. *Stranger in a Strange Land*. This alien comes to earth. Not like he's invading or anything, shooting people with a ray gun. It wasn't that kind of story. Anyway, this alien, he could change his sense of time. You go to the dentist, you speed things up and the visit goes by in seconds. You're making love, you slow it down.' Freddy laughed. 'I could use *that*, slow things down, I'm saying. Sometimes.'

'That was in the book?'

'Not the dentist or the sex. It was a classy book. Science fiction but classy.'

'*Stranger*—'

'—*in a Strange Land*.'

Nick liked the concept. 'That's just what it's like, yeah. Everything speeding up now I'm out. Get freaked some.

I read a lot inside. But never heard of that one. I'll read
it. Want a beer?'

Freddy was looking around the room. Nick had kept it
as organized as his cell. Clean. Polished. Ordered. It was
about as sparse as the cell too. He was going to borrow
a car and go to Ikea. Inside, he'd dreamed about shopping
there. Then Freddy glanced at his watch. 'We should leave
soon. But sure, one beer.' And he looked relieved that it
seemed the serious conversation was on hold.

Nick got a couple of bottles of Budweiser. He church-
keyed them, sat down and handed one over.

'You have booze inside?' Freddy asked.

'You could get 'shine. Expensive. Bad, real bad.
Probably poison.'

'They call it moonshine?' Freddy asked. This seemed
to tickle him.

'They did where I was. Most cons went for Oxy or
Perc. Easy to smuggle in. Or just buy from a guard.'

'Stay away from them both.'

'I hear that. Got beat up once, some bullshit thing.
Really hurt, broke a finger. Med center doc said he could
get me a couple of pills. I said no. He was surprised. I
think he wanted me to pay him.'

Judge Judy was harping about something. Nick shut the
show off. 'So who is this guy can help me out?' he asked.

'Name's Stan Von. I don't know him good. But he's
vouched for.'

'Von. What is he, German?'

Thinking of Amelia again.

'I don't know. Maybe Jewish. Could still be German.
Don't know.'

'Where're we meeting him?'

'Bay Ridge.'

'He's got the names? J and Nanci?'

'I don't know for sure. But he said what he's got'll point you in the right direction.'

'He's not warranted, right?'

'Nope. I checked.'

'I can't see him if he is.'

Freddy reassured, 'He's clean.'

'And no weapons.'

'I told him. Absolutely.'

Nick remembered life in prison and he remembered life on the streets. 'So what's he want out of this?'

'A meal.'

'A . . . Is that like code or something?' Thinking: 'M' for a thousand bucks. Or 'M' for megabytes, as in a shitload of money.

Freddy shrugged. 'Dinner is what it means.'

'That's all?' Nick was surprised. 'I was thinking five bills.'

'No, I've done his boss some favors. So, no cash involved. Anyway, some guys, doing something for somebody, they just want a meal. It's more, I don't know, intimate or something.' Nick shot him a look and Freddy chuckled. 'No, not *that* kind of intimate. I just mean it's more like a good thing they're doing.' The amphibian guy chugged the last suds of his beer. 'Or, who knows, maybe he's just hungry.'

'It's not bad. A bit of burn. I was under the line of fire.'

In Rhyme's parlor, Sachs was responding to Rhyme's question about her condition.

She displayed her left arm, where the steam from the microwave had kissed the skin, which was now slightly reddish. For the treatment – ointment, it seemed – she'd removed her blue-stone ring. She apparently now remembered it, fished the jewelry from her pocket and reseated it gingerly. Flexed her fingers. And nodded. 'Fine.' The bandage on her forearm was modest.

'So what happened?' Sachs asked. The question was directed toward Juliette Archer, who had, by voice command, just disconnected a phone call. They knew, of course, that the unsub had turned the microwave power way up but neither Rhyme nor Sachs had guessed how that could create a virtual bomb.

The intern replied, 'The consumer products specialist at the microwave manufacturer.' Nodding at the phone. 'He said it looks like our unsub used the DataWise to override the control panel and up the power exponentially. He said it would be a lot – probably by forty or fifty times. Whatever he was making, tea or coffee, was superheated. When he opened the door, the air was a lot colder and it vaporized the liquid inside *and* the moisture in the porcelain mug itself – all ceramic absorbs liquids to some extent. The mug exploded like a hand grenade.'

Archer nodded to the screen. 'Even with microwaves that haven't been tampered with you get the same effect, if you overheat something. But that takes time. Our unsub? He basically caused fifteen minutes of high-power radiation to happen in about sixty seconds.'

Rhyme had no idea such a ubiquitous device could be so dangerous.

Sachs's phone hummed and she read a text. 'He's published another message.' A few keystrokes and an email appeared on the high-def monitor near them.

Greetings! Are you learning about the EVIL results of your unbridled lust for convenience?? Now, every time you want to heat up some soup or coffee, you'll run the risk of five hundred degree steam and deadly bits of ceramic and glass piercing your bodies! Will it be the microwave in you're home? Or office? Or your son's dorm room?

Are you finally seeing that I'm doing nothing more to you than what your doing to Mother Earth! Do you know the impact your obsene love of THINGS have on the atmasphere, the waters? The landfills, You are injecting our environment with toxins.

As yee buy, so shall yee reap.

Until tomorrow, I remain –

The People's Guardian

Nothing to be drawn from the message, other than he was continuing to front he was more ignorant than he actually was, Rhyme concluded.

Yee . . .

Nothing that is, except the substance of the rant: that more attacks were planned.

Mel Cooper said, 'An exploding microwave . . . That's going to get attention.'

It already was.

Since the first story appeared, written up by the reporter Sachs had spoken to, a flurry of coat-tail articles and broadcast news stories had appeared, looking at the danger of Internet of Things products. A number of writers and talking heads speculated that sales of smart appliances and equipment would soon be slumping, returns rising, and people simply not using products that might turn on them.

Rhyme, Sachs and the team were perhaps protecting some potential targets but Unsub 40 was also winning battles in his war against consumerism.

Sachs and Rhyme had had a follow-up conversation with Vinay Chaudhary, of CIR Micro, and he told them that every one of its customers had again received the security patch that would stop anyone's hacking into the network and taking control of the embedded product. The chief executive himself had personally sent a memo or called to remind them of the importance of updating.

In addition he was ordering that the code of all of his future products be modified to provide for automatic updates from CIR's own server.

'What else do we have?' Rhyme asked, gazing at the evidence bags Sachs had brought from the Times Square scene.

'A rich contact site,' she told him. Referring to the place where their unsub had escaped from the jobsite, after reprogramming the microwave. This had been on the opposite side of the site, on 47th Street, where he'd had to use a crowbar to break through a padlock and chain. In crime scene work a rich contact is anywhere the perp engages in multiple or time-consuming activities. A victim or police officer, for instance, wrestling with a perp, an unsub dismembering a body (it takes time and effort) or an escapee breaking through a well-protected door or window.

'Friction ridges?'

'A hundred,' Sachs said, but she'd already sent them through IAFIS. She'd gotten back a few hits but the prints belonged to individuals arrested for minor violations long ago – workers employed by the construction company or delivery people.

'Footprints?'

'Yes. One matches his. We got a bit of trace from the treads.'

'What was it?' Rhyme wheeled closer to Mel Cooper, who was on the optical microscope. A low magnification. One mistake Rhyme had found was common among newbies in crime labs: cranking the 'scope to 100 power. That kind of voyeurism generally got you nowhere. Examining a bit of trace at 5X or, at most, 10X was all you needed. If you wanted a more micro view there was always the scanning electron microscope.

Looking at the screen, Cooper said, 'More sawdust.'

Sachs: 'I got it at the jobsite, where he was standing, but it's different from the rough-cut particles indigenous to the site. It's much finer. Very similar to the mahogany at the earlier scene. Sanded again. Different wood, though.'

Rhyme looked it over. 'Walnut, I'd guess. No, I'm sure. Cellular structure and color temperature. Five thousand Kelvin.'

Cooper agreed.

Archer asked Sachs, 'Did you search the workshop at the theater?'

'No.'

Rhyme observed that Sachs glanced at her closely, eyes settling briefly on the gold Celtic bracelet encircling her left wrist, strapped to the armrest of the Storm Arrow wheelchair. Sachs's gaze returned to the evidence chart.

A pause. Archer said, 'He might've gone inside there to check out the brand of microwave before the attack. We know he was in the Theater District earlier.'

'I didn't need to search it.' Sachs, studying the bits of sawdust, answered absently.

Archer looked from Sachs to Rhyme. 'Don't you think . . .' she began, implicitly questioning Sachs's decision.

The detective replied, 'The workshop has a two-day-looping security video. Lot of souvenir thieves in theaters in New York. I had the security company review it. The perp wasn't inside on any of the existing tape . . . and the floors're mopped every night.'

'Oh. I—'

Sachs said, 'It was a reasonable question. And in a perfect world with unlimited resources I would have searched it. You play the odds.'

Rhyme would probably have had someone search the scene. But Sachs was right about resources. Besides, he wasn't taking one woman's side against the other.

Rhyme: 'Mel? What else?'

Cooper found more trace and examined it. 'More glass splinters, probably from the same batch as before, and more glazing compound.'

'What's that? In that bag?' A tiny plastic one.

'A fleck of something . . .'

'Let me see.'

Cooper mounted it and projected the image onto the screen. It looked like a tiny opaque fish scale. A piece of the sawdust was stuck to it. Cooper said, 'I can GC it. But there's not enough to preserve for court.'

Rhyme said, 'We'll have plenty of evidence to make a case against him. But we have to find him first.' A nod toward Mel. 'Burn it.'

Cooper ran the sample through the gas chromatograph/ mass spectrometer. A few moments later he scanned the computer screen. 'Ammonium rhodanide and dicyandi- amide, urea, collagen.'

Rhyme said, 'Glue of some sort. I'll bet used in wood- working.'

'That's it,' Cooper said, after running the quantities of the found substances through a database. 'Bond-Strong liquid hide glue. Mostly for musical instruments but woodworkers in any field use it.'

Archer leaned forward, stony-faced, staring at the evidence bags. 'Instrument making? What do we think?'

Rhyme was doubtful. 'That's a rare hobby or profes- sion. And if so he'd probably be a musician too. But we haven't found any other trace that suggests that. No resin from strings, no horsehair from violin or cello bows – they shed hairs abundantly, by the way. No tuning gear lubricants. No felt from bridges. No callus skin cells sloughed off – from fretboard or fingerboard use.'

'You're a musician, Lincoln?' Archer asked. 'I mean, were a musician?'

'Never touched an instrument.'

'How do you know all that?'

'It pays to know the tools of the trade of potential perps and potential victims. Minimize the time you need to look up sources. It might make the difference between collaring the unsub and attending his next crime scene. So I'm leaning in favor of furniture making or fine carpentry. But: hobby or profession? Don't know which. And what exactly does he make with his varnish and glue and sandpaper and exotic woods? Keep going, Mel.'

'A bit of vegetation,' he called. 'Stem or a leaf.'

Rhyme looked it over. He laughed. 'Then sometimes, Archer, despite all your diligent homework, you don't have a goddamn idea what you've found. Send a picture of the cellular structure and color temperature to the Horticultural Society Research Databank.'

Cooper emailed jpgs of the sample to the HSRD. 'Should have it back within a day or so,' he said, reading the return email.

'Light a fire,' Rhyme snapped. 'Urgent, life or death . . . Don't care about John Doe's doctoral thesis on Venus flytraps. This has priority.'

Cooper sent a follow-up and then turned back to the bags. 'Okay, something else. A fragment of black, flexible plastic with some printing on it. Too small to make out any letters.'

'Put it up.'

Gazing at the screen, Rhyme could see instantly that it was wire insulation. 'Our boy's done some electrical work. The wire's cut with a razor knife. Don't you think, Sachs?'

But she was looking at her phone, reading a text.

Archer said, 'So he's not a pro.'

'Why would you say that?'

'A pro would use a stripping tool, not a knife. Those plier-like things, I'd think.'

'Good. Yes. But let's say *probably* not a pro. He might've had to leave his regular tool belt at home and found he had only a sharp blade to do some work with. Or, non-pro with two question marks?'

Archer smiled. Cooper started to write the punctuation marks. Rhyme said, 'That was a joke.'

He regarded the chart. Too many mysteries here. Rhyme decided to get some outside analysis from an expert and had the digitized files and photographs uploaded to a secure server, then sent the link to the man he had in mind. A moment later a text came back.

Yah, yah. Tomorrow.

Amused at the irreverence but irritated that he had to wait, he texted back, 'K. I guess.'

He thought: Well, beggars can't be . . . But shot the cliché dead before he completed it. And turned his chair to the parlor doorway as he detected the footfall of Ron Pulaski, who'd just let himself in with a key.

'Where've you been, Rookie? You have Gutiérrez in custody yet?'

'Had to see somebody about a lead. Could've waited but I thought it was better to do it now, meet with this guy. Get it over with. And—'

'Fine, fine, fine. Amelia said you ran the canvass in Times Square. What'd you find?'

'The unsub, he got out through the far side of the jobsite.'

'We know that. Tell me something I'm ignorant of.'

'He was in a Carhartt jacket, one of those brown things contractors wear. And a hard hat. But he must've ditched 'em. We swept the area and didn't find them. And nobody matching his descrip was seen.'

'That's not a word, "descrip." There's "nondescript" and there's "description." But there's no "descrip."'

'Well, it's in common usage on the street.'

'So is methamphetamine. That's no reason to embrace it.'

'Now, nothing on the subway CCTVs or any of the cameras in the COC. My thinking is he got a bus north or south. His height wouldn't be so prominent that way, sitting. I've sent a memo to Transit. Officers'll canvass all the drivers to see if they saw somebody fitting the *description*. Some of the buses have video and they'll look at those too.'

'Good. The jobsite workers?'

'A couple of people saw him but they just said tall and skinny. Had a tablet of some kind.'

'His weapon. That's what he used to sabotage the microwave.' Rhyme backed up and continued to stare at the evidence chart. 'Think, everybody. Speculate. The answer's there.' His eye caught Archer's; she was looking his way with a smile. He recalled that this was how he'd begun his lecture at the college the other day. 'Let's find it.'

Crime Scene: 438 W. 46th Street/ Construction site across street

- Offense: Attempted assault.
- Victim: Joe Heady.
  - Union carpenter, Broadway. Was electrician and autoworker a few years ago in Detroit. Suffered only minor injuries.
- Means of attack: Hacked into microwave, fitted with DataWise5000 controller.
- Evidence:
  - Sawdust from walnut. Cut with same blade as mahogany. Probably a handheld saw or other tool, not electric.
  - Bond-Strong liquid hide glue. Mostly used in making musical instruments, but craftsmen in any field use it.
  - Glass splinters, probably from same batch as before.
  - Additional glazing compound.
  - Fragment of leaf. Sent out for analysis. Waiting for return.
  - Fragments of electrical insulation, cut with razor knife.
- Additional elements of profile of suspect:
  - Probably not a professional electrician.
  - Fine woodworker or musical instrument maker (probably former).
  - Wore Carhartt jacket, hard hat. Probably discarded.
  - Additional message from People's Guardian.

CHAPTER 35

A cool spring evening.

Pleasant. Nick Carelli and Freddy Caruthers were walking down Fourth Avenue in Bay Ridge. Past a yoga store, past Rent-Your-Kilt, which drew a double take from Nick. Yep. That was the name.

From here you could see a bit of the Verrazano's crown. One hell of a bridge. After he'd been arrested he'd thought about jumping off it. But thinking about and doing are two very different animals. Would've upset his brother and mother too much. After the mad urge had passed he was ashamed he'd even considered it.

'There.' Freddy pointed.

A block away. The Bay View Café. The diner looked pretty decent though the sign lied; there was no view of the bay. For one thing, it faced east, the opposite direction. And it offered no view of any water – harbor or ocean or drainage canal or puddle.

'Should call it the Bay Somewhere Nearby Café.'

'Huh?' asked Freddy. Then he got it. 'That's good. Ha.'

The place was clean inside. Nick looked around, noting where the hostess station was, what kind of cash register they had, where the kitchen was located, the doors that opened into it, what the Daily Special board looked like, how many servers and busboys there were – and if they looked like they spoke English as a first, second or third language. Or didn't speak it at all. Where the food was stored. Big cans of tomato sauce sat stacked against a back wall. Were they empty and just decorative?

Nick knew he had a lot to learn about the restaurant business. Still, he felt good about the prospect. He really hoped Vittorio Gera would come through and accept his offer.

Freddy tapped Nick's arm and directed him to a booth in the back, where a skinny guy in jeans and a black T-shirt under a brown sport coat sat sipping a Sam Adams from the bottle. He wasn't using the frosted glass the waitress had brought and the empty mug was sweating.

'Stan. I'm Freddy.'

'Yo.'

'This's Nick.'

Hands were shaken and Nick sat down opposite Von, who had thick black hair that could've used a shampooing and trim. His right palm, Nick had felt upon the clasp, was callused. Wondered what his job was. Knuckles red. Maybe he boxed; he had the muscles for it. Nick the cop made observations like this. Nick the prisoner had too. He wasn't going to quash that instinct now that he was neither.

Nick scooted over so Freddy could join him on his side of the booth. But Freddy said, 'I gotta make some calls. Be five, ten minutes. Leave you guys to it.'

'You know what you want to eat?' Nick called.

'I don't care. Burger. You guys order. Don't wait for me.' He fished his phone out and headed to the front of the restaurant, punching in a number. He smiled as he struck up a conversation with the person who'd picked up. Some people did that, smiled or frowned when talking, even though the guy on the other end of the line couldn't see them.

'So, you and Freddy go way back?' Von was reading the menu like there'd be a test later.

'School.'

'School.' Von's voice seemed to hint that that was a waste of time. 'You drive cars, Nick?'

'I . . . You mean as a job?'

A laugh. 'Naw, just you drive cars?'

'I can drive. I don't have one.'

'Yeah?'

'Really.'

Von laughed once more, as if that were the funniest thing in the world.

'What're your wheels?' Nick asked.

'Oh, whatever.' And Von went back to the menu.

Nick too looked it over, wondering what would be the fastest thing to order. He wanted this to be over soon. Wasn't Von's bizarre personality. Well, it was partly that. Mostly Nick's gut told him that, despite what Freddy's homework showed, Von might be connected or whoever he worked for was, and one or both of them might have a record. That was a no-fly zone for Nick, a violation of his parole. He didn't want to ask Von because, if the answer was yes, then he'd know for certain. He wanted to tell his PO that he'd had no clue.

Best get the info about J and Nanci, buy the guy the best steak on the menu and shut up to let him eat it as fast as possible. Then get the hell out.

But even with the urgency there were the rituals that had to be obeyed, of course. The men chatted about sports, about the neighborhood, about business, even the goddamn weather. Von kept laughing at things that made no sense to laugh about. 'There's a high-rise going up where the Knights social club used to be. You believe it, son-o?'

That was worth a yuk or two.

Nick caught the waitress's eye and she approached. 'We're ready.'

Von ordered a salad to start, extra Thousand Island dressing, and chicken Parmesan.

Nick got a burger. 'Rare.'

Von gazed at him with grinning astonishment. 'You're not worried, worms and shit?'

Nick, gripping patience tightly, said, 'I'm not worried.'

'Suit yourself.'

'No fries,' Nick said.

Von blinked, reared back. 'You're fucking crazy. They're great here, the best. I mean, the best.'

'Then I'll take 'em,' Nick said.

'You won't be regretting it, son-o. Bring him a salad too. He needs a salad. Same dressing.' A grin as he turned to Nick. 'They make their own here. You could call it *Two* Thousand Island, it's so effing good.'

Nick smiled back coolly and ordered the same thing for Freddy. 'Two beers.'

'And me, top her off, Lucy,' Von said, tapping the beer, even though the woman's name tag read *Carmella*. Unsmiling, she turned and left.

Nick said, 'Thanks for doing this.'

'My boss owes Freddy. You notice?' Von's voice dropped. 'He looks like a frog?'

'Never did, no.'

'He does. Well, glad to help. Only I don't know how helpful it's gonna be.'

'You know Flannigan's?'

'Did some work at the place last month. You handy?'

'Some. I can do electrical. Plumbing.'

'Plumbing?' A laugh. 'I frame like a motherfucker. I was framing there, Flannigan's. Old man Flannigan gave me a bonus. Pretty sweet. Said it was the best framing he'd ever seen. Anyway, I started to hang there. I got to know some people, the bartenders, the staff.' Von didn't bother to lower his voice now. 'They're all right. They're us, you know. Not from some other countries, like you see in a lot of places.' A nod toward Lucy/Carmella.

An urge to wash his hands came over Nick.

'I got to know people there, I was saying. People like to talk to me. I got the gift of gab. Got that from my father. So, I asked around, put two and two together. About what Freddy was asking. And put together this list, might be the guy you're looking for. A bunch of guys named J. Nothing about a Nanci. But they all got bitches they're married to or're fucking. Ha, or both. Here.' He dug into his pocket to retrieve a slip of paper, pulling his jacket aside.

Oh, Jesus Lord. Nick actually gasped.

Von was carrying.

Nick saw the wood grip of something small. Probably a little .38.

Man, this was bad. Freddy'd said there was no way he'd have a gun on him.

Maybe Von'd forgotten. Or lied.

Nick took the grimy sheet of limp paper.

'You okay, son-o?'

Nick couldn't say anything. He looked around. Nobody else had seen the piece.

'Yeah. Haven't eaten all day. I'm starving.'

'Ah, well, here we go.' The salads arrived, both drenched in dressing. No appetite whatsoever.

Von peered at Nick and said in a loud voice, real loud: 'What's a four-letter word that ends in K and means intercourse?'

Carmella had heard; Nick knew the joke was for her benefit.

Nick said, 'I don't know.'

'How 'bout you, Lucy?' Von asked the waitress, who blushed. He roared, 'Ha! The answer's "talk"! Get it?'

She nodded and gave a polite laugh.

Nick started to chow down fast. Breathless.

'Easy, son-o. You'll choke to death . . . You see that? She *didn't* get it. She didn't know "intercourse" also means "talk." That's what I'm talking about, with *them*.'

Lord, I'm sitting across from a man with a gun. No, an idiot with a gun.

Nothing to do but hope for the best.

Nick ate a few disgusting forkfuls as he scanned the names Von had brought him. Jackie, Jon, Jonny. There were ten altogether.

'Not much of a shortlist,' Von said, chewing. A bit of dressing launched itself tableward.

'No, man. It's good. Appreciate it.' Names and some addresses, some businesses. Nothing jumped out. He would have to do more homework but he'd pretty much figured he'd have to.

Von continued, 'According to my boys – and girls – these dudes hang at Flannigan's some. Or used to. They're all kinda quiet about what they do. You get what I'm saying. Quiet. Get it?'

'Great. Sure.'

More salad, wolfed down.

Von said, 'You are one hungry son of a bitch.' That eerie giggle.

'Yeah, like I said.' Chewing, swallowing, trying not to puke. And a goddamn hamburger on its way.

Nick cased the list into his jeans pocket.

And that was when he saw the figure outside.

A guy, in a suit, one that didn't fit so well. Gray. Blue shirt, button-down collar and a tie. Crew cut. He was walking past the restaurant, looking in, a neutral expression on his face. He stopped, squinted and leaned forward, peering through the window.

No . . . oh, no . . . Please.

Nick stared down at his salad.

Another plea.

Another prayer.

It wasn't answered.

The door to the restaurant opened and closed and he felt, as much as heard, the big man make his way to the booth. Coming straight for them.

Shit.

Didn't matter if Nick glanced at the newcomer or not; he was making a beeline for the two men. He decided it was probably better to glance his way – it'd look less guilty. He did this now and studied the face, keeping his own as emotionless as possible. He couldn't summon the name. Not that it mattered. He knew what the guy did for a living.

'Well, if it ain't my old buddy, Nick Carelli.'

He nodded.

Von looked him over.

'The hell you up to, Nick? They let your ass outa the system, did they? What happened? You stopped giving guards blow jobs with those pretty little lips of yours.'

Von swallowed his immense chew of salad and said, 'Fuck off, asshole. We're—'

The gold NYPD shield stopped about a foot from Von's face. 'Do *what*?'

Von, who would face a mandatory year in prison for the gun, even if he had no priors, shut up and looked back to his salad. 'Sorry, man, I didn't know. You're just busting his chops. Whataya mean, let him outa the system?'

Von would know, of course. He just wanted to inflate his innocence preserver.

But Detective Vince Kall – Nick got the name – turned away from Von to his prey of choice. 'So you didn't answer me. What're you doing here, Nicky Boy?'

'Come on, Vince. Give me a break—'

'Or I could give you a third chance to answer the question.'

'Having dinner with a friend.'

'Your PO know about it?'

Nick shrugged. 'If he asks I'll tell him whatever he wants to know. I always do. It's just dinner. Why're you busting my ass?'

'You reconnecting with your friends?'

'Look, I'm not hassling anybody. I did my time. I'm legit now.'

'No, bad cops're never legit. Once bad, always bad. Like a whore. She may give up the business but she'll always be somebody who got dicks up her ass for money. Am I right?'

'I just want to get a job, something going, get on with my life.'

'How's the guy you beat the crap out of, Nick, you got busted for? I heard he had brain damage or something.'

'Come on, please.' Nick wasn't going to give Kall the I'm-innocent speech. A shield like this'd never believe it and it'd only rile him up more.

Kall turned to Von, who was concentrating – way too much – on his salad.

'And who is your little friend here? What's your name?'

Von swallowed, looking guilty as sin. 'Jimmy Shale.'

'Whatta you do for a living, Jimmy?'

'Can you ask me that?'

'I can ask you what you beat off to at night. I can ask you where your boyfriend likes you to kiss him. I can ask—'

'General contracting and construction.'

'For who?'

'A bunch of companies.'

'Most guys I ask, they give me a straight answer. They say Helmsley or Franklyn Development. You say a bunch of people.'

'Well, Officer—'

'Detective.'

Von was leaning back and staring up coldly now, attitude flowing from his eyes. 'Well, Officer Detective, the fact is I work for a lot of people. Because *I'm* good at my job and a lot of people want me. And I'm not real happy, the way you're talking to me.'

'Really? And your happiness counts why, Jimmy?'

Nick'd been thinking the worst that could happen was that the cop would find Von's gun, bust him and then word would get back to Nick's PO that they'd been together and there'd be a hearing and Nick might very well get his ass kicked back inside for the violation. But there was one step past worse: Von would decide Kall had pushed him too far and would pistol whip him or even empty five blunt .38 slugs into the asshole detective's body. No, *four* into his body and *one* into his face, just in case he was wearing a vest.

Nick tried, 'Look, Vince, let's just take this down a notch, okay? I'm—'

'Shut up, Carelli.' Leaning toward Von. 'You, asshole. Lemme see some ID.'

'ID. ID. Sure.' Von, that weird grin on his face, wiped his fat lips with his napkin and placed it back in his lap. Then he started to reach for his pocket. 'I'll show you some fucking ID.'

Yes, he was going for his gun. Kall was dead.

And so was Nick.

He assessed angles. From the depth of the booth he couldn't leap forward and wrestle the gun from Von's hand. If he shouted to Kall that Von was armed, he'd be admitting he knew.

Von started to rise, hand near the piece.

But just then a staticky voice crackled from Kall's belt.

'All units. Ten thirty. Carjacking in progress. Four One Eight Fourth Avenue, Bay Ridge. Two black males, twenties, believed to be armed. Silver Toyota. Late model. No tags at this point.'

'Shit.' The cop was looking out the window. The address was virtually across the street.

He yanked the radio off his belt. 'Detective Seven Eight Seven Five. At the scene of the ten thirty. Bay Ridge. Send backup. K.'

'Roger Seven Eight Seven Five. Two RMPs en route. ETA four minutes. K.'

Nick lost the rest of the transmission. The detective was headed outside, hand on his weapon. He pushed out the door, turned left and vanished from sight.

Freddy, head down, entered before the door closed. He stormed up to them. 'Come on, you guys. Get out. Now!' He tossed two twenties on the table. Von leapt from the booth, Nick behind him, and they followed Freddy through the kitchen and out the back door into a pungent, trash-filled alley.

'This way.'

Nick said to Freddy, 'You called it in? You did that?'

'Had to do *something*. Didn't look good, whatever was going down. We gotta move, though. He'll find out it was fake in about five minutes.'

'They'll trace you,' Von said.

'A burner. Jesus, you think I was born yesterday?'

They walked into a backyard and kept going west.

Freddy said, 'Look for a gypsy cab. Not metered, a gypsy. The hell happened?'

'The shield recognized me,' Nick said. 'Gave me some lip. Would've been okay . . . Only, only our boy here's got a piece.'

'Yeah, so?' Von was defensive.

Freddy turned on him, furious. '*What?* I told Art: No weapons. Period. My man here just got out.'

'Art didn't say nothing to me. I don't know. I was meeting some stranger in the Ridge. I'm not stupid.'

'Well, you're stupid enough to get mandatoried one year in Rikers, for the piece. How'd that sit with you?'

'All right, all right.'

'He get your name?' Freddy asked Von.

'No,' Nick said. 'But he'll come back, looking. And he does have your descrip, Von. And he knows me. Ditch the piece. And I mean now. In the water.'

'These things cost money.'

Freddy said, 'No. I don't trust you. Give it to me. I'll do it myself.'

'Man . . .'

'You want me to call Art?'

'Shit.' He handed over the gun, which Freddy took in a wad of tissue.

'It's cold?' Freddy asked.

'Yeah, yeah, can't be traced.'

Freddy asked, 'You got the list, Nick?'

'Yeah.'

Freddy said, 'Thanks for that, Von. But now, separate ways.'

'I didn't get my meal.'

'Jesus.'

Von grimaced and started off along the dark sidewalk.

'I'm going to the bay, get rid of this.' Freddy tapped his pocket.

'Thanks, man . . . You're the best.'

'The list look good?'

'It's something. A good start. I'll just have to do a little more detective work.'

'Hell, you *were* a detective. Piece of cake.'

'Thanks, Freddy. Man, I owe you. Big.' A faint smile.

Freddy touched his forehead, a half salute, then headed west, to the shore, where he'd pitch the gun into the Narrows. A few minutes later Nick found a gypsy cab; they were more plentiful in the outer boroughs since medallion cabs were harder to find. He settled into the seat and inhaled deeply. Then his phone hummed and he panicked, thinking the detective from the restaurant was following up and wanted him to come downtown. But he looked at caller ID.

Felt a thud in his gut all right. Though a different sort than the kind he'd just experienced.

He answered.

'Amelia. Hi.'

CHAPTER 36

Rhyme and Archer sat in their chairs before the evidence boards. They were alone.

The speculation, the guesswork, the suppositions had gone on for several hours – several extremely unproductive hours – before the team called it quits for the night. Pulaski and Cooper were gone. Sachs was in the hallway making a phone call. Her voice was low and he wondered whom she was speaking to. Her face looked grave. The shooting incident at the mall seemed resolved largely in her favor. What else could it be?

She ended her call and walked back into the parlor, offering nothing about the conversation. She didn't remove her Glock – again she'd be staying in Brooklyn. Sachs pulled her jacket off a hook.

'Better go.'

She glanced at Archer then back to Rhyme and seemed about to say something.

Rhyme cocked an eyebrow. The equivalent of a taciturn man, which he was, saying, 'Talk to me. What is it?'

A moment of debate within Sachs. Then she balked, snagged her purse, slung it over her shoulder and nodded farewell. 'I'll be back early.'

'See you then.'

''Night, Amelia,' Archer said.

''Night.'

Sachs strode into the hallway and Rhyme heard the front door as it opened and closed.

He turned back toward Archer. Had she fallen asleep? Her eyes were closed. Then they opened.

She said, 'Frustrating.'

Looking at the board. 'Yes. Loose ends. Too many of them. This riddle's not that easy.'

'You figured it out? Ours?'

'The letter "e."'

'You didn't cheat? No, you wouldn't. You're a scientist. The process is the most important part of solving a problem. The answer's almost secondary.'

This was true.

She added, 'But I'm not speaking of the case. The frustration in general.'

The life of the disabled, she meant. And she was right. Everything takes longer, people treat you like pets or children, there's so much in life that's not accessible – in all senses, more than just second floors and restrooms: love, friendship, careers you otherwise would have been perfect for. The list goes on and on.

He'd noted her struggling with the phone not long before, trying to call her brother for a ride back to his apartment. The unit was on speaker but not recognizing her commands. She'd given up and used the controller with her right hand, angrily entering the digits. Her Celtic bracelet jangling with each number. Her jaw had been trembling by the time she got through.

'You fall into a rhythm,' he said. 'And you learn, you plan ahead, you take the route where you minimize frustrations. You don't need to make unnecessary challenges for yourself. Most stores are accessible but you learn which ones have narrow aisles and protruding endcaps and you avoid them. Things like that.'

'A lot to learn,' she said. Then seemed uncomfortable with the topic. 'Oh, Lincoln. You play chess.'

'I did. Haven't for a long time. How did you know?' He didn't own a physical chess set. When he played, he did so online.

'You've got Vukovic's book.'

Art of Attack. He glanced at the bookshelf. The title was at the far end, where the personal, not forensic, books were kept. He himself couldn't read the spine from here. But he recalled that eyesight – and fingernails – were among her God-given strengths.

She said, 'When we were together, my ex and I played quite a bit. We did bullet chess. It's a form of speed chess. Each player has a total of two minutes to make a move.'

'Per move?'

'No, the entire game, first move to last.'

Well, she was an aficionado of an esoteric form of chess *as well as being* a riddle-mistress. Not to mention well on her way to being a damn good criminalist. Rhyme could not have asked for a more interesting intern.

'I never played that. I like some time to strategize.' He missed the game. There was no one to play with. Thom had no time. Sachs had no patience.

Archer continued. 'We also played a limited-move variant. Our goal was to win in twenty-five moves or fewer. If we didn't, we both lost. Say, if you'd like to play sometime . . . I don't know anybody who's really into it.'

'Maybe. Sometime.' He was looking at the evidence charts.

'My brother won't be here for fifteen minutes or so.'

'I heard that.'

'So,' Archer said, a coy lilt to her voice, 'I can't hold two pieces behind my back for you to pick black or white. But I won't cheat: I'm thinking of a number one through ten. Even or odd?'

Rhyme looked her over, not understanding at first. 'Oh, I haven't played for years. Anyway I don't have a board.'

'Who needs a board? Can't you picture one?'

'You play in your head?'

'Of course.'

Well . . . He was silent for a moment.

She persisted. 'Even or odd?'

'Odd.'

'It's seven. You win the virtual toss.'

Rhyme said, 'I'll take white.'

'Good. I prefer defense . . . I like to learn as much about my opponent as I can. Before I trounce them.'

The gold Celtic bracelet clinked against the controller as her fingers maneuvered her chair close to his and faced him, about three feet away.

He asked, 'No time limit, you said.'

'No. But the game has to result in a mate or draw – in which case black wins – in twenty-five moves or fewer. Otherwise . . .'

'We both lose.'

'We both lose. Now' – she closed her eyes – 'I'm seeing the board. Are you?'

Rhyme continued to gaze at her face for a moment, the freckles, the narrow brows, the faint smile.

She opened her eyes. He looked away quickly and closed his, nestled his head back in the rest. The chessboard, fully loaded, was as clear as Central Park on a crisp spring afternoon, as today's had been. He thought for a moment. 'E2 pawn to e4.'

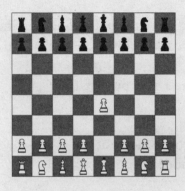

Archer said, 'Black pawn e7 to e5.'
Rhyme imagined:

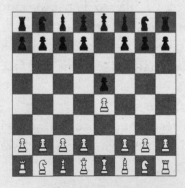

He shot back with, 'White king's knight to f3.'

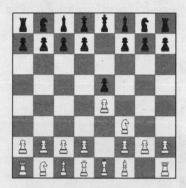

Archer: 'Black queen's knight to c6. You're seeing it clearly?'

'Yes.'

Well, she was certainly aggressive. Rhyme was pleased. No uncertainty. No hemming or hawing. He said, 'White king's bishop to c4.'

Archer snapped, 'Black queen's knight to d4.'

Her knight was now nestling between Rhyme's bishop and pawn.

How many moves were they up to? he wondered.

'Six moves,' Archer said, unknowingly responding to his question.

He said, 'White king's knight takes black pawn on e5.'

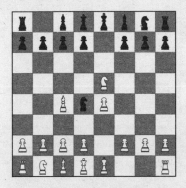

'Ah, yes, yes.' Archer then said, 'Black queen to g5.' Bringing her most powerful piece into the middle of the field. Vulnerable. Rhyme was tempted to open his eyes and see her expression. He opted for concentration.

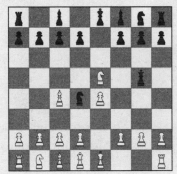

Rhyme saw an opportunity. 'White king's knight takes black pawn on f7.' In position to take her rook. And safe from her king, because the piece was guarded by his bishop.

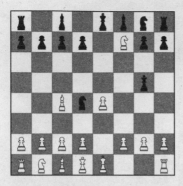

'Black queen takes white pawn on g2.'

Rhyme frowned. He'd have to abandon his tactics in the upper right-hand corner of the board. Her brash moves were bringing the assault to his home territory – with most of his pieces not even in play.

He said, 'White king's rook to f1.'

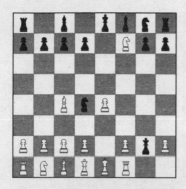

Archer's buoyant voice said, 'Black queen takes white pawn on e4. Check.'

Eyes still closed, Rhyme could clearly see where this was going. He chuckled. And said what he had to: 'White king's bishop to c2 to block the check.'

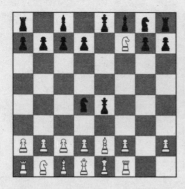

And there was no surprise when Juliette Archer said, 'Black queen's knight to f3. Checkmate.'

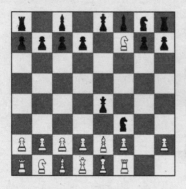

Rhyme studied the board tucked into his mind. 'Fourteen moves, I think.'

'That's right,' Archer confirmed.

'Is that a record?'

'Oh, no. I've won in nine. My ex in eight.'

'The game, it was elegant.' Lincoln Rhyme was a loser gracious on the surface but filled with knobby resolve not to be one again. 'A rematch soon?'

After he'd practiced.

'Love to.'

'But now – the bar's open! Thom!'

She laughed. 'You're teaching me forensics. You're teaching me how to be a productive gimp. But I think you're also teaching me some bad habits. I'll pass.'

'You're not driving,' Rhyme said. 'Well, not exactly.' A nod at the Storm Arrow motor, which could propel her along the pavement at a zippy seven mph.

'Better keep a clear head anyway. I'm seeing my son tonight.'

Thom poured Rhyme's Glenmorangie and glanced at Archer, who shook her head. The doorbell hummed. It was Archer's brother, who, when Thom escorted him into the parlor, greeted them cheerfully. He seemed like a nice guy. 'Fellow' was the word that fit. Rhyme wouldn't want to spend much time with him, but he seemed the rock that his sister would need facing life as a quad.

She wheeled toward the archway. 'I'll be back early tomorrow,' she said, echoing Sachs's farewell.

He nodded.

She wheeled out the door, her brother behind her.

The door closed. And Rhyme was suddenly aware of the immense silence of the room. He had a curious feeling. 'Hollowness' was the word that came to him.

Thom was back in the kitchen. The sound of metal against metal, wood against ceramic, water filling pots, emanated from there into the parlor. But no sound of human voices. Unusual for him, Rhyme didn't care for this manifestation of solitude.

A sip of the scotch. Rhyme was aware of the scent of garlic, meat and the perfume of vermouth, heated.

Something else too. A fragrant smell. Appealing, comforting. Ah, Sachs's perfume.

But then he recalled that she didn't wear any – why give the perp a clue as to your position in a potential firefight? No, the scent would have to be that, of course, of whatever Juliette Archer had worn that day.

'Dinner is served,' Thom said.

'On my way,' Rhyme said and left the parlor, instructing the controller to shut out the lights as he did so. He wondered if the voice-controlled lighting system in the town house happened to be embedded with a DataWise5000.

CHAPTER 37

'Just a fast one.'

'Honey, no.'

Her husband persisted, 'Twenty minutes. Arnie said he's got a new scotch. From the Isle of Skye. Never heard of it before.'

If there was a scotch that Henry was unfamiliar with it must've been something.

They'd finished dinner, Ginnie surprised that he'd actually complimented her on the chicken fricassee (though there *had* been: 'Good fix over last time, dear'), and she was rinsing dishes.

'You go,' Ginnie told him.

'Carole wanted you to come too. They're starting to think you don't like them.'

I don't, Ginnie thought. While she and Henry were transplants to the Upper East Side, Arnie and Carole were natural products of the effete neighborhood. She found these neighbors up the hall arrogant and pretentious.

'I really don't want to. I've got to clean up here. There's that project for work.'

'Just thirty, forty-five minutes.'

Double what it had been a moment ago.

Of course there was more to this than a neighborly

visit. Arnie was head of a small tech start-up and Henry wanted him as a client for his law firm. Her husband didn't admit it but this was obvious to her. She knew too that he liked to have Ginnie accompany him as he tried to win over people like Arnie – and not because she was smart and funny, but because of what she'd overheard him say once to a fellow attorney, when he didn't know she was nearby: 'Let's face it, a potential client's on the borderline, who's he going to sign with? The partner with the wife he can fantasize about fucking.'

The absolute last thing that Ginnie wanted to do, go have drinks with the Bassetts. He'd probably make her try the scotch.However expensive all tasted like dish soap to her.

'But we just got Trudy down.' The two-year-old could be a fitful sleeper and sometimes impossible to get to fall asleep at a reasonable hour. Tonight, the 7 p.m. target had been a bull's-eye.

'We've got the Nanny.'

'But still, you know I don't like leaving her.'

'Forty-five minutes, an hour. Just to say hi. Sip a little whisky. Did you know about the spelling. Whiskey with an "e" is bourbon. Irish too. Without it is scotch. Who thought that up?'

Henry was oh-so good at deflecting.

'Really, can't we take a pass, honey?'

'No,' Henry said, grit to his voice. 'I told them yes. So. Go scoot and throw something on.'

'It's just drinks,' Ginnie said. Glancing at her jeans and sweatshirt. Then realizing she'd caved.

Henry turned his handsome face toward her (yeah,

yeah, they *were* the perfect-looking couple). 'Ah, for me, honey? Please. That little blue thing.'

Gaultier. Thing.

He gave her a seductive wink. 'You know I like it.'

Ginnie went into the bedroom and changed, peeked at their daughter, still asleep, an angel with golden ringlets of hair, and then walked silently to the window, which faced a quiet side street, one flight below. Made sure the window was locked – though she'd checked it earlier – and drew the shades. Curiously Trudy might wake up at the sound of a cooing pigeon on the sill but would sleep through a fire engine siren and blaring intersection horn. She wanted to kiss the girl or touch her cheek. But that might wake her and disrupt the impromptu get-together. Henry wouldn't be happy.

Of course, if the child *were* to wake, that would be an excuse for Ginnie not to go.

Yes, no?

But she couldn't do it, use her daughter as a ploy against her husband. Still, she smiled to herself, thinking: It *had* been a good plan.

Five minutes later they were up the dimly lit hall, ringing the Bassetts' doorbell. The door opened. Cheeks were bussed, hands gripped, pleasantries exchanged.

Carole Bassett was in jeans and T-shirt. Ginnie's eyes dipped to the outfit then to Henry but he missed the telling glance and accompanying grimace of her thin glossy lips. The men veered to the bar, where the magic potion sat, and – thank goodness – Carole apparently remembered that Ginnie drank wine exclusively and thrust a Pinot Gris into her hand. They clinked, sipped and headed into the living room, which offered a partial view of Central Park. (Henry was resentful that the Bassetts, new to the building, had happened to decide to move here just as that particular unit became vacant. Henry's and Ginnie's faced plebian 81st Street.)

The men rejoined their mates.

'Ginnie, you want to try some?'

'Sure, she will. She loves scotch.'

And Palmolive is my favorite label. Right next to Duz. 'Already have wine. Don't want to spoil the experience.'

'You're sure?' Arnie said. 'Cost eight hundred a bottle. And that's because my guy got me a deal. And I mean *deal*.'

Carole said in a low voice, eyes wide, 'He got us a Pétrus for a thousand.'

Henry barked a laugh. 'You are shitting me?'

'Cross my heart.'

Ginnie noted her husband glance at the spot on her body where Carole was doing just that. It was just a T-shirt, yes, but quite tight and made of thin silk.

Arnie: 'The Pétrus? It was heaven. I nearly came.' He pretended to looked shocked at his own words. 'Listen to this: We *bribed* the maître d' to let us sneak it into Romance. They don't have a corkage policy, you know.'

'I didn't,' Ginnie said with mock astonishment. 'Oh, my God.'

Arnie added, 'I know. A restaurant like that.'

The couples sat and conversation meandered. Carole asked about Trudy and the schools they had planned for her (not as outrageous as it seemed, Ginnie had learned; Manhattan parents must plan early for their offsprings' education). The Bassetts were a few years younger – early thirties – and were just thinking about children now.

Carole added, 'Next year sounds good. For conceiving, I mean. It'll be a convenient time. The company's putting a new maternity leave plan in place. A friend of mine in HR told me about it. He said he wasn't supposed to say anything, but I should wait to get pregnant.' She laughed wickedly. 'It's sort of like *insider* trading!' and studied Ginnie's face to see if she got the risqué joke.

Got it and stepped on it till it was dead.

'Have to give up the wine,' Carole had said. 'That'll be hard.'

'You won't miss it. Only eighteen months.'

'Eighteen?' Carole asked.

'Breast-feeding.'

'Oh. That. Well. It's pretty much optional nowadays, isn't it?'

The men talked about business and Washington and all the while examined their glasses as if the amber liquid inside were unicorn blood.

Carole rose, saying she wanted to show off a new print she'd gotten from her 'favorite' gallery in SoHo. Ginnie wondered: How many galleries did she have?

They were halfway across the living room floor when a man's voice intruded.

'*Hi, there, little one.*'

Everyone froze. Looking around.

'*Aren't you a cute little petunia.*'

The baritone words oozed from the speaker of Ginnie's phone, sitting on the coffee table. Her wineglass tumbled to the floor and shattered into a hundred pieces and she lunged for the Samsung.

Arnie said, 'Wasn't the Waterford. Don't worry—'

'What is that?' Carole asked, nodding to the phone.

It was what Henry and Ginnie called the 'Nanny' – actually a state-of-the-art baby monitor. The microphone was next to Trudy's crib and sensitive enough to pick up the child's breathing and heartbeat.

And could also pick up the voices of anyone in the room.

'*You're coming with me, honeybun. I know somebody who wants to give you a whole new home.*'

Ginnie screamed.

She and Henry bolted for the door, flung it open and sprinted down the hall, followed by the Bassetts. Henry raged at her, 'Did you lock the fucking window?'

'Yes, yes, yes!'

'*Stay asleep, little one.*'

Ginnie's mind was a swirling tornado. Tears streamed and her heart vibrated in her chest. She lifted her phone and touched VOICE on the monitor app. She shouted into the microphone – it was a two-way system: 'The police are here, you son of a bitch. Don't you touch her. I'll kill you if you touch her.'

A pause, as perhaps the intruder was noticing the monitor. He chuckled. '*Police? Really? I'm looking out Trudy's right window and there's not a cop to be found. Better be going. Sorry, your little dear's still snoozing; I'll have to say goodbye for her. Bye-bye, Mommy. Bye-bye Daddy.*'

Ginnie screamed again. Then: 'Now! Now! Open the door!'

Henry fumbled the keys and Ginnie ripped them out of his hand, shoving him aside. She unlatched the door and pushed it in. She detoured into the kitchen to grab the first butcher knife in the block and charged to her daughter's room, swung it open, flipped the overhead light on.

Trudy stirred slightly at the intrusion. But didn't wake.

Henry pushed inside an instant later and they both scanned the small room. No one. The window was still locked. And the closet was empty.

'But . . .'

She handed the husband the knife and picked up and clutched her child.

Arnie and Carole were right behind them. Relief flooded their faces, seeing the baby girl.

'Is he here?' Carole asked in a tremulous voice, looking around.

But Arnie, the high-tech entrepreneur, was shaking his head, picking up the monitor near Trudy's crib. 'No, he's not. He could be a hundred miles away. He hacked into the server.' He SET the device back onto the table.

'So he could hear us now?' Ginnie cried, grabbing it and shutting it off.

Arnie said, 'That doesn't always cut the connection.' He unplugged it and added, 'People do it just to mess with you. Sometimes if there's a video monitor they do screenshots of the kids or videos and post them online.'

'What kind of sick fuck'd do that?'

'I don't know what kind. I just know how many. A lot of them.'

Arnie asked, 'You want me to call the police?'

'I'll take care of that,' Ginnie said. 'Just leave please.'

Henry said, 'Honey, really.' Glancing at his friends.

'Now,' she snapped.

'Sure. Really sorry,' Carole said. She embraced Ginnie with what seemed to be true concern.

'And,' Arnie offered, 'don't worry about the wineglass.'

After they were gone, Ginnie took the knife once more and, carrying still-snoozing Trudy, checked every room, Henry with her. Yes, all the windows were locked. There could have been no physical intrusion.

Back in their bedroom, Ginnie sat on the bed, wiped tears and fiercely cradled her daughter. She glanced up and saw her husband dial three numbers on his mobile.

'No.' She half rose and took it from him. Hit disconnect.

'What're you doing?' he snapped.

She said, 'It's going to ring in a minute. Nine one one'll call back. You tell them you hit it by mistake.'

'The fuck would I do that for?'

'If I talk to them, a woman, they'll think it's a domestic and might send somebody anyway. You have to tell them it was a mistake.'

'Are you crazy?' Henry raged. 'We *want* them to send somebody. We got hacked. That asshole fucked up our evening.'

'The police are *not* going to hear that we left our daughter alone to go drink some overpriced liquor with two idiots just because you want a new client. Do you *really* think that's a good idea, Henry?'

The phone rang. No caller ID number. She handed the unit to him. Glared into his eyes.

He sighed. And hit accept call. 'Hello?' he answered pleasantly. 'Oh, I'm really sorry. Nine one one is first on my speed dial, I hit it by mistake, calling my mother. She's number two . . . Yes, it's Henry Sutter . . .' He gave the address, apparently in response to another question. 'I'm really sorry . . . Appreciate your following up like this, though. Good night.'

Ginnie walked into Trudy's nursery and, one-handed, pulled the crib after her into the guest room. 'I'll sleep here tonight.'

'I think we should—'

She closed the door.

Ginnie tucked her daughter into the crib, nearly – but not quite – smiling that the girl had managed to sleep through the excitement. She pulled off the thousand-dollar dress and angrily flung it into the corner of the room. Then she climbed into bed without moisturizing her face or brushing her teeth. She shut out the light, knowing that, unlike for her daughter, sleep would be a long time in coming tonight. If at all.

But that was okay. She had lots to think about. Most important: what she would say to the lawyer tomorrow, the one she'd talked to a couple of times about the possibility of divorce. Until tonight she'd waffled. Tomorrow she would be telling him to proceed as quickly and as relentlessly and brutally as he could.

CHAPTER 38

Unprofessional, I guess.

But sometimes you do things for yourself. Because you have to.

I'm walking away from the Upper East Side coffee shop, near Henry and Virginia Sutter's apartment. I was across the street. It was *some* building, I'll tell you. Can't imagine living in a place like that. Wouldn't want to, probably. Beautiful people live there. I wouldn't be welcome. A den of Shoppers.

Doing things for yourself.

It was all pretty easy, visiting vengeance on the Shopper. I'd simply followed Henry home from the Starbucks in Times Square where we'd collided that afternoon.

You'd spilled this on me, it would've cost you big time, you Walking Dead asshole. This shirt cost more'n you make in a month. I'm a lawyer . . .

Once I found his address, I cross-referenced deeds with DMV pictures. And got his ID. Mr Henry Sutter. Married to Virginia. I was stymied briefly – data mining records didn't show they own anything with a CIR DataWise5000 inside. But then I peeked at Facebook. Henry and Ginnie, her preferred nic, had actually posted pictures of two-year-old Trudy? Fools . . . but good for me. Babies in the city equal baby monitors. And, yep, a simple scan of the house revealed the IP address and a brand name. I executed a handshake exploit with the network then ran Pass Breaker on my tablet and in no time at all, I was in. Listening to Trudy's soft breath and coming up with a script for my conversation with the young 'un that was sure to destroy Mom's and Dad's peace of mind for the immediate future.

(Opens up a world of possibilities. After all, I'm not wedded to the DataWise5000 idea. Other options are good too.)

I keep walking, loping really. I pass by the subway entrance. It's a long way to Chelsea but I have to use shanks' mare (my mother's mother's expression, even though I don't think she ever saw a mare in the flesh or walked more than a few hundred feet from car to her grocery store Piggly Wiggly); I'm worried about getting recognized. Those damn CCTVs. Everywhere.

What about dinner? I wonder. Two, no three sandwiches tonight. Then I'll work on my new miniature project, a boat. I don't usually make them. There's a whole world of seafaring model makers (like airplane and train people – this obsession with transportation has bloated the field). But Peter said he liked boats. So I'm making a Warren skiff for him. A classic rowboat with reciprocating oars.

Then maybe Alicia will come over. She's been upset lately, the past returning. The scars – the inside scars – aching. I'm doing what I can to make it better. But sometimes I just don't know.

Then I'm thinking again of the fun I've just had,

recalling his face earlier in the day, all sneery and handsome, after we collided outside of Starbucks.

Walking Dead . . .

Well, Henry, that's a good line. Clever. But I'm thinking of a better one:

It has to do with the last laugh.

'Hey.'

Amelia Sachs walked inside Nick Carelli's apartment. Sparse but clean, ordered.

'You got a TV.'

When they were together, Sachs recalled, they'd never owned one. Too much else to do.

'I've been watching some of the cop shows. You watch those?'

'No.'

Too much to do now too.

'They ought to do a show about you and Lincoln.'

'He's been approached. He's said no.'

She handed him the big cardboard moving box she'd brought. It contained some of his personal effects from when they lived together: yearbooks, postcards, letters, hundreds of family photos. She'd called him to say she'd found these things in her basement, thought he'd want them.

'Thanks.' He opened it up, rifled through the contents. 'I thought this stuff was gone for good. Hey, look.' Nick held up a photo. 'Our first family vacation. Niagara Falls.'

The family of four, the classic cascade behind them and a rainbow from the particles of water. Nick was about ten, Donnie seven.

'Who took it?'

'Some other tourists. Remember pictures back then? You had to have them developed.'

'Always tense when you got them back from the drugstore. Were they in focus, the right exposure?'

He nodded. More foraging. 'Oh, hey!' He picked up a program.

New York City
Police Academy
Graduation Ceremony

At the bottom was the date he'd graduated. The cover featured a seal: *Training Bureau. Preparing the Finest.*

His smile faded.

Sachs was recalling her own graduation ceremony. That had been one of the two times in her life when she'd worn white gloves. The other had been at the police department memorial honoring her father after his death.

Nick put the program back in the box, gazing at it fondly for a moment. He closed the carton up and asked, 'Glass of wine?'

'Sure.'

He stepped into the kitchen and returned with a bottle of wine and a beer. He poured her a glass of Chardonnay.

Another memory, of the two of them, triggered by the smell and the tap of metal on glass and his fingers brushing hers.

Boom . . .

She shot the recollection dead. She'd been doing a lot of sniping like this lately.

They sipped the oaky wine and the beer and he showed her around the place, though there wasn't much to see. He'd gotten some furniture out of storage. Picked up a few things, borrowed from cousins, bought on the cheap. Some books. Several boxes of documents. And then there were the case files of *People of the State of New York v. Nicholas J. Carelli*. The many documents were spread out on the kitchen table.

Sachs looked over the framed pictures of his family. She liked it that he had them on the mantelpiece for all to see. Sachs had spent a lot of time with his mother and father and had enjoyed their company. She thought too about Donnie. He'd lived in BK, not far from Nick. After he was arrested Sachs made an effort to keep up with the Carellis, Nick's mother in particular. Eventually, though, the contact grew wispier and finally ceased altogether. As often happens when the fulcrum of common connection between two people vanishes – or one of them goes to prison.

Nick poured more wine.

'Just a little. I'm driving.'

'How do you like the Torino versus the Camaro?'

'Prefer the Chevy, but it got turned into a cube of metal.'

'Hell, how'd that happen?'

Sachs explained about the perp who worked for a data mining company and had invaded every part of his victims' lives – including hers. Having the beautiful Camaro SS towed and pressed into scrap had been as simple for him as tying his shoes.

'You nailed him?'

'We did. Lincoln and I.'

There was a pause. Then: 'Can I say? I liked seeing Rose. I wasn't sure she believed me. About my brother. What really happened.'

'No, we talked later. She believed you.'

'From what you said before, I thought she'd look sicker. She was pretty good.'

'There are women who won't go out of the house without quote putting their face on. *That's* her healthy complexion. Maybelline.'

Nick sipped the beer. '*You* believe me, don't you?'

Sachs cocked her head.

'About Donnie and everything. You never said.'

Sachs gave him a smile. 'I wouldn't've given you the file if I didn't. I wouldn't be here now.'

'Thank you.' Nick looked down at the carpet, which was worn in a particular configuration that she attributed to heels of the shoes worn by a heavy person's outstretched legs. She remembered when they would sit on the couch – yes, this very couch – it had a slip-cover on it back then, but she could tell from the shape that it was the same. He put the carton of artifacts away. 'How's the case coming? The guy screwing around with the appliances? Which is pretty sick, by the way.'

'The case? Slow. He's smart, this perp.' She sighed. 'These controllers – they're in everything now. Our Computer Crimes contact said there'll be twenty-five billion embedded products in a few years.'

'Embedded?'

'Smart controllers. Stoves, refrigerators, boilers, alarm systems, home monitors, medical equipment. All of them, with Wi-Fi or Bluetooth computers in them. He can hack into a pacemaker and shut it off.'

'Jesus.'

'You saw what happened with the escalator.'

'I'm taking stairs now.' Nick wasn't making a joke, it seemed. He added, 'I saw a thing in the paper about what he's doing. And how these companies should fix their servers or something. In the cloud. To keep him out. Not all of them're doing it. You see that?'

She laughed. 'I'm responsible.'

'What?'

'I tipped a reporter off. There's a security patch that'll make it impossible for the unsub to hack into the controllers. But not everybody's installing it, looks like.'

'I didn't see a press conference from One PP.'

'Well, I didn't exactly share I was doing it. Going through channels would've taken too long.'

'Some things in policing never change.'

She lifted her wineglass to that.

'Domestic terrorism? That's his agenda?'

'The way it's looking. Ted Kaczynski sort.'

After a moment, Nick asked, 'How is he doing?'

'Who?'

'Your friend. Lincoln Rhyme.'

'Healthy as can be expected. There are always risks.' She told him about some of them, including potentially fatal dysreflexia, the rapid spike in blood pressure that can lead to stroke, brain damage and death. 'But he takes good care of himself. He exercises—'

'What? How can he do that?'

'It's called FES. Functional electrical stimulation. Electrodes in the muscles . . .'

'*Fifty Shades of Grey* . . . Oh, hell, sorry. That was way out of line.' He seemed to be blushing, not a typical aspect of Nick Carelli.

Sachs smiled. 'Lincoln doesn't have pop culture on his compass much but if he knew what the book is, or the movie, he'd laugh and say, Hell yes. He's got a sense of humor about his condition.'

'Hard for you?'

'Me? Yep. I saw the movie with a girlfriend. It was pretty bad.'

Nick laughed.

She chose not to speak any more about Rhyme and herself.

Sachs rose and poured more wine, sipped, feeling the warmth around her face. She looked at her mobile: 9 p.m. 'What've you found?' Nodding at the case file.

'Some good leads. Solid. Still a lot of work to do. Funny, it's just as hard to prove you're innocent as it is to make a case against a perp. I thought it'd be easier.'

'You're being careful?'

'Got my buddy, the one I told you about, to do most of the legwork. I'm bulletproof.'

What was said about him when he'd been on the force. Bulletproof. Sachs remembered Nick being not only a good cop but a risk taker. Anything to save a victim.

They were a lot alike in that way.

'You want . . .' he began.

'What?'

'Some dinner? You eaten already?'

She shrugged. 'I could use something.'

'Only problem. I didn't get to Whole Foods.'

'You *ever* shop at Whole Foods?'

'Once. I felt the need to spend eight dollars for a fruit salad.'

She laughed.

He continued, 'I've got frozen curry in the freezer. D'Agostino's. It's not bad.'

'No, but I'll bet it'd be better if we heat it up.' And she poured herself another glass of wine.

What *is* that noise?

The sixty-six-year-old soon-to-retire printing press operator was in the hallway of his apartment building, a decades-old, work-a-day dwelling typical of this unglamorous part of New York City. He was walking unsteadily after a drink or two at Sadie's. Nearly midnight. He'd been thinking that Joey, from the bar, was a dick, the politics and all, but at least he didn't insult you, you said I'm voting this way or that. It'd been fun to argue with him.

But his recollection of the evening, and its four drinks or five, faded as he slowed to a stop and listened to the sound coming from the apartment he was now walking past.

Edwin Boyle leaned closer to the door.

TV.

Had to be TV.

But, even with the new sets, the new sound systems, TV sounded different from this. It wasn't the same. Live was live. And *this* was live.

Besides, on TV and in movies, the sound of a couple

making love was either short and sweet (and usually there was music) or it went on and on and on, like in porn.

This was the real thing.

Boyle was grinning. Fun.

He didn't know the guy whose apartment this was, not very well. Seemed decent, if quiet. Wasn't the sort to hang out at Sadie's and get into talks about politics or anything else. Had that same kind of quiet you saw in private eyes. At least in the movies. The printer had never known a private eye.

Now the woman was whispering something. The rhythm was faster.

The man was saying something too.

And Boyle was wondering: If he made a recording who could he send it to?

Well, of course Dirty Old Tommy on the board cutter. Ginger in Accounting – she was always talking about sex, always flirting. Jose in Receivables.

Boyle pulled out his phone and edged close to his neighbor's door, then recorded the sounds. Smiling to himself.

Who else would appreciate it?

Well, he'd think about it. But he sure wouldn't send the recording to anyone tonight – not after a few hours at Sadie's. He might end up sending it to his ex or his son by mistake. Tomorrow, at work.

Finally his neighbor and whoever his squeeze was sped up and it was over with – a long sigh, which might've been him or might've been her or might've been his imagination.

Boyle shut the recorder of his iPhone off and slipped

it away. Staggered up the hall to his apartment. He tried to remember the last time he'd been laid, and couldn't – that's what seven or eight drinks did to you – but he was sure it was sometime during the previous administration.

SATURDAY

V CHECK . . .

CHAPTER 39

Eight a.m.

Amelia Sachs yawned. She was tired, and her head was throbbing. She'd had, to put it mildly, a restless night. No. Turbulent.

She had left Nick's apartment an hour before and was now in the war room at One PP, where for the second time in a few days, she was reviewing the file of a case that was not on her docket.

First, it had been Nick's.

And now this, a much smaller file, unrelated to his situation.

The hour was early but she'd read it three times already since she'd downloaded it from the archives not long ago. Looking for some positive nuggets that might explain what she suspected. Finding none.

She looked out the window.

Back to the file, which wasn't cooperating in the least.

No gold nuggets. No salvation.

Goddamn it.

A figure appeared in the doorway.

'Got your message,' Ron Pulaski said. 'Got down here as soon as I could.'

'Ron.'

Pulaski walked inside. 'Empty. Different.' He was

glancing around the war room. The evidence charts were in the corner but they were incomplete, now that the two cases – Sachs's and Rhyme's – were in fact just one and this facility was no longer part of the Unsub 40 operation. Sunlight poured harshly in, an acute angle.

Pulaski looked uneasy. Sometimes he was uncertain – mostly because of the head injury. It had robbed him of confidence and, yes, a little cognitive skill, which he more than made up for in persistence and street instinct. After all, the solutions to most crimes were pretty obvious; police work was built on sweat more than Holmesian deduction. But today? Sachs knew what the issue was.

'Sit down, Ron.'

'Sure, Amelia.' He glanced at the file open on the table in front of her. He sat.

She turned the folder around and pushed it forward.

'What's this?' the young blond officer asked.

'Read it. The last paragraph.'

He scanned the words. 'Oh.'

She said, 'The Gutiérrez case was closed six months ago. Because Enrico Gutiérrez died of a drug overdose. If you're going to lie, Ron, couldn't you at least have checked the facts?'

The phone woke him.

Humming, not ringing or trilling or playing music.

Just humming as it sat on his JCPenney bedside table. The dream helped, having kept him near waking; inside, he had dreams about being out; outside, he dreamed about his cell. So sleep was watchful, busy as water spiraling down a drain.

'Hello? Uhm, hello?'

'Yes, hi. Is this Nick?'

'Yeah, yeah.'

'I didn't wake you, did I?'

'Who's this?'

'Vito. Vittorio Gera. The restaurant.'

'Oh, sure.'

Nick swung his feet around, sat up. Rubbed his eyes.

'I wake you?' Gera asked again.

'Yeah, you did. But that's okay. I've gotta get up anyway.'

'Ha, honest. Most people woulda said no. But you can always tell, right? They sound groggy.'

'Do I sound groggy?'

'Sort of. Listen, speaking of, you know, being honest. I'll get right to it, Nick. I'm not going to sell the restaurant to you.'

'You had a better offer? I can work on that. What're we talking?'

'It's not the money, Nick. I just don't want to sell to you. I'm sorry.'

'The record?'

'What?'

'Me being in jail.'

Gera sighed. 'Yeah, the record. I know you were saying you were innocent. And, you know, I believe that. You don't seem like a crook. But still word'll get out. You know how that works. Even rumors, even they're lies. You know.'

'I do, Vito. Okay. If that's the way it is. Hey, you had the balls to call me yourself. It wasn't your lawyer calling my lawyer. A lotta people would've handled it that way. Appreciate it.'

'You're an okay guy, Nick. I know things'll work out for you. I got a feeling.'

'Sure. Hey, Vito?'

'Yeah?'

'Does this mean I can ask your daughter out?'

A pause.

Nick laughed. 'I'm messing with you, Vito. Oh, and by the way, that take-out order the other day? My friends said it was the best lasagna they'd ever had.'

A pause. A guilty pause, probably. 'You're okay, Nick. You'll do all right. Take care.'

They disconnected.

Hell.

Sighing, Nick rose and walked stiffly to his dresser, on which his pants lay in a pile. He tugged them on, swapped yesterday's T-shirt for a new one and brushed his hair. More or less.

Amelia Sachs had left the apartment an hour before, the footsteps and closing door waking him briefly.

He walked into the living room, thoughts of her prominent in his mind as he made a pot of coffee, poured a cup and sat at the kitchen table to wait for it to cool. But then, looking over the files she'd given him, the images of Amelia, the disappointment about the failed restaurant deal were replaced by memories of his days as a cop.

Now, like back then, something clicked in his mind when he was starting an investigation. Like turning on a switch, snap, he was in a different mode. Suspicious, for one thing. Sifting, picking out what could be believed and letting the rest sprinkle away. This wasn't hard for Nick Carelli.

And, more important, making leaps. His mind making those weird leaps. That's what nailed the perps.

'You told me you drove out to Suffolk.'

'Right, Detective Carelli. That's where I was. Seeing my friend. He vouched for me. You talked to him.'

'It's a hundred and ten miles round trip.'

'So?'

'Your gauge when I stopped you? Showed nearly full.'

'So again. Here's where I say, I refilled.'

'You drive a turbo diesel. Here's where I say there's no diesel along the route you say you took.'

'Oh. Ah. I wanna talk to my lawyer.'

Making that leap – calling the stations and checking for diesel pumps – was just something that occurred to him naturally.

Detective then, detective now.

He pulled the list of J names toward him, the people from Flannigan's that Von had said were regulars – one of whom, Nick prayed, could help him turn his life around.

Jack Battaglia, Queens Boulevard Auto and Repair

Joe Kelly, Havasham General Contracting, Manhattan

JJ Steptoe

Jon Perone, J&K Financial, Queens

Elton Jenkins

Jackie Carter, You Stor It Self Storage, Queens

Mike Johnson, Emerson Consulting, Queens

Jeffrey Dommer

Gianni 'Jonny' Manetto, Old Country Restaurant Supply, Long Island City

Carter Jepson Jr., Coca-Cola distribution

He'd never heard of any of them. Though he was amused to speculate that one in particular surely had had a tough time growing up, with a name close enough to a serial killer's for the kids to torment him mercilessly.

The cop mind was firing on all cylinders but that wasn't enough. He needed input, research. So get to work. Nick went online and began to check out the names. Google and Facebook and LinkedIn. He also logged onto the People Finder site Freddy had told him about. Jesus, there was a lot of information. When he was on the force, it would've taken him weeks, not hours, to get all this stuff. And he was astonished too at how much people posted about themselves. One guy, JJ Steptoe, was shown proudly smoking pot in a Facebook picture. A link led to a YouTube video that showed Jepson in the Caribbean, staggering around drunk and falling into a pool. Then climbing out and puking.

As for the wife of 'J,' Nanci, no luck there, for any of them.

But maybe Mr 'J' was divorced from Nanci. Or Nanci

was a girlfriend. There were probably ways to find out, maybe programs at the NYPD that linked people even if not married or related. If 'J' had done time, there might be a record of a Nanci coming to visit him in prison.

But he didn't have access to anything like that and he sure wasn't going to ask Amelia to search for him. He was already pushing the limits there.

He skimmed the data he'd downloaded. Nick had been hoping 'J' was somebody involved in law enforcement, with a knowledge of the hijacking operations back when he'd been arrested. But none of the men were law enforcement. The next best thing – somebody with underworld ties (even though he knew he'd need to be very, very careful about contacting them). That didn't pan out either, though. Jenkins had been arrested – misdemeanor and a long time ago. Two others had been the subject of civil investigations – SEC in one case, IRS in the other – but nothing came of these.

Nick sat back and sipped his lukewarm coffee. A glance at the clock. The work had taken three hours. A ton of info but nothing to show for it.

Okay. Think better. Think like a gold shield. Sure, the list could be useless and Stan Von had pulled together enough random names to buy himself an over-breaded chicken Parmesan. But it's all you got, the list, so work it. Just like the flimsiest lead on the street, the way you used to do. Turn it to something sweet.

He decided to look more carefully into the businesses the men operated or were employed by; were any of them more likely than others to have a potential connection to hijacking or receiving stolen? Von's list didn't have all of their outfits but Nick was able to find most of the others. Transportation and wholesale companies were the heart of hijacking operations but there were none of those. (Battaglia's operation was used car sales and repair.) Jackie Carter, who owned a franchise of self-storage facilities, seemed like a possibility. And Jon Perone's J&K Financial Services intrigued him; they might've lent money to any number of people involved in shady deals. And Johnson's consulting business? Who knew what they were up to?

Nick took a long slug of tepid coffee. The cup froze in midair. He set it down and sat forward, staring at the list. He laughed. Oh, man. How did I miss it? How the hell did I miss it?

He read: Jon Perone, J&K Financial, Queens.

Fi NANCI al.

'Nanci' wasn't a wife or girlfriend. It was from the name of his *company*. The detective's faded notes were to blame for his misreading.

Nick was suddenly filled with the thrill he remembered from his days running cases, when you had a breakthrough like this.

Okay, Mr Perone, who exactly are you? He'd found no suggestion of any criminal activity. Perone seemed to be upstanding, a legit businessman, generous, a giver-back to the community, active in the church. Still, Nick would have to be careful. He couldn't risk linking his own name with the man's if Perone were, in fact, involved in any underworld activity. He remembered his promise to Amelia.

If there's anybody who can help me and there's any risk, or it even looks like they're connected, I'll use, you know, an intermediary to contact them, a friend . . .

He found his phone and called Freddy Caruthers.

CHAPTER 40

Ron Pulaski stared at the Gutiérrez file sitting between him and Amelia Sachs.

He fidgeted in the chair across the table from her in their war room.

Hell. Why hadn't he checked to see if Gutiérrez was still around? There was an answer to that: Mostly because he believed nobody would know or care what he was up to.

Got that one wrong, didn't I?

Hell.

'Ron. Work with me here. What's going on?'

'Have you talked to IA?'

'No. Not yet. Of course not.'

But he knew that if she found he'd committed a crime, she'd report him to Internal Affairs in an instant. That was something about Amelia. She'd bend regs. But when you stepped over the razor wire of the New York Penal Code, that was a sin. Unforgivable.

And so he sat back, sighed and told her the truth. 'Lincoln shouldn't quit.'

She blinked, not understanding where this was going.

He could hardly blame her. 'He shouldn't. It's just wrong.'

'I agree. What does that have to do with anything?'

'Everything. Let me explain. You know what happened. He pushed the Baxter case too far.'

'I know the facts. What—?'

'Let me finish. Please.'

Funny about beauty, Pulaski was thinking. Amelia Sachs was no less beautiful than yesterday but now it was the beauty of ice. He looked past her out the window, unable to stand the beam of her eyes.

'I checked out the Baxter file. I've read it a thousand times, been through every word of testimony, every sentence of forensic analysis, all the detectives' notes. Over and over. I found something that didn't make sense.' Pulaski sat forward and despite the fact that his cover was blown and his mission in peril – Amelia by rights should put an end to it immediately – he felt the rush of being on a hunt that wasn't yet over. 'Baxter was a criminal, yes. But he was just a rich man screwing over other rich men. At the end of the day: He was harmless. His gun was a souvenir. He didn't have bullets in it. The gunshot residue had ambiguous sources.'

'I know all this, Ron.'

'But you don't know about Oden.'

'Who?'

'Oden. I'm not sure who he is, black, white, age, other than that he's got some connection with the crews in East New York. There was a reference to him in the notes of one of the detectives that ran the Baxter case. Baxter was tight with Oden. I talked to the detective, and he never followed up on Oden because Baxter was killed, and the case was dropped. The gang unit and Narcotics haven't heard the name. He's a mystery man. But I asked on the street and at least two people said they'd heard about him. He's connected with some new strain of drugs. Called Catch. You ever hear of it?'

She shook her head.

'Maybe he was smuggling it in from Canada or Mexico. Maybe financing. Maybe even fabricating it. I was thinking that might be the reason Baxter was killed. It wasn't a random prison fight. He was targeted because he knew too much about this stuff. Anyway, I've been working undercover . . . No, not sanctioned, just on my own. I told people I needed this stuff Oden was making. I was claiming my head injury was really bad.' He felt he was blushing. 'God'll get me for that. But I've got the scar.

'And?'

'My point was to prove to Lincoln that Baxter wasn't innocent at all. He was working with Oden, financing fabrication or importing of Catch. That maybe Baxter *did* use his gun. That people were dying because of the shit he was involved in.' Pulaski shook his head. 'And Lincoln would realize that he didn't screw up so bad – and he'd un-quit.'

'Why—?'

'—didn't I tell anyone, why make up the story? What would you have said? To give it up, right? An unauthorized undercover op, using my own money to score drugs—'

'To *what*?'

'Only once. I bought some Oxy. I dumped it in the sewer five minutes later. But I needed to make the buy. I had to build some street cred. I dropped a weapons charge to get some banger to vouch for me. I'm walking a line here, Amelia.'

He looked at the Gutiérrez file. Stupid. Thinking: Why didn't I check it?

'I'm close, I'm really close. I paid two thousand bucks for a lead to this Oden. I've got a feeling it's going to work out.'

'You know what Lincoln would say about feelings.'

'Has he said anything, now he's helping on Unsub Forty, getting back to work for the NYPD?'

'No. He told me nothing's changed.' She grimaced. 'He's working with us mostly to make a civil case for Sandy Frommer.'

Pulaski's own face remained stony. 'I wish you hadn't found out about this, Amelia. But now you know. Only I'm not stopping. I'll tell you right up front. I've got to play this out. I'm not letting him retire without a fight.'

'East New York, that's where this Oden hangs?'

'And Brownsville and Bed-Stuy.'

'The most dangerous parts of the city.'

'Gramercy Park is just as dangerous if that's where you get shot.'

She smiled. 'I can't talk you out of this?'

'No.'

'Then I'll forget all about it on one condition. You don't agree, I'll report you and get your ass suspended for a month.'

'What condition?'

'I don't want you on this alone. You go to meet Oden, I want somebody with you. Anybody you know who can back you up?'

Pulaski thought for a moment. 'I've got a name in mind.'

Lincoln Rhyme dialed Sachs's mobile.

No response. He'd called twice already this morning, once early – at 6 a.m. She hadn't picked up then either.

He was in the lab with Juliette Archer and Mel Cooper. The hour was early but they were already looking over the evidence chart and kicking ideas back and forth like players in a soccer game. A simile Rhyme had used coyly, given the sedentary nature of two of the participants.

Cooper said, 'Got something here.'

Rhyme wheeled over to him, his chair nearly colliding with Archer's.

'Sorry.' He looked at the screen.

'It's the varnish that Amelia found at one of the earlier scenes. It just came in from the bureau's database.'

Braden Manufacturing, Rich-Cote.

'Took their sweet time.'

Cooper continued, 'Used in fine furniture making. Not for floors or general carpentry. Expensive.'

'Sold in how many stores?' Archer asked.

The appropriate question.

'That's the bad news,' Mel Cooper offered. 'It's one of the most common varnishes on the market. I make it a hundred twenty retail locations in the area. And they sell it in bulk direct to furniture operations. Big ones and small. And – not to brighten everyone's day – they also sell it online through a half-dozen resellers.'

'Write it up on the chart, would you?' a discouraged Lincoln Rhyme muttered to Archer.

Silence filled the parlor.

'I, uh.'

'Oh, right,' Rhyme said. 'Sorry. Forgot. Mel, write it up.'

The officer added the brand and manufacturer in his fine penmanship.

Archer said, 'Even if there're a lot of outlets I'll start canvassing stores that sell it. See if anybody recognizes our unsub.'

Rhyme said, 'There's also a chance that the unsub—'

Archer continued, '—works for the store. I've thought of that. I figured I'd do some preliminary. Check out the shops and see if they have employee pictures. Their websites, Facebook, Twitter. Maybe softball teams. Charities, blood drives.'

'Good.' Rhyme wheeled again to the charts and examined them. He felt prodded by urgency. Now that they'd confirmed that the People's Guardian, their Unsub 40, was a serial performer, they had every reason to suspect that he would move again soon. That was often the nature of multiple criminals. Whatever motivated them, sexual pleasure or terrorist statement, lust tended to accelerate the frequency of their kills.

Until tomorrow, I remain . . .

There came the sound of a key in the lock, the door opening and footsteps in the front hall . . .

Sachs and Pulaski had arrived. Sometimes the kid was in uniform, sometimes street clothes. Today he was dressing down. Jeans and a T-shirt. Sachs looked tired. Her eyes were red and her posture slumped.

'Sorry I'm late.'

'I called.'

'Busy night.' She walked to the charts and looked over them. 'Well, where are we?'

Rhyme gave her a synopsis of the varnish, what Archer was doing – canvassing stores for customers who'd bought the substance. Sachs asked, 'Anything more on the napkins?'

'Didn't hear from HQ,' Mel Cooper replied.

She grimaced. 'Still missing.'

Rhyme too was scanning the charts.

The answer's there . . .

Except that it wasn't. 'There's *something* we're missing,' Rhyme snapped.

A man's voice boomed from the doorway. 'Of *course* there is, Linc. How many times I have to tell you, you gotta look at the big picture. Do I *always* need to hold your goddamn hand?'

And with that, rumpled NYPD detective Lon Sellitto limped slowly into the room, assisted by a dapper cane.

CHAPTER 41

Waiting for his ride, looking at the sheets on the couch of his apartment, Nick Carelli smiled. Not to himself, an actual full-faced smile.

He'd been the gentleman last night, when Amelia was over. They'd sat together on the couch – the dining table was cluttered with Operation I'm Innocent paperwork – and eaten the curried chicken and finished the wine, down to the last bit, a good bottle he'd bought knowing she was coming over.

Sitting close to her, yes, but a gentleman. When she said, a bit woozy, that she couldn't drive home and should call a cab, he'd said, 'You want the couch? Or the bed, and I'll take the couch? Don't worry. I'm not hitting on you. You just look, well, you look like you needed to fall asleep an hour ago.'

'You don't mind?'

'Nope.'

'Couch.'

'I'll even make it up right.'

He hadn't. But neither had she minded the sloppy job. In five minutes she'd been asleep. Nick had just stared at her beautiful face for two or three minutes. Maybe longer. He didn't know.

Nick now pulled the sheets off the couch, took them

into the bedroom and pitched them into the laundry hamper. He got the pillowcase too, lifted it to his face and smelled it, feeling a thud in his gut at the aroma of her shampoo. He'd been going to launder this too but changed his mind and set it on the dresser.

His mobile beeped with a text. Freddy Caruthers had arrived. He rose, pulled on his jacket and left the apartment. In front of the building he jumped into his friend's SUV – an Escalade, an older one but well cared for. He gave Freddy an address in Queens. Freddy nodded and started off. He turned this way and that, a dozen times. He wasn't using GPS. Freddy seemed to know the area cold. The guy looked tiny behind the big wheel of the Caddie, but less toady this morning, for some reason.

Nick sat back in the crinkly leather and watched the urban vista mellow as they headed east. The ambience morphed from bodega and walk-up to 7-Eleven to bungalows to larger single-families surrounded by plots of lawn grass and gardens. You didn't have to drive far in Queens to see the change.

Freddy gave him the folder. 'Everything I could get on Jon Perone and his company. His contacts. Man is brilliant.'

Nick read. Took some notes. Compared what Freddy'd found to what he himself had pieced together. His heart tapped solidly. Yes, this could be just what he needed.

Salvation. Another smile.

He slipped the papers into his inner jacket pocket and the two men made small talk. Freddy said he was going to take his sister's kids to the ball game this weekend.

'The Mets. They're twelve and fifteen.'

'The Mets?'

'Ha. The boys. Attitude some but not with me so much. And you're fifteen without an attitude, something's way wrong.'

'Remember when Peterson caught us with that pint in the gym?'

Freddy laughed. 'What'd you say to him? It was . . . I don't remember. But it didn't go over good.'

Nick said, 'He was like what the hell're you doing with booze? Don't you know it's bad for you? And I just went: "Then why'd your wife give it to me?"'

'Jesus, that's right! What a line. He decked you, didn't he?'

'Shoved me is all . . . And suspended me for a week.'

They drove in silence for a few blocks, Nick relishing the memories of school. Freddy asked, 'What's the story with you and Amelia? I mean, she's with that guy now, right?'

Nick shrugged. 'Yeah. She's with him.'

'That's kinda weird, don't you think? He's a cripple. Wait. Can you say that?'

'No, you can't say that.'

'But he is, right?'

'Disabled. I looked it up. You can say disabled. They don't like handicapped either.'

'Words,' Freddy said. 'My dad, he called blacks coloreds. Which you weren't supposed to. But now you're supposed to say "persons of color." Which is a lot like coloreds. So, I don't get it. You guys made a nice couple, you and Amelia.'

Yeah, we did.

Nick glanced in the side-view mirror and stiffened. 'Shit.'

'What?' Freddy asked.

'You see that car behind us?'

'The—'

'Green, don't know. Buick, I think. No, Chevy.'

'Got a look. What about it?'

'It's been making the same turns as us.'

'No shit. What's that about? Nobody after me I know about.'

Nick looked in the mirror again. He shook his head. 'Goddamn it.'

'What?'

'I think it's Kall.'

'Is—'

'Vinnie Kall. That asshole detective hassling us at the Bay View with Von.'

'Shit, staking out your place. That's low. I ditched the gun. They'll never find it. And you didn't do nothing. You could say you didn't know he had a piece, even if it comes up. And Von didn't give his real name. What's it about?'

'He's a dick, that's what it's about. Just riding me maybe. Man, I don't want him to screw this up, with Perone. It's too important. It's the only way I'm going to prove I'm innocent.'

He looked around. 'Look, Freddy. He's got nothing on you. He doesn't know you called in that false alarm. Do me a favor.'

'Sure, Nick. You got it.'

He looked around. 'Pull into that garage.' Pointing ahead.

'Here?'

'Yeah.'

Freddy spun the wheel fast. Tires squealed. It was a four-story parking garage attached to an enclosed shopping center.

'I'm getting out here. Just hang for a half hour, forty minutes.'

'What're you going to do?'

'I'll go through the stores, get a cab to talk to Perone. Meet you back here. I'm sorry about this.'

'No, it's cool. I'll get some breakfast.'

Freddy pulled to a stop near one of the entrances to the mall. Nick asked, 'You saw him at the restaurant, right? Kall?'

'Yeah, I remember him.'

'If he comes up and wants to know about me—'

'—I'll tell him I can't talk. I'm waiting for his wife.' Freddy winked.

Nick grinned and slapped the little man on the shoulder. He jumped out of the SUV and vanished into the mall.

There was no security – no *human* security – in the lobby of J&K Financial, only a mundane intercom. Nick pressed a button and announced himself.

A pause.

'Do you have an appointment?' a woman's voice asked.

'No. But I'd appreciate a chance to speak to Mr Perone.'It has to do with Algonquin Transportation.'

Another pause. Longer.

The door lock buzzed with what Nick thought was a jarringly loud sound.

He stepped into a small elevator and on the third floor he entered a surprisingly nice office, given the neighborhood and the scruffy façade of the building. Jon Perone did okay for himself, it seemed. The receptionist was a beautiful woman with deep mocha skin.

Behind her two offices were visible through open doors. Both occupied by men, large men with short brownish hair. Their large torsos were encased in pressed dress shirts. One was lost in a phone call. The eyes of the other, in the near office, swiveled to Nick. The bigger of the two, he wore yellow suspenders over a pale-green shirt. His stare was cool.

The receptionist set down her landline. 'Mr Perone will see you now.'

Nick thanked her. He walked inside the largest office in the suite, filled with books and spreadsheets and business documents, along with memorabilia and photos. Hundreds of photos. On the wall, on the desk, on the coffee table. A lot of them appeared to be of family.

Jon Perone rose. He wasn't a tall man and was solidly built. Like a column. Wearing a gray suit, white shirt and tie the color of the sea surrounding a Greek island. Black hair, slicked back. He'd cut himself shaving and Nick wondered if he used a straight razor. He seemed the sort who might. A gold bracelet encircled his right wrist.

'Mr Carelli.'

'Nick.'

'I'm Jon. Have a seat.'

Both men lowered themselves into supple leather chairs. Perone eyed him carefully.

'You mentioned Algonquin Transportation.'

'I did. You've heard of it?'

'It's not in business anymore but I believe it was a private trucking company.'

'That's right. It transported pharmaceuticals and cigarettes in unmarked semis for big brand manufacturers – unmarked because, of course, hijackers would target trucks with Philip Morris or Pfizer logos on them.'

'I'm aware of that practice. What does that have to do with me?'

'Fifteen years ago an Algonquin semi carrying two million dollars' worth of prescription drugs was hijacked near a bridge over the Gowanus Canal.'

'Was it?'

'You *know* it was. The hijacker stashed the drugs in a warehouse in Queens but before he could get back and fence them to his buyers he got busted. Somebody in a Brooklyn crew found out about the 'jacked merchandise and stole the whole shipment from the warehouse. It took me a while but I found out those guys worked for you.'

'I don't know anything about that.'

'No? Well, I do.'

Perone said nothing for a moment. Then: 'How're you so sure?'

'Because I was the hijacker.' Nick let that sit for a minute. 'Now. My take from the job was going to be seven hundred K. Which you robbed me of. Inflation and interest? Give me a million and we're square.'

CHAPTER 42

'Well, look at this.' Mel Cooper was grinning, running a hand through his thinning hair.

Stepping into the parlor, moving slowly, Lon Sellitto nodded to those present. He'd been Rhyme's partner for some years when the criminalist was on the NYPD. Of recent, Sellitto had fed Rhyme consultancy work, helping Major Cases with forensics and other investigative services.

'Lon!' Pulaski was on his feet and pumping the detective's hand.

'All right, all right. Take it easy on an old man.' In fact, Sellitto was comfortably lounging somewhere in middle age.

Thom, who'd let the officer in, said, 'Anything for you, Lon?'

'Hell yes. If you baked it, I'm all over it.'

The aide smiled. 'Anyone else?'

The others declined.

Sellitto was a Cliffs Notes version of himself, having been sidelined for a long time thanks to a perp who'd poisoned him. He'd nearly died and had undergone a great deal of treatment and therapy. He had dropped, Rhyme guessed, forty pounds over the past year. His thinning hair was graying. With his lithe new physique he looked even more rumpled than usual. The clothes didn't fit and some of the newly emptied skin was baggy too.

Sellitto walked farther into the room, eyes on Juliette Archer. 'What is this . . .' His voice faded.

Rhyme – and Archer – laughed. 'You can say it.'

'I . . .'

Archer cocked her head. 'A wheelchair showroom?'

Sellitto, blushing one of the few blushes Rhyme had ever seen on his cheeks, said, 'I was gonna say convention. But yours is funnier.'

Rhyme introduced them.

She said, 'I'm an intern.'

Sellitto cut a glance toward Rhyme. '*You*? Are a mentor? Jesus, Juliette, good luck with *that*.'

Sachs hugged Sellitto. She and Rhyme saw the detective and his girlfriend Rachel with some frequency but, now that Rhyme wasn't doing criminal work and Sellitto had been on medical leave, they hadn't worked together for a long time.

'Ah.' His eyes glowed as Thom brought a tray of Danish into the parlor. Sellitto scarfed. Thom handed him a coffee.

'Thanks.'

'You don't want sugar? Right?'

'Yeah, I do. A couple.' Sellitto's idea of losing weight had been to choose black coffee to accompany the dough-nuts. Now, slim, he was indulging.

The Major Cases detective looked over the parlor with a critical eye, half the equipment covered with plastic. The dozen whiteboards, turned against a far wall. 'Jesus,

I take a break and everything goes to hell.' Then he smiled. 'And you, Amelia, heard about your big-game hunting, escalators in BK malls.'

'What exactly *do* you hear? I got the incident report to the team on time.'

'All good,' the detective added. 'They're holding you up as Miss Ingenuity. And better'n good. Madino's got cred – he just got tapped for a spot at One PP – so you've got a power hitter rooting for you.'

Rhyme said sourly, 'Fans root for hitters, Lon, not the other way around.'

'Jesus. Did kids in school regularly beat the crap out of you, Mr Hand-Up-First-With-The-Right-Answer?'

'Let's get caught up *later* on irrelevant issues, shall we? Lon, you were saying, big picture?'

'I read what you sent.'

Sellitto was the expert Rhyme had uploaded the Unsub 40 case file to. He smiled to himself at the man's laconic response.

Yah, yah. Tomorrow . . .

'First, this is one sick fuck.'

Accurate but irrelevant. Rhyme said with subdued impatience, 'Lon?'

'So. What we have. He's got this thing for products, for consumer products that we bring into our houses and turn on us. Now, my take? He's agendizing in two ways.'

'What did you say?' Rhyme started, reflexively.

'I'm fucking with you, Linc. Couldn't resist. Been months without you breaking my balls with a grammar lesson. Pardon my French.' Directed at Archer.

She smiled.

Sellitto continued: 'Okay. He's got two agendas. Using the controller things to make a statement or to target rich people who buy expensive shit or whatever. That's his weapon of choice. Fucked up but there it is. Agenda two: self-defense. He needs to stop people who're after him. I.e., us. Well, you. He's been at the scenes to type in the code to work the controller, right?'

'Right,' Archer said. 'You can hack into the cloud server from anywhere in the world. But he seems to want to be close. We think he may have some moral element – making sure he doesn't hurt kids or maybe poorer folks who *don't* spend lots of money on indulgent products.'

'Or,' Sachs said, 'he gets turned on by watching.'

'Well, that means he might've stayed around to see who was after him. The Evidence Collection Team, you – Amelia and Ron.'

'I was at a scene too,' Rhyme said. 'When he destroyed the office of the man who taught him how to hack the controllers.' He grimaced. 'And he saw Evers Whitmore there.'

'He on the force?' Sellitto asked.

'No, a lawyer. I was working with him – the civil case, the escalator accident. Before we knew it was a homicide.'

Sellitto sipped coffee, then added another sugar. 'Wouldn't be hard for your unsub to ID him. And you, you're too public, Linc. Easy to track you down and all your little chickies. I'd get protective details on everybody. I can handle that.'

Rhyme ordered the computer to print out Whitmore's address and phone. Sellitto reminded that he had Cooper's and Sachs's personal information and he'd get a detail to their residences. Archer said it was unlikely she was at risk but Rhyme was emphatic. 'I want somebody at your brother's anyway. Unlikely doesn't mean impossible. From now on, we all have to assume we're in his sights.'

On the agenda for today: The People's Guardian has more mischief planned.

And a beautiful day for it too.

I've spent some time with Alicia, comforting her. She's off to do some work (she's a bookkeeper, a sort-of accountant, though I couldn't tell you where she works or exactly what she does. Fact is, she's not excited about it and therefore I'm not either. We're not a typical couple; our lives do not, of course, completely coincide). I'm enjoying first one then a second breakfast sandwich at the window of my apartment in Chelsea. Tasty, full of salt. My blood pressure is so low that a doctor asked joking during a checkup if I was still alive. I smiled, though it was not really funny coming from a medico. I was inclined to crack his skull but I didn't.

I chew the second sandwich down fast and get ready to go out.

Not quite ready for PG's full-on assault, though; I have an errand first.

New outfit today – no cap for a change, my blond crew cut is there for the world to see. A running suit, navy blue, stripes along the legs. My shoes. Nothing to do about them. I need a special size. My feet are long, like my fingers, the way my skinny body is tall. The condition is Marfan syndrome.

Hey, Vern, sack of bones . . .

Hey, Bean Boy . . .

Can't reason with people, can't say: Wasn't my choice. Can't say, God blinked. Or He played a joke. Doesn't work to point out that Abraham Lincoln was one of us. Doesn't work to say what's the big deal?

So you let it go, the taunts. The punches. The pictures slipped in your locker.

Until you choose not to let it go. Red's partner, this Lincoln Rhyme, his body's betrayed him and he copes. A productive member of society. Good for him. I'm taking a different path.

Backpack over my shoulder, I head out onto the street, radiant on this glorious spring day. Funny how beauty blossoms to fill the world when you're on a mission.

So. I go west toward the river and the closer I get to the gray Hudson the farther back in time I go. Chelsea east and central, near me, is apartments and boutiques and chic and *New York Times*–reviewed restaurants. To the far west it's industrial – like it was in the 1800s, I imagine. I see the building I'm looking for. I pause, pull on cloth gloves and on the prepaid I make a call.

'Everest Graphics,' a voice answers.

'Yes, Edwin Boyle, please. It's an emergency.'

'Oh. Hold on.'

Three minutes, three solid minutes, I wait. How long would it be if this *weren't* an emergency – which it isn't but never mind.

'Hello, this is Edwin Boyle. Who's this?'

'Detective Peter Falk. NYPD.' Not so much into TV, no, but I loved *Columbo*.

'Oh. What's wrong?'

'I'm sorry to report your apartment's been broken into.'

'No! What happened? Druggies? Those kids hanging out on the street?'

'We don't know, sir. We'd like you take a look and tell us what's missing. How soon can you be here?'

'Ten minutes. I'm not that far away . . . How did you know I work here?'

I'm prepared. 'Found some business cards on the floor of your place. It was ransacked.'

Such a great word.

'Okay. I'll be right there. I'm leaving now.'

I disconnect and examine the sidewalk. Other companies and commercial operations squat here. One pathetic ad agency, striving to be cool. Sidewalks pretty deserted. I step into the loading dock of an abandoned warehouse. It's no more than three minutes before a figure steams past, sixty-ish Edwin Boyle, eyes forward, concern on his face.

Stepping forward fast, I grab his collar and yank him into the shadows of the loading dock.

'Oh, Jesus . . .' He turns toward me, eyes wide. 'You! From up the hall! What the hell?'

We're neighbors, two apartments away, or three, though we don't say much to each other. Just a nod hello occasionally.

I don't say anything now. What's the point? No quips, no chance for last words. People can get snaky at times like that. I just bury the round end of the ball-peen hammer in Edwin's temple. Like with Todd Williams while we were on our way to have a drink commemorating our joint venture in making the world safe from smart products too smart for our own good.

Crack, crack.

Bone separates. Blood appears.

On the ground, he's squirming, eyes unfocused. Pull the hammer out – it's not easy – and do the same thing again. And again.

The squirms stop.

I look onto the street. No pedestrians. A few cars but we were deep in obscuring shadow.

I drag poor Edwin to a supply cabinet of the abandoned warehouse's abandoned loading dock and open the warped plywood door. Muscle him inside. Then crouch down and get his phone. It's passcode-protected but that doesn't matter. I recognize it from last night. Alicia and I were making love on the couch, beside the fish tank. I glanced up at the security monitor and saw Edwin, returning home drunk, like most nights, outside my door, recording our sounds. Didn't tell her, didn't say anything. It would upset her, a woman whose resting state is upset.

But I knew I'd have to crack Edwin's bones for what he did. Just knew it. Not that there was any evidence that could be used to track me down. Just because doing that – recording us – was cruel. It was the act of a Shopper.

And that was reason enough for the man to die. Wish it had been with more nociceptive pain but you can't have everything.

Crack the bones of his mobile too – can't take the battery out very easily on these models – and I'll dispose of it later.

I notice a few intrigued rats nearby. Cautious but sniffy. Nice way to eliminate evidence, it occurs to me, hungry rodents, digesting trace evidence from the corpse.

Stepping out onto the sidewalk, I inhale deeply. Air is a bit ripe, this part of town. But invigorating.

A good day . . .

And soon to get better. It's time for the main event.

'Stand up,' Jon Perone said, smoothing his jet-black hair. Was a bottle involved? Probably.

Nick knew the drill. Pulled up his shirt and spun around slowly. Then dropped his pants too. And underwear. Perone glanced down. Impressed, dismayed? A lot of men were.

Nick buttoned and zipped and tucked.

'Shut your phone off. And battery out.'

Nick did this too. Set them on Perone's desk.

He glanced at the door. The man in suspenders was there. Nick wondered how long he'd been present.

'It's okay, Ralph. He's clean.'

Nick stared into Ralph's eyes until the man turned and left the room. Back to Perone. 'Just to connect the dots, Jon. A friend of mine tracked down a friend of *yours* – Norman Ring, presently guest of the state, doing five to eight up in Hillside. He earned himself serious time because he agreed to keep quiet when he could've rolled over on you. I've got enough, though, to put you two together.'

'Jesus, man. Fuck.' Perone's complexion, ruddy from weekend golf and vacationing, Nick guessed, grew ruddier yet under the painted hair.

'It's all in a letter to my lawyer, to be opened in the event of my getting fucked. You know the rest of it, right? So let's not get indignant here. Or blustery. Or trigger-happy.

Let's just talk business. Didn't you ever wonder where the merch you stole came from?'

'Algonquin?' Perone was calmer now. 'I kept waiting for somebody to come out of the woodwork. But nobody did. What was I gonna do, take out an ad? Found: two million bucks' worth of Oxy and Perc and propofol. Call this number.'

'No harm done. But time for my money.'

'You didn't need to come on like the fucking Godfather.'

Nick screwed up his face. 'All respect, Jon. What happened to the owner of the warehouse where I stored the shit? Stan Redman?'

Perone hesitated. 'Accident. Construction site.'

'I heard you buried him alive after he tried to move the merch himself.'

'I don't recall any such occurrence.'

Nick shot him a wry glance. 'Now the money. I earned it. I need it.'

'I'll go six.'

'We're not negotiating, Jon. Even you went to the hardest-ass fence in the city, you cleared fifty-five points. That's over a million. And I'll bet you didn't. You're not a discount kind of guy at all. You sold it on the street. You probably walked away with three M. Pure profit.'

Perone shrugged. The equivalent of: Yeah, pretty much.

'So here's the deal. I want a million. And I want paper-work shows it as a loan – from a company that can't be traced to you or anybody with a record. Only we have a side agreement, written, that the debt's forgiven. I'll worry about the IRS if it comes to that.'

Perone's grimace was more reluctant admiration. 'Any other fucking thing you want, Nick?'

'As a matter of fact, yeah, there is. The Algonquin 'jacking, the Gowanus? I want you to put the word out on the street that it wasn't me did it. It was my brother. Donnie.'

'Your brother? You're diming him out?'

'He's dead. He won't give a shit.'

'Whatever people hear on the street, nobody's reversing a conviction.'

'I know that. I just want some people who're in the loop to hear it.'

Perone said, 'I knew that merch'd come back to haunt me. Are we through?'

'Almost.'

'Oh, Christ.'

'Now, there's a guy named Vittorio Gera. Owns a restaurant in BK. The place is his name. Vittorio's.'

'Yeah?'

'I want you to have somebody visit him, tell him he's going to sell the place to me. For half of what he's asking.'

'And if he doesn't?'

'Have that somebody lean on his wife and daughters. I think he's got grandchildren too. Just get some pictures of them in the park and send them to him. That should do it. If not, have somebody visit his youngest daughter. Hannah. She's the one looks like a slut. Just take her for a ride around the block.'

'You do have a style, Nick.'

'You robbed me, Perone. I don't need any shit from you.'

'All right. I'll get the paperwork put together.' Then Perone was frowning. 'How'd you tip to me, Nick? Couldn't've been that easy. I cover tracks real good. Always have. Who's this friend of yours?'

'Freddy Caruthers.'

'So he could put me together with the Algonquin heist merch. And put you and me together.'

Nick said, 'Which brings me to my last request.'

Perone was nodding slowly. His eyes remained on something behind Nick, on a hat on the coatrack or on a grease spot on the wall or a photo of him playing golf at Meadowbrook.

Or maybe on nothing at all.

'Freddy drove me partway today. I told him I was worried there was a cop after me and we ducked into the garage at Grand Central Center, the mall. I took a cab the rest of the way.'

'Cop?'

'No, no, I made it up. I just wanted Freddy to cool his heels.' Nick'd had an idea this was how it was going to shake out.

Perone said softly, 'We can take care of that.' He made a call. A moment later Ralph, of the solid chest and flamboyant suspenders and icy glare, was back.

'Nick Carelli, Ralph Seville.'

A moment of mano eye lock, then hands were shaken.

'Got a job for you,' Perone said.

'Sure, sir.'

Nick pulled out his phone, slipped the battery in, turned it back on. He texted Freddy; he didn't want to hear the man's voice.

On way back. Any sign of Kall?

There wouldn't be, of course.

Nope.

Nick typed and sent:

Where R U?

The reply was:

Purple level near Forever 21 door.

Nick's next message was:

C U in 15.

From Freddy:

All good?

Nick hesitated then typed.

Gr8

Nick gave Ralph the information about Freddy's location. 'He's in a black Escalade.' He then cut a glance toward Perone. 'No buried-alive shit. Fast, painless.'

'Sure. I don't need to send messages. This is just loose ends.'

'And I don't want him to know it was me.'

Ralph gave a grimace. 'I'll do what I can. But.'

'Just try. The phone's got my texts. And my prints're in his SUV.'

'We'll take care of everything.' Ralph nodded. And left the office. Nick caught sight of a large, nickel-plated automatic pistol in his waistband. Thinking one of those bullets would be in his friend's brain in a half hour.

Nick rose and he and Perone shook hands. 'I'll get a cab back to the city.'

'Nick?'

The man paused.

'You interested in doing some work with me?'

'I just want to open my business and settle down and get married. But, sure, I'll think about it.' Nick walked out of the office, lifting his phone and dialing a number.

CHAPTER 43

Rhyme was looking at Amelia Sachs when her phone rang.

She glanced away from him and stepped to the recesses of the parlor to take a call. Her back was to the room. He wondered if it was her mother. Her shoulders were slumped. Was all okay? He knew the troubled history of mother and daughter but also knew that it had improved with the years. Rose had mellowed. Sachs had too, with regard to her mother. Years go by, edges dull. Entropy. And now, of course, the woman's illness. Someone's physical condition, as he well knew, can change all.

He couldn't hear or deduce much. Finally: 'restaurant' and 'worked out' and 'congratulations.' She sounded enthusiastic. Then, after she'd listened for a time: 'I have faith in you.'

Not Rose. Then who?

He turned back to the evidence charts, wheeled closer. His meditation was interrupted by Lon Sellitto. 'Anything close in NCIC?'

'No,' Rhyme said. The fourteen people files and the seven property files in the National Crime database were geared toward individuals with outstanding warrants or who were otherwise suspects and toward stolen property; it was possible to run a profile of a crime or pattern of crimes and shoot out a few names but that wasn't what the FBI's system was designed for.

Juliette Archer said, 'In the media and academic sites I found plenty of stories or reports of instances of hacking smart systems. Mostly for the sake of hacking. Nature of the hobby, my son tells me. The challenge. Nobody's intentionally weaponized an appliance, though some hackers've taken control of cars and stoplights.'

'Stoplights. That's a scary thought.' From Sellitto.

She continued, 'It's cheaper to use wireless controls in them – public works doesn't have to dig and lay cables.'

Sellitto said, 'Solid backgrounding. You'd make a good cop.'

'Passing the physical'd be a problem.'

Sellitto muttered, 'Linc sits on his ass all day long. You can consult. Give him some competition. Keep him sharp.' The rumpled detective was once more scanning the charts. 'The hell's his profile? Maybe explosives but we ain't had any bangs lately. Toxins but nobody's been poisoned. He's a fine woodworker. What's he build, do you think? Cabinets or bookshelves? With the glass, maybe that's it.'

'No,' Rhyme said, 'the glass fragments were old. And Amelia found glazing compound. I don't think furniture glass is mounted with glazing. That's for residences. Besides, see the rubber? It was found with the ammonia. That told me he replaced a broken window and cleaned the new one with a squeegee and paper towel.' His voice faded as he looked at the chart. 'Window.'

Pulaski said, 'Even psycho killers need to do home repairs. Probably it's not related to the case.'

Rhyme mused, 'But he'd just recently repaired it. The trace was fresh and found with other evidence from the scene. Just speculating here but if you were going to break into somebody's house or an office—'

'You could front you were a repairman,' Sellitto said.

Sachs said 'Put on coveralls. Carry a new piece of glass with you. Break in, get what you need inside, then replace the glass, clean it and leave. Anybody looking would think you were the super or'd been hired to do repairs.'

Archer added, 'And he pretended to be a workman once before – in the Theater District.'

Sellitto said, 'Maybe he broke in somewhere to find out if there was some device that had one of those controllers in it. That DataWise thing.'

'He doesn't need to,' Archer pointed out. 'His first vic, Todd Williams, downloaded the list of products with controllers and the people or companies who bought them.'

Did she actually say 'vic'? Rhyme was amused.

'Yeah, yeah,' Sellitto said. 'That's right.'

Rhyme said, 'I could see it if the shards of glass we found were frosted – he'd replaced the glass with clear so he could see his kill zone. But the broken pane was clear. Old or cheap but clear. I want to work with this. Assuming our window repairman scenario is valid and – let's be *bold* here – he's planning another attack, then it's because there's no embedded product at the target location.'

Sachs quickly said, 'And that's because he's going after somebody who's not *on* the list. A specific person, rather than a random consumer.'

'Good,' Rhyme said. 'Let's work with that.'

'But why?' From Archer.

Rhyme's eyes closed momentarily. Then opened fast. 'Somebody who's a threat. What Lon was just suggesting. It's his *second* mission. To stop those who're after him or a threat to him. Us. Maybe a witness, somebody who knows him and might be growing suspicious. Anything on the charts that might suggest a victim unrelated to the products, nothing to do with his manifesto against consumers?'

He scanned the charts. Although the source for some items had not been isolated (*Queens??*), everything had been identified – except one thing.

'Damn it, Mel. What the hell is the plant? We asked the Horticultural Society ages ago.'

'It was yesterday.'

'Ages, like I said,' Rhyme snapped. 'Call. Find out.'

Cooper looked the number up once more and placed the call. 'Professor Aniston? This is Detective Cooper. NYPD. I sent you that sample of vegetation trace evidence we found at a crime scene. Have you had any luck? We're under some time pressure . . . Sure.' Cooper glanced toward them. 'He's looking it up now.'

'Which suggests it wasn't a *particularly* burdensome request in the first place,' Rhyme muttered, probably louder than he should have.

Cooper's body language changed as the call resumed. He wrote on a pad beside him. 'Got it, thanks, Professor.' He disconnected. 'It's rare. You don't find it very often.'

'That's what rare means, Mel. What the hell is it?'

'It's a fragment of leaf from a hibiscus. But what's rare is that it's a blue one. There'll be limited sources—'

'My God!' Sachs pulled her phone out, hit speed dial. 'This is Detective Five Eight Eight Five. Sachs. I need officers at Four Two One Eight Martin Street, Brooklyn. Possible ten thirty-four in progress. Suspect is white male, six two to six four, weight one fifty. Possibly armed . . . I'm en route.'

She hung up, grabbed her jacket. 'My mother's house. I got her a blue hibiscus for her birthday. It's in her backyard, right by a window to the basement. He rigged something there.'

Sachs sprinted for the door, making a second call.

A circuit breaker had popped.

Rose Sachs was now in her Brooklyn town house's dank basement, the place redolent of mold. She was making her way slowly to the panel. Slowly not because of her cardiac condition, but because of the clutter.

Looking over the boxes, the shelves, the racks of plastic-wrapped clothing.

Even here she felt good – the 'even' because she was dodging a spider's elaborate web.

Good.

Spending some time in her own house for a change.

She loved her daughter, appreciated everything Amie did for her. But the girl – the *woman* – had been such a, well, mother hen about the surgery. Stay at my house, Mom. Come on. No, I'll drive you. No, I'll pick up dinner.

Sweet of her. But the fact was Rose wasn't going to break apart in the days leading up to the operation. No, it was obvious what Amie was thinking – that Rose might not wake up from the deep sleep while the surgeon was slicing out components of her heart and replacing them with little tubes from a lesser part of her body.

Daughter wanted to spend as much time with mother as possible – just in case Part A didn't get along with Part B, which, by the way, God never did intend.

Upstairs her mobile phone was ringing.

They could leave a message.

Or maybe Amelia's persistence – and insistence – was simply her uncompromising nature.

And for this, Rose thought smiling, she herself was to blame. She was thinking of the turbulent days with her daughter. What had been the source of Rose's moods, her paranoia, her suspicion? Thinking that father and daughter were conspiring to get away from Mom?

But that wasn't paranoia at all. They *were* conspiring.

As well they should have. What a shrew I was. Who knew what was the reason . . . There were probably meds I could have taken, probably therapists I could have shared with. But that would have been a weakness.

And Rose Sachs had never done well with weakness.

At this moment, lost in these reflections, she felt a burst of pride. Because the upside of that attitude was that she'd created a strong daughter. Herman had given the girl heart and humor. Rose had given her steel.

Uncompromising . . .

The lights here in the cellar were working – it was on the second floor that the lamp had gone out. She wondered why the breaker had popped. She hadn't turned anything on, no iron or hair dryer. She'd been reading. And pop, out went the lights. But the house was old; maybe one of the breakers was bad.

Now the home line was ringing – an old-fashioned *ring, ring, ring*.

She paused. Well, there was voice mail on that one too. Telemarketer on the landline probably. She didn't use that phone much anymore, mostly her cell phone.

Welcome to the twenty-first century. What would Herman have thought?

Moving aside a few boxes to clear a path to the breaker box, she thought of Nick Carelli.

Rose supposed that the story was true, that he'd taken the blame for his brother. That seemed good, that seemed noble. But, as she'd told her daughter, if he'd really loved Amie, wouldn't he have found a better way to handle it? A cop had to accept that you did things the right way when it came to the law. Her husband had been a lifelong policeman, a portable – a foot patrolman – walking the beat in a number of places, mostly in Times Square. He'd done his job with calm determination and was never confrontational, defusing conflicts, not fanning flames. Rose could never see Herman taking the fall for anybody. Because, even if for a good cause, that would have been a lie.

A tightening of her lips. Another matter: Her daughter was wrong, wrong, wrong to have any contact with Nick at all. Rose had seen his eyes. He wanted them to get back together, clear as day. Rose wondered what Lincoln knew about it. Rose's advice would have been for Amie to drop Nick instantly, even if the mayor himself gave him a big, fat blue ribbon saying *Pardon*.

But such was the nature of children. You bore them, shaped them as best you could and then turned them out into the world – bundles that contained all your gold stars and all your cinders.

Amie would do the right thing.

Rose hoped.

Continuing toward the breaker box, she noticed the window next to it was quite clean, for a change. Maybe the gardener had washed it. She'd have to thank him when he came next week.

Rose passed some old boxes labeled *A's High School*. Rose laughed softly, remembering those crazy years, Amie spending her free hours on car repair and fielding modeling jobs for some of the top agencies in Manhattan (remembered how one time the seventeen-year-old girl had had to wear black polish at a fashion shoot not because the scene involved gothic chic but because it had proven impossible to dig out the General Motors grease from under her nails).

Rose decided she'd take one of the boxes upstairs. What fun to look through it. They could do that together. Maybe tonight, after dinner.

And she began to slide boxes out of the way to clear a path to the breaker box.

CHAPTER 44

Sitting on a doorstep, in overalls and cap, I'm a workman once more, taking a workman's break. Newspaper and coffee at hand, lingering before I have to get back to the job.

And glancing through the basement window of Mrs Rose Sachs's town house in idyllic Brooklyn. Ah, there she is, coming into view.

It's worked well, my plan. The other day, staking out Red's town house, just six blocks away, I'd spotted an elderly woman stepping from the police girl's doorway and locking the dead bolt. A clear resemblance. Aunt or mother. So I followed her here. A little touch of Google . . . and the relationship became clear.

Hi, Mom . . .

Red needs to be stopped and needs to be taught a lesson. Killing this woman will do the trick nicely.

Rose, a lovely name.

Soon to be a dry, dead flower.

I would have liked to use one of my trusted controller exploits again but the other day I scanned diligently and found no embedded circuits begging to be let into the network or shooting data heavenward. But, as I know from woodworking, sometimes you must improvise. Brazilian rosewood, short supply? So go with Indian.

Not as rich. Not as voluptuously purple. Cuts differently. Smooths differently. But you make do.

And occasionally the pram, the dresser, the gingham-dressed bed works out better than you'd planned.

So. Let's see now if my improv here works out. It really was quite simple. I rigged a circuit from a garage door opener to short out a light in Rose's living room. A few minutes ago I pressed the opener button on the remote, which popped the breaker. And Rose started downstairs to find the box and reset it.

Normally she'd have an easy job of simply flicking the switch back into the on position.

Let there be light . . .

Except that won't happen. Because I also diverted the main line from the incoming wire to the circuit breaker box itself. The metal door is, in effect, a live wire, carrying 220 volts and many wonderful heart-stopping amps. Even if she's inclined to do the wise thing, the *safe* thing and cut off the main power before resetting the breaker, she'll still have to open the door to do that.

And zap.

Now she's feet away from the breaker box. Then, unfortunately, she moves out of view.

But it's clear where she is. And she'll be reaching for the handle now . . .

Yes!

Anticlimactic. But I see it's worked perfectly.

When she completed the circuit with her body the main line shorted out, extinguishing all the electricity to the house — the upstairs and basement and front door lights went dark.

I imagine I heard a growling buzz but that would have to be in my mind's ear. I'm too far away for that.

Goodbye, Rose.

Rising and hurrying away.

A block down this pleasant street I hear sirens. Getting louder. Curious. Are they coming here? Could it be they're en route to me?

Has Red figured something out? That I was about to visit the wrath of Edison upon Momma?

No, impossible. It's just a coincidence.

I can't help but be delighted with the handiwork. Have you learned your lesson, Detective Red? I am *not* someone to bully.

What a day, what a day.

He was so looking forward to getting home.

Dr Nathan Eagan eased the big sedan through traffic in Brooklyn, Henry Street in the Heights. Not too congested. Good. He stretched, heard a joint pop. The fifty-seven-year-old surgeon was tired. He'd been in operating suites for six hours today. Two gallbladders. One appendectomy. A couple of others. Didn't need to. But the kid with the scalpel needed some help. Some medicine was about diagnostics and referrals and business. Some was about slicing open the human body.

That young resident wasn't that sort.

Nathan Eagan was.

Exhausted. But more or less content. He felt good, he felt purged. Nobody scrubbed and buffed as much as doctors, surgeons especially. You ended your shift – and it *was* a shift, just like an assembly-line worker's – you ended your shift with the hottest of hot showers. The most astringent of soaps. Your body tingling, a humming sound in your ear from the fierce stream.

The memory of the bile and blood washed away, he was now in his husband-and-parent frame of mind. Enjoying the pleasant drive through a pleasant part of the city he loved. Soon he'd see his wife and, later tonight, his daughter and his first grandchild. A boy named Jasper.

Hm. Jasper.

Not his first choice when his daughter told him. 'Jasper, really? Interesting.'

But then, seeing the wrinkled little blob before him and touching his tiny, tiny fingers and toes and delighting in the perplexed infant grin, he decided any name was wonderful. Balthazar, Federico, Aslan. Sue. It didn't matter. Heaven was here on earth and he remembered at that moment, eye-to-eye with his grandson, why he had taken the Hippocratic oath. Because life is precious, life is astonishing. Life is worth devoting yours to.

Eagan clicked on satellite radio and hit a preselect button, one of the NPR channels, and began listening to Terry Gross's wonderful show.

'This is *Fresh Air* . . .'

Which was when his car went insane.

Without warning, the engine began to scream, as if he'd floored the accelerator; the cruise control light blinked on spontaneously – his hands hadn't been anywhere near the switch! – and the system must've been instructing the engine to accelerate to a hundred!

'Jesus, no!'

The tachometer redlined and the car surged forward,

tires smoking, rear end wobbling like a drag racer's.

Eagan cried out in panic as he wove into the oncoming traffic and, at the moment, empty lane. The vehicle hit fifty, sixty – his head bouncing back against the rest, his eyes unfocused. He slammed his foot on the brake but the engine surge was so unrelenting that the car slowed hardly at all.

'No!' The panic was on him completely. He let up on the brake and jammed down again over and over. He felt a metatarsal in his foot snap. Now at sixty mph and climbing, his auto continued to skid and weave. Cars veered from his path, horns blaring.

He jammed the start/stop button for the engine but the motor kept up its demonic roar.

Think!

The gearshift! Yes! Neutral. He shoved the lever to the central position, and, thank God, that did the trick. The engine still howled but the transmission was disengaged. He pitched forward as the car slowed, dropping to sixty-five, sixty.

Now the brakes.

Which were not working at all.

'No, no, no!' he cried.

Consumed with panic, paralyzed, he could only stare forward as the car raced, against a red light, toward the intersection ahead, noting the vehicles stopped or slowly crawling in the cross-traffic lane, perpendicular to him. Cars, a garbage truck, a school bus. He would strike one of them broadside at close to fifty mph.

A splinter of rational thought: You're dead. But save who you can. Hit the truck, not the bus! Go right, just a bit! But his hands couldn't pace his mind, and tweaking the wheel sent the car veering directly toward a Toyota sedan. He gaped at the panicked face of the driver of the tiny car he was speeding directly for. The elderly man was as frozen as Nathan Eagan.

Another twitch of the wheel and the doctor's car struck the rear driver's side of the Japanese vehicle, a few feet behind the man at the wheel.

The next thing that Eagan knew he was coming around, after the air bag had knocked him unconscious. He was frozen in position, embraced by bones of steel from the crumpled car. Trapped. But alive, he thought. Jesus, I'm alive.

Outside, people running. Mobile phones were filming the accident. Pricks . . . Had at least *one* person had the decency to call 911?

Then, yes, he heard a siren. Would he end up in his own hospital? That would be rather ironic, maybe the same ER doctor he'd helped out . . .

But wait. I feel so cold. Why?

Am I paralyzed?

Then Nathan Eagan realized that, no, he had complete sensation; what he was feeling was liquid cascading over his body from the mangled rear portion of the Toyota he'd virtually cut in half.

Gasoline was drenching every inch of his body from the waist down.

CHAPTER 45

Amelia Sachs hit eighty on the FDR.

This was not easy to do. Incurring horn blares and extended fingers, Sachs ignored the protests and concentrated on finding gaps between cars, braking furiously, zipping through lane changes. Keeping the revs high, high, high. Fifth gear at the most. Fourth – she called it the gutsy gear – was better. And the meat and potatoes, third.

When you move they can't getcha.

And the corollary: When you move they can't get *away.*

'No,' she was saying into the hands-free, speaking to the patrolman from the precinct near her mother's town house. 'He's there somewhere nearby. It's his MO. He . . . oh, shit.'

'What's that, Detective?' the officer asked.

She controlled the skid as she swept past the car that had braked hard to make a sudden exit that neither its driver, nor she, had been planning on. The Torino and the Taurus, distant relatives, missed a potentially deadly kiss by two inches, tops.

Sachs continued, 'His MO is he's nearby when there's an attack. He could rig an accident and leave but he doesn't. He probably flipped the switch and waited to make sure the vic' – her voice choked – 'to make sure my mother would get to the trap. He's only had a ten-minute start and we don't think he's got a car. Gypsies a lot.'

'We're sweeping, Detective. Just—'

'More bodies. I want more bodies out there. He can't get that far!'

'Sure, Detective.'

She missed what else he said, if anything. Concentrating on fitting between two vehicles in a space no third vehicle was meant to pass through. Over the roar of the Torino's engine she couldn't tell if contact was made. Horns blared. Sue me, sue the city, she thought. And, irritated that she'd lost seconds braking, she downshifted hard and explored the redline zone once again.

'More people on site,' she repeated to the patrolman and disconnected. Then said into the mobile: 'Call Rhyme.'

He answered immediately. 'Sachs. Where are you?'

'Just onto the Brooklyn Bridge . . . Hold on.'

She veered around an idiot on one of those low bicycles you recline upon, a flag fluttering over your head. It wasn't much of a skid; the surface of the bridge gripped her tires well, and she turned sharply into it. The Ford righted itself. Then she had a clear field ahead of her and sped up again.

'Lon's already called COC. Nothing yet. Checking subways too.'

'Good. And . . . Oh, Jesus Christ.'

Clutch in, brake full, shift to second just in case you need it, hand brake up, take a skid to buy some space . . .

'Sachs!'

The Torino stopped two feet behind a taxi, forty-five

degrees in the lane – well, lane and a half, since she was, yes, at an angle. A massive traffic jam extended past the cab she'd nearly slammed into.

'Traffic's stopped, Rhyme. Damn it. Completely stopped. And I'm in the middle of the bridge. Can you have Mel or Ron get me a route once I get off? One without traffic?'

'Hold on.' Rhyme shouted, 'Lon, I need a route, no traffic from the east end of the Brooklyn Bridge to Amelia's mother's place.'

She climbed out of the car and peered ahead. A sea of vehicles. Motionless.

'Why now?' she muttered. 'Why the hell now?'

Her phone hummed with a number she recognized. The patrolman she'd been speaking with not long before. She put Rhyme on hold and took the call. 'Officer, what've you got?'

'I'm sorry, Detective. Got a dozen RMPs en route and ESU's sending a truck. Only weird. Traffic's totally fucked up. Sorry. Totally screwed up. The Heights, Carroll Gardens, Cobble Hill. Nobody's moving.'

She sighed. 'Keep me posted.' She flipped back to Rhyme's call.

'. . . you there, Sachs? Can you—?'

'I'm here, Rhyme. What's the story?'

'You're going to be stuck for a while. Looks like five bad accidents all around the same time. Near your mom's place.'

'Shit,' she spat out. 'I'll bet it's him. Unsub Forty. Remember what Rodney said? He can fuck up cars with the controller. That's what he did. I'm parking here and

getting a train. Tell Lon to have a crew pick up my wheels.
Keys'll be under the back floor mat.'

'Sure.'

Not bothering with the walkway, Sachs started east
along the bridge. Two trains and a jog later – a half hour
– she was at her mother's town house, charging into the
living room, nodding to the officers, the medics. Then
she paused.

'Mom.'

'Honey.'

The women embraced. The mother's flesh and bones
troublingly frail under the daughter's grasp.

But she was all right.

Sachs stepped back and examined her. Rose Sachs was
pale. But that was probably from the fright. She'd suffered
no physical harm from Unsub 40 – the medics were here
because of her heart condition. A precaution.

It had been, however, such a very close call. Rhyme
had explained to Sachs that when they'd realized Rose
was a possible target, he and the team had speculated
that the unsub had – possibly – rigged some kind of
electrical trap in her house since they'd found evidence
of stripped electrical wires.

At first they hadn't known how to handle it – other
than telling Rose to get out. But the woman wasn't picking
up the phone. And the neighbor Sachs had called wasn't
home. They'd been trying to guess exactly what the perp
had done to attack Rose, when Juliette Archer had blurted,
'We have to do what Amelia did with that saw in the
Theater District. Cut the power. The grid! Just cut the
entire grid for her block.'

Rhyme had ordered Lon to do just that.

And they'd been in time – but barely. The respondings found that the unsub had sabotaged the circuit breaker box, which Rose had been reaching for at the instant the grid went down. The power was back on in the neighborhood now – Sachs didn't want to think of the complaints, lost computer data and communications. But they'd have to deal with it; her mother was alive.

'I'm sorry this happened, Mom.'

'Why would he want to hurt me?'

'To get to me. It's become like a chess game between us. Move for move. He must've thought we wouldn't consider you'd be a target. Now one of these officers is going to take you to my house and stay with you. I've got to run the scene here, in the basement, where he broke in. Maybe he was in the rest of the house too. Will you be okay without me for a while?'

Rose took her daughter's hands. The woman's fingers were not, Sachs noticed, trembling in the least. 'Of course, I'll be fine. Now get going. Catch that son of a bitch.'

Drawing smiles from both Sachs and one of the patrol officers present. Daughter embraced mother, and Sachs walked outside to see her into a squad car and await the arrival of the CSU bus.

Back in the Toy Room now. For the comfort of it. Working on the Warren skiff for my brother.

I'm making it of teak, a difficult wood. Therefore it's more challenging. Therefore the end result will make me particularly proud.

The news is on and I've learned that I did not in fact

incinerate Red's mother. I know this not because she was mentioned but because of the story that the electric grid in that part of Brooklyn went down briefly. Of course Red the Shopper did that. She or her police friend figured out what I was going to do and pulled the plug.

Smart. Oh, they are so very smart.

The other story, being reported to death (I call TV news Humpty Dumpty; every report is 'breaking'), was about a string of serious car accidents, surely a co-inky-dink — one of my brother's favorite words — that had nothing to do with the grid glitch; the accidents weren't related to the stoplights going out. No, the carnage was thanks exclusively to *moi* and the lovely DataWise5000s.

I'm surprised no clever reporters have brought up everybody's favorite target: the smart controller.

I wasn't sure my escape plan would work. I'd never tried hacking a car. Todd taught me how but it wasn't helpful for my mission at the time. I'd thought the cloud system in vehicles was used just for diagnostics — or you lose your key and need to start it, you call an 800 number the car company provides and tell them what happened, give them a code. They can start your car and disable the steering wheel lock. But, oh, no, you can do all sorts of wonderful things. Cruise control, brakes.

The problem was that I had no way of knowing which cars in Brooklyn had a DataWise. Maybe a lot, maybe few.

Few, it turned out. Walking quickly away from Rose's town house, hearing sirens, I decided they might signal visitors coming just for me. So I began running the automotive controller software. Nothing, nothing, nothing.

Until finally: From about a block away from where I was I heard the huge roar of an auto engine revving high followed ten seconds later by a massive crunch.

Traffic began backing up immediately.

Wonderful. I'm actually smiling at the memory.

A few blocks farther along I heard another hit – literally! It turned out to be a lovely rear-ender. I stopped a car mid-block. One Japanese import versus one cement truck. Guess who won?

A quarter mile east, one more.

Nothing for a few minutes but finally another car on the Brooklyn Queens Expressway. A stretch limo, I later learned.

So. A nice new trick I've learned. A shame Red drives such an antique car. Would be fitting for her to break her bones in an auto crash. Well, there'll be other options for my friend.

Now, peering through the loupe, I examine the Warren skiff. The boat is done. I wrap it carefully. And set it aside. Then I turn back to the diary and begin to transcribe.

The graduation party. Frank and Sam's and mine.

Maybe forty people there. The sports crowd, pretty nice most of them. A few look at me like, him? But mostly nobody stares. Nobody whispers.

And I'm playing music – took me like ages to try to figure out what to play, what everybody'd like – and Sam says come on back here. And in the parlor or den there's Karen DeWitt, who smiles at me. I've seen Karen, she's a junior and is sort of pretty, skinny too but not like me. Her nose is big but who am I to talk? The parlor's dark and she starts touching me on the shoulder and arm. And I'm like, what is this? Only I know of course what it is, even though I never thought this would happen, at least not for years, even though half the guys in the class have been laid.

And she unzips me and does what she does with her mouth.

Then some other people come into the parlor and Karen says let's get out of here, there's a bedroom over there. She's going to pee and then I'll meet her and we can do it. So I wait a few minutes and she calls me into the room and it's dark and there she is, no clothes, bent over the bed and I start to do it. I'm inside her and everything.

And then. No, no, no – lights come on. And there's Sam and Frank and Karen only she's not the one on the bed. The person bent over the bed is Cindy Hanson. And she's passed out, sheet around her mouth all wet, she's been drooling.

And Sam is taking pictures of me and Cindy with a Polaroid. Getting it all – her drugged sleepy face and my string-bean body and my you know. Other people too are there. Laughing and laughing.

I'm grabbing clothes and putting them back on and crying. 'What are you doing, what are you doing, what are you doing?'

Frank and Sam are looking over the pictures and laughing ever harder and one of them says, Hey, you're a natural born pornstar, String Bean!

Frank still laughing hard lifts up Cindy's head by her hair, 'You like it after all, bitch?'

I got it then. Remembering them coming out of Cindy's house a month ago, seeing them on my secret route home, talking to them for the first time. Cindy had told them no.

No fucking, no blow job, get out of my house. Or something.

And that's when they'd thought of it. Seeing me. How to get even with Cindy Hanson.

The 'Epic' was a lie. The Alien Quest was a lie. Music at the party was a lie.

All of it, a lie.

CHAPTER 46

Amelia Sachs entered the parlor, set down the evidence cartons gathered at her mother's town house, and walked straight up to Juliette Archer. Threw her arms around the surprised woman, nearly dislodging the wrist strapped to the Storm Arrow's armrest.

'I—' the woman began.

'Thank you. You saved my mother's life.'

'We all did,' Archer said.

'But,' Rhyme said, 'she's the one who came up with the blackout strategy.'

'I don't know how to thank you.'

A shrug, similar to the ones Rhyme was capable of.

Sachs looked from the intern to Rhyme. 'You two make a good team.'

Rhyme, with typically little patience for the sentimental, or the irrelevant, asked Mel Cooper, 'What's the latest?' The tech was just hanging up the phone from a conversation with someone in the Traffic Division.

He explained that there had been no fatalities. The closest brush with death had been a doctor whose sedan crashed into the rear end of a Toyota and ruptured the gas tank. He and the other driver were inundated with fuel but pulled out by passersby before the two cars vanished in flames. (To be doubly safe the doctor had stripped naked in the middle of the street, flinging his drenched clothing away.)

A half-dozen people, however, had been badly injured.

Rhyme now called Rodney Szarnek to ask about the incident. 'Any way to trace the signal?'

The computer cop went into a long explanation about cell towers, public Wi-Fi and VPNs.

'Rodney.'

'Sorry. The answer's no.'

He disconnected. 'One hell of a weapon,' Sachs said to Rhyme and Archer.

Sellitto, downtown, called and reported that everyone on the team – and their family members – was now under protective detail. 'It's UAC-prioritized,' he muttered.

Rhyme had given up trying to stay on top of New York City Police Department shorthand. 'Which is?'

'It'll be in place Until the Asshole is Caught,' Sellitto said.

Archer laughed.

Sachs and Cooper were unpacking evidence she'd collected from her mother's house – the garden, the house itself and the steps across the street, where witnesses had seen a skinny worker taking a break, reading the paper, sipping coffee.

Rhyme looked around the parlor. 'Where the hell's the rookie?' he grumbled. 'That other case?'

'That's right.' Sachs was nodding. But offered nothing more.

'Somebody just find this Gutiérrez and shoot him, please.'

For some reason Sachs smiled at this. Rhyme was not amused.

Sachs itemized the evidence. 'Not much. Wire, electricians' tape on the circuit breaker panel. He rigged a lamp with this.' She held up a plastic bag with a small electric circuit board inside. 'When he triggered it, two wires in the lamp crossed and that blew the breaker. It was to get Mom downstairs to the box. Ambient trace. Naturally, no friction ridges or hairs other than mine or Mom's. Some fibers. He's wearing flesh-colored cotton gloves.'

'You found copper bits earlier but now we have the actual wire,' Cooper said.

It was eight-gauge, according to the American wire gauge standard, about 0.128 inch in diameter.

Rhyme said, 'Can carry pretty high voltage. What, Mel? Forty amps?'

'That's right, at sixty degrees Celsius.'

'What about the manufacturer?'

There were, Rhyme could see, letters on the black insulation.

Cooper looked up the initials. 'Hendrix Cable. Popular brand. Sold a lot of places.'

Rhyme scoffed. 'Why don't perps shop at unique stores? . . . And he used a razor knife again to strip it?'

'Right.'

'And electricians' tape?'

'Probably good quality,' the tech said, touching part of it with a steel needle probe. 'Good adhesive, strong. Cheaper tape tends to have uneven coverage and it's thin.'

'Burn a bit. See if we can get a brand name.'

After the gas chromatograph worked its magic, Cooper looked over the results and displayed them to the room on a monitor.

Archer said, 'They seem generic. Aren't those ingredients found in every brand of electrical tape?'

'Quantity,' Rhyme said. 'Quantity is everything.'

Cooper explained further, 'I'm running the *amounts* of each of those substances through a database. Micrograms make all the difference. It should give us an answer in . . . Ah, here we go now. It's one of these.'

On the screen:

- *Ludlum Tape and Adhesive*
- *Conoco Industrial Products*
- *Hammersmith Adhesives*

'Good, good,' Rhyme muttered.

Sachs was examining the bag she'd held up earlier. The remote relay that had shorted out Rose's lights. Cooper mounted the device on the reflecting stage of a low-power microscope. They examined the monitor. He said, 'Antenna here.' He pointed. 'Signal comes in and closes the switch here. It's not an off-the-shelf switch. It's a component part of something else. See? The base? He fatigued through the circuit board. Got a code number on it,' he announced. Rhyme hadn't been able to see it.

Keeping his eyes on the monitor, Cooper touch-typed as fast as falling marbles. A moment later they turned to the screen.

'Home-Safe Products Atlas garage door opener,

extended-reach model. Opens the door from fifty yards. He took the switch out and threw the rest away, I'd guess.'

The remaining trace revealed more walnut sawdust, some glass fragments from Rose's town house, more glue associated with adhesive from an earlier scene, but nothing else new.

'Put everything up on the boards.'

Crime Scene: 4218 Martin Street, Brooklyn

- Offense: Attempted Assault.
- Suspect: Unsub 40.
- Victim: Rose Sachs, unharmed.
- Means of attack: Rigged circuit breaker box to electrocute.
- Evidence:
  - No friction ridge, DNA.
  - Insulation from Hendrix Cable.
  - Additional adhesive, as from earlier scene.
  - Walnut sawdust.
  - Glass shards associated with earlier scene (this location).
  - Unsub wore flesh-colored cotton gloves.
  - Electricians tape from one of:
    - Ludlum Tape and Adhesive.
    - Conoco Industrial Products.
    - Hammersmith Adhesives.
  - Home-Safe Atlas garage door opener.

'Everything common, Mel?' Rhyme asked.

'Yep. Sold in a hundred stores in the area. Not very helpful.'

Two voices: 'But he was improvising the attack at your mother's town house, Sachs.' At the same time Archer said, 'But he didn't plan your mother's attack ahead of time, Amelia.'

Rhyme laughed at their tripping over each other's words yet again. He explained to Sachs, 'The unsub's planned out all the other attacks against his victims ahead of time. But he made a last-minute decision to attack your mom. He hadn't figured you'd be so persistent, so much of a risk to him. Which means he bought the tape, the electric wire, the glass and glazing compound and the garage door opener around the same time. Likely some or all at the same place. It would have been smart to buy them separately over a period of days or weeks but he didn't have a choice. He had to stop you.'

Archer looked over the chart. 'Maybe the parts for the gas bomb that he used downtown too – to destroy Todd Williams's office.'

'Very possibly,' Rhyme said. 'Let's start with the garage door opener, don't you think? Sachs?' He'd been speaking to her.

'What's that?' She'd been distracted, reading a text.

'The garage door opener. Get a list of retail locations, then canvass to see if anybody bought the other items there.' Rhyme added, 'Start with Queens. Expand from there.'

Sachs called Major Cases and put together a canvass

team to start searching for the purchases. She then disconnected and emailed them a list of the items Unsub 40 would have bought. Rhyme noted she looked out the window for a moment. Then turned and walked close to him.

'Rhyme. You have a minute?'

One of those useless expressions. Why not just say: I want to talk to you. Let's lose the bystanders. But of course he nodded. 'Sure.'

He wheeled toward her and together they headed into the parlor across the hallway. She remained silent for a moment. He knew her well. When someone is your lover and your professional partner little of her psyche remains hidden. She was not being dramatic. She was weighing what she wished to say the way one would carefully measure a drug found in a bust to most accurately determine the charges against the suspect. Sachs was certainly given to impulse in some things. But matters close to her heart were swathed in thick deliberation.

She sighed and turned. Then sat. 'There's something I have to talk to you about.'

'Yes. Go ahead.'

'I could have told you a few days ago. I didn't. I'm not sure why I didn't. Nick is out.'

'Carelli? Your friend.'

'My friend, yes. He was released from prison. He contacted me.'

'And he's well?'

'Pretty much. Physically. I'd think being inside would change you more.' She shrugged and it was clear to

Rhyme she didn't want to go down this path. 'There's something I debated about telling you. I didn't. But now I have to.'

'A preface like that, Sachs? Pray continue.'

SUNDAY

VI ... AND MATE

CHAPTER 47

At 11:30 a.m. the canvass team looking into the unsub's purchases for his improvised weapons, in the attempt on Rose Sachs's life, had a hit.

Rhyme was frustrated that it had taken so long but then they'd made the discovery about the garage door opener and the other purchases only late last night, when most of the hardware stores were closed. And few opened early today, Sunday morning.

'Fucking blue laws,' he'd snapped.

Ron Pulaski, apparently on hiatus from the Gutiérrez case, had said, 'I don't think the Puritans've pushed through legislation about late opening times for hardware stores on the holy day, Lincoln. Salespeople probably just want to sleep in one day of the week.'

'Well, they shouldn't do it when I. Need. Answers.'

But then Sachs got a call from one of the officers on the canvass. She sat slightly more upright as she listened. 'I'll put you on speaker.'

A click. 'Yes, hello? Jim Cavanaugh. Major Cases Support.'

'Officer,' Rhyme said, 'this is Lincoln Rhyme.'

'Detective Sachs told me you're working the case. An honor, sir.'

'Okay, sure. Well, what do you have?'

'A store on Staten Island.'

So, not Queens. Archer gave Rhyme a wry smile.

With two question marks . . .

'The manager said a man fitting the description of the unsub comes in two days ago, wanted a garage door opener that would work at a distance of about thirty-five feet, maybe more. Also bought glass, glazing compound, electricians' tape and some wire. All matching the products you mentioned.'

Here's hoping . . . Rhyme asked, 'Credit card?'

'Cash.'

Of course.

'Did the manager know anything about him? Name, where he lives?'

'Not that, but he did find out a few things, Captain.'

'"Lincoln" is fine. Go on.'

'The unsub saw some tools the store had for sale and asked about them. They were specialized ones. Like the kind used for crafts.'

Sachs asked, 'Crafts? What sort of crafts?'

'Hobbies. Model airplanes, things like that. Razor knives and saws and very small sanders. He bought a set of miniature clamps. He'd been looking for ones like them. The store he usually shops at didn't have them in stock.'

'Good. I like "usually." That means he's a regular. Did he mention the name?'

'No. Just said it was in Queens.'

Rhyme shouted, 'Somebody find me all the crafts stores in Queens. Now!'

'Thanks, Officer.' Sachs disconnected the call.

A moment later a map was on the biggest of the monitors. There were sixteen crafts stores indicated in the borough of Queens.

'Which one?' Rhyme muttered.

Sachs leaned forward, her hand on the back of his chair. She pointed. 'That one.'

'How do you know?'

'Because it's three subway stops away from the MTA station near the White Castle in Queens, where he always went for lunch after shopping.'

Crafts 4 Everyone didn't quite live up to its name.

No yarn, no floral art foam, no finger paints.

But if you wanted to build model ships or spacecraft or doll house furniture this was your emporium.

Fragrant with the smell of paint and wood and cleansers, the shop featured jam-packed shelves of supplies and tools. More Dremel power tools and balsa wood than Amelia Sachs had ever seen in one place. A lot of *Star Wars* characters, creatures and vehicles. *Star Trek* too.

She showed her gold shield to the young man behind the counter, good looking, more like an athlete than a, well, clerk in a nerd store.

'Yes?' His voice did, however, crack.

She explained she was trying to find a customer for questioning in connection with a series of crimes. She described the unsub, asked if anyone had recently bought mahogany, walnut, Bond-Strong and Braden Rich-Cote varnish. Craft tools too.

'He'd be smart,' Sachs said. 'Well spoken.' Thinking of

the unsub's attempts to obscure his intelligence in his
rants against consumerism.

'Well, you know,' the clerk said, swallowed and
continued, 'there *is* somebody. But he's quiet, polite. I
can't imagine he'd do anything wrong.'

'What's his name?'

'I just know his first name. Vernon.'

'He fits the description?'

'Tall and thin, yeah. Kind of weird.'

'Any credit card receipts?'

'He always pays cash.'

She then asked, 'You have any idea where he lives?'

'Manhattan, I think in Chelsea. He mentioned that once.'

'How often does he come in?'

'Every couple of weeks.'

'No phone number he left for special orders?'

'No, sorry . . . Now you're asking me, he always seemed
kind of paranoid, you know. Like he didn't want to give
away too much.'

She handed him a card and asked him to call her if
Vernon returned. No more 911 intermediaries. She walked
around a father and son poring over a carve-your-own-
Jedi display and left the store. Sachs dropped into the
front passenger seat of the unmarked car that had accompanied her here. The detective from the local precinct,
an attractive Latina, asked, 'Success?'

'Yes, and no. The perp's name is Vernon. No other
name yet. I want you to stay here on the chance he comes
back. The kid – the clerk – was so nervous all Vernon
would have to do was look at him and he'd know something was up.'

'Sure, Amelia.'

She thought now about how to narrow down an address in the relatively large neighborhood of Chelsea. She spun the detective's computer around and typed real estate databases. No one with a first name Vernon owned property in Chelsea and those two people with that name on deed records were much older than the perp and both were married, a status that seemed extremely unlikely for this type of perp. So, if the kid was right about the name, their perp would be renting.

An idea occurred to her: She ran stats in Chelsea to see about recent crimes. Something interesting turned up. A homicide, just reported yesterday, on West 22nd Street. A man named Edwin Boyle, a printing company employee, had been killed and his body shoved into a storage cabinet in an abandoned warehouse. His wallet and cash were still in his possession. Only his phone was missing. The cause of death was 'blunt force trauma.'

She called the Medical Examiner's Office and got through right away. She identified herself.

'Hi, Detective,' said the woman technician. 'What do you need?'

'That homicide, Boyle? Yesterday. Chelsea. You have anything more on the blunt force? Type of weapon?'

'Hold on. I'll check. I didn't do the PM.' A few moments later she came back on the line. 'I have it here. Funny, it's similar to another PM we handled not long ago. Something you don't see very often.'

Sachs said, 'Murder weapon was a ball-peen hammer?'

The tech barked a laugh. 'Sherlock Holmes. How'd you know that?'

'Can't tell, Detective. He's got shutters on the bedroom window. Metal, have to be. Can't read through them. K.'

Near an ESU van parked up the street from the target apartment, Amelia Sachs spoke into her stalk mouthpiece in reply: 'Any light getting through?'

The S&S officer was on the roof opposite, his sophisticated equipment aimed at the second-floor, two-bedroom apartment on West 22nd Street. 'Negative, Detective. No thermal readings but with the shutters he could have a candle-lit card game going on there, everybody smoking cigars and I couldn't tell you. K.'

'Roger.'

The unsub was no longer one. He was an *Identified* Subject.

Vernon Griffith, thirty-five, was a resident of New York. He'd owned a house on Long Island, which he'd inherited and recently sold. He'd been renting here in Chelsea for about a year. Some juvie offenses for school-yard fights, but no rap sheet as an adult. And – curiously – no history of social activism, until he started using consumer products a few days ago to murder the good citizens of the city of New York as the People's Guardian.

Edwin Boyle had been his neighbor until, for reasons yet unknown, Griffith had hammered him to death a few blocks away, in the same inelegant manner as he had Todd Williams.

'We're locked down. The whole block.'

This from Bo Haumann, head of the NYPD's Emergency Service Unit – the city's SWAT team. The lean, grizzled man, with an etched face, and Sachs looked over a layout of the apartment building on his laptop. The schematic had come from the Department of Buildings and was old, about ten years, but New York City apartments rarely underwent major internal renovation. Landlords wouldn't want to pay for that. Only when eyeing the gold mine of converting a building to co-ops or condominiums did the owners get out the checkbooks for structural improvement.

'Don't have much choice,' Haumann said, meaning there was essentially only one strategy for entry to collar Griffith. There was a single entrance into the building from 22nd Street and one door in the back alley. Griffith's apartment itself had one door, opening onto the living room. There were two bedrooms opposite the entry door and a small kitchen to the right.

Haumann called a half-dozen officers over. Like Sachs they were in tactical outfits – helmets, gloves, Kevlar vests.

Tapping the computer screen, he said, 'Three friendlies in the back. Four-man entry through his front door.'

'I'm one of them,' Sachs said.

'Four-*person* entry through his front door,' Haumann corrected, to smiles. 'One breacher, other three in serially. One right, one left, one center, covering.'

The weapons they'd be armed with were the same as the one that had been used to kill Osama bin Laden: H&K 416s. This model was the D14.5RS carbine, the numbers referring to the length, in inches, of the barrel.

They acknowledged the instructions blandly, as if their boss were giving them details of a new coffee break plan at the office. To them this was all in a day's work. For Sachs, though, she was alive. Completely attuned to the moment. Good at crime scene work, yes – she enjoyed the mind game of tricking evidence to life. But there was *nothing* like a dynamic entry. It was a high unlike anything else she'd experienced.

'Let's move,' she said.

Haumann nodded in confirmation, and the teams formed up.

In five minutes they were sprinting along the sidewalk, motioning bystanders to leave the area. With a screw-end lock pop, one officer opened the front door of the building in a single deft pull and Sachs and the other three streamed inside. Through the lobby and corridor to Griffith's unit.

With hand signals, Sachs stopped the team fast. She pointed to the video camera above the suspect's door. All four officers moved back, out of view of the lens.

On the radio: 'Team B, in position in alley. It's clear.'

'Roger,' said the Team A leader, a lean, dark-complected man whose name was Heller. He was beside Sachs. 'He's got a camera above the door. We'll have to go in fast.' The conversation occurred in whispers and was delivered through state-of-the-art headsets and microphones.

Normally they'd move silently up on their rubber-soled boots, then the breaching officer would wait while one cop slid a tiny camera on a cable under the door. But now – with the perp's surveillance of *them* a possibility – they'd have to race to the door and move in fast.

Heller pointed to Sachs and to the right. Then to another officer and aimed a thumb to the left. Then to himself and moved his hand up and down, like a priest offering a blessing. Meaning he'd take the center.

Sachs, breathing hard, nodded.

The breacher lifted the battering ram – a four-foot

piece of iron – from his canvas bag. And at a nod from Heller, all four ran to Griffith's apartment. The breaching officer slammed the metal hard into the knob and lock plate, and the door crashed inward. He stepped back and unslung his H&K.

The three other officers stepped inside, Sachs and the other flank officer spreading out, sweeping their weapons around the sparsely furnished room.

'Kitchen clear!'

'Living room clear!'

The left bedroom door was partially open. Heller and the other officer moved forward, Sachs covering. They entered the small room. Heller called, 'Left bedroom, clear.'

They returned and approached the closed door of the front bedroom, which had both a number-pad lock and a dead bolt.

Heller said, 'S and S report. The front bedroom's sealed. We're about to enter. Any sign of life? K.'

'Still can't tell, sir. Too well shielded.'

'K.'

Heller regarded the number lock knob. There would be no element of surprise now, after their noisy entry, so Heller pounded on the door and said, 'NYPD. Is anyone in there?'

Nothing.

Again.

Then he motioned over to the officer with a stalk camera. He tried to jimmy it under the door but the gap was too small; the device wouldn't fit.

This doorway was narrower. Only one officer could

go in at a time. Heller pointed to himself and held up a single finger. To Sachs, two. The other officer, three. Then he motioned the breacher forward. The burly cop arrived with his ram and they got ready for the final stage of the entry.

CHAPTER **48**

Weird. I had just been writing in my diary:

The worst day.

That had been in the past, *that* day. But now, today, was just as bad.

Not *worst*, no. Because I haven't been arrested, haven't been shot to death by Red and the Shoppers.

But pretty fucking bad. I've known the People's Guardian couldn't go on forever. But I thought I could slip away from the city and remain anonymous. Get on with my life. Now they have my name.

I'm wheeling two suitcases, a backpack holding my most important worldly possessions. Some of my miniatures. The diary. Some photos. Clothes (my size, hard to find). My hammer, my wonderful Japanese razor saw. A few other things.

Lucky, lucky.

Just a half hour ago. Was back home, Chelsea, thinking of my next visit to a Shopper, planning to scald, when I got, imagine this, a call.

'Vernon, listen.' The crackly-voiced kid from Crafts 4 Everyone.

'What's wrong?' I asked him. Because something was wrong.

'Listen. The police were just here.'

'Police?'

'Asking about things you bought. They found some notes with your name on them. I didn't say anything.'

The kid was lying. There was no reason there'd be any notes with my name on them. He sold me out.

'They didn't find your last name. But.'

But, yeah.

'Thanks.' I hung up and began to pack. Had to leave fast. The kid at the crafts store would die and painfully. He was a Shopper, after all. I'd thought he was a friend. But there's no time to worry about that now.

I finished packing, rigged some surprises for Red and the Shoppers who'd be there soon enough.

Now, head down, slumping to hide the sack-of-bones height, I'm heading downtown with two big suitcases like a tourist from Finland who's just arrived at the Port Authority and needs a hostel room. Appropriately I find such a place now, well, a cheap hotel, not hostel, and I step inside. Inquire about rates and, when the desk clerk steps away I go to the bell captain and check my bags, telling him my flight's not till this evening. He cares about the five dollars more than the explanation, and I leave again, carrying only my backpack.

In twenty minutes I'm at my destination, an apartment not dissimilar to mine, which makes me sad. My womb in Chelsea, my fish, my Toy Room. All gone. Everything ruined. My whole life . . . Red did it, of course. I shiver with fury. At least anybody slipping into the Toy Room will get a lovely surprise. I hope Red's the first one in.

Now I stare up at the dirty white façade for a moment,

then look around. No one to notice me. I hit the intercom button.

The superintendent was in his basement unit, taking care of his own plumbing for a change, a toilet issue, when he heard a thud upstairs.

And then a scrabbling sound.

Sal wasn't sure what a scrabble actually sounded like – a big crab from a horror film maybe, somebody on all fours scurrying away from a spider. Who knew? But that was the word that came to mind. He returned to fixing the chain to the ball cock and got it snapped into place. Just as he did, there was another thud, more of a crash of things falling, and then voices. Loud.

He rose, wiped his hands and walked to the open back window. The voices, from the apartment directly above his, were more or less distinct.

'I don't . . . I don't . . . You did that, you did what you're telling me, Vernon?'

'I had to. Please. We have to go now.'

'Are you . . . Vernon! Listen to what you're saying!'

Alicia Morgan, the occupant of 1D, was crying. She was one of the better tenants. Quiet, paid on time. Timid. Something fragile about her. Was this her boyfriend? Sal had never seen her with anybody. What was the fight about? he wondered. She didn't seem like the sort who would fight with anyone.

Fragile . . .

The man – 'Vernon' apparently – said in a shaky voice, 'I shared things with you! Private things! I've never done that with anybody.'

'Not this! You didn't tell me you'd done this, you hurt people!'

'Does it matter?' The man's voice wasn't much lower than hers. It sounded weird. But he could hear the anger in it. 'It's for a good cause.'

'Vernon, Jesus . . . Of course, it matters. How can you—?'

'I thought you'd understand.' Now the voice was sing-song – and all the more threatening for it. 'We were alike, you and me. We were so much alike. Or that's the way you wanted it to seem.'

'We've known each other for a *month*, Vernon. A month. I've stayed over once!'

'That's all I mean to you?' There was a huge crash. 'You're one of them,' the man shouted. 'You're a fucking Shopper. You're no better than any of them!'

Shopper? Sal wondered. He didn't get exactly what was going on but he was growing quite concerned with the escalating dispute.

Alicia was sobbing now. 'You just told me you've killed some people. And you expect me to go away with you?'

Oh, hell . . . Killed somebody? Sal fished out his mobile.

But before he could hit 911, Alicia screamed – a sound that was cut short in a grunt. Another thud as she, or her body, hit the floor. 'No,' came her voice. 'Don't. Vernon, please, don't! Don't hurt me!'

Another scream.

Then Sal was moving, grabbing his aluminum baseball bat. He flung open his door and charged up the stairs to Alicia's apartment. He used his master key and shoved inside. The knob smacked the wall so hard, it dug a crater in the plaster.

Panting from the sprint, Sal stared, wide eyed. 'Jesus.'

The tenant lay on the floor, a huge man standing over her. Easily six three or four, skinny, sick looking. He'd hit her in the face, which was bleeding from her cheek, swollen badly. Tears poured as she sobbed and held up her hands to protect herself, uselessly, from what he held – a ball-peen hammer, poised over his head about to crack her skull open.

The attacker spun around and stared at the super with mad, furious eyes. 'Who're you? What're you doing here?'

'Asshole, drop it!' Sal snapped, nodding at the hammer and brandishing the bat. He outweighed the guy by thirty pounds, even if he was six inches shorter.

The assailant squinted and looked from the super to Alicia and then back again. His breath hissed from his throat as he drew back and flung the hammer toward Sal, who dropped to his knees to avoid it. The scrawny man grabbed a backpack and ran to the open rear window, tossed the bag out and jumped out after it.

The breacher gripped the heavy battering ram and Heller again pointed out the order of entry into Griffith's front bedroom, the one protected by the number lock. They all nodded. Sachs set down the H&K submachine gun and drew her pistol.

The choice of weapons was always the tactical officer's to make. She felt more comfortable with a handgun in a confined space.

The breacher was drawing back the ram when Sachs held up a hand. 'Wait.'

Heller turned.

'I think he's rigged something. A trap. It's his style. Use that,' she said, pointing into the breaching officer's canvas bag. Heller looked down. He nodded, and the officer withdrew the small chain saw.

Sachs pulled a flash bang stun grenade from her pocket. Nodded.

The breacher fired up the growly tool and sliced a two-by-four-foot hole in the door, kicked in the cut piece. Sachs pitched in the live grenade and, after the stunning explosion – disorienting but not lethal – Heller and Sachs, remaining outside still, went to their knees, pointing their weapons and flashlights inside.

Scanning.

The room was empty of humans.

But it *was* booby-trapped.

'Ah.' Heller was pointing to a piece of thin wire that was attached to the inside doorknob. If they'd bashed the door in, it would have slackened the wire and released a gallon milk jug, cut in half horizontally, filled with what seemed to be gasoline, spilling the contents onto a hot plate that sat smoking on a workbench by the window, sealed by the thick shutters.

The officers entered and dismantled the device. Then they cleared the room – the connected bathroom too.

Heller radioed Haumann. 'Team A. Premises secure. No hostile. Team B, report.'

'Team B leader to Team A leader. No hostiles in back. We'll sweep the other apartments. K.'

'Roger.'

'Sachs,' she heard through her earpiece. Surprised to

hear Rhyme's calm voice. She hadn't known he was patched in to the tactical frequency.

'Rhyme. He's gone. Rabbited. We should've thrown the Crafts For Everyone guy in protective detention to keep him from talking. That's how Griffith got tipped off, I'm sure.'

'The nature of democracy, Sachs. You can't tie up and gag everybody who ought to be tied up and gagged.'

'Well,' she said, 'we've got a pristine scene. When he left he didn't take much. We'll find something here. We'll get him.'

'Walk the grid, Sachs, and get back soon.'

CHAPTER 49

An hour later Sachs was on the doorstep of Vernon Griffith's apartment, sweating in the Tyvek bodysuit.

Reading aloud from a notebook.

It's society thats the problem. They want to consume and consume and consume but they don't have any idea what that means. Collecting objects collecting things is what we focus on. In other words, dinner SHOULD BE about people, families getting together to commune at the end of a work day. Its not about having the best oven, the best food processor, the best blender, the best coffee maker. We focus on those things not on our friends!!! Not on our family.

'You still there, Rhyme?'

'Somewhat. It's a rant. Like the others. The People's Guardian.'

'It's his full manifesto. The title's *The Steel Kiss*.'

Poetic, she reflected.

She put the book back into an evidence bag. 'Got lots of trace. Some paperwork. Lon's running vitals. Sold his family house in Manhasset and no other residences show up positive at this point. Lon'll have some people follow the public records.'

'Anybody else's friction ridges?'

'One more than others. A woman's, I'd guess. Or a small man's. But probably a woman's. I found shoulder-length blond hairs. Seem to be dyed blond with traces of gray. And the alternative light source? He had a pretty active sex life. I mean, busy boy.'

The ALS imaged bodily fluids that would otherwise have been invisible.

'So, he has a girlfriend.'

'But no evidence that she lived here. No women's clothing or cosmetics, toiletries.'

'He may be there now,' Rhyme muttered. 'Wonder where the hell she is. Get the prints back here ASAP, Sachs, we'll IAFIS them. I want to move.'

'I'll be a half hour.'

Her phone rang just as she disconnected. She recognized the number from NYPD Dispatch. 'Detective Sachs.'

'Amelia, it's Jen Cotter. Wanted you to know, there was a nine one one of an assault in Midtown West. Vic's hurt but'll live. Respondings say she's ID'd her attacker. Vernon Griffith.'

Well. 'Who's the vic?'

'Alicia Morgan, forty-one. Don't know the exact relationship with the perp but they knew each other.'

'She there, or the hospital?'

'Still there, far as I know. This just happened.'

'The perp?'

'Got away.'

'Give me the address.'

'Four Three Two West Three Nine Street.'

'Tell the respondings I'm on my way. I want to talk to

the vic. If they take her to a hospital, let me know which one.'

'Will do.'

Sachs reported the developments to Rhyme and hurried to her car. Fifteen minutes later Sachs and Haumann's tac teams were parked at the corner of Eighth Avenue and 39th, before a five-story apartment building.

It was unlikely Griffith was anywhere near here but he was obviously unstable, if not psychotic, and he might very well have stayed around after the assault. Hence the firepower.

Two EMTs, a detective and a uniform were standing over a slim woman in her early forties lying on a gurney. Her face was bandaged and bloody. Her eyes were red from crying and she had an expression that Sachs could describe only as sorrowful bewilderment.

'Alicia Morgan?' Sachs asked.

The victim nodded, then winced from the pain.

'I'm Detective Sachs. How're you feeling?'

The woman stared at her. 'I . . . what?'

Sachs displayed her shield. 'How are you?'

Her voice was a whisper. 'It hurts. Really hurts, I'm dizzy.'

A glance at one of the EMTs, a solid African American. 'He hit her, with his fist, at least once. Pretty bad. Probably a fracture and a concussion. We'll need X-rays. We'll take her in now.'

As they wheeled her to the ambulance Sachs asked, 'How did you know Vernon?'

'We went out some. Did he really kill those people?'

'He did, yes.'

Alicia cried softly. 'He was going to kill me too.'

'Do you know why?'

She started to shake her head and then gasped at the pain. 'He just showed up and wanted me to go away with him. He told me he was the one who was in the news. Who killed the man in the escalator and burned up that other one in the gas explosion! I thought it was a joke at first. But, no, he meant it. Like it wouldn't matter to me that he was a killer.' She closed her eyes and winced. Then carefully wiped tears.

'When I said no, I wouldn't go away, he snapped. He started to beat me, and then got a hammer. He wanted to kill me with it! Sal showed up just in time. The Super. He had a baseball bat. He saved my life.'

Sachs noticed some scars on the woman's neck and her arm was slightly deformed, as if from a bad break. Maybe the victim of an assault some time ago. Domestic abuse? she wondered.

'Does Vernon own or have access to a car?' Griffith didn't have one registered in New York.

'No, he uses cabs mostly.' Wiping tears again.

'And no idea about places he'd go?'

Her wide eyes stared at Sachs. 'He was so nice to me. He was so gentle.' More tears. 'I—'

'Alicia, I'm sorry,' Sachs said, pressing. 'I need as much information as you can give us. Any other residences or places he'd go?'

'He had a house on Long Island. Manhasset, I think. But I think he sold it. He never mentioned anyplace else. No, I don't know where he'd go.'

They arrived at the ambulance. 'Detective, we better get her in now.'

'Which hospital?'

'We'll do Bellevue.'

Sachs took out one of her cards, circled her number and added Rhyme's, as well as his address on the back. She gave it to Alicia. 'When you feel up to it we'll need to talk to you some more.' She was sure the woman had some insights that could help them find their prey.

'Okay,' she whispered. Breathed deeply. 'Sure. Okay.'

The ambulance doors shut and a moment later the vehicle took off through traffic, the siren pulsing urgently.

Sachs walked up to Bo Haumann and reported what she'd learned – which wasn't much. He in turn told her that canvassing had revealed no sightings. 'He had a fifteen minute lead,' the ESU man said. 'How far does that buy you in the city?'

'Pretty damn far,' she muttered.

And Sachs walked to the superintendent, Sal, sitting on the stoop, to interview him. He was a good-looking Italian American, thick black hair, solid muscles, clean-shaven. Reporters were shooting pictures and asking him to hold up the baseball bat with which he'd driven off the killer. Sachs could picture the punning tabloid headline already: *'Hero-super' Bats a Thousand*.

CHAPTER 50

Rhyme watched Amelia Sachs cart in the evidence from Vernon Griffith's apartment. She had yet to search Alicia Morgan's place and the warehouse where Griffith had bludgeoned to death his neighbor, Boyle, but Rhyme wanted to get started on the clues from what was probably the most fruitful scene that would lead to his whereabouts: his apartment in Chelsea.

She walked to the evidence tables and, pulling on blue gloves, began to organize the evidence she and the ECTs had collected.

Juliette Archer too was here, though Cooper was absent. Rhyme said to Sachs, 'Mel's going to be a couple of hours – some terrorist thing the FBI wanted him to look in on. But we can get started. Any more word on Alicia?'

'She should be released soon. A fractured cheekbone, loose tooth, concussion. She's shaken up but willing to talk.'

As one would expect when your boyfriend tries to beat you to death with a hammer.

Rhyme examined the evidence collected at Griffith's apartment. Unlike from the earlier scenes, here was a trove.

'But first, the documentation,' Rhyme said. 'Any luck

with real property, tickets to anywhere regularly, plane or train?'

Sachs reported that the findings were negative, so far. 'I've looked over banking and financial information. He'd sold the house on Long Island but there was no record of him buying another place. Banks and credit card companies, insurance, taxes – they all sent statements and correspondence to a P.O. box in Manhattan. He had a business – selling his miniatures and dollhouse furniture. But it was handled out of his apartment, not from an office or workshop.'

Archer noted a slip of paper in a clear plastic envelope. 'This could be another potential victim. In Scarsdale.'

The upscale suburb north of New York City was undoubtedly filled with many high-end products equipped with DataWise5000 controllers and owned by the rich consumers that Vernon Griffith despised.

Archer was reading from the note, '"Henderson Comfort-Zone Deluxe water heater."'

And Rhyme cross-referenced the list of products that had DataWise controllers inside; yes, the water heater was one of them.

'Who lives there?'

'No indication from the note. Just have the address at this point. Griffith's been ID'd so I doubt he'll go for another attack but, on the other hand, he's pretty fanatical. So who knows?' Rhyme asked Sachs to call Westchester County and have troopers stake out the house.

'And find out who lives there, Sachs.'

She did so, searching records and DMV. A moment later she had the answer. William Mayer, a hedge fund manager. He was a friend of the governor and there were a few articles about him that hinted at political aspirations.

Archer said, 'Water heater? What was he going to do, do you think? Turn the heat up and scald somebody to death in the shower? Todd Williams blogged about something like that, remember? Or maybe build up the pressure and close a valve, so that when somebody goes down to see what's wrong, it blows up? Gallons of two-hundred-degree water? Jesus.'

She wheeled closer and looked over the half-dozen plastic bags of miniatures. Furniture, baby carriages, a clock, a Victorian house. They were very well made.

Rhyme too studied them. 'He's very good. Let's see if he took classes anywhere.'

Sachs had thought of this, it seemed. 'I've got a body at One PP checking out Griffith's bio in depth. They might turn up a workshop or two he went to. School he studied at recently.' Then Sachs was frowning. She picked up a small toy. 'Something familiar about this. What is it?'

Rhyme squinted at the toy. 'Looks like a caisson. A wagon artillery soldiers tow along with the cannon. Holds the shells. The song, that line: "And the caissons go rolling along."'

Sachs studied it closely. Rhyme said nothing more. He let her thoughts play out on their own. Archer, too, he noted, held back any questions.

Finally Sachs, still studying the caisson, said, 'It's connected to a case. The past couple of months.'

'But not Unsub Forty?'

'No.' It seemed that a thought hovered. And flitted away. A hiss of breath at the frustration. 'Might've been one of mine, might've been another in Major Cases and I saw the file. I'll check.' In a gloved hand she lifted the delicate creation out of the plastic bag and set it on an examination sheet. With her phone she took a picture and sent it off. 'I'll have somebody in Queens look through the logs of evidence collected in the past few months, see if anything shows up. Let's hope they do better with that than our missing White Castle napkins.'

She rebagged the toy. 'Okay, you two keep going here. I'll get to Alicia's now. And the warehouse where he killed Boyle. Walk the grid.' Then she was out the door. A moment later the powerful chug of her Ford's engine resonated along Central Park West. He believed it shook one of the large plate-glass windows in the parlor. A falcon looked up from its nest on the window ledge, peeved at the sound, which seemed to have disturbed the fledglings.

Rhyme turned once more to the miniatures. He thought: Why would somebody so talented, who could make such beautiful things, who had such skill, turn to homicide? An irrelevant question, but persistent.

Archer too, close to Rhyme, was looking over Vernon Griffith's creations. 'So much work. So fastidious.' Silence between them momentarily. She continued her examination, eyes on a tiny chair. Absently Archer said, 'I used to knit.'

He wasn't sure how to respond to that. After a beat: 'Sweaters, things like that?'

'Some. More art, hangings. Like tapestries.'

Rhyme was glancing at the photos of Griffith's apartment. 'Landscapes?' he asked.

'No, abstract.'

He observed a softening of her facial muscles. Wistfulness, sadness. He fought to find something to say. He finally settled on: 'You could do photography. Everything's digital now anyway. Just pressing buttons. Or voice-commanding buttons. Half the young people out there are as sedentary as we are.'

'Photography. It's a thought. I might.'

A moment later Rhyme said, 'But you won't.'

'No,' she said with a smile. 'Like if I have to give up drinking I won't switch to fake wine or beer. I'll take up tea and cranberry juice. All or nothing. But it'll be the best tea or cranberry juice I can find.' A pause and she asked, 'You ever get impatient?'

He laughed, a sound that contained his stating-the-obvious grunt.

She continued, 'It's like . . . tell me if this is what it's like: You don't move, so your body isn't bleeding off the tension, and it seeps up into your mind.'

'That's exactly what it's like.'

'What do *you* do?' she asked.

'Stay busy. Keep the mind going.' He tilted his head toward her. 'Riddles. Make your life about solving riddles.'

A deep breath and a look of pain, then one of panic crossed her face. 'I don't know if I can handle it, Lincoln. I really don't.' Her voice caught.

Rhyme wondered if she'd start to cry. She wasn't the sort for whom tears came easily, he guessed. But he knew too that the condition she was facing pushed you to places you couldn't imagine. He'd had years to build up a sinewy guard around his heart.

New to the game . . .

He swiveled his chair to face her. 'Yes. You. Can. I'd tell you if it wasn't in your core. You know me by now. I don't sugarcoat. I don't lie. You can do it.'

Her eyes closed and she inhaled deeply once. Then she was looking at him again, her remarkable blue eyes driving into his, which were far darker. 'I'll take your word for it.'

'You have to. You're my intern, remember? Everything I say is gold. Now let's get to work.'

The moment passed and together they began to catalog what Sachs had recovered at Griffith's apartment: hairs, toothbrush (for the DNA), reams of handwritten notes, books, clothing, printouts on hacking and technical details about breaking into secure networks. Even pictures of fish in an aquarium (Sachs had sifted in the sand at the bottom for buried clues – this was a common hiding place – but found none). Many items were from what turned out to be his profession – making and selling the miniatures: stores of wood and metal, tiny hinges, wheels, paint, varnish, pottery. Many, many tools. Had they been sitting on the shelves of Home Depot or Crafts 4 Everyone, they'd be benign; here the blades and hammers took on a sinister air.

The Steel Kiss . . .

Since the documentation offered no leads to Griffith's whereabouts Rhyme and Archer concentrated on the trace evidence from his apartment.

But after a half hour of 'dust work,' as Archer rather

charmingly dubbed their efforts, referring to criminalist Edmond Locard, she wheeled back from the envelopes and bags and slides. She glanced at Griffith's notebook, the manifesto. He noted she'd braked to a stop and was now staring out the window. Finally she turned back to him. 'You know, Lincoln, part of me doesn't believe it.'

'What's that?'

'Why he's doing this. He's against consumerism. But *he's* a consumer too. He had to buy all these tools and the supplies for his work. He buys food. He special-orders his shoes for his big feet. He benefits from shopping. And he makes his living selling things. That's consumerism.' She turned her chair to face him, her beautiful eyes sparkling. 'Let's try an experiment.'

Rhyme looked at the evidence bags.

'No, I don't mean a physical experiment. A hypothetical. Let's say there *is* no evidence in the case. An exception to Locard's Principle. Imagine a case where there isn't a single lick of PE. How's this? A killing on the moon. We're on earth and we have no access to the evidence at all. We know the victim was murdered up there. There are suspects. But that's it, no trace, no physical evidence. Where do we go from there? The only approach is to ask, why did the perp kill the victim?'

He smiled. Her premise was absurd, a waste of time. But perhaps he found her enthusiasm charming. 'Go on.'

'If this were an epidemiological investigation, and you and I were presented with unidentified bacteria killing some people but not others, we'd ask: Why? Is it because they've been to some country and contracted it? Is it because there's something about the victims physically that makes them and not others vulnerable to the disease? Have they engaged in certain behaviors that have exposed them to the bacteria? So let's look at *Vernon's* victims. I'm not buying the theory they were targeted because they were rich consumers, buying expensive stoves or microwaves. What else is common among them? Why he killed them might lead to how he knew them might lead to where he met them . . . and to where he's sitting right now. You with me?'

The criminalist within him was resistant, but Lincoln Rhyme had to admit the logician was intrigued. 'Okay. I'll play along.'

CHAPTER **51**

Juliette Archer was saying, 'Who were the people that Griffith targeted? Other than Amelia's mother and the drivers of the cars he took control of – those were to stop us from catching him. His main victims. Greg Frommer, Abe Benkoff, Joe Heady. And the potential victim in Scarsdale, the hedge fund manager, William Mayer.'

'Well, what about them?' Rhyme was happy to co-operate but he was compelled to add a spoonful of devil's advocacy into the stew.

'Okay . . .' Archer wheeled to a spot in front of the charts. 'Frommer was a store clerk in Brooklyn and a volunteer at a homeless shelter, among other charities. Benkoff was account manager for an ad agency in New York. Heady is a carpenter for a Broadway theater. Mayer is into finance. None of them seems to know the others. They don't live near each other.' She shook her head. 'No connection.'

'Oh, well, that's not enough to ask,' he said softly. 'You have to go deeper.'

'How do you mean?'

'You're looking at the surface. Pretend those people you mentioned are bits of trace evidence . . . No, no,' he chided, seeing her scowl. '*You* play along with *me* now. The people aren't people but bits of trace evidence. On the surface one's gray metal, one's brown wood, one's cloth fiber, one's a fragment of leaf. What do they have in common?'

Archer considered this: 'Nothing.'

'Exactly. But, with evidence, we keep digging. What kind of metal, what sort of wood, what type of fiber, what plant is the leaf from? Where did they come from, what's the *context*? You put them altogether and, bang, you've got an upholstered lawn chair sitting under a jacaranda tree. Different is suddenly same.

'You want to analyze the victims, Archer, good, but we need to approach your inquiry the same way. Details! What're the details? You have present careers. What about the past? Look at the raw data Amelia collected. The charts are only summaries. Residences and careers, anything that seems relevant.'

Archer called up Sachs's notes and read from the screen.

As she did, Rhyme said, 'I can fill in about Greg Frommer. He was a marketing manager for Patterson Systems in New Jersey.'

'What does Patterson do?'

Rhyme recalled what the lawyer had told him. 'Fuel injectors. One of the big suppliers.'

She said, 'Okay, noted. Now Abe Benkoff?'

'Amelia told me – advertising. Clients were food companies, airlines. I don't recall.'

Archer read from Sachs's and Pulaski's notes. 'He was fifty-eight, advertising account executive. Pretty senior. Clients were Universal Foods, U.S. Auto, Northeast Airlines, Aggregate Computers. He was a New York City resident, lived here all his life. Manhattan.'

Rhyme said, 'And Heady, the carpenter?'

Archer read: 'He grew up in Michigan and worked in Detroit on an assembly line. Moved here to be closer to his kids and grandkids. Didn't like retirement so he joined the union and got a job at the theater.' She looked up from the computer screen. 'Mayer is a hedge fund manager. Works in Connecticut. Lives in Scarsdale. Wealthy. Can't find anything about his clients.'

Rhyme said, 'Wife.'

'What?'

'Why do we assume that *he's* the target? Is he married?'

Archer clicked her tongue. 'Damn. Forgive my sexism.' Typing. 'Valerie Mayer. She's a Wall Street trial lawyer.'

'Who are her clients?'

More typing. 'No names. But her specialty is representing insurance companies.'

Rhyme, gazing at the screen. He smiled. 'We'll have to wait until we do more research about Valerie, about her clients. But the others – they sure as hell have something in common.'

Archer looked over the chart and the notes. 'Cars.'

'Ex-actly! Benkoff's client was U.S. Auto. Heady was on an assembly line and I'll bet that's whom he worked for. Did U.S. Auto use Patterson fuel injectors?'

With voice commands, Archer did the search. And, yes, Google dutifully reported that Patterson had been a major supplier of U.S. Auto . . . until about five years ago.

He whispered, 'Around the time Frommer quit the company.'

Archer asked, 'And Valerie Mayer?'

The criminalist turned to the microphone near his head: 'Call Evers Whitmore.'

The phone responded instantly and after two rings a receptionist answered. 'Evers Whitmore, please. Now. It's urgent.'

'Mr Whitmore is—'

'Tell him Lincoln Rhyme is calling.'

'He's actually—'

'That's Lincoln, first name. Rhyme, second. And, as I said, it's urgent.'

A pause. 'One moment.'

Then the lawyer's voice was saying, 'Mr Rhyme. How are you? How's—?'

'Don't have time. You were telling me about a case, a personal injury case, involving a car company. Some internal memo said that it would be cheaper to pay wrongful death claims than fix some dangerous defect in a car. Was it U.S. Auto? I can't recall.'

'Yes, you're correct. It was.'

'Valerie Mayer, a trial lawyer in New York. Did she defend the company?'

'No.'

Hell. There went his theory.

Then Whitmore said, 'She represented the insurer who *covered* U.S. Auto against liability suits.'

'Was Patterson Systems involved?'

'Patterson? You mean the company Mr Frommer worked for? I don't know. Hold on a moment.'

Silence. Then the lawyer came back on the line. 'Yes, the main suit was against U.S. Auto but Patterson was also a defendant. The claim was that both the automaker and the parts supplier knew about the fuel system defect and decided not to change the injectors and the interface with the motors to make them safer.'

'Mr Whitmore, *Evers*, I need everything you can send me about the case.'

A pause. 'Well, that is somewhat problematic, Mr Rhyme. For one thing I didn't work on the suit so I don't have any source material. Besides, you don't have room. Or the time to read everything. There were hundreds of cases revolving around the defect, and they went on for years. There have to be ten million documents, I would estimate. Perhaps more. May I ask why—'

'We think our killer – the one using the DataWise controllers as a murder weapon – was targeting people with connections to U.S. Auto.'

'My. Yes, I see. He was injured in one of the accidents because of the fuel system failure?'

'We think so. He's at large, and I was hoping there might be something in the case files that'll give us a clue where he's gone.'

'I'll tell you what I can do, Mr Rhyme. I'll have my paralegal send over whatever I can find in the legal press and I'll get as many of the publicly filed pleadings and discovery documents as I can. And you should check popular reports too. This story, naturally, made the news.'

'I need them ASAP.'

'I'll make sure it's done right away, Mr Rhyme.'

CHAPTER 52

Rhyme and Archer were both online reading about the U.S. Auto case as quickly as they could.

Whitmore had been right. There were more than twelve million hits on Google.

A half hour later the emails from Whitmore started arriving. They divided up the court pleadings and supporting documents and began reading these, as well as the press accounts of the case. There were, as Whitmore had mentioned, scores of plaintiffs, those injured in accidents and the relatives of those killed when the cars were engulfed in flames because of the defective fuel system. In addition, the incidents spawned more than a hundred business-related lawsuits for lost revenue by the manufacturers and component parts makers. The more troubling accounts – in the sometimes lurid popular media and in the cold, clinical court documents – were those of lives shattered. He read testimony about horrific pain from burns and collisions after the gas lines ruptured, scanned accident scene pictures of scorched and shattered bodies and photos of dozens of plaintiffs who'd been injured. Some were hospital pictures of their burns and lacerations. Some were of them stoically marching into and from courthouses. He reviewed them carefully, looking for Griffith's name or likeness, on the chance that he'd been a victim or related to one.

'Any references to a Griffith?' he called to Archer. 'I'm not seeing anything yet.'

'Nothing,' Archer replied. 'But I've read fifty pages out of looks like a hundred thousand.'

'I'm doing a global search for the name. Nothing yet.'

She said, 'That works *within* a document but I don't know how to search in unopened ones.'

'Maybe Rodney has a program,' he said. Before he could call the computer expert, though, the doorbell buzzed. Rhyme glanced at the monitor. A woman wearing a nondescript rumpled brown jacket and jeans stood at the front door. She had a bandage on her face.

'Yes?' he called.

'Is this Lincoln Rhymes? With the NYPD?'

Rhyme had no nameplate on the door; why make it easier for your enemies? He didn't bother to correct the woman. 'Who is this?'

'Alicia Morgan. A police officer, Amelia Sachs, asked me to come by and give a statement. About Vernon Griffith?'

Excellent. 'Sure. Come on in.'

He commanded the door to unlock and a moment later he heard footsteps approaching. They paused.

'Hello?'

'We're in here. To the left.'

The woman walked into the parlor and did a double take, seeing two people in elaborate wheelchairs . . . and scientific equipment worthy of a university research lab. She was petite, attractive, and had short blond hair.

Sunglasses partially covered the bruise that peeked from underneath thick bandages. She removed the glasses and Rhyme studied her damaged face.

'I'm Lincoln Rhyme. This is Juliette Archer.'

'Well, hello.'

Archer said, 'Thanks for coming by.'

Rhyme's eyes strayed back to the computer, on which he could see several of the accounts of the cases against U.S. Auto and the fuel injector supplier. He continued to scroll through them.

'How are you?' Archer asked as she was scanning the woman's injuries.

'Not too serious.' The woman focused on the wheelchair-bound pair. 'Hairline fracture, cheekbone. Concussion.'

Rhyme paused the documents on his monitor and turned to Alicia. 'You and Vernon dated?'

She set her purse on the floor and sat in a rattan chair, wincing. There seemed to be a stunned air about her. 'That's right, if you could call it dating. I met him a month or so ago. He was easy to be with. He was quiet and sometimes he would get a little odd. But he was nice to me. Like he never thought anybody would ever go out with him. He's kind of odd looking, you know. But I never had any idea he'd be dangerous.' She whispered, eyes wide, 'Or would kill those people. Officer Sachs told me what he'd done. I couldn't believe it. He was so talented, making his miniatures. Just . . .' She shrugged. Then winced. She searched in her pockets and found a bottle of pills. Shook two out. She asked Rhyme, 'Do you . . . ?' An awkward moment. 'Have an assistant? Could I get some water?'

Before Rhyme could say anything Archer said, 'No, he's away now. But there, there's a bottle of Deer Park. It's not opened.' She nodded to a shelf.

'Thanks.' Alicia rose and took what would be something to combat the pain. She returned to the chair but remained standing, collecting her purse and then slipping the pill bottle into it.

'What happened in your apartment?' Rhyme asked. 'Earlier today.'

'He showed up, unexpected. He wanted me to go away with him and confessed what he'd done.' A dismayed whisper. 'He actually thought I'd understand. He thought I'd support him.'

Rhyme said, 'You were lucky someone was nearby. The superintendent of the building, I think Amelia said.'

Yet, as calm as his words were, Lincoln Rhyme's mind was racing. He was trying to come up with a strategy that would allow him and Archer to survive the next few minutes.

Because the woman he was smiling at right now was someone whose picture he had just seen – in one of the press reports on the U.S. Auto case. It was this page that he now found again and paused his scrolling. He glanced at it quickly. The photo depicted a woman in a black dress walking from a courthouse on Long Island. He hadn't recognized her outside the team house just now; had he done so, he wouldn't have let her in. When she'd asked if anybody was here to bring her water, he'd been about to say his aide was in the back room, along with another officer, but Archer had pulled the rug out from under that ploy.

Alicia Morgan had sued U.S. Auto and Patterson Systems for the death of her husband and for her own personal injuries – some burns and deep lacerations – from when the fuel system of the car her husband was driving caught fire, causing the car to crash. Rhyme could see scars above the high collar of her blouse.

He now had a good idea of what had happened: Alicia had hired Vernon Griffith to kill those involved in making, marketing, and selling the defective car, and Valerie Mayer, the lawyer who had defended them. Or, in lieu of payment, maybe Alicia had seduced Griffith into doing so for her; Sachs's search of the crime scene revealed significant sexual activity. Griffith and Alicia had been surprised when Rhyme and the team had learned his identity, and they'd come up with a new endgame; they'd arranged the 'assault' in front of a witness, the superintendent of the building.

And the reason for that?

For one, to remove any suspicion that she was involved.

But then why was she here?

Ah, of course. Alicia had a plan of her own. She'd steal any evidence that might implicate her and then kill Rhyme and anyone present, planting other clues that would implicate Vernon in the murders. She'd then meet the man and kill him.

And Alicia Morgan, satisfied in her revenge against the auto company, would be home free.

In her purse would be a gun, he guessed. But now that she'd noted her victims were disabled, she'd probably use one of Griffith's tools to kill him and Archer. Tidier for the case against him.

And Mel Cooper wouldn't be here for hours. Sachs either. Thom would return in about two hours or so, he guessed. Alicia had plenty of time for murder.

Still, he'd have to try. Rhyme glanced at the clock. 'Amelia – Detective Sachs – should be back at any moment. She's much better at interviewing than I am.'

Alicia gave a very faint reaction. Of course, she'd probably just spoken to Sachs and learned that the woman wouldn't be back for hours.

Rhyme looked past her and said to Juliette Archer, 'You're looking tired.'

'I . . . I am?'

'I think you should go in the other room. Try to sleep.' He looked to Alicia. 'Ms Archer's condition is more serious than mine. I don't want her to push herself.'

Archer gave a slight nod and manipulated the controller with her finger. The chair turned. 'I think I will, if you don't mind.'

Motoring toward the doorway.

Alicia, though, stood, strode forward and blocked her. The chair stopped fast.

'What . . . What're you doing?' Archer asked.

Alicia glanced at Archer as if she were an irritating fly and, grabbing the woman by the collar, pulled her from the chair and let her fall onto the floor. Archer's head smacked the hardwood.

'No!' Rhyme cried.

Archer said desperately, 'I need to be upright! My condition, I—'

Alicia's response was to deliver a stunning kick to the woman's head.

Blood pooled on the floor, and, eyes closed, Archer lay still. Rhyme couldn't tell if she was breathing or not.

Alicia opened her bag, pulled on blue latex gloves and stepped forward fast, ripping the controller from Rhyme's chair. She walked to the pocket doors to the parlor and closed and locked them.

Rummaging through her bag, she extracted a razor knife – which would, of course, be Vernon's. It was in a plastic tube and she popped the plastic top off and shook out the tool. Alicia turned the blade Rhyme's way and stepped closer to the wheelchair.

CHAPTER 53

'I know about you, Alicia. We made the connection between Griffith's victims and the U.S. Auto case. I saw your picture in one of the stories.'

This gave her pause. She stopped and cocked her head, clearly considering these implications.

He continued, 'I figured right away that you and Griffith faked the assault in your apartment. You made sure the super could hear your fight and come and supposedly rescue you. The minute I saw you outside I hit a special phone code. A speed dial for emergencies.'

Alicia looked past Rhyme to the computer. She typed until she found the call log. No outgoings in the past ten minutes and the most recent callee had not been 911 or NYPD Dispatch but Whitmore's law firm. She redialed it and they heard through the speaker the matter-of-fact receptionist say, 'Law office.' Alicia hung up.

Her face relaxed, as she would be concluding that Rhyme had just now made the connection and that no one else knew the truth. She looked around the room. Rhyme noted she wore her age well. Pale eyes, freckles. Few wrinkles. Her hair, blond with gray streaks, was voluminous and rich. The scars were prominent but did not diminish her attractiveness. Vernon would be putty in her hands.

'Where's the evidence you collected at Vernon's apartment?'

She'd be afraid he'd collected some articles about the U.S. Auto case or that he had some other evidence of what the real motive was, which could ultimately lead to her.

'I tell you, you'll kill us.'

A wrinkle of brow. 'Of course. But I give you my word I'll leave everyone else alive. Your friend Amelia – Vernon was pretty obsessed with her. I was almost jealous. She'll be fine, Amelia. And her mother. And the others on your team. But you're dead. Obviously. Both of you.'

'What you're asking isn't that easy. Some of the evidence's in processing in Queens, the main Crime Scene Unit. And—'

'My other option is to burn this place down. But that'll attract a lot of attention and I might miss some things. Just tell me.'

Rhyme was silent.

Alicia looked around the parlor: at the file cabinets, boxes of paper and plastic bags, shelves, instruments. She walked to a cabinet, opened it and peered in. Closed the drawer. Tried another. Then she perused the broad, white examination tables, and flipped through the boxes that contained plastic and paper bags of the evidence. She unfurled a garbage bag, the deep green of a body bag from the coroner, and tossed some notebooks and clippings inside.

She continued collecting evidence that seemed likely to have references to her and the litigation and then extracted a paper bag from her purse and began depositing the contents carefully, just as he'd thought: hairs,

Griffith's, of course. A scrap of paper; it undoubtedly held his friction ridge prints. And then – well, she'd certainly thought this out carefully – one of Vernon's shoes. She didn't leave it; she left several impressions on the floor near Rhyme's chair.

Rhyme said, 'It's terrible what happened to you and your husband. But none of this will fix that.'

She snapped, 'The cost-benefit analysis. I think of it as the who's-it-cheaper-to-screw analysis.' When she bent forward at one point to press the shoe to the floor, her blouse fell away and he could see clearly the leathery and discolored scar on her chest.'

'You won your case, the article said.'

Rhyme noted, in a detached state, that several of the evidence bags had come open when she'd tossed them into the garbage bag. Even facing death, Lincoln Rhyme was riled by the contamination.

'I didn't win. I settled. And I settled before the memo came to light. Michael, my husband, had been drinking before the accident happened. That had nothing to do with the fuel injector hose splitting. But the alcohol would've worked against us at trial. And there was evidence that he made *my* injuries worse – he broke my arm pulling me from the burning car before he died. And my lawyer said they'd spin that . . . and the drinking. The jury might give us nothing. So I took a settlement.

'But it's never been about money. It was about two companies who murdered my husband and scarred me forever and never came to justice. Nobody was ever indicted. The company paid out a lot of money to plaintiffs but the executives went home to see their families that night. My husband didn't. Other husbands and wives and children didn't either.'

'Greg Frommer quit the company and went on to do volunteer work,' Rhyme said. 'He felt guilty about what happened with the fuel injectors.'

The sentence tripped leadenly off his tongue and deserved the Oh-please look that Alicia gave him.

'The People's Guardian. That was all nonsense, right?'

Alicia nodded. 'Vernon isn't the most attractive man in the world. It wasn't hard to get him to do what I wanted. I needed people responsible for Michael's death to die the way he and the others had. Because of products. Because of greed. Vernon was happy to go along and we decided to turn it into a political issue as a cover. To keep people from thinking about U.S. Auto and maybe making a connection to me.'

'Why *The Steel Kiss*, the name for his manifesto?'

'He came up with that. Thinking of his tools, saws and knives and chisels, I think.'

'How *did* you find him?'

'I've been planning this for years, of course. The hardest part was finding a fall guy. I was one of the parties to a suit against the automaker, so I couldn't kill anyone myself. But one night I was in Manhattan having dinner, and I happened to see Vernon get in a fight with a man. Some Latino guy. He'd made fun of Vernon – he's very skinny, you know. Vernon just snapped. Went crazy. He ran and the man chased him. But Vernon had it planned. He spun around and killed the man, used a knife or razor. I've never seen anybody more frenzied. Like a shark. Vernon jumped into a gypsy cab and vanished.

'I couldn't really take in what I'd just seen. A murder right in front of me. I kept thinking about it for days. Finally I realized he was someone who might be able to help me. I checked with the restaurant it seemed he'd been eating in. They didn't know his name but told me that, yes, he ate there about once a week. I kept coming back and finally saw him.'

'And you seduced him.'

'Yes, I did. Then the next morning I told him I'd seen him kill that Latino. It was a risk but I had my hook in by then. I knew he'd do whatever I wanted. I told him I understood why he'd killed him. He'd been bullied. I told him *I'd* been bullied too, in a way — the car company taking my husband away from me and ruining my body with the scars from the accident. I wanted to get even.'

'The man who taught Vernon how to hack the DataWise controllers, the blogger he killed, also got him a list of customers who'd bought embedded products. You searched them for the names of people connected to U.S. Auto. Right?'

She nodded. 'I couldn't kill everybody connected to the companies. I just wanted a half dozen or so. Frommer, Benkoff, Heady . . . that leech of an attorney, Valerie Mayer.'

'So,' Rhyme asked, almost nonchalantly, 'how are you going to kill Vernon Griffith?'

She didn't seem surprised he'd deduced this. 'I don't know yet. Probably have to burn him alive. Make it look like he was creating some booby trap or another. Gasoline. He's oddly strong for such a skinny man.'

'So you *do* know where he is?'

'No, after he left my place, he wasn't sure where he was going. A transient hotel somewhere. He'd be in touch, he said. And he will be.'

Rhyme said, 'It was tragic what happened to you and your family. But what does this get you?'

'Justice, comfort.'

'You will be found out.'

'I don't think so.' A glance at her watch, then Alicia stepped closer to Rhyme and turned the blade up, eyeing his jugular. She had the steady hand of a butcher or surgeon.

Rhyme looked away from the blade, lifted his head and said, 'Yes, go ahead. But hard. It has to be hard. You'll only have one chance.'

Alicia paused. Frowned in confusion.

But Rhyme wasn't speaking to her. His eyes were focused on Juliette Archer, unsteadily walking up behind the woman, holding an examination lamp, which had a heavy iron base. She nodded, acknowledging Rhyme's instruction, and swung the fixture, hard indeed, directly into the base of Alicia's skull.

CHAPTER 54

The medics reported that the injuries the two women had sustained were not life threatening, though Alicia Morgan's were more severe by far.

She was presently in the hospital wing of Manhattan's detention center, close by Central Booking and the courthouse downtown.

Juliette Archer was sitting in one of Rhyme's rattan chairs in his parlor, her face bandaged, with an impressive bruise spreading out from under the gauze, similar to Alicia's when she'd arrived. An EMS tech was finishing up his artistry on a second wound, to her jaw.

'Is it ready yet?' Rhyme asked Thom, who was re-assembling the controller that Alicia had ripped from his wheelchair. 'I mean, it's been ten minutes.'

You ever get impatient . . .

'I volunteered to get the service people here,' the aide replied languidly. 'Do you remember that? But do we think that might've taken, oh, until tomorrow?'

'It looks finished to me. Just turn it on. I have phone calls to make.'

At the younger man's glare, Rhyme fell silent.

Three minutes later he was functional again.

'Seems to be working pretty well.' He tooled around the parlor. 'Turns are off slightly.'

'I'll be in the kitchen.'

'Thank you!' Rhyme called to the aide's receding back.

Stepping back and eyeing the intern's face, the EMT said to Archer, 'Mostly superficial. Dizzy?'

She rose from the rattan chair where she'd been sitting and paced up and down the parlor. 'A little but not any worse than what I usually have.' She returned and lowered herself into her Storm Arrow wheelchair. Then she restrapped her left arm to the rest by herself.

The tech said, 'Okay. Stable. Good. You're moving pretty good there. Got to say.' He regarded the power chair. He was understandably confused.

Neither Rhyme nor Archer explained to the man how she had come to use as her sole means of conveyance a wheelchair rigged for someone who was a full quad when she in fact was not. Not yet, in any event. As she'd explained to Rhyme after class the first week – and to Thom when she'd started her internship here – she was only partially disabled at this point. Yes, there was a tumor embracing her spinal cord. But the consequences of the condition were not complete debilitation. However, she had decided to prepare for the day when, after her surgery, she would most likely be rendered a full quad.

Thom had indeed played the *role* of caregiver, but only up to a point; she returned to the non-disabled world for bathroom detail at home and at Rhyme's, and she would dress herself. Rhyme had noted too that her golden bracelet, with the runic characters, might appear on one arm in the morning and the other in the afternoon; she would swap the accessory from time to time if it was irritating her skin. The jewelry had been a present from her son and, accordingly, she insisted on wearing it constantly.

The only other time she had forsaken the playacting was, of course, just moments ago to rise to her unsteady feet and save Rhyme's and her own life.

After the EMT signed off and left, she piloted closer to Rhyme.

'You didn't miss a beat,' he said, of her performance. When he'd mentioned to Alicia Morgan that Archer's condition was worse than his and suggested she should get some rest, she'd deduced immediately that something was wrong regarding their visitor – since, of course, she *had* no condition, at least not one as grave as Rhyme had suggested.

Archer nodded. 'I was going to call the police as soon as I was out of the parlor.'

Rhyme sighed. 'I didn't think she'd tackle you. I knew she was here to kill me – and anyone else – but I thought we could buy some time.'

Archer added, 'I saw where Amelia keeps that gun on your shelf, but I don't really know how to use one. And, with the tumor, my hands aren't very steady.'

'And you don't need to cock a lamp or make sure it's loaded,' Rhyme conceded.

Archer said, 'But we still have one more perp.'

'You like that word, don't you?'

'Nice feel to it. Perp.' Archer added, 'Alicia said she didn't know where Griffith is. He was going to contact her. I suppose we could monitor her cell.'

Rhyme shook his head. 'He'll use a burner phone. And in a few hours he'll know she was busted. He'll go to ground.'

'So where do we look to find him?'

'Where else?' Rhyme asked, nodding toward the evidence boards.

The answer is there . . .

CHAPTER **55**

He wasn't going to propose.

Nick Carelli was tempted to, felt that draw, that urge within. Just say it, fast. And, if Ame said no, which of course she would, back off.

But he'd keep at it. If it took a long time then it would take a long time. One way or the other he'd ease his way back into Amelia's heart.

Thinking of Freddy's words:

Find a lady, Nick. Man needs a woman in his life.

Oh, I'm working on that . . .

Nick was heading home, walking down the tree-lined sidewalk in BK, his gym bag over his shoulder. Odd, but he was pretty close to whistling. He didn't; actually he didn't know many people who whistled (though when he was inside he read in the papers about a case Amelia had run, in which a professional killer was an accomplished whistler).

The bag contained a small painting, wrapped in gold gift paper. It was a landscape, no, a *cityscape* it was called, since it showed the Brooklyn Bridge with the early-morning sun making the metal glow and casting shadows toward Manhattan. The artwork, which he'd found in a small gallery on Henry Street, was similar to a painting Amelia had liked when they'd been together. It had been in a Manhattan gallery and they'd discovered it on a cold Sunday after brunch. That one, on the pure-white wall of the pretentious space (SoHo; enough said), was expensive as shit. No way could he afford it. He'd thought about blustering his way into the gallery around closing time, flashing his shield and claiming he had to take it into evidence on suspicion of its being stolen. It would then 'disappear' from the evidence room, and it'd be sorry, sorry, to the gallery owner. But Nick couldn't figure out a way to make it work.

Well, the one in his gym bag was just as nice. Better, actually. Bigger and the colors were brighter.

She'd love it. Yeah, Nick was feeling good.

Whistling . . .

Jon Perone had left a message that he was getting Nick's money together, writing up the fake loan documents. Nick would look them over carefully. He had to make sure the deal appeared legitimate, so that anyone close to him – well, mostly his parole office and *Amelia* – would believe he came by the cash legitimately. He'd convince them. And he knew Ame would accept it. He knew this because he'd seen in her eyes that she *wanted* to accept it.

Then Vittorio, the restaurant owner, would accept the offer, because Perone and his minder Ralph Seville, the suspender guy, would make sure he did. He'd get the place up and going – new paint, better uniforms – secure a liquor license waiver and rename the joint Carelli's Café. Nick would slip into legitimacy. His past buried. No one the wiser.

As for his quest to prove his innocence, Nick would just let it peter out. Tell Amelia and her mother and their friends that the leads had dried up, that one witness from back then was dead, that another had Alzheimer's and couldn't remember anything. He'd get a long face and look sad that the search wasn't working. Hell, and I tried so hard . . .

Ame would take his hand and say it was all right. She knew in her heart he was innocent – and she'd already been hearing the word on the street, thanks to Perone, that Nick hadn't been guilty after all. He felt bad lying to her – making up that crap about Delgado, who couldn't have run a 'jacking operation if his life depended on it – but some sacrifices had to be made.

A half block later he thought of Freddy Caruthers again.

Ralph Seville, Perone's minder, had called Nick and told him that Freddy's corpse was in Newtown Creek, wrapped in chain link and decorated with thirty-pound barbells. Nick supposed Seville knew what he was doing but he'd picked a hell of a resting place for Freddy. That body of water, separating Brooklyn and Queens, was one of the most polluted in the country and had been the site of the infamous Greenpoint oil spill, worse than that from the *Exxon Valdez*.

Well, now, shit. A real shame about Freddy. The guilt prodded. And the man a father too.

Twins're boys. The four- and five-year-old're girls . . .
That hurt.

But sorry. There had to be some casualties. Nick was owed. What had happened to him had been so unfair

– a little hijacking, a little pistol-whipping (the driver of the tractor-trailer he'd hit had been a complete asshole) and the system had come down on him with both feet, when he'd done pretty much what everybody did. The whole fucking world got away with all kinds of shit. And what was he rewarded with? Years and years of his life stolen.

I'm owed . . .

Nick waited for a light and then crossed the street. He felt the gym bag, with the cityscape inside, pressing lightly on his back, like a loving arm. He was picturing Amelia, her fashion model's face, her straight red hair, full lips. He couldn't get her out of his mind. Remembering her asleep the other night, fingers in a partial fist, breathing shallow and soft.

He turned onto his block and as he did he thought of someone else: Lincoln Rhyme.

Nick had nothing but respect for the man. Hell, if Rhyme'd been running the 'jacking cases, Nick and the crews he fenced to would've been busted months before – and the charges would've been a lot worse. You couldn't help but admire a mind like that.

And Rhyme cared for Amelia. That was good.

Sure, it'd be tough to take her away from him. But, of course, Nick took solace in the fact that she really couldn't love him. How could you love somebody who was . . . well, like that. She was with him out of sympathy, had to be. Rhyme would have to know that. He'd get over it.

Maybe in the future they could all be friends.

*

Amelia Sachs had finished walking the grid at Alicia Morgan's apartment, which had revealed few, if any, clues as to Vernon Griffith's whereabouts, and she was in a reflective mood, thinking – of all things – about the nature of evil.

Bad had so many different faces.

Alicia Morgan was one manifestation. Lincoln Rhyme had called and told her what happened at the town house, how Alicia was the mastermind of the product liability killings. That her motive was revenge for a terrible injustice seemed to put the evil she'd perpetrated in a different category from that of, say, a serial rapist or a terrorist.

Then there was yet another evil: Those in the stream of commerce who had decided not to correct a vehicle that they knew might injure or kill. Perhaps greed or perhaps the layers of corporate structure shielded them from conscience, the way an exoskeleton protects the liquid heart of a beetle. And maybe the car and fuel injector executives had truly hoped, or even prayed in their spotless suburban churches on Sunday, that the worst would not come to pass and the passengers who drove about in their gadgety and sleek ticking-time-bomb cars would live long, unhurt lives.

Then there was Vernon Griffith, seduced – literally – by a woman who had preyed on his insecurities.

And what is the *worst* evil? Amelia Sachs asked herself.

She was sitting on a couch at the moment, leaning back against the well-worn leather. Thinking now: Where are you, Vernon? Hiding out a mile away? Ten thousand?

If anyone could determine his whereabouts it would be herself, Rhyme and Cooper. Oh, and Juliette Archer too. The intern. She was good for a newbie. Her mind was quick and she displayed a detachment that was *so* Lincoln Rhyme. And so necessary to this odd world of forensic analysis. Rhyme had been good before his accident, Sachs was sure, though she hadn't known him then, but she believed that his condition had allowed him truly to soar as a criminalist. Juliette would excel in the field if the surgery she was facing in a few months rendered her a quad, which seemed likely, Rhyme had explained.

You two make a good team . . .

She looked around this apartment. The place seemed washed out; there were no lights on and the overcast illumination from the street filtered in. This was one interesting aspect of city life – so little direct sunlight. It bled into your home or office, mostly by bouncing off windows and walls and signs and storefronts and other façades. For only two or three hours a day were most city spaces illuminated by actual sun, apart from the abodes of the blessed rich, dwelling at lofty heights. Sachs had imagined a phrase some time ago: Living in reflected light. This seemed to describe the urban experience.

My, aren't we thoughtful today?

Wonder why . . .

Just then from the front door came a jangle of keys. One click, then another. In suburbia or rural America one can get away with a single lock. In cities, New York at least, a knob lock and dead bolt are the minimum.

A faint squeak sounded as the door pushed inward. And Sachs drew her Glock smoothly and aimed it, steady, on her target's chest.

'Amelia.' A shocked whisper.

'Drop the bag, Nick. And get on the floor, facedown. I don't want either hand out of my sight for one second. Do you understand me?'

CHAPTER 56

Two Pulaskis sat in a deli in Greenwich Village, not far from the 6th Precinct.

The 6 was Tony Pulaski's house and the twin brothers came here pretty frequently.

He and Ron were nursing coffee in thick cups. Thick so that if they got banged up, which happened a lot and loudly in this dive of an eating establishment, they wouldn't chip so much.

Ron's, however, was missing a heart-shaped chunk from the lip. He minded the sharp edge with every sip.

'So,' Tony was saying, 'just to get this straight. You're running an unauthorized undercover op, using your own buy money, though you're not buying, or if you are you flush the evidence right after. You have no Major Cases or ESU backup. Is that about it?'

'Pretty much. Oh, and it's in the worst part of New York. Statistically.'

'Good to add that to the mix,' Tony said.

People would turn their eyes onto the brothers occasionally. They were used to it, being identical twins in nearly identical uniforms. Tony had a few more decorations. He was older.

By seven minutes.

Amelia Sachs had told Ron to have somebody watching

his back when he went in for the meeting with the drug czar Oden, in his quest to find out what the man's connection was with Baxter and about this new drug Catch. And the only person Pulaski could think of was Tony.

'You're doing this for Lincoln, then?'

Ron nodded. Didn't need to repeat what Tony already knew. That after the head injury Ron would've left the force if Rhyme hadn't gotten him to stay – by saying bluntly, Get off your ass and get back to work. Rhyme hadn't played the look-at-me card: me, the gimp still catching bad guys. He just said, 'You're a good cop, Rookie. And you can be one hell of a good crime scene investigator if you stick to it. You know that people depend on you.'

'Who?' the officer'd asked. 'My family? I can get another job.'

Rhyme had twisted his face up, in that way only Lincoln Rhyme could do, when people didn't get what he was saying. 'Who do you think? I'm talking about the vics who're going to die because you were doing public relations or some shit and not walking the grid at scenes in the field. Do I have to spell it out? Get off your ass and get back to work. Last. Word. From. Me.'

So Ron Pulaski had gotten back to work.

'What's your plan, you meet this Oden? Wait. Isn't that a god or something? Like in Germany?'

'Norse, I think. Spelled different.'

'Does that mean he's from Norway. Wouldn't that be Norwegian?'

'I don't know.'

'Oh. What's the plan?'

'I've got the name of somebody, some kid knows where he hangs.'

'Oden the Norse dealer.'

'Are you listening? I'm serious.'

'Go on,' Tony said and looked serious.

'I meet Oden. I'm going to say I knew Baxter. He was going to hook me up with him, Oden, but then Baxter got busted.'

'Hooked up for what?'

'That's just to get in the door. Then I'll make a buy, this Catch stuff. The super drug. I bust him. You come in. Ta-da. We negotiate. He tells us what Baxter did and we let him go. I'm betting Baxter bankrolled him. I tell Lincoln and he realizes Baxter was really a dangerous shit. Not that he deserved to die. But he wasn't a lamb. And Lincoln un-retires.'

Tony scowled. 'That isn't much of a plan.'

Ron scowled back. 'Any other thoughts? I'm happy to entertain them.'

'Just saying. It's not much of a plan.'

'So?' Pulaski asked. 'You up for it?'

'What the hell,' Tony muttered. 'I haven't risked my job, my pension, my reputation and – what else? – oh, yeah, my life in the last couple days. Why not?'

'What is this?'

Nick was speaking not to Sachs but to her backup, a uniform stepping out of the kitchen, a slim African American borrowed from the 84. The officer frisked Nick carefully. A grimace toward Sachs as he removed a Smittie hammerless .38 from the man's jacket pocket.

'That. Wait. I can explain.'

Sachs grimaced. The gun alone was enough to put him away for five years. She'd have thought he was smarter than that.

'Cuffs?'

'Yes,' Sachs replied.

'Hey, you don't need . . .' Nick's voice faded.

The patrolman handed the weapon to Sachs then cuffed Nick's hands behind him and helped him up. She emptied the rounds from the weapon and slipped it into an evidence bag. The cartridges went into another. She set them on a table, well out of Nick's reach.

'I was going to report it,' Nick blustered, his voice higher, in the register of guilt, as Sachs thought of it. 'The piece. I was going to turn it in. I wasn't carrying.'

Though, yeah, he pretty much was.

'You don't understand,' he continued. The desperation was thick. 'I've been on the street, trying to find that man I told you about, who could help me. Could prove I was innocent. I was in Red Hook and this guy comes out of nowhere, pulled that Smittie, going to mug me. I took the piece away from him. I couldn't toss it. Some kid might've found it.'

Sachs didn't even bother to run down the lie. 'Jon Perone,' she began. And let that sit.

Nick gave absolutely no reaction.

'When you met with Perone we had a team outside his office.'

The man tried to take this in. Then: 'Well, yeah, Perone was the one had information about Donnie. He was going to do some digging, find what he needed to prove I wasn't anywhere near the 'jacking—'

'We turned Ralph Seville, Nick. Perone's muscle. The one you two sent to kill Freddy Caruthers.'

Mouth open slightly. Eyes zipping throughout his apartment. She thought of the tiny fish in Vernon Griffith's aquarium.

She added, 'Two of our people followed Seville to the mall where you had Freddy waiting. He moved on Freddy, in the garage, and they nailed him. He dimed you both out.'

'But—?'

'Seville told Perone he bodied Freddy. That was the script. Perone doesn't know we've got Seville. Freddy's in protective custody for the time being.'

Nick's face remained adamant. 'Lying. That son of a bitch is lying. Seville. He's a prick.'

'Enough,' Sachs whispered. 'Enough.'

With that, Nick changed. Instantly. He became a wolf. 'How'd you get a team to Perone's? Bullshit. You're fucking bluffing.'

She blinked at his fury. His words stabbed like a blade. 'We knew you'd be smart, switching cars in a garage or leading us off. The night I stayed here? I got a tracker app on your phone after you fell asleep. We followed you to Perone's. I couldn't get a warrant – we couldn't hear what you and Perone said. But Seville told us you *did* 'jack the Algonquin truck near the Gowanus back then and you *did* pistol-whip the driver. Donnie had nothing to do with it. And the reason you wanted the case files: to get your money from whoever'd ended up with 'jacked drugs.'

His shoulders slumped in defeat, and he reverted to pathetic. 'I go back and I'm dead, Amelia. Either I'll kill myself or somebody'll do me.' His voice cracked.

She looked him over, head to knees. 'I don't want you to go back, Nick.'

Relief, like a hurt child collected in his mother's arms.

'Thank you. You have to understand. What happened a few years ago. I didn't want to do it. The 'jacking. You know, Mom was sick, Donnie was having problems. All that merch is insured. It wasn't that big a deal. Really.'

Sachs's phone buzzed. She regarded the screen, and sent a reply text. A moment later the front door opened and a tall, lean man, dark-skinned, walked inside. He was wearing a brown suit, yellow shirt and bold crimson tie. The colors may have clashed but the garb fit well.

'Well, lookie here. Lookie this. Caughtcha, din't we?' He ran long fingers over his short salt-and-pepper hair.

Nick grimaced. 'Shit.'

Fred Dellray, a senior FBI special agent, was known for several things. One, his love of philosophy, a subject in which he was somewhat famous in academic circles. Two, his outlandish fashion choices. Then there was his unusual vocabulary. Dellray-speak, it was called.

'So, Mr Nick, you been doing some naughty oops stuff, considerin' you're still hot off the presses from prison.'

Nick remained silent.

Dellray turned a chair around and sat, the back between him and Nick, and looked him over, even more intensely than Sachs had done.

'A-melia?'

'Fred?'

'M'I allowed to push the plunger.'

'Do what you need.'

Dellray teepeed his fingers. 'By the power vested in *her*, thanks to the great state of New York, Detective Sachs here will be arresting you for a large number o' things. Many, many come to *my* mind, at least, hers too, I'll betcha. Shhh, shhh, don't make your mouth go that way, 'bout to form words. I'm speaking. She will be arresting you and then with the agreement of her boss and my boss, *way* high ups, you will be working for me, call me the great eagle of the federal government.'

'What're you—'

'Shhh, shhh. You miss that part? You'll be a CI for me, a *con*-fidential informant. And oh what a dangle you'll be. Former cop, former con. The plan is you produce for us. Five years or so, doing just what you're sposta – which's what I tellya, and all's happy, happy. Then off you go to house arrest, and pretty soon you'll be free to become a Walmart greeter. If they hire former felons. Hm. Have to check that.'

Dellray, a former undercover agent, was now the foremost runner of informants in the Northeast.

'You want Perone.' Nick was nodding.

'Hell-*o*. That boy's suspendered minder, Seville, has burned him nice and toasty already. But he's jus' a starter, an appetizer, an *aperitivo*. We'll go onward and upward from there. The world awaits. Now what I wanta hear, *all* I wanta hear, is Yessir, I'm on board. I don't, I'll be squeezing some parts of your life you *don't* want nail marks in. We all together on that?'

A sigh. A nod.

'Delighted. But . . .' Dellray said, his dark face furiously screwed up. 'Can't hear you and more important, the *micro*-phones can't hear you. Of which we got more than the sets o' *The Bachelor* and *Survivor* combined. So?'

'I'll do it. I agree.'

Sachs pulled out her mobile and called another detective, who was parked outside in an unmarked car. 'Need transport down to Central Booking.' She looked at Nick and read him his rights. 'Lawyer?'

'No.'

'Good call.'

The detective arrived in the doorway, a solid Latina whom Sachs had known for years. Rita Sanchez. The woman nodded to Sachs.

'Rita. Get him downtown. I'll be there soon to handle the paperwork. Call the US attorney too.'

The woman stared coolly at Nick. She knew the story of their relationship. 'Sure, Amelia. I'll handle it.' Her tone was saying: Jesus, I'm sorry, honey.

'Amelia!' Nick was pausing at the door, Sanchez and the uniform slowing. 'I'm . . . I'm sorry.'

What's the worst evil?

She looked past him, to the detective, and nodded. Nick was led from the apartment.

'Whatsis?' Fred Dellray asked, nodding at the gym bag Nick had with him.

Sachs unzipped it and extracted a painting. Well. Took a deep breath. The canvas was similar to one that she'd admired years ago. One she'd wanted so very badly but hadn't been able to afford. Remembered the freezing cold Sunday they'd seen it in the SoHo gallery, after brunch on Broome and West Broadway. Remembered the night, back in their apartment, snow tapping on the window, the radiator clicking, lying beside Nick, thinking about the painting. Sorry she couldn't buy it but much, much happier she was a cop than someone with a more lucrative job who could've plunked down the Visa and bought the canvas on the spot.

'I don't know,' she said, replacing the painting in the bag. 'No idea.'

And, turning away, she wiped one small tear from the corner of her right eye and sat down to write up the rest of the report.

CHAPTER **57**

'Ah, Amelia,' Thom said as she walked into the parlor. 'Wine?'

'Gotta work.'

'You sure?'

'Yes.' She noted that both Rhyme and Archer had whiskies in their cup holders. 'I mean, no. I mean, yes, I'll take one.'

The aide returned a moment later. He glanced at the bottle of scotch nearby. 'Wait.'

'Wait,' Rhyme said, attempting to preempt. 'What does that mean? I hate it when people say that. "Wait." Wait *what*? Stop moving? Stop *breathing*? Stop their mental processes?'

'Okay, what "wait" means is that somebody has done something unacceptable, something of which I am only now aware and about which I am lodging a protest. You raided the booze.'

Archer laughed. 'He commanded me to stand up, walk over there and pour some. No, Lincoln, I'm not taking the fall for you. I'm just a lowly intern, remember?'

Rhyme grumbled, 'If you'd given me a decent amount to begin with, there would've been no issue.'

Thom snagged the bottle and left the parlor.

'Wait!' Rhyme called. 'And that's the *proper* use of the word.'

Sachs gave a smile at the exchange and returned to the evidence, pacing as she looked over the packets and regarded the charts. She did this often, the pacing, to bleed off energy. When he was capable of it, Lincoln Rhyme used to do exactly the same when considering an intractable problem with a case.

The doorbell sounded and Rhyme heard Thom's footsteps zip to the door. The nearly subaudible greeting of the visitor explained to Rhyme who had come a-calling.

'Time to get to work,' Rhyme said.

Sachs nodded to Mel Cooper, who walked into the parlor shucking his jacket. He'd heard about Alicia Morgan, and Rhyme now explained about her contamination of the evidence. The tech shrugged. 'We've been up against worse.' He looked over the evidence from Griffith's and Morgan's apartments. 'Yes, yes. We'll find some answers in here.'

Rhyme was pleased to see Cooper's eyes shine with the intensity of a prospector spotting a thumb-sized nugget.

Sachs was digging latex gloves from her pocket when her phone dinged. An incoming text.

She read the message. She sent back another text and then walked to the computer. A moment later she opened an email. Rhyme saw the official heading. It was an evidence file from NYPD Crime Scene headquarters.

'They found what I was trying to remember – from that earlier case.' She held up the caisson that Vernon

Griffith had made. The wheels were identical to those depicted in the picture she'd just received from CSU.

She said, 'Alicia said she'd met Vernon when he killed somebody who bullied him.'

'Right.'

'I think the vic was Echi Rinaldo, the drug dealer and transport man – the homicide I haven't made any progress on.'

Archer said, 'Yes, the wheels match, toy wheels.'

'That's right. Also, Rinaldo was slashed to death with what might've been one of those.'

She nodded at the razor saws and knives they'd recovered from Griffith's apartment.

'All right, good,' Rhyme said. 'Another scene involving Griffith. Anything about *that* case that might give us an idea where he's hiding?' He and Sachs had worked it together briefly but then Rhymes had retired before they had progressed very far.

She ran through what she knew, concluding: 'Just that he jumped into a gypsy cab and headed to somewhere in the Village. Nothing more specific than that.'

'Ah,' Rhyme said softly, gazing up at the board. 'That puts us in a slightly different position.'

'But the Village,' Archer said, 'is huge. If there's no way to narrow it down . . .'

'Always question your assumptions.'

Sachs: 'Happy to. Which one?'

'That Vernon was referring to *Greenwich* Village.'

'What other village is there?'

'Middle Village.' He glanced at Archer. 'A neighborhood in Queens.'

She nodded. 'The one you called – because of the humus and the other trace. And I was skeptical of.'

'Correct.'

'I guess we didn't need two question marks after all.'

Sachs was looking over an online map of Middle Village. It wasn't a small area. 'Got any idea where exactly he might be?'

'I do,' Rhyme said, looking over the map himself, hearing Juliette Archer's words.

The answers to riddles are always simple . . .

'I can narrow it down.'

'By how much?' Cooper asked.

'To about six feet.'

St John Cemetery in Queens is the permanent resting site of a number of notables.

Among them: Mario Cuomo, Geraldine Ferraro, Robert Mapplethorpe and, no less, Charles Atlas. But Amelia Sachs knew it mostly through a quasi-professional connection, you might say. The Catholic cemetery held the bodies of dozens of the most famous gangsters in history. Joe Colombo, Carmine Galante, Carlo Gambino, Vito Genovese, John Gotti, and the quintessential Godfather, Lucky Luciano.

Sachs now parked her Torino at the entrance on Metropolitan Avenue, in Middle Village, pastoral by New York City standards. The main building was a structure that both Bavarians and Elizabethan country folk would have found familiar. Steepled, turreted, with leaded windows and brick walls framed by trim.

She climbed out and, from habit, unbuttoned her jacket

then touched her Glock grip with open palm to orient position. If you'd asked her a moment later if she'd done this, she couldn't have told you.

There were two unmarked cars parked nearby, from the local precinct. They were, she was pleased to note, *highly* unmarked. No buggy whip antennas or computers occupying the interstitial portion of the front seat. Real license plates, not government or permanents.

A young patrol officer, name of Keller on the breastplate, nodded to her from his vantage point near the entrance.

'Can we walk?' she asked.

'Yes, and it's better.'

She understood he'd be referring to the fact that any car would arouse attention in the largely open cemetery.

'We should move fast, though. It'll be dark soon. We've got the entrances covered, but . . .'

They started off, silently, through the entrance and then along the asphalt drive. The spring evening was mild as a greeting card and a number of people were here, leaving flowers. Some were alone, widows and widowers probably. Mostly elderly. There were couples too, flowering their parents' graves or perhaps their children's.

In five minutes they came to a deserted section of the cemetery. Two ESU officers, compact crew-cut men in tactical gear, looked up. They were taking cover behind a mausoleum.

She nodded. One of the tac cops said, 'He got here a half hour ago and he hasn't budged. We had an under-cover move people away. Told them there's going to be a state funeral later and we wanted to keep the area clear for security.'

Sachs looked past them to a grave about fifty feet away, at the back of a man sitting on a bench near a tombstone.

'If he rabbits,' she asked, 'other teams?'

'Oh, we're covered. There, there and there,' Keller said, pointing. 'He's not going anywhere.'

'No car?'

'No vehicle, Detective.'

'Weapons?'

'Didn't present.' This from one of the tac officers. His partner shook his head. Added, 'But there's a backpack beside the bench. In reach.'

'He took something out of it. Set it on the tombstone, there, see it? I looked with the binoculars. Seems like it's a toy. A ship or something. A boat.'

'It's a miniature,' Sachs said without looking closely. 'Not really a toy. Back me up. I'm going to take him.'

Vernon Griffith did not resist.

He would have been a formidable opponent; he was truly skinny but she could see muscles under the close-fitting shirt and he was tall, with a very long reach. And the backpack probably contained another deadly ball-peen or maybe a blade or saw like the ones she'd found in Chelsea.

The Steel Kiss . . .

He'd been clearly surprised at the officers' sudden presence and, after half rising, dropped down on the bench once more, holding his strikingly long hands up, straight in the air. Keller directed him onto his knees and then the ground, where he was cuffed and frisked. And the backpack searched. No guns, no hammers, nothing that might be used as a weapon.

Sachs guessed that he'd been lost in a meditation about his brother, Peter, whose grave he was sitting in front of. Or, if he believed in that sort of thing, maybe Griffith actually thought they were engaging in a conversation.

On the other hand he might simply have been thinking of practical matters. What was to come next? After the events of the past few days he'd have some thinking to do.

Then, helped to his feet and flanked by the ESU officers, he and Sachs walked to the front of the cemetery office. Griffith was deposited on another bench, this one featuring a verdigris dove. They were waiting for a prisoner transport van; Griffith would have been very cramped in the back of one of the unmarkeds. Besides, he had hurt people in such clever and unpleasant ways that you wouldn't want him behind you in a squad car, much less a Ford Torino, even cuffed.

Sachs sat next to him. She took out her tape recorder, clicked it on, then recited his Miranda rights. Asked if he understood them.

'I do. Sure.'

Griffith had long fingers, to match the feet, whose size they knew, of course. His face was lengthy too but the pale, beardless visage was nondescript. His eyes were hazel.

She continued, 'We know that Alicia Morgan had you kill certain individuals connected with the U.S. Auto vehicle that was defective and killed her husband. But we'd like to know more. Will you talk to us?'

He nodded.

'Could you state yes, please?'

'Oh, sorry. Yes.'

'Tell me in your words what happened. She's told my partner some things but not everything. I'd like to hear it from you.'

He nodded and without hesitation explained how Alicia had approached him, after seeing him kill someone on the street. 'Someone who was attacking me,' he added emphatically.

She recalled that Rhyme had told her Griffith had goaded Rinaldo to attack. But she nodded encouragingly.

'You said she had me kill the Shoppers who'd made and sold the car that killed her husband.'

Shoppers? she wondered.

'But I did it because I wanted to help her. She was burned and cut and, you know, changed forever by what happened. I agreed.'

'She wanted the people she felt were to blame to be killed by a product?'

'Things, yes. Because that's what killed her husband and injured her.'

'Tell me about Todd Williams.'

He confirmed what they'd guessed. That Williams, a digital activist, was a genius of a hacker and had taught Griffith how to crack the DataWise5000s. And, pretending he worked for an ad agency, he bought the databases of the products containing the controllers and of people or companies who had purchased the specific items.

Griffith added that he and Alicia had searched the list for anyone employed by U.S. Auto, the fuel injector company, the agency creating their ads or the lawyers defending them. 'Greg Frommer, Benkoff, Joe Heady. The woman insurance attorney in Westchester.'

'Afterward, where were you and Alicia supposed to be going?'

'Don't know. Upstate maybe. Canada'd be better. This all happened so fast. Didn't plan anything out. How'd you get here?' he asked. 'I never told Alicia about my brother.'

Sachs explained, 'A case from a while ago. The victim you killed named Echi Rinaldo.'

'The Shopper.'

Again, that word.

'He was a drug dealer,' Sachs said.

'I know. I read the story after. But still. How?'

'That case was on my docket. One of the pieces of evidence from the scene where you killed him was a wheel from a toy. You had a caisson in your apartment in Chelsea. It had the same wheel.'

Griffith nodded. 'I'd made one for Peter, a caisson.' Nodding back toward his brother's grave. 'I had it with me that night at dinner. I left the restaurant and was coming here to put it on his grave.' He shivered with disgust or anger. 'He broke it.'

'Rinaldo?'

A nod. 'He was walking back to his truck and wasn't looking where he was going. Knocked into me and it got crushed, the caisson. I shouted at him and he came after me. I killed him.' Griffith shook his head. 'But here, how'd you figure here?'

Sachs explained that after they'd connected Vernon and Rinaldo, with Rhyme making the Middle Village leap, it hadn't taken much to speculate that the evidence from the various scenes – the humus, the large quantities of fertilizer and pesticides or herbicides, along with the phenol, an ingredient in embalming fluid – might mean he'd visited this famed cemetery.

To about six feet . . .

A call revealed that Peter Griffith, Vernon's brother, was interred here. Sachs had called the director and asked if they had records of Vernon visiting the grave. He said he didn't know about visits, but there had been some odd occurrences around the Griffith plot: Someone would leave miniature furniture or toys at the grave site. The director told her the pieces were extremely well made. The man supposed some visitors took them. The ones that were turned in he kept in the office, waiting for someone to claim them. The combination had all the makings of an urban legend: miniatures and a cemetery.

'When he was alive Peter always liked what I made for him. The boy things, of course. Medieval weapons, tables and thrones for castles. Catapults and war towers. Cannon and caissons. He would have liked that boat, the Warren skiff. On his tombstone. Where is it?'

'In an evidence bag.' She felt compelled to add, 'It will be well taken care of.'

'You police, you were watching the grave?'

'That's right.'

Sachs had noted that his brother was only twenty when he passed. She commented on this. Then asked, 'What happened to him?'

'Shoppers.'

'You've said that. What does that mean?'

Griffith looked at his backpack. 'There's a diary in there? My brother's diary. He dictated it to an MP3 player. I've been transcribing it, thinking I was going to publish it someday. There's some remarkable things Peter's said. About life, about relationships, about people.'

Sachs found the leather book. It contained easily five hundred pages.

Griffith continued, 'In high school, Manhasset, some of the cool kids made friends with him. He thought they really meant it. But, uh-uh, they just were using him to get even with a girl who wouldn't have sex with them. They drugged her, convinced Peter it was somebody else, and they got pictures of him with her in bed. You know, you can imagine.'

'They posted them online?'

'No, this was before phone cameras. They took Polaroids and passed them around school.' He nodded toward the battered leather-bound volume. 'The last page. The last entry.'

Sachs found it.

Some things don't really go away. Never ever. I thought it would. Really believed it would. Tell myself I don't need friends like Sam and Frank. They're slugs, they're useless. They're garbage. As bad as Dano or Butler. Worse really 'cause they say one thing and do something else. Tell yourself they're not worth thinking about. But it doesn't work.

And nobody believed me that I didn't know it was Cindy. Everybody in school, the police, everybody, thought I planned it.

No charges, but didn't matter. Reinforced I was a freak.

Vern went crazy, wanted to kill them. My brother always had that temper, always wanted to get even with anybody who crossed him or me. Mom and Dad always had to keep an eye on him. His Shoppers, wanted to kill the Shoppers.

What happened with Frank and Sam and Cindy and everything – I'm not mad, like Vern. I'm just tired. So tired of the looks, so tired of the notes in my locker. Cindy's friends spit on me. She's gone. She and her family moved.

So tired.

I need to sleep. That's what I need, to sleep.

'He killed himself?'

'Not technically. Couldn't be buried here if he had. It's Catholic. But he drank himself into a stupor and went for a drive on Route Twenty-Five. Hit a hundred. Was twenty years old.'

'And "Shoppers"? What does that mean?'

'Peter and me? We're built different, we look different. It's Marfan syndrome.'

Sachs wasn't familiar with it. She assumed the condition was the cause of his height and disproportionately low weight, long hands and feet. To her, the condition wasn't particularly odd, simply another body type. But bullies in school? Well, they rarely needed much ammunition.

Griffith continued, 'We got made fun of a lot. Both of us. Kids're cruel. You're pretty. You wouldn't know that.'

Yes, she would. In her teens Sachs, more boyish than most of the boys, more competitive than any of them, had certainly been bullied. And later bullied too in the fashion industry because she was a woman. Same when she joined the force . . . and for the same reason.

He said, 'Most boys're bullied in gym class. But for me, it was mechanical arts – shop. It started because I had a crush on this girl, eighth grade. I heard she had this neat dollhouse. So for assignment, while all the other boys were making bookshelves and boot scrapers, I made her a Chippendale desk. Six inches high. Perfect.' His light-colored eyes shone. 'It was *perfect*. The boys gave me crap for that. "Skinny Bean's got a dollhouse. Slim Jim's a girl."' He shook his head. 'I still finished it. Gave it to Sarah and she looked all funny, you know. Like when you do something real nice for somebody and it's more than they want. Or they don't want anything at all. Makes them feel uncomfortable. She said, "Thanks," like thanking a waitress. I never talked to her again.'

So, that was it. Not 'shoppers' as in those who buy products. As in students in shop class.

'And the people who were responsible for the defective car Alicia and her family were in, you thought of them as Shoppers.'

'They were. Bullies, arrogant. Thinking only about themselves. Selling defective cars and knowing they were dangerous. Making money. That's all that mattered to them.'

'You must have loved your brother a lot.'

'I kept my old phone with his voice mail messages on it. I listen to them all the time. It's some comfort.' He turned to her. 'Any comfort in this life is good, don't you think?'

Sachs believed she knew the answer to her next question. 'Those boys who took pictures of your brother and that girl. What happened to them?'

'Oh, that's why I moved into the apartment in Chelsea. Easier for me to do what I'd decided to – find them and kill them; they worked in the city. One I slashed to death. Sam. The other, Frank? Beat him to death. The bodies're in a pond near Newark. I can tell you more about those, if you want. She was going to kill me, wasn't she? Alicia.'

Sachs hesitated.

The story would come out, sooner or later. 'Yes, Vernon. I'm sorry.'

Resignation on his face. 'I knew. I mean, deep down, I knew she was using me. Anybody who wants you to kill people, just comes out and asks you, after you've slept together.' A shrug. 'What did I expect? But sometimes you *let* yourself be used because . . . well, just because. You're lonely or whatever. We all pay for love one way or another.' Another searching gaze of her face. 'You're nice to me. Even after I tried to kill your mother. I don't think you're a Shopper after all. I thought you were. But you're not.' After a moment he continued, 'Can I give you something?'

'What?'

'In the backpack. There's another book.'

She looked inside. Found a slim volume. 'This?'

'That's right.'

The Nutshell Studies of Unexplained Death.

She flipped through it, examining the pictures of crime scene miniatures. Sachs had never seen anything like it. Frances Glessner Lee was the creator of the dioramas.

Sachs gave a soft laugh, looking at the tiny doll, a corpse, lying in a kitchen.

'You can have it. I'd like you to.'

'We're not allowed. You understand.'

'Oh. Why not?'

She smiled. 'I don't know. A police rule. But we're not.'

'Sure. Maybe you could buy one, now that you know about it.'

'I'll do that, Vernon.'

Two uniformed officers approached. 'Detective.'

'Tom,' she responded to the taller of the two.

'Bus's here.'

She said to Griffith, 'We'll take you to booking. You're not going to be a problem, are you?'

'No.'

Sachs believed him.

CHAPTER 58

'He in there.'

Ron Pulaski looked from the boy, no more than fifteen, to the building the kid was pointing at. The place was bad, worse than most in East New York. Ron and his children had seen *The Hobbit* not long ago and at one point the dwarves and Bilbo were heading for a cave. That's what this place reminded him of. One of those old stone structures, dried-blood brown, and with windows black and sunken as corpse eye sockets. Some broken. Some dotted with bullet holes.

Seemed appropriate, this dim, forbidding place, for Oden to be dealing from. Or where he fabricated his infamous Catch. The drug of drugs.

Or maybe he did that elsewhere and it was here that he tortured rivals and suspected informants.

'He alone?' Ron asked.

'Dunno.' The boy's wide brown eyes twitched around the street. Ron had dressed down again – as always on the Save-Lincoln-Rhyme operation – but he still looked just like who he was: a white cop in a black 'hood, dressing sorta-kinda undercover. He was forcing himself not to peer behind him, into the alley where Tony was waiting with his Glock drawn.

He asked the kid, 'Oden? Is he armed?'

'Look, man, just my green. K?'

'I'm paying you one large. Does Oden usually carry?'

'This ain't my 'hood. I don't know this Oden, don't know his crew. All's I know: Word come from Alpho, at Richie's, vouching for you, saying you lay down some green, I find this Oden bitch for you. I heard he in there, that building. All I know. I'm saying. You sure you ain't a cop?'

'Not a cop.'

'Okay. I done what I'm s'posed to. Now: green.'

Pulaski dug into his pocket, wrapped his fingers around a week's take-home – in fives to make the roll sing.

'Wait.' The kid was speaking urgently.

'Whatta you mean wait?'

'Don't gimme no cash *now*.' As if the cop had belched during mass.

Ron sighed. 'You just said—'

'Hold on, hold on . . .'

Looking around.

Ron was too. The hell was this?

Then he spotted three young men, two Latino, one black, walking down the opposite side of the street, smoking, laughing. Their age would make them early college in some places, but here they might still be in high school, if not dropouts.

'Wait, wait . . . No, no, don't look at 'em, lookit me.'

Sighing again. 'What are you—?

'K. Now. Gimme. The green.'

Ron handed the money over. The boy dug into his pocket and handed him a crumpled pack of cigarettes.

Ron frowned. 'What's in there? I don't want to score anything. I just want to talk to Oden.'

'What's in there is cigarettes, man. Just take it. Put it away like there's three G of rock. Careful. Hide it. Now!'

Ah. Ron understood. The kid wanted to make it seem like he was dealing. Build his street cred. Ron glanced across the street and saw that the three young men had noticed. They gave no reaction and continued on their way.

Ron looked over the building. 'Okay. Oden. What unit's he in?'

'Dunno. Just he in there. I was you, I'd start One A and work yo way up.'

Ron started across the street.

'Yo.'

'What?'

'My ciggies.'

'I just bought 'em.' He crushed the pack and tossed it into the street. 'Give it up, they're not good for you.'

'Fuck that, man.'

After the kid vanished Tony joined him. He was wearing his own brand of undercover garb – black jeans and a T-shirt, a gray leather jacket, Yankees cap swiveled backward. Together they headed toward the mouth of the alley next to the Orc Cave building.

'What goes on in there?'

'No idea. The kid swears Oden's in there now. Well, he didn't swear. He *thinks* he's in there. And it's the only lead we've got. So here's hoping.'

'Feels like a meth house.'

Ron hoped it wasn't. Both meth- and crackheads could get wound up like superheroes. The junk gave them crazy strength and unmeshed their thinking. If Ron and Tony were lucky Oden wasn't retail; he sold in bulk. Maybe even to Charles Baxter directly, the perp Rhyme had put in Rikers. After all, brokers and Wall Street lawyers had to get smack and C someplace.

Tony said, 'If he's dealing he's not going to be alone and they're all gonna have weapons. Did you ask the kid?'

'Yeah, I did. Not helpful.'

Dunno . . .

'We've been here forty minutes. Nobody in or out. I think it's cool.'

'Oh?' Tony asked. 'You don't maybe think Oden and his three minders, and their AK-Four-Sevens, might've got here forty-*five* minutes ago?'

'Tone.'

'I'm just saying. K. We go.'

Unzipping the jacket to better access his now-holstered Glock, Tony looked over his brother. 'Where's your piece?'

'Ankle.'

'No. In your waistband.'

Pulaski hesitated then tugged up his jean cuff. He lifted the Bodyguard out of the holster and slipped it into the pocket where he kept the rest of the buy money. His brother nodded, a concession that, okay, the tiny .380 would probably fall out of the waistband or slip down to Ron's crotch.

Tony touched his arm. 'Just, one last time. You sure this's worth it?'

Ron smiled.

And together, they eased up to the front door of Oden's building. It was unlocked. To be exact, it was no-locked. A gaping hole where a dead bolt had been.

'Which apartment?'

Dunno . . .

Ron shook his head.

But they didn't have to look very far. On the second floor, the apartment in the back, 2F, had a handwritten card beneath the buzzer button, in the center of the door, which was red and scuffed.

O'denne.

Under other circumstances Ron might've laughed. An Irish, not a Norse, drug dealer.

Tony stood to the side of the door.

Ron didn't. When one looks out a peephole and sees nobody in the hall that means the visitors are cops. He put a stony look on his face and hit the bell. He was sweating. But he didn't wipe the rivulets off. Too late.

Silence for a moment then footsteps from inside.

'Who is it?' came the gruff voice.

'Name is Ron. I was a friend of Baxter's. Charles Baxter.'

Ron could see shadows moving under the door. Was O'denne pulling a gun from his pocket and debating just shooting the visitor through the door? It didn't seem smart to do that in your residence. But Ron realized O'denne might not be particularly stable and might therefore be unconcerned about wasting an intruder close to home. And as for anyone else nearby, he guessed gunshots were more or less common here and therefore largely ignored.

'What do you want?'

'You know Charles's dead.'

'What do you want?'

'He told me about you. I want to pick up with you where he left off.'

A click from the other side of the door.

A gun cocking? Or de-cocking?

But the sound turned out to be one of several locks' snapping open.

Ron tensed, his hand slipping toward his pistol. Tony lifted his Glock.

The door opened and Ron looked inside, scanning the man who stood before him, backlit in light from a cheap lamp with a torn shade.

Ron's shoulders slumped. All he could think: Oh, man . . . What do I do now?

CHAPTER 59

Lincoln Rhyme heard the front door of his town house open and close. Footsteps approached.

'It's Amelia,' Juliette Archer said. They were in the parlor.

'You can tell from the sound. Good. Yes, your hearing, vision, smell will improve. Some doctors dispute it but I've run experiments and I'm convinced it's true. Taste too, if you don't kill off your sapictive cells with excessive whisky.'

'The what? Sapictive?'

'Taste receptor cells.'

'Oh. Well, life's a balance, isn't it?'

Amelia Sachs walked inside, nodding greetings.

'A confession from Griffith?' he asked.

'More or less.' She sat down and told him a story of two brothers bullied – the younger one to death – and his sibling's growing instability and desire for revenge. Griffith's account aligned perfectly with what Alicia Morgan had told them.

'"Shoppers,"' Archer mused after hearing the story. 'Well, didn't see that one coming.'

While the mental makeup of a perp was largely irrelevant to Rhyme, he now had to admit to himself that Vernon Griffith was one of the more complex suspects he'd ever been up against.

'Not unsympathetic,' Sachs offered.

Stealing the very words Rhyme had been about to offer.

She explained that there would probably be a plea deal. 'He admitted we got him dead to rights. He doesn't want to fight it.' A smile. 'He asked if I thought they'd let him make furniture in prison.'

Rhyme wondered if that was a possibility. It seemed that felons incarcerated for murder might not be allowed access to saws and ball-peen hammers. The man might have to settle for making license plates.

Then he was gazing at the evidence boards, reflecting how the two cases that had seemed so different were in fact as genetically linked as twins. *Frommer v. Midwest Conveyance* and *The People of the State of New York v. Griffith* and, now, *v. Alicia Morgan.*

Sachs 'deweaponed' herself (the verb had been in an NYPD memo on firearm safety that she'd shared with Rhyme; they'd had a good laugh). She poured coffee from a service Thom had set up in the corner. She sat. Just as she took her first sip her phone sang out. She read the text and gave a laugh. 'CSU in Queens found the missing napkins. The White Castle napkins.'

'I'd forgotten about those,' Archer said.

Rhyme: 'I hadn't, though I had given up on them. And?'

Sachs read: '"Negative for friction ridges, negative for DNA. Positive for confectionery milk-based beverage in proportions that suggest source was White Castle restaurant chain."'

'But didn't the—' Archer began.

'—napkins have *White Castle* printed on them? Yep, they did.'

Rhyme said, 'Nature of our profession – yours now too, Archer. Every day we deal with missing evidence, evidence never properly identified, evidence contaminated. Deductions botched completely. And deductions made that don't need to be. Missed clues. Happens in epidemiology, I would imagine.'

'Oh, yes. Myopic children, remember?' She told Amelia Sachs the story of the study that incorrectly asserted causation between children's sleeping with lights on and vision problem.

Nodding, Sachs said, 'Heard this story on the radio – people used to believe that maggots spontaneously generated from meat. Don't remember the details.'

Archer said, 'Sure. Francesco Redi, seventeenth-century scientist, was the one who disproved that. It was because fly eggs were too small to be seen. Father of experimental biology.'

Sachs glanced at the evidence boards, apparently at the section about the civil suit. She asked, 'Your case, the original one, Mrs Frommer's? Can she recover anything?'

'Very doubtful.' Rhyme explained that the only cause of action would be against Alicia and Griffith for the wrongful death of Greg Frommer. Whitmore was looking into their finances, but neither of them seemed very wealthy.

Archer's phone rang. She commanded, 'Answer.'

'Hey, Jule. Me.'

'Randy. You're on with Lincoln and Amelia.'

Her brother.

Greetings shot back and forth.

'Be there in ten.'

She said, 'We closed the case.'

'Seriously? Well, I'm impressed. Billy'll love to hear all about it. Between you and me, he loves the idea of Cop Mom. He's doing a graphic novel. You're the heroine. But you didn't hear me say that. It's going to be a surprise. Okay. I'm in traffic without a hands-free. Don't tell the police. Ha!'

They disconnected.

Archer was looking not at Rhyme but toward Sachs. 'When I signed up for Lincoln's course, I knew about you, of course, Amelia. Anybody who follows New York crime knows about you. You're epic, as my son would say. I'd go with "famous" but, well, "epic" seems to fit better. And I knew you worked with Lincoln and that you were his partner but I didn't know you were *that* kind of partner too. Seeing you the past few days, I found out.'

'We've been together for a long time. Both ways,' Sachs said with a smile.

'I wasn't sure what to expect. But you're just like any other couple. Happy, sad, irritated.'

Rhyme chuckled. 'We fight, sure. We've been having one for the past few weeks.'

Sachs wasn't smiling when she said, 'I'm mad he resigned.'

'And *I'm* mad she's mad that I resigned.'

She added, 'And mad he stole my lab tech.'

'You got him back in the end,' Rhyme groused.

Archer said, 'When I was diagnosed I decided that I'd live alone. Oh, with Billy part of the time, under the

custody agreement, and with a caregiver, of course –
somebody like Thom. Though I don't know if I can find
somebody like him. He's a gem.'

Rhyme glanced at the doorway. 'None better. But that
goes no farther than this room.'

Archer gave a coy smile. 'As if he doesn't know.' She
continued, 'I decided that I'd never be in a relationship,
never even think about that. Get my new profession, one
that was fulfilling, challenging. Raise my son as best I
could. Have friends who could deal with quadriplegia.
Not the life I'd planned on or wanted but a decent life.
Then – don't you love the way fate works? – then I met
somebody. It was about three months ago, just after the
neurologist confirmed that the disability would probably
be as severe as they'd thought. Brad. That was his name.
Met him at my son's birthday party. Single father. An
MD. It really clicked between us. I told him right up front
about the tumor, the surgery. He's cardio but knew generally about the condition. He didn't seem to care and we
went out for a while.'

Sachs said, 'But you broke it off.'

'I did, yes. I was probably going stone-cold gimp in a
year. He was a jogger and a sailor. Now, that is a combination you don't really find in the same column on Match
Dot Com or eHarmony, do you? Brad was pretty upset
when I told him. But I knew it was best. For both of us.'
She gave a wisp of a laugh. 'Can you see where this is
going?'

Rhyme didn't. Not at all. But he noticed Sachs had a
faint smile on her face.

Archer continued, 'Then I saw you two together.

Began to think maybe I'd made a mistake. I called him back last night. We're going out this weekend. Who knows? Maybe in six months we'll be engaged. Like you two. Have you set a date yet?'

Sachs shook her head. 'Not yet. Soon.'

Archer smiled. 'Did he propose romantically?'

'Hardly got down on one knee, now, did I?' Rhyme muttered.

Sachs said, 'I think it was, "There seems to be no objective or practical reason for not getting married. What's your thinking on the subject?"'

Archer laughed.

Rhyme frowned. 'Nothing funny about that. I gave an accurate assessment of the situation, coupled with a request for further data that might be helpful in reaching a conclusion. Made perfect sense to me.'

Archer was glancing at Sachs's left hand. 'I was noticing your ring. Beautiful.'

Sachs held up her ring finger, displaying the two-carat blue stone. 'Lincoln picked it. It's from Australia.'

'Sapphire?'

'No, a diamond.'

'Not particularly valuable,' Rhyme said analytically. 'But rare. A class two-b. I was intrigued by the color. Blue because of scattered boron in the matrix. A semiconductor, by the way. The only diamond that has that characteristic.'

'You having a honeymoon?'

Rhyme said, 'I was thinking Nassau. The last time I was in the Bahamas I was almost shot and almost drowned. Both within five minutes. I'd like to go back and have a more peaceful time of it. And there's a friend I'd like to see. His wife makes excellent conch fritters.'

'I expect an invite to the wedding.'

Sachs tilted her head. 'There're some openings for the wedding party.'

'Just ask, I'll be there.'

The doorbell buzzed. Rhyme glanced at the screen. Archer's brother had arrived to pick her up. Thom let Randy into the room. He greeted Rhyme and Sachs with a nod and hurried to his sister. 'You all right, Jule? Your face!'

'No, no, it's okay. A little bruised.'

Archer turned her chair to Rhyme. 'I'm going out of character again.'

He lifted an eyebrow.

She rose from the chair, walked to Rhyme and put her arms around him, hugged hard. At least, that was his deduction, since he couldn't feel the pressure. A similar embrace for Sachs, then she dropped back into the Storm Arrow and, with her brother behind, wheeled out.

'Back tomorrow early,' Rhyme called.

He laughed as she lifted her left arm and gave a thumbs-up.

When they'd left, Rhyme said, 'I talked to your mom. She's in good spirits. When's the surgery?'

'Tomorrow afternoon.'

He observed her wan face, peering out the window. 'The other situation?' He was referring to Nick. Several night's ago she'd told Rhyme everything about his re-appearance – and her suspicion of him. And about spending the night at Nick's to place a tracking app on his phone.

A preface like that, Sachs? Pray continue . . .

No reaction for a moment. She was immobile, looking out over Central Park.

'Turned out the way I was afraid it would. Worse, actually. He tried to order a hit on somebody.'

Rhyme grimaced and shook his head. 'I'm sorry.'

'Fred'll run him for a while. We'll get a half-dozen others, high-ups in the OC chain. Then cut him loose.'

'One thing you never told me, Sachs.'

The rattan chair she sat in gave its unique caw as she turned his way. She tilted her head, brushed her hair back. Rhyme liked her wearing it down, rather than in a bun.

'What's that?'

'*Why* did you get suspicious of Nick? Everything he told you, how he acted . . . it sounded credible. To me, at least.'

After a moment she said, 'Intuition. How you hate that word, I know. But that's what it was. I couldn't quite put my finger on it. Something was off about him. It was Mom who brought it into focus. Nick said he took the fall for his brother. But she said that if he'd really cared for me, he never would've done that. Nick was a decorated cop; he had cred all over downtown. His brother gets busted, he could've worked with the DA on sentencing, helped Donnie get into a program in prison. Organized an operation to nail Delgado – that was all a lie, by the way. But he wouldn't have taken the fall.' She smiled, her full lips, free of color, forming a mild crescent. 'Didn't have a splinter of evidence, just a gut feel.'

'No,' Rhyme said. 'Not gut. Heart. Sometimes that's better than evidence.'

She blinked.

'But you didn't hear me say that, Sachs. You never heard me say that.'

'I better get to Mom.' She kissed his mouth hard. 'That woman's got to get well fast. I miss sleeping here.'

'I miss that too, Sachs. I really do.'

CHAPTER **60**

Rhyme looked up from his monitor, on which he was engaged in a chess match against a smart, but largely unimaginative computer program.

He said to the visitor dawdling in the parlor doorway, 'Come on in.' And to the microprocessor: 'White queen to e-seven. Check.'

Rhyme let the software cogitate on *that* move and wheeled away from the work station, facing Ron Pulaski. 'Where've you been, Rookie? You missed the climax, the crescendo, the *denouement* of the Griffith case. Here you are, arriving for the coda. How dull.'

'Well, that other case. I was multitasking.'

'Do you know how much I detest that word, Pulaski? Using "task" as a verb is as mortifying as using "ask" as a noun. Unacceptable. *And* tacking on the prefix "multi" is unnecessary. "Tasking," if you're going to accept it as a predicate, includes a single endeavor or a dozen.'

'Lincoln, we live in the era of the—'

'If you say "sound bite," I will not be happy.'

'—the, uhm, era of the frequent use of a contracted phrase or single word to convey a complex concept. *That's* what I was going to say.'

A stifled laugh and he reminded himself not to sell the kid short. Rhyme needed someone to ground him.

But through the repartee Rhyme could see he had something important on his mind. 'You heard from Amelia? About Griffith?' Rhyme asked.

A nod. Ron sat in the rattan chair. 'Sad character. Sad story.'

'Was, yes. But in the eyes of the law, revenge is no more acceptable as a motive than sexual lust or terrorism. Now I'm tired of being pretentious. Since the case is over, there's no reason for you to be here. So. What's up?'

The young officer's eyes remained on a miniature dresser of Griffith's. Then he looked at a kitchen table. He studied this until, apparently, it was time to talk.

'The other case.'

'Gutiérrez.'

Pulaski looked at him. 'The way you said that, Lincoln. You know it wasn't Gutiérrez.'

'I made the supposition. Wasn't hard.'

'Jenny calls me transparent.'

'A bit of that in you, Rookie, yes. Not that it's bad.'

Pulaski didn't seem to care if it was good or bad. 'The other case?'

'Go on.'

'It was the *Baxter* case.' Accompanied by an unnecessary glance at the whiteboard in the corner, whose back was turned to them.

This revelation Rhyme had not guessed. Ideas formed, but it was his colleague, not Rhyme, who had center stage.

'I went through the case files. I know it was closed but I went through them anyway. And I found some loose ends.'

Rhyme recalled Archer's questioning observations: Why

the outside storage space that Baxter had neglected to tell investigators about?

Rhyme asked, 'Which were?'

'Well, one was pretty interesting. I looked over the detectives' notes and got the names of everybody Baxter met with over the past year or so. One in particular seemed interesting. Someone named Oden.'

'Never heard of him.'

'The name was in a transcription of a witness's statement so they wrote O-D-E-N. Turns out the name was actually O apostrophe D-E-N-N-E.'

'Irish not a misspelled Norse deity,' Rhyme observed.

'I asked around, checked more notes. There wasn't much. But I did find this O'denne had some connection to the drug world in Brooklyn. He was behind some kind of new drug people were talking about on the streets. Synthetic. Seemed like the name was Catch. But detectives on the case never pursued the lead. I guessed it was because Baxter . . .'

'You can say it, Rookie. Died.'

'That's right. But *I* did. I followed up.'

'Unofficially?'

'Sort of.'

'She's sort of pregnant.'

'Finally got an ID. O'denne was in East New York. Why would Baxter – a financial bigwig – have anything to do with this gangbanger in East New York? I went to talk to O'denne and find out—'

'—if Baxter was more than just a scam artist.'

'Exactly. I wanted to prove he was bankrolling this new drug. That he'd actually used the gun you found –

that he'd killed people. The evidence was ambiguous, remember, Lincoln. There were questions. Maybe he *was* dangerous.'

Rhyme said softly, 'So then it would have been proper procedure for him to go into Violent Offender Detention.'

Pulaski nodded. 'So you *wouldn't've* been responsible for an *innocent* man's death; you'd've put a dangerous perp away. And if I could show you that, then you'd give up this bullshit about retirement. Which it really is, Lincoln.'

Rhyme exhaled a faint laugh. 'Well, quite the sixty-four-thousand-dollar question, Rookie. And what's the answer?'

'My brother and I tracked down O'denne. East BK.'

A raised eyebrow.

'He's a priest, Lincoln.'

'A . . .'

'Father Francis Xavier O'denne. He runs a storefront clinic in Brownsville. The drug he was connected with?' He shook his head with a grim smile. 'A new form of methadone to treat addicts. And it's not called "Catch." *That's* the name of Father O'denne's clinic. Community Action Treatment Center for Hope.' Pulaski sighed. 'And Baxter? He was one of the main benefactors of the place.'

So the gun *was* Baxter's father's, a souvenir from one of the milestones in the man's life. And the gunshot residue came from a stray twenty-dollar bill, the drugs from that or another bill. The oil from the sporting goods store where he'd bought his son the last present he would ever buy for the boy.

'And, I guess I'll tell you everything, Lincoln. The center

may have to close, if Father O'denne can't find somebody else to back it.'

'So, I'm responsible not only for an innocent man's death but for preventing how many people from getting off the street and into productive lives?'

'Shit. I just wanted to help, Lincoln. Get you back on the job. But . . . well, that's what I found.'

Which is the thing about science; you can't ignore the facts.

Rhyme turned his chair and looked again at the tiny pieces of furniture that Vernon Griffith had so carefully and perfectly created.

'Anyway,' Pulaski said. 'I understand now.'

'Understand what?'

'Why you're doing this. Retiring. If I fucked up, I'd probably do the same thing. Back out. Quit the force. Take up something else.'

Rhyme kept his eyes on Vernon Griffith's miniatures. He said in a gusty voice, 'Bad choice.'

'I . . . What?'

'Quitting because of a screw-up – a thoroughly bad idea.'

Pulaski's brows narrowed. 'Okay, Lincoln. I don't get it. What're you saying?'

'You know who I was talking to an hour ago?'

'No clue.'

'Lon Sellitto. I was asking him if there were any cases he needed some help on.'

'Cases? Criminal?'

'Last time I looked he wasn't a social worker, Rookie. Of *course* criminal.' He wheeled around to face the young officer.

'Well, I hope you can understand why I'm a little confused.'

'A foolish consistency is the hobgoblin of narrow minds.'

'I like Emerson too, Lincoln. And I think it was "little minds."'

Was it? Probably. Rhyme nodded in concession.

'But that still doesn't explain why.'

Lincoln Rhyme suspected the answer was this: If you tallied up all the reasons for not pursuing what you know in your heart you're meant to pursue, you'd be absolutely – he relished the word – paralyzed. Which simply meant that you had to ignore every voice within clamoring for you to quit, to retire, to hesitate or pause or question, whether it was a clue that stymied you or exhaustion tempting you to rest or the stunner that a man lay dead in a grave that you had thoughtlessly dug for him.

But he said, 'I don't have a clue, Rookie. None at all. But there it is. So go clear your calendar. I'll need you in early tomorrow morning. You and Amelia. We've got to finish up the Unsub Forty case and then see what else Lon has on the – forgive me – front burner.'

'Sure, Lincoln. Good.'

As he headed out the door, Pulaski was blushing and the look on his face was best described as beaming.

Which was a form of expression that Rhyme believed no one should ever succumb to.

MONDAY

VII PLAN A

CHAPTER 61

The door buzzer sounded and Rhyme glanced at the screen. Lon Sellitto and his cane.

Thom walked to the entry hall and let the detective in. He noted that Sellitto stayed on course toward Rhyme, not diverting to the tray of cookies that Thom had made earlier, the air still redolent of hot butter and cinnamon. But the glance toward the pastry revealed regret; maybe he'd gained a pound or two in the past few days and the old Lon Sellitto – Let the Dieting Begin – was back.

'Hey.' A nod to Thom, then moving stiffly to the chair, the shoes tapping, the cane silent on its worn rubber tip. 'Linc, Amelia.'

Sachs nodded. She'd come here to drop off the evidence from the early part of the Unsub 40 case – what had been stored in Queens. She'd been concerned that, like the White Castle napkins, some of it might go missing. So she had personally collected the evidence early this morning and delivered it to Rhyme's.

Her stay here wouldn't be long; she was taking Rose to the hospital for her surgery in a few hours.

'Nothing?' Thom asked the detective. 'Coffee?'

'Nup.' Looking up, avoiding their eyes.

Hm. Rhyme scanned the man's face. Something was up.

'That escalator. You oughta leave it, Linc. Good conversation starter.'

And good conversation deflector, Rhyme thought. He was impatient. There was evidence to organize. He was meeting with the prosecutor in the cases against Griffith and Morgan, and Mel Cooper would be arriving soon.

'What's up, Lon?'

'Okay, gotta tell you.'

Rhyme looked toward him. But Sellitto's eyes were on Sachs.

She finished assembling the evidence and then peeled off the tight latex gloves. Blew on her fingers. For years Rhyme had not experienced the relief that a small act like that brought, after hours of being gloved, but he remembered the sensation clearly.

'Go ahead, Lon.' Amelia Sachs wanted her news straight and fast – bad news, at least. He reflected that she never seemed to have much use for the good.

'You've been suspended.'

'What?'

'The fuck is this about?' Rhyme snapped.

'A problem at One PP.'

Sachs was closing her eyes. 'I leaked the story, right? About the smart controllers? And didn't tell the brass. But I had to, Lon.'

Rhyme said, 'This is bullshit. She probably saved lives. Companies shut down their servers and Griffith wasn't able to hack in.'

Sellitto's doughy face registered confusion. 'What're you talking about?'

Sachs explained about her clandestine meeting with the

reporter, who broke the story that some companies were hesitant, for financial reasons, to go offline to upgrade their cloud servers with the new CIR security updates.

Sellitto gave a sour look. 'Whatever. But that ain't it. Sorry, Amelia. It's Madino.'

Rhyme recalled. The captain from the 84th Precinct, who'd convened the Shooting Team after Sachs had shot a round into the escalator motor to save Greg Frommer's life.

'Turns out there were some reporters got on the case.'

'And he told me they went away.'

'Well, they didn't go very far. It's a big deal now, police firing weapons.'

'At unarmed kids, yeah,' Rhyme snapped. 'Not at industrial machinery.'

Sellitto held up two palms. 'Please, Linc. I'm the messenger is all.'

Rhyme recalled his exchange with Sachs a few days ago.

As long as there're no reporters trying to make their careers with stories on cops shooting guns in malls, I'll be cool.

I don't think that's much of a journalistic subspecialty . . .

It had seemed funny at the time.

Sachs said, 'Go on.'

'The reporters, they kept at him about what happened, who was involved. They threatened to go over his head.'

She smirked. 'And he was afraid that'd jeopardize his plush new office in One PP if he didn't throw me to the wolves.'

'In a nutshell, yep.'

'Bottom line?' she muttered.

'Three months, no pay. Sorry, Amelia. I gotta do the weapon and shield thing. Just like the fucking movies.' He appeared genuinely disgusted by the whole affair.

A sigh, then she handed them over. 'I'll fight it. Talk to the PBA lawyer.'

'You can. Sure.' His tone was like quicksand.

She eyed him closely. 'But?'

'My advice. Take the wrist slap and move on. Madino could make it bad for you.'

'I'll make it bad for him.'

Silence for a moment. Then the reality of NYPD politics – well, every governmental body's politics – appeared to seep in, and a look of resignation stilled her face.

Sellitto continued, 'Everybody'll forget about it in a few months. You'll be back on track. You fight, it'll drag out. Make more press. They do not want that. Could sideline you for a long time. You know how the system works, Amelia.'

Rhyme said contemptuously, 'This is bullshit, Lon.'

'I know it, you know it, *they* know it. The difference is they don't care.'

She said, 'But we've got the Griffith/Morgan case to wrap up.'

'Effective immediately.'

She pulled off her lab jacket, swapped it for her sport coat, the dark-gray one, cut to accommodate both her figure and her Glock 17. A tricky job of tailoring, Rhyme had always thought.

Her voice contained a shrug, as she said, 'Not the worst timing, I guess. Gives me a chance to take better care of Mom over the next couple of weeks. Maybe it's a blessing.'

But it wasn't, of course. And Rhyme could easily see she didn't feel that way at all. She was facing an empty, and edgy, quarter year and mad as hell about it. He was certain of this because it was how *he* would have felt under these circumstances. Working is what we're made for – dogs, horses, humans. Take that away and we're diminished, sometimes irreversibly.

'I have to get her to the hospital now.' She strode out and left the town house.

Rhyme heard the front door shut and not long after that the big engine of her Torino fire up. He wasn't surprised that the acceleration was modest. For Amelia Sachs, unleashing her vehicle's horses was done only out of joy, never anger.

CHAPTER 62

At first Lincoln Rhyme didn't recognize the man who stepped into his parlor.

He glanced at Thom, irritated. Why no warning that a stranger had arrived?

But in a few seconds he realized: This was Evers Whitmore, Esq., the stiff, understated attorney with the precise handwriting and more precise mannerisms.

The reason for the missed identification was that the man was incognito: wearing gray wool slacks, a blue plaid shirt sans tie, and a green sweater (he should have tipped immediately; the sweater was a cardigan, all three buttons done in the best style of a 1950s sitcom father, patiently enduring his children's mischievous but benign antics). On the man's head was a Titleist golf cap, bright green and yellow.

'Mr Rhyme.'

'Mr Whitmore.' Rhyme had, as he put it to himself, given up on given names.

The lawyer was aware of Rhyme's scan of his outfit. 'I'm coaching a soccer game in an hour. My sons.'

'Oh, you have a family. I didn't know.'

'I choose not to wear my wedding ring most of the time because it tends to give away a fact about me to opposing counsel. I myself would not use another attorney's personal information tactically but there are some who don't feel the same. As I'm sure will be no surprise to you.'

'You said sons?'

'I also have daughters. Three of each.'

Well.

'The boys are triplets, and they're all on the same soccer team. It tends to confound the opponents.' A smile. Was this his first? In any event, it was small and brief.

Whitmore looked around. 'And Detective Sachs?'

'At the hospital. Her mother's having surgery. Bypass.'

'My. Any word?'

Rhyme shook his head. 'But she's a feisty one. If that's indicative of a good prognosis.'

The literal-minded attorney didn't seem to comprehend. 'When you talk to Detective Sachs, wish her my best. And to her mother, as well.'

'I will.'

'I understand that you had a run-in with the suspect. A firsthand run-in.'

'That's right. I wasn't injured. Juliette Archer was, but it's not serious.'

Without unbuttoning his sweater, the man sat pristinely in a chair and hoisted his briefcase to his lap. A double click of the spring clasps and then he lifted the lid.

'I'm afraid I have bad news. I'm sorry to report that I've had my investigator take a thorough look at the finances of both Alicia Morgan and Vernon Griffith. She had a savings account worth about forty thousand dollars and he had about one hundred and fifty-seven thousand in assets, plus a retirement plan – but that's protected against creditors.'

'So a total of about two hundred thousand.'

'I'll pursue it but, if there are other plaintiffs, and there will be, I assure you, that will have to be divided among all the other survivors and family members. Abe Benkoff's wife. Todd Williams's survivors. Even the carpenter who was injured at the Broadway theater.'

'And the people ruined forever because they can't take escalators,' Rhyme added, referring to the bandwagon clients Juliette Archer had initially mentioned and that Whitmore had assured them will be standing in line, hat in hand.

The lawyer continued, 'And there'll be my contingent fee. Mrs Frommer will collect perhaps twenty thousand at most.'

The check to be delivered to a garage in Schenectady.

Whitmore was setting documents on a nearby rattan coffee table, probably his investigator's financial analysis of the two perpetrators, carefully ordered. Rhyme didn't know why he was delivering them. He believed the lawyer's PI had done his homework and that the results were accurate. There was no need for proof.

'So,' Whitmore said, ordering the paperwork even more precisely. 'We'll have to go with Plan A.'

'Plan A.'

The plaintiff's team hadn't established any alphabetized contingencies that Rhyme was aware of, but after the Midwest Conveyance bankruptcy and the absence of any culpability by CIR Microsystems, he'd assumed that the only recourse was to target the conspirators' own assets, a strategy that was now defunct.

Rhyme mentioned this. And Whitmore regarded him

through a thin gauzy veil of confusion. 'No, Mr Rhyme. That was Plan *B*. Our first approach – product liability against the manufacturer – has always been viable. Here.' He pushed forward one of the documents he'd just off-loaded and Rhyme wheeled closer to the table to read it. He saw it was not, in fact, a financial analysis.

SUPREME COURT OF THE STATE OF NEW YORK
COUNTY OF KINGS

– *x*

SANDRA MARGARET FROMMER,
           Plaintiff,

                              COMPLAINT

       - vs. -   *Index No.:*

CIR MICROSYSTEMS, INC.,
           Defendant.

– *x*

TO THE SUPREME COURT OF THE STATE OF NEW YORK
The complaint of the Plaintiff, SANDY MARGARET FROMMER, respectfully shows and alleges as follows:

With his right hand Rhyme clumsily flipped through the lengthy complaint. There was a second batch of documents, similar, in the name of her son, for wrongful death, and a third in the name of Greg Frommer himself for the pain and suffering in his last fifteen minutes on earth. And many, many adjunct documents.

The demand for judgment – the ad damnum clause – was for fifty million dollars.

Rhyme looked up from the documents. 'But . . . I assumed there was no suit against the controller manufacturer.'

'Why would you think that?'

Rhyme shrugged. 'Vernon Griffith was—'

'An intervening cause?'

'Yes.'

'Ah, but a *foreseeable* intervening cause, one they should have guarded against. Negligence is determined by multiplying the likelihood of injury by the severity of that injury and comparing that against how much it would have cost to prevent it. Learned Hand. Second Circuit Court of Appeals. *United States v. Carroll Company.*

'Applying that rule, I take the position that, one, the probability of hacking a smart product is extremely high, given the number, ingenuity and motivation of hackers today. Two, the gravity of the injury can be extremely high. Mr Frommer and Abe Benkoff are dead. *Res ispa loquitur.* And, three, the burden of adequate precautions is minimal. CIR could easily have provided for *automatic* security updates, as they themselves admitted and, indeed, are doing now. They should have foreseen that a hacker would cause serious injury and it would have been a simple fix for them. So, CIR is negligent in the deaths.

'I'll also claim the controllers are defective under the law of strict products liability. Your associate told me – and I have experts researching this further – that the software in embedded products is antiquated.'

True. Rodney Szarnek had told them that it was cheaper

and easier for the smart controller companies to use old, easily hacked software, stripped of certain functions, than write new code, to save money and get the products to market sooner.

The spamming refrigerators . . .

'So, negligence and strict liability. I'll probably add that breach of warranty claim too. There's nothing wrong with the kitchen sink strategy when suing a wealthy defendant.'

'You'll try for a settlement, of course.'

'Yes. They know I'd bring into evidence all of the other incidents – Mr Benkoff's stove, the microwave in the theater, the cars taken control of. It would be a public relations nightmare for CIR to fight us in court. And I could get a jury to bleed them anemic, if not dry, with punitive damages. Like a vampire.'

Ah, the somber lawyer had a sense of humor after all.

'I won't get fifty million but I'll negotiate a reasonable amount. Which brings me to why I'm here. There are some evidentiary issues that you'll have to address before I send the complaint to Mr Frost, the CIR attorney, and begin the horse trading.'

A pause.

'I'm afraid I can't help you with that.'

'No? May I ask why not?'

'I'm helping the DA prepare the criminal case. There'd be a conflict of interest if I were to continue helping you.'

'I see. Of course. I'm sorry to hear that. True, I don't want to jeopardize the civil trial.'

'No.'

'I must say, though, it's important to marshal our cause of action as formidably as we can. There cannot be any gaps in the case we present to the defendant. And the evidence is vital to that. I need an expert. Is there anyone you can think of, Mr Rhyme? Anyone at all?'

'Hello, Rose.'

The elderly woman opened her eyes. 'Lincoln. You came for a visit. Good to see you.'

With her non-IV'd arm she brushed at her hair, though it was perfectly well assembled. Amelia Sachs had fixed her sleeping mother's coiffure when she and Rhyme had arrived in the recovery room not long before.

'Where's Amie?'

'Talking to the doctor about when you get to go home. What you can do and can't.'

'I'm supposed to start walking tomorrow. Who would have thought? Cut you open, fix your ticker . . . and start you on marathons. Hardly fair. I wanted to bask in sympathy for a while.'

Rose didn't look as pale as he'd expected. In fact, she looked healthier. The improved circulation, Rhyme supposed. He thought momentarily of Alicia Morgan. A small, obscure object, a product within the family car, had changed her life for the worse, forever. And small obscure objects here, in a hospital, had just added years to a life that, otherwise, could have ended abruptly at any minute. In the same way a variety of *things* kept Rhyme himself alive and functioning.

Then he chuckled at the overwrought thinking. He was here to visit his future mother-in-law.

Rose's room was a good one, and happened to look out over a park across the street, a portion of it at least. He commented on the view.

She glanced through the window. 'Yes, it is. It is. Though I must say I was never one of those people who went for a room with a view. What occurs *in* rooms is far more interesting, don't you think?'

He couldn't have agreed more.

No questions about how she was feeling, the hospital food, the trivia that visitors ask patients by rote. Rhyme had noted on the nightstand one of Stephen Hawking's books. He'd read it some years ago. They fell into a lively discussion about the big bang theory.

A nurse arrived, a handsome man, solid, with a rich Caribbean accent.

'Mrs Sachs. Ah, you have a famous visitor.'

Rhyme was inclined to offer a dismissive grimace but for her sake simply nodded and smiled.

The man looked her over, the incision site, the IVs.

'Looking good, looking very good.'

Rose said, 'And Mr Herrando knows what he's talking about. Now, Lincoln, I think I'll get some rest.'

'Sure. We'll be back tomorrow.'

Rhyme left the room and headed up to the nurse's station, where Sachs was finishing a call.

He said, 'She's good, getting some sleep.'

'I'll peek in.'

Sachs stepped into her mother's room and returned to Rhyme a moment later.

'Like a baby.'

Together Sachs and Rhyme walked and wheeled down

the corridor. Not that he cared much, but Rhyme noted that he received not a single glance his way, unlike on the streets of the city. Here, of course, one would expect to find someone in a fancy wheelchair. Nothing extraordinary, nothing worth staring at. Indeed *he* was mobile and moving breezily down the hall beside a companion, far more fortunate than many of the people in the dim, silent rooms they passed.

In regione caecorum rex est luscus, he thought.

In the land of the blind, the one-eyed man is king.

Side by side, they negotiated the crowded lobby and headed out into the overcast spring afternoon, turning toward the van, which was sitting in the disabled zone.

'So,' Rhyme asked Sachs. 'Any more thoughts on what to do during your three-month retirement?'

'Aside from being pissed off?'

'Aside from that.'

'Taking care of Mom. Working on the Torino. Shoot a hell of a lot of lead through paper out on the range. Take up cooking.'

'*Cooking?*'

'Okay, not that.'

As they approached the van she said, 'I have a feeling you're agendizing something.'

Rhyme chuckled. Ah, Lon Sellitto . . . what would we do without him?

'Evers Whitmore came to see me, the lawyer. You know I'm not working for him anymore on the Frommer case. Conflict of interest, now that I'm handling the criminal side.'

'What's this about, Rhyme?'

'I need a favor, Sachs. You're going to want to say no, but just hear me out.'

'This sounds familiar.'

His eyebrow rose. 'Hear me out?'

Sachs put her hand on Rhyme's and said, 'Deal.'

ACKNOWLEDGMENTS

With undying gratitude to: Will and Tina Anderson, Ciccly Aspinall, Sophie Baker, Giovanna Canton, Francesca Cinelli, Jane Davis, Julie Deaver, Jenna Dolan, Kimberly Escobar, Jamie Hodder-Williams, Kerry Hood, Mitch Hoffman, Cathy Gleason, Emma Knight, Allegra Le Fanu, Carolyn Mays, Claire Nozieres, Hazel Orme, Abby Parsons, Seba Pezzani, Michael Pietch, Jamie Raab, Betsy Robbins, Katy Rouse, Lindsey Rose, Roberto Santachiara, Deborah Schneider, Vivienne Schuster, Ruth Tross, Madelyn Warcholik. You're the best!

ABOUT THE AUTHOR

A former journalist, folksinger and attorney, Jeffery Deaver is an international number-one bestselling author. His novels have appeared on bestseller lists around the world, including the *New York Times*, *The Times* of London, Italy's *Corriere della Sera*, the *Sydney Morning Herald* and the *Los Angeles Times*. His books arc sold in 150 countries and translated into twenty-five languages.

The author of thirty-seven novels, three collections of short stories and a nonfiction law book, and a lyricist of a country-western album, he's received or been shortlisted for dozens of awards.

His most recent novels are *Solitude Creek*, a Kathryn Dance novel; *The October List*, a thriller told in reverse; *The Skin Collector* and *The Kill Room*, Lincoln Rhyme novels. For his Dance novel *XO* Deaver wrote an album of country-western songs, available on iTunes and as a CD; and before that, *Carte Blanche*, a James Bond continuation novel, a number-one international bestseller.

Deaver has been nominated for seven Edgar Awards from the Mystery Writers of America, an Anthony, a Shamus and a Gumshoe. He was recently shortlisted for the ITV3 Crime Thriller Award for Best International Author. *Roadside Crosses* was on the shortlist for the Prix Polar International 2013.

JEFFERY DEAVER

His book *A Maiden's Grave* was made into an HBO movie starring James Garner and Marlee Matlin, and his novel *The Bone Collector* was a feature release from Universal Pictures, starring Denzel Washington and Angelina Jolie. Lifetime aired an adaptation of his *The Devil's Teardrop*. And, yes, the rumors are true; he did appear as a corrupt reporter on his favorite soap opera, *As the World Turns*. He was born outside Chicago and has a bachelor of journalism degree from the University of Missouri and a law degree from Fordham University.

Readers can visit his website at www.jefferydeaver.com.

Author's Note

I thought my readers in the UK and Commonwealth might like to see a few memos regarding Lincoln Rhyme's first foray into crime solving on their turf.

The Preliminary Report

Jeffery Deaver

TOP SECRET

21 March, 2016
From: Lincoln Rhyme
To: Peter Quiller, Director General, Security Service,
Thames House, Millbank, London
Re: Alexander Litvinenko

Introduction

I am submitting here, as requested, a preliminary report
on my analysis of certain evidence relevant to the inquiry
into the death of Russian expatriate Alexander Litvinenko
in London, 2006.

Background

For the past two weeks I have been lecturing on various
topics of forensics at the London College of Criminal

Science in conjunction with John Marshall College of Criminal Justice in New York and the British Academy of Forensic Sciences.

I was approached following one of my talks (the subject: Predictive Exotoxicology as it Relates to Crime Scenes at Industrial Sites) by two officers with the Security Service and asked if I might consult in an ongoing investigation. I expressed an interest in doing so and, thereupon, they explained that the matter would have to remain strictly confidential. I agreed to that stipulation and they then told me that the case in question was the death of Russian expat Alexander Litvinenko, former KGB, then FSB, security service officer, who died following polonium-210 poisoning at a hotel in London in 2006. While a Russian agent was originally identified as the killer, Moscow denied that this was the case and, in any event, declined to extradite. It was by no means clear that this man was in fact the perpetrator, however; a number of other potential suspects have been suggested: former FSB agents, enemies Litvinenko had made in Spain and Italy, Russian oil oligarchs, pro- and anti-Kremlin interests and expats in London. It was even suggested that the death was accidental and resulted from Litvinenko's attempts to profit by smuggling radioactive material into England.

The case has remained dormant for a time, but recently the Home Secretary ordered a public inquiry into Litvinenko's death to see if the true perpetrator could be identified.

The question posed to me was could I assist in the forensic examination of some of the evidence gathered at the hotel where Litvinenko apparently received the fatal dose of polonium. While much of the forensic evidence gathered by the Security Service and the Metropolitan Police Service at the time had to do with the polonium itself, a great deal of other trace was discovered as well, including soil, fibers, metal shavings, cosmetics, medicines and substances consistent with various types of food.

Since my specialty is the analysis of such trace evidence, the officers informed me, it was hoped that I might bring some new insights to the investigation. Further, since the issue had been raised that British intelligence services could have done more to prevent Litvinenko's death, and therefore might have an interest in the outcome of any inquiry, my efforts as an impartial analyst would be particularly appreciated.

Accordingly, using the facilities at London College's forensic laboratory, I've spent six days analyzing the evidence gathered at the scene in London, and, at my request, additional samples of various materials from sites in London and Manchester in the UK, as well as some in Spain, Rome and Moscow. The Security Service and MPS obtained the samples within the UK; the Secret Intelligence Service was responsible for the foreign samples. By the way, I must express my gratitude for their fine efforts – in the face of what I'm sure was, at times, my rather impatient demeanor.

Conclusion

My preliminary findings are these: I am able to state with 90 percent certainty that the individual who killed Alexander Litvinenko continues to have a presence in London, though I believe that this individual travels abroad with some frequency, primarily to destinations other than the Western Hemisphere and Africa. I am confident that additional analysis will identify at least the neighborhood of that person's residence and most likely the address itself. Similarly, I am close to discovering the perpetrator's race and gender, as well as significant identifying characteristics. And I will have direct links between this person and Litvinenko's murder. I should have all of these details within twenty-four to forty-eight hours.

I am pleased to be of some assistance in this matter and, as we discussed, will submit to you an invoice for my services, at my standard rate, upon my return to the United States.

TOP SECRET

23 March 2016
From: Peter Quiller
To: Lincoln Rhyme
Re: Alexander Litvinenko

I am writing to update you regarding your efforts in our inquiry into the Litvinenko death.

As a preliminary matter, the Home Secretary and I wish to thank you for your invaluable assistance, and indeed in your creation of the plan that, we hope, will bear fruit and see the perpetrator of this horrific crime brought to justice.

When our officers first approached you, it was indeed with the hope that you might bring your analytical skills to bear on the additional evidence gathered from the crime scene in 2006. And we were, accordingly, disappointed when, upon your review of the files and evidence itself, you reported that "that vein has been thoroughly mined," and that we and the MPS had done all that could be done to wrest insights from the trace.

Hardly did we think that you might conjure a very different plan to identify the killer.

Let me report here how we have proceeded, based on your strategy.

• I sent an email to the heads of station at our embassies or consulates in Moscow, Rome, and Madrid, bearing the unencrypted heading *Litvinenko Update*. I attached your memo of 21 March. The body of the memo was encrypted but in a weak algorithm created by our GCHQ. This rendered it easily hacked by both Kremlin security services and corporate and political interests regularly monitoring UK government signals traffic, one of which, as you suggested, might be behind Litvinenko's death, or have an interest in relaying the memo's contents to the person or persons responsible.

• Simultaneously, armed Specialist Operations officers of the MPS and our organization began around-the-clock surveillance of the forensic laboratory at London College of Criminal Science.

• Three hours ago, two suspects wearing hats and sunglasses were spotted near the entrance door to the forensic laboratory. They took several pictures on their phones and left. Our officers on site are certain that they or their superiors have learned of the contents of your memo and are planning a break-in in search of your or your fictional evidence. They will, of course, receive quite a surprise reception when they do so.

I know you are returning to the United States presently but I will keep you apprised of the investigation. Let me thank you again for your assistance in this matter, Captain Rhyme. And on a personal note, let me say how much I enjoyed dining with you, Detective Amelia Sachs and your associate Mr Thom Reston the other night. And I am delighted you enjoyed your visit to the Palace. I do hope you return to London in the near future; I assure you we will not put you to work quite as arduously as we have on this visit.

Lincoln Rhyme will return in

THE BURIAL HOUR

Coming 2017

Read on for an exclusive look at the first chapter

CHAPTER 1

"Mommy."

"In a minute."

They trooped doggedly along the quiet street on the Upper East Side, the sun low this cool autumn morning. Red leaves, yellow leaves spiraled from sparse branches.

Mother and daughter, burdened with the baggage that children now carted to school.

In my day . . .

Claire was texting furiously. Her housekeeper had—wouldn't you know it?—gotten sick, no, *possibly* gotten sick, on the day of the dinner party! *The* party. And Alan had to work late. *Possibly* had to work late.

As if I could ever count on him anyway.

Ding.

The response from her friend:

Sorry, Carmellas busy tnight.

Jesus. A tearful emoji accompanied the missive. Why not type the Goddamn "o" in "tonight"? Did it save you a precious millisecond? And remember apostrophes?

"But, Mommy . . ." A nine-year-old sing-songy tone.

"A minute, Morgynn. You heard me." Claire's voice was a benign monotone. Not the least angry, not the least peeved or piqued. Thinking of the weekly sessions: sitting in the chair, not lying back on the couch—the good doctor didn't even have a couch in his, office—Claire attacked her nemeses, the anger and impatience, and she had studiously worked to avoid snapping or shouting when her daughter was annoying (even when she behaved that way intentionally, which, Claire calculated, was easily one quarter of the girl's waking hours).

And I'm doing a damn good job of keeping a lid on it.

Reasonable. Mature. "A minute," she repeated, sensing the girl was about to speak.

Claire slowed to a stop, flipping through her phone's address book, lost in the maelstrom of approaching disaster. It was early but the day would vanish fast and the party would be on her like a nearby Uber. Wasn't there someone, *anyone*, in the borough of Manhattan who might have decent help she could borrow to wait a party? A party for ten friggin' people! That was nothing. How hard could it be?

She debated. Her sister?

Nope. She wasn't invited.

Sally from the club?

Nope. Out of town. And a bitch, to boot.

Morgynn had slowed and Claire was aware of her daughter turning around. Had she dropped something? Apparently so. She ran back to pick it up.

Better not be her phone. She'd already broken one. The screen had cost $187 to fix.

Honestly. Children.

Then Claire was back to scrolling, praying for

waitperson salvation. Look at all these names. Need to clean out this damn contact list. Don't know half these people. Don't like a good chunk of the rest. Off went another beseeching message.

The child returned to her side and said firmly, "Mommy, look—"

"Ssssh." Hissing now. But there was nothing wrong with an edge occasionally, of course, she told herself. It was a form of education. Children *had* to learn. Even the cutest of puppies needed collar-jerk correction from time to time.

Another ding of iPhone.

Another no.

Goddamn it.

Well, what about that woman that Terri from the office had used? Hispanic, or Latino . . . *Latina*. Whatever those people called themselves now. The cheerful woman had been the star of Terri's daughter's graduation party.

Claire found Terri's number and dialed a voice call.

"Hello?"

"Terri! It's Claire. How are you?"

A hesitation then Terri said, "Hi, there. How're you doing?"

"I'm—"

At which point Morgynn interrupted yet again. "Mommy!"

Snap. Claire spun around and glared down at the petite blonde, hair in braids, wearing a snug pink leather Armani Junior jacket. She raged, "I am on the *phone*! Are you blind? What have I told you about that? When I'm on the phone? What is so f—" Okay, watch the language, she told herself. Claire offered a labored smile. "What's so . . . *important*, dear?"

"I'm trying to tell you. This man back there?" The girl nodded up the street. "He came up to another man and hit him or something and pushed him in the trunk."

"*What*?"

Morgynn tossed a braid, which ended in a tiny bunny clip, off her shoulder. "He left this on the ground and then drove away. She held up a cord or thin rope. What was it?

Claire gasped. In her daughter's petite hand was a miniature hangman's noose.

Morgynn replied, "*That*'s what's so—" She paused and her tiny lips curled into a smile of their own. "*Important*."